ELVEN DOOM

DEATH BEFORE DRAGONS
BOOK FOUR

LINDSAY BUROKER

Elven Doom: Death Before Dragons Book 4
Copyright © 2020 Lindsay Buroker. All rights reserved.

www.lindsayburoker.com

No part of this book may be reproduced, scanned, or distributed in any printed or electronic form without permission. Please do not participate in or encourage piracy of copyrighted materials in violation of the author's rights. Thank you for respecting the hard work of this author.

This is a work of fiction. Names, characters, places and incidents are either the product of the author's imagination or used fictitiously. No reference to any real person, living or dead, should be inferred.

Edited by Shelley Holloway
Cover and interior design by Gene Mollica Studio, LLC.

ISBN: 978-1-951367-06-0

ELVEN DOOM

Acknowledgments

Thank you for continuing on with the adventures of Val and Zav and their friends, family, and mortal enemies. Before you start this new novel, please allow me to thank those who continue to help me put these books together, my editor, Shelley Holloway, and my beta readers, Sarah Engelke, Rue Silver, and Cindy Wilkinson. Also thank you to Vivienne Leheny for narrating the audiobooks and Gene Mollica for the cover art.

And now, onward to the new adventure!

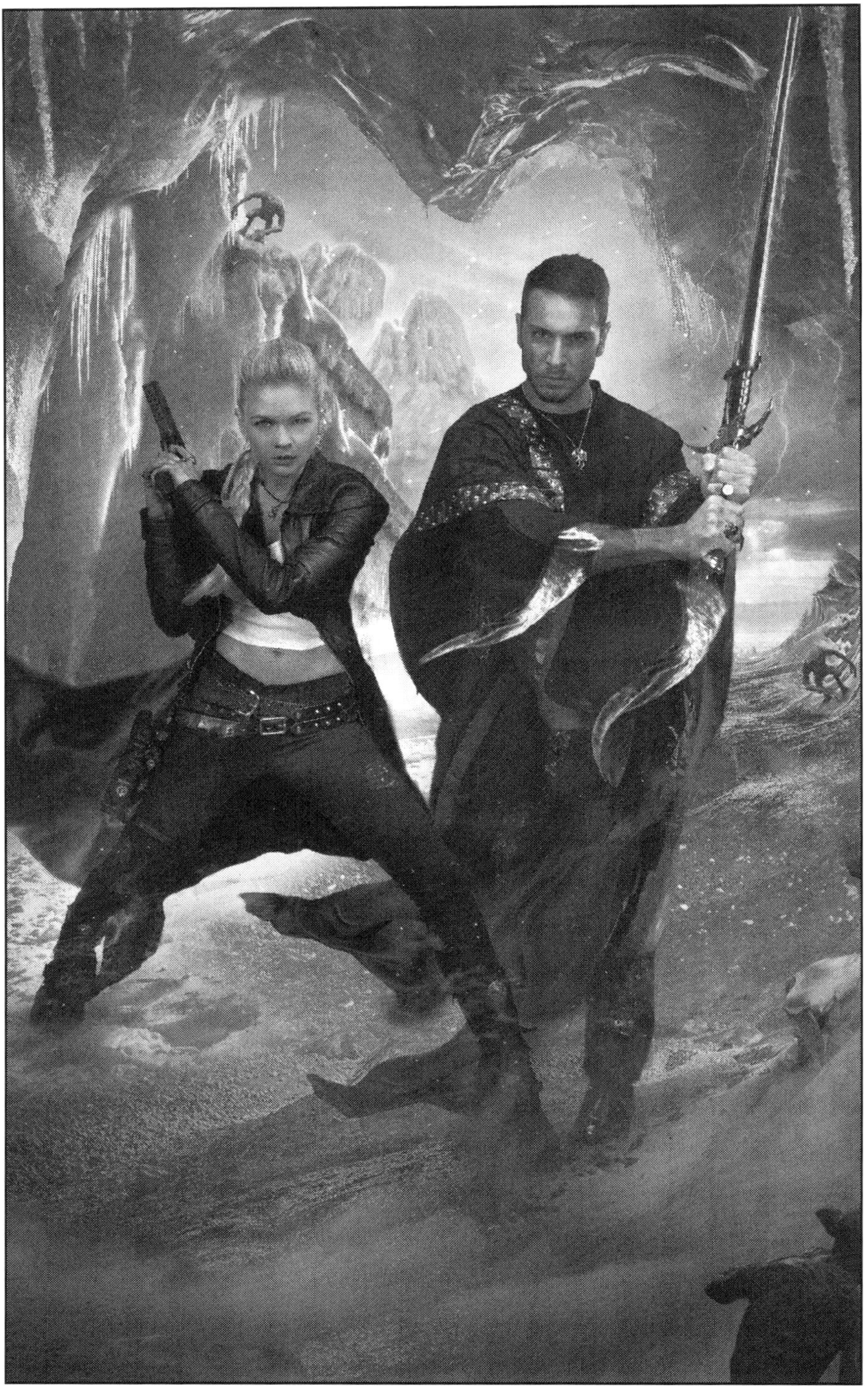

Chapter 1

Condemned by order of the health inspector. Do not enter.

I stared at the sign on the door to Rupert's bar for longer than it took to read it. Cars honked at the nearby intersection, and tourists and locals hurried down the sidewalks with their collars turned up against the rain pelting down from above. But this alley was empty of life, as if nobody knew it was here.

My phone buzzed. Thinking it was my boss, Colonel Willard, I pulled it out, but when I saw the identity of the caller, I grimaced and stuck it back in my pocket. My therapist's office. No doubt it was the perky receptionist reminding me of my next appointment. She could leave a message. Work got priority over my niggling health issues.

I rested a hand on the cold metal door and willed one of the magical trinkets on the leather thong around my neck to open the lock. Nothing happened. I tried the handle. The door creaked open. Silly me, thinking the troll owner would have locked up his establishment before abandoning it.

My half-elven senses told me there wasn't anyone with magical blood inside. That was vastly different from when I'd visited only two weeks earlier. Then, shapeshifters, orcs, goblins, and other magical beings had been dancing and drinking as they enjoyed the only bar in Seattle dedicated to serving their kind—while doing its best to make sure the rest of the world didn't know it existed.

As I stepped inside, a faint rustling drifted up the dim cement stairway that led down to the basement establishment, barely detectable over the street noise outside. I left Fezzik, my custom-made submachine pistol with magical bullets, in its thigh holster and drew Chopper, my dwarven-made longsword, from its scabbard on my back.

The rustling stopped. Darkness descended as the door closed behind me, and I walked down the stairs, wrinkling my nose at the lingering scents of spilled beer and sludge—an orc drink made from fermented moss. A hint of mildew underlaid the other odors.

At the bottom, I found and flipped a light switch near the wooden doorframe that numerous knives had been thrown into over the years. One had almost found my head the last time I'd come.

The lights didn't come on. I activated another of my charms, one that gave me night vision. With a word, I could have made Chopper glow brightly enough to illuminate the room, but my ears told me I wasn't alone down here, and I didn't want to make myself more of a target.

As the charm turned the room from black to green, the details muted and sometimes fuzzy, I picked out blankets and clothing under some of the tables. Homeless people? A couple of pairs of eyes were turned toward me, but more people remained hunkered in their damp piles, ignoring my entrance.

If I didn't find what I'd come for, I would bribe a couple of the squatters and see if they had any information. Most likely, they had come after the place had been shut down and knew little.

I headed down the hallway in the back, passing mostly empty rooms to the sides. A few of the couches, previously meeting spots for orcs, gnolls, and trolls who'd been chatting or necking, were occupied by sleeping humans. Someone had pushed their shopping cart full of belongings down the stairs and into one of the rooms.

The bank-vault-style door at the end of the hall was closed, and my hopes rose. Maybe Rupert, the troll owner, had left the dark-elf artifact inside when he closed down his place. If so, I could, as Willard had asked, bring it to her office for study.

This door was locked. I hesitated before using my charm on it, remembering the power the orb had to pull people to it with promises of pleasurable experiences. Someone had been dead on the floor the night I'd come and, according to Willard's reports, others had died from long-term use here and in other locations that had housed the so-called pleasure orbs. Once the door was open, its power would flow out, and all those homeless people might be drawn back to their eventual deaths.

No, if it was inside, I was taking it with me. One way or another.

My charm worked, and the heavy lock thunked. I pulled open the door to an empty storeroom.

The orb was gone. A faint hint of lingering power remained in the air, like the scent of an animal after its passing, but it was nothing like the magic that had filled the room when the artifact had hung suspended in the middle.

My phone buzzed again. The therapist's office. Why didn't she leave a message?

I stepped into the storeroom, turned off the night-vision charm, and whispered, *"Eravekt"* to activate Chopper. There might be clues in here that only light would reveal.

Such as the chalk outlines on the floor. I stared at them as a rat skittered under a shelving unit. Six outlines had been drawn around the room. Did that mean the police had taken the orb? Or had the dark-elf scientists, specifically the pair Willard had me hunting down, returned to retrieve it?

On the third call, I answered the phone with an exasperated, *"What?"*

"Val?" It was Mary, my therapist, not her receptionist.

"No, it's the goblin work leader I hired to screen calls for me." I walked between the chalk outlines, examining the floor, the ceiling, the shelves... anything that might give me a clue.

"Someone was here asking for your record."

I froze. "Who?"

Someone from Willard's office? Willard knew I'd seen a doctor about my newly developed asthma and a few other concerns, and that I'd been directed to speak to a therapist to learn how to lower the stress in my life—hah. The military didn't have any reason to snoop.

"She didn't give a name to my receptionist, Gina, just demanded the reports on the half-elf. We wouldn't have known that was you except..." Mary cleared her throat delicately. "Your file is gone."

"It's gone? Gina gave it to this person?"

"She says she didn't, but she also says her memory got fuzzy after this young lady made her demand. She remembers unlocking the door to my office and going in but nothing after that until she was back at her desk and the next client came in."

Ugh, that sounded like someone being directed by a magical compulsion. I thought of my new enemy, Shaygorthian, a silver dragon inquisitor from the Dragon Justice Court. He'd stalked me all over northern Idaho, trying to read my mind to see if I'd been responsible for his son's death, and, as I knew from personal experience, dragons could place magical compulsions on even those with strong minds.

"I'm very sorry about this, Val. It is not our policy to share a patient's records. We take privacy very seriously. I must apologize deeply about this."

"You said it was a woman? Is Gina sure about that?"

Dragons could shape-shift into numerous forms, but I'd never seen one change sexes before.

"Yes," Mary said. "I gather this woman was distinct. Young with purple hair, black leather clothing, and nose piercings."

"That's not the usual style for a government agent." The only person I knew who came close was Nin, but only because she'd dyed her hair purple before. She didn't have any piercings or black leather that I'd seen in the years I'd known her.

"Not even an undercover one?"

"When they go undercover, they try *not* to stick out. Look, thanks for letting me know, but I'm in the middle of something." Actually, I was at a dead end. I hoped Zav, my dragon ally and provisional partner, was having better luck hunting down the dark-elf scientists.

"Will you still come for your appointment tomorrow? I apologize again for this unforgivable transgression and hope you'll continue to see me."

If someone with magical power had diddled the receptionist's mind, it was forgivable. It wasn't like she could have stopped it.

"Unless something comes up, I'll be there. I had some new developments while I was in Idaho that would probably be good to talk about." Reluctantly. I hated opening up, but I'd finally spoken to my daughter and ex-husband after almost ten years of avoiding them. And I'd been claimed by a dragon as his mate. These seemed like important life events to discuss with someone.

"Good. I look forward to listening. I'll make sure going forward that your records are only electronically stored and behind a password nobody except for me knows."

That just meant the magical intruder would diddle *her* mind next time. I didn't point this out.

"That's fine. Thanks."

As I left the storeroom, unlocking the owner's office and checking the hidden viewing room I'd been in before, I tried to think of who, with the power to magically coerce people, might be researching me this week. Dragons weren't the only ones who could do that trick.

More rustling noises and a few muttered words from the main room reminded me to stay alert. I almost called Sindari, my magical tiger companion, but if someone powerful was looking for me, I had better save him. The time he could spend on Earth each day was limited.

Back in the main room, someone had lit a dented camp lantern. The unnatural white light revealed six men and a tattooed woman standing between me and the stairs leading out. Two of the men had pistols stuffed in their jeans waistbands, a couple had knives, and the woman had a baseball bat with fang marks chomped in the end.

"This is our place," the woman said. "You can't come down here uninvited. And you can't leave with that jacket."

I snorted. If the lighting were better, she could see how often my leather duster had been patched after being stabbed, shot, and scorched by enemies. It wouldn't fetch a high price at a consignment shop.

But she was serious. They all were. I sighed, as a fight seemed inevitable.

A shadow stirred in the stairwell, and for the first time, I sensed someone with magical blood. More than that, the person was carrying something magical, something with a signature that reminded me of the dark-elven artifact.

I could barely make out a young, blue-skinned troll crouching on the steps, peering toward the group. Was this someone who knew Rupert? And where he'd gone? If so, I wanted to question him, not deal with these idiots.

But the woman slapped the baseball bat into her palm. This group wasn't going to let me out.

Chapter 2

"I'm from the health inspector's office," I told the group of toughs, hoping to escape without a fight.

Usually, I didn't mind brawls, but my job was to assassinate criminals, not homeless street people. Besides, the young troll I wanted to talk to might flee if there was a fight.

"Did you see the rats back there?" I pointed a thumb over my shoulder. "I'm afraid I'm going to have to report that the business still can't reopen."

"Health inspector." A man snorted and looked me up and down. "Sure."

I was in my usual work clothes: combat boots, jeans, tank top, magical vest armor, and the apparently desirable duster. I didn't know what health inspectors wore, but maybe this wasn't it. My magical weapons weren't visible to mundane people unless I set them down. That was sometimes a boon, sometimes a curse, and probably the latter this time. These people wouldn't have harassed me if they'd seen Fezzik. Though Chopper was the weapon more likely to cleave off an ogre's balls.

"I'm done with my inspection. I'm walking out that door now. You can get in my way or not. If I were you, I'd make the decision based on what you're actually hoping to accomplish here and how much ibuprofen you have in your stash." I sheathed Chopper and strode toward the door.

Willard wouldn't forgive me if I cleaved body parts off normal human citizens, and I didn't think I would need to. But I did keep a close eye on the men with pistols in their waistbands. Even though they looked more likely to blow off their own balls than kill anyone else.

The woman with the baseball bat and two of the men faded back, on the fence about attacking. The four other men lunged for me as I got close.

I sprang to one side of the group, making sure they couldn't all attack me at once, before launching a kick that sent one thug sprawling into the others. One man evaded the tangle and jumped at me, slashing with a knife.

To someone used to battling preternaturally fast shapeshifters, the group's movements were like molasses. I easily evaded the slash and caught the man's wrist. I slid in and jammed my hip into his gut, then threw him into the tables along the nearest wall. Two more kicks sent two more of my attackers in the opposite direction.

One of the gunmen yanked out his pistol, but I got to him before he could aim it. I grabbed his wrist, slammed a palm strike into his chest, and disarmed him as he tumbled back. The other would-be gunman had been reaching into his waistband, but he ran toward the hallway.

Worried he was being smart and putting distance between us before he turned to shoot, I flipped on the safety on the handgun I'd acquired and threw it at him. It spun like a poorly weighted knife, the butt striking him in the back of the head. The force sent him sprawling, his own handgun flying behind the bar. Hopefully, somewhere he would have trouble finding it.

The rest of the toughs skittered back like rats alarmed by someone turning on a light. They raised their hands. They were done.

But the young troll was gone. Damn it.

I sprinted for the stairs. My senses told me he was still in the alley. Maybe I could catch up to him.

As I ran out, he sprang atop a dumpster, leaped across the alley, and scurried up the side of the three-story building, as fearless as a squirrel. Grumbling, I climbed after him. An adult troll wouldn't have been light enough or agile enough to climb a building, but this kid hadn't put on his grown-up mass yet.

But I could climb faster and had almost caught him by the time he reached the flat rooftop. He pulled himself over the edge and ran. I swung up and sprinted after him, feeling like a truant officer.

"I'll give you twenty dollars if you answer a few questions," I yelled, not wanting to tackle a kid. I was trying to improve my reputation among the magical community, not make it worse. "That's all I want."

He didn't slow down, but I caught up with him on the opposite side of the rooftop. When I grabbed him by the upper arm, he whirled, trying to throw a punch, but I yanked his arm behind his back in a lock and immobilized him. His head only came up to my chin. Granted, I was six feet tall, but this made me feel like a bully.

His body tense, he tried to jerk away, but he had to be careful. He was by the edge of the building, staring down at a thirty-foot drop into traffic.

"Twenty dollars in cash," I promised.

"Just kill me if you're going to," he said, in an attempt at a snarl, but his voice was too high-pitched to pull it off. "I will die nobly like a warrior."

"Or you could take the money I'm offering, go get a Slurpee, and be the ten-year-old that you are."

"I'm only eight!"

"An even better reason to enjoy a sugar high." I pulled him back from the edge and patted him down for weapons.

He didn't have any, but he did have a bunch of junk in his pockets, including bottle caps, matchbooks from hotels, and a shard of something like lavender glass in his pocket. It radiated the magic I'd sensed, and it looked like a piece of the orb, but it didn't ooze any kind of attraction now.

I turned it over in my hand and let go of the boy.

"I'll give you twenty dollars if you answer my questions and another twenty for this." I held up the shard. "Do you know Rupert? Is he a relative?"

The kid spat on the puddle-drenched roof and showed me his fangs. They were impressive compared to a human's canines, but nothing like a vampire's or shifter's. And they lacked the fear-inspiring quality of orc tusks.

"What were you doing sneaking down into the bar?" I pulled out the money clip I kept for bribing informants and slid two twenties off the stack.

Someday, Willard would accept that I spent most of the money she paid me on replacing broken equipment, buying ammunition, and bribing people. Maybe then, she would give me a raise.

His stone-gray eyes watched the money. "I left something there when we had to leave. I think those *nokgorooks* stole it."

"What was it?"

The rest of the orb? Did he know who had taken it and where?

"My LEGO speeder bike."

"Ah, yes. I hear those are catnip to homeless people."

He scowled at me.

"Where do you live now?"

"I'm not telling you."

"Are you sure?" I pressed the twenties into his hand.

He hesitated, then took them and stuffed them into a pocket. He didn't ask for the shard back or even react to it. Maybe he believed it a simple piece of junk he'd picked up to add to his collection.

The kid started to open his mouth but then whirled toward the edge of the building. Afraid he would jump, I grabbed him by the collar of his jacket. But he didn't jump; he stared into the solid gray sky to the north.

"Dragon," he whispered, awe and fear mingling in his tone.

Zav? I couldn't see his black form against the clouds, nor could I yet sense him, but a full-blooded troll would have better range for that than I.

"It's all right." I assumed Zav was coming to see me. He was also searching for the dark-elf scientists. Maybe he'd found something. "He won't—"

I halted as my senses picked up the powerful aura in the sky. A dragon *was* flying this way, but it wasn't Zav.

Chapter 3

The dragon grew visible against the gray sky, a shadowy shape at first, the rain making it hard to pick out details. Most of the humans going about their lives in the city below wouldn't sense it, wouldn't even see it unless the dragon wished to be seen. But the troll boy and I had no trouble detecting it.

The dragon's scales were purple. No, *lilac*. With a start, I recognized the aura. I'd seen this dragon on the rocky slope of a ski mountain in Idaho. Zav's sister. She had come through a temporary portal with Zav's mother, and for a time, there had been seven dragons on Earth, six of whom had been determined to take me back to be punished for killing Dobsaurin, even though it had been honorable and in battle. By claiming me as his mate, at least in the eyes of his people, Zav had found a loophole in their laws and kept them from collecting me.

The sister—I'd never gotten her name—had only telepathically spoken a few words that I'd heard. It had been right after he claimed me, and they had been a warning to Zav not to make the same mistake again.

Tendrils of unease slithered through my gut as the lilac dragon flew straight toward us. What if she'd come to kill me or take me to her world while Zav wasn't around? To make *sure* he couldn't repeat the same mistake.

I released the troll and drew Chopper. The kid didn't hesitate to drop to his belly, slither over the edge, and climb down the side of the building. He sprinted across the street, almost being hit by cars, and disappeared into another alley.

"I guess that won't work for me." The dragon would chase me if I fled, and she could fly faster than I could run.

She ignored the troll and arrowed toward me. She pulled in her leathery wings—they were as lilac as her damp scales—and dove toward the rooftop, as if I were a fish she planned to snatch out of a lake to eat.

"Sindari." I touched his charm and summoned him. "I may need some help."

While he formed in the silvery mist that appeared, I trotted toward a metal door in a cement stairwell structure, the only access to the building below and the only place I could put my back to. I thought about picking the lock and running into the building, but I doubted I could avoid facing Zav's sister. None of my charms could keep a dragon from using its magic to hold me in place—as I had found out several times.

Sindari solidified into the great seven-hundred-pound tiger he was, but when my visitor landed on the corner of the rooftop, she made him appear small in comparison. Her eyes were the same color of violet as Zav's, but they lacked the haughty calmness I usually saw in his. She looked pissed.

I do not think I can give the kind of help you require, Sindari spoke telepathically into my mind as he took in the situation.

I was afraid of that.

Despite his words, he loped over to stand beside me, and we faced the dragon together. She hadn't moved since she'd landed, and an uncomfortable scraping feeling raked at the mental barrier of my mind. Was she trying to read my thoughts? The way Shaygor had?

I suggest you be very polite and acquiescing. Sindari must have read the same anger in her eyes.

"Hi!" I waved my sword. "I'm Val. This is Sindari. We didn't catch your name. Who does your scales? You're a less gloom-and-doomy shade of dragon than most. Is it natural or kind of like dying your hair?"

Sindari looked at me.

What? That was polite. And friendly. Girls like to talk about fashion.

I have never heard you discuss such things.

Well, I'm not a typical girl. I can fake it though.

The presence in my mind faded, and the dragon shifted form, melting down into a human woman. A human woman with purple hair—no, *lilac* hair the same color the scales had been—black leather pants and jacket, and two silver rings in each of her outer nostrils.

"Oh." So that was who'd stolen my file from Mary.

How could some strange dragon from another world have known about my therapy? Or where it took place? Or anything about me at all?

She walked slowly toward us, her violet eyes narrow.

My phone buzzed. Normally, I would ignore it when a dragon was stalking toward me, but I pulled it out, having a hunch. It was my general practitioner, Dr. Brightman.

"This is Val. Are you reporting that someone came in and stole my file this morning?"

After a startled pause, he said, "Yes."

"Purple hair? Nose rings?"

"Yes. We couldn't stop her. She had some kind of power."

"No kidding. I'll update you later."

I hung up, stuffed my phone in my pocket, and leaned Chopper's tip against the rooftop beside my foot. Zav's sister stopped in front of me, ignoring Sindari altogether. I lifted my chin and met her hard gaze, refusing to appear intimidated.

"Is there a reason you're researching me like an obsessed stalker?" I asked when she didn't speak. "Are you a fan of my work? Maybe we could get coffee and I could sign a napkin for you. Do dragons drink coffee? I haven't seen Zav do so." Maybe bringing up Zav's name would be helpful here. "I'm not sure he needs caffeine though. He's a little high-strung already."

Sindari swatted me in the back with his tail. A warning to be more polite? What was I supposed to do? Prostrate myself in the puddle between us and kiss the tips of her pointed boots?

"*Zav*," she spoke her first word, which was followed by a lip curl. "You disrespect him by not using his proper name."

"I can't pronounce his proper name."

"That is *pathetic*. At least the elf princess used his full name."

"The elf princess who tried to assassinate him? Yeah, I'm sure she was a big step up from me."

Her eyes flared violet, and I braced myself for magic that would fling me off the rooftop—or incinerate me.

"My name is Zondia'qareshi, and I will not allow you to harm my brother."

Oh, good. Another name I couldn't pronounce. Someday, a dragon named Bob would introduce himself, and I would fall over in surprise.

"I hadn't planned to, so we're good." I smiled and leaned casually on Chopper. Showing weakness only got you in trouble with predators. "You can go find someone else to stalk. And if you wouldn't mind returning the records you stole, that would be fabulous. I'm a deeply layered and complex individual. Without my medical history, my providers will be flustered and helpless."

"You have little wealth as your world measures it, mediocre health, and no power in your society. Your ruse is clear to all those who are not smitten by human female attributes." She curled her lip again and waved at my chest.

"My ruse?"

"To pretend loyalty to my brother until such time as you can coerce him into a compromising position and murder him. Then you will have power and fame among your people."

"My people don't know dragons exist, so that can't be true."

"Impossible!"

"Look, Zav is the one who claimed me. Not the other way around. I don't—" I caught myself before saying I had zero intention of obeying him, having sex with him, or anything else that being claimed entailed. If I let any of the dragons know that Zav had only claimed me to protect me, and that we weren't actually rutting like rabbits, I might yet end up in front of their Dragon Justice Court. "I don't plan to kill him. I'm pretty sure he would laugh at the idea that I could."

"Males often let their egos put them in danger."

"Oh, you've noticed that too?"

Her eyes narrowed further. "Shaygorthian did not get all of your thoughts."

"No, and that's fine with me."

She—Zondia, I decided to call her—strode toward me, lifting her hand toward my face. Sindari growled and stepped between us. She flicked her fingers, and a burst of power hurled him across the roof.

Snarling, I dropped into a fighting stance and whipped Chopper up, but my hand froze before I got the blade fully pointed at her. Though I gritted my teeth and tried to use my weak half-elven power to break the hold, nothing happened. My entire body froze. I couldn't even move my eyes.

"I will take your thoughts." She lifted her hand, and this time, her slender fingers, cold and damp from the rain, reached my temple.

I seethed inside, tired of dragons doing this to me, but a part of me wondered if it would be for the best if I let her have whatever thoughts she wanted. Then she would know I didn't intend to betray Zav. So far, Zav was the only dragon I'd met that I didn't detest. Why would I hurt him?

But she would also see that Zav's claiming had been a ruse and wasn't anything I'd agreed to. Could that get him in more trouble with his people?

Glaring into her eyes, I willed my mind to stay away from those thoughts and tried to keep her from digging in.

She lowered her hand. At first, I thought I'd done something to convince her to leave me alone, but she sighed and gazed off toward the west, toward the sky above the downtown skyscrapers. Dare I hope that her mother had stuck her head out of a portal and was calling her home for dinner? If her human form was anything to go by, Zondia was young. Like a teenager.

I sensed Zav flying this way from the west, and triumph and relief flooded through me. But only for a second, until I remembered that the female dragons ruled their society and the males served them. At least that was what Zav had hinted at. Whether that was because the females were more powerful or that was simply how their society had developed, I didn't know, but it might mean that his lilac little sister was stronger than he was.

He came into view, powerful wings carrying him toward us faster than a car would have ripped down a speedway. As he dipped toward the rooftop for a landing, Zondia stepped back and propped her fists on her hips.

A flutter of anticipation teased my stomach as Zav's gaze met mine. Not, I told myself firmly, because I hadn't seen him for several days and missed him. But because he had put a stop, at least for now, to his sister's machinations.

Sindari returned to my side. *That was embarrassing.*

Being thrown across a rooftop by a dragon? That happens to all of us. Thank you for trying to stop her.

Zav was arrowing down at me, not his sister, and even though I trusted him not to accidentally send me flying off the roof as he landed, I braced myself.

He seamlessly transformed into his human form and dropped down at my side, his shoulder touching mine as he faced Zondia.

As usual, he wore his silver-trimmed black robe, but vibrant yellow-, pink-, and green-colored sneakers poked out from under the hem. Later, I would ask him about them, but now, I merely looked at his sister with him and hoped he could handle this.

"You will speak out loud so she can hear you," Zav said, making me realize their discussion had already started. His violet eyes were hard, his strong jaw set. Power radiated from him, crackling over my skin with its usual intense energy. "And you will not attack her, threaten her, or touch her without my permission."

I lifted a finger. "Ideally without *my* permission."

Which I would not give.

"I will communicate with you as I see fit." Zondia's lip curled again, and she ignored me as she glared at her brother. "How can she be the daughter of a powerful elf king and not be able to grasp a telepathic conversation going on around her?"

"She is half human and does not know how to employ her elven power."

"Are you sure about that? Maybe that's what she told you, so you'll think she's helpless."

I lifted my finger again, irritated that they were ignoring me. "I'm *not* helpless, and your mom knows more about my elven heritage than I do."

Something that I was starting to resent. If some of this elven power I had supposedly inherited could be used to keep dragons out of my mind, I would love to learn how to use it. But so far, I'd only met one light elf and only in passing. My elven father had left Earth long ago.

"If her feminine wiles sway you when you are in human form," Zondia went on, still ignoring me, "then remain yourself for a time. You will forget that she interested you."

"It is not her *wiles* that interest me." Zav wrapped an arm around my shoulders.

Though I hated being the recipient of the this-female-is-mine behavior, I didn't move. He was risking his reputation and more to make his people believe we were an item and all to protect me. Besides, even if it wasn't wise, I didn't mind his touch or having the magic of his aura running over my skin and sparking my nerves. The electric presence of other dragons never felt appealing to me. I didn't want to think too much about why Zav's always had.

"Val has battled at my side several times now, and she has proven her loyalty to me." Zav's voice was fierce, almost a growl, and it sent a little shiver through me. "She vexes my enemies and pleases me. *That* is why I have claimed her."

His gaze shifted from his sister to me, his eyes smoldering. They reminded me of when we'd been nude in that hot tub and where things might have gone if that goblin hadn't shown up.

You don't need to make this quite so convincing, I thought quietly in my mind, worried Zondia would be as apt to hear my thoughts as Zav.

He did not look away. The intensity of his focus should have been off-putting to someone like me, who saw a stare as a challenge and didn't care for hugs, but I found myself stepping closer to him, resting a hand on his chest. To convince Zondia that I had feelings for him, nothing more.

Zondia rolled her eyes and snapped her fingers, trying to pull Zav's attention back to her. A petty part of me liked that he was ignoring her now. Let her see how it felt.

"Of course she is pretending to be loyal to you for *now*. Wasn't your elf princess the same way? She let you bed her for months before she tried to kill you." Zondia gave me a triumphant look, as if she thought the information was new to me and it would make me angry to learn that Zav had enjoyed the embrace of some previous lover. No, what made me mad was that the elf had pretended to care for him while secretly plotting to kill him. Who would do that and why? There were so many more obnoxious dragons one could plot against.

Not that Zav didn't have his obnoxious moments, but he wasn't cruel, just arrogant. And, as I'd learned, he cared about doing the right thing.

I reached up and ran my fingers along his jaw, rubbing my thumb over his short, neatly trimmed beard. Zav froze, his gaze growing even more intense. His mouth wasn't far from mine now. It would be easy to kiss him.

Zondia made an unfeminine noise akin to hacking up a loogie. "How can you not see that she's using you, brother? You are supposed to be older and wiser than I, but you are being a fool in this matter. What will Mother do if she loses you as well?"

"She will not lose me." Zav glanced at his sister, and some of the spell that had held me captive weakened.

I lowered my hand from his face back to his chest and put notions of kissing out of my head. This ruse was going to end up getting me in trouble. I didn't think Zav was intentionally using his power to compel me to want to kiss him or please him—I well remembered what it had felt like when he had magically coerced me to do his wishes—but a dragon's magnetic allure was problematic even without magic being involved.

"She will if this mongrel drives that blade into your chest when you're in the middle of some gross human sex act. Have you seen into her mind? Has she let you? Do you have any idea what her plans truly are?" Zondia turned her glare on me, and her fingers twitched, as if she wanted to rip me out of Zav's embrace.

"Whatever her plans," Zav said, "they are mine to worry about. I have claimed her. You have no right to question her or force your way into her mind. If you do so again, I will challenge you."

I expected Zondia to sneer again and tell him to bring it on. Her face was flinty. But it softened slightly, the glow fading from her eyes.

"I do not want to challenge you, brother. I want you to be safe. Treachery is all over the Cosmic Realms now, and you better believe it is also on this backward vermin-infested planet."

"I am aware of that," Zav said.

"I do not want to lose another brother. Even a self-important half-brother with delusions of the virtues of nobility."

"Meet me at the spire. We will discuss this further. In private."

"An excellent idea. Leave your female prize out of the affairs of dragons." Zondia shifted back into her natural form and sprang off the roof as if the wet cement were burning her feet. She flew west, toward the Space Needle.

I almost laughed, imagining a dragon tête-à-tête in front of the windows where people were dining. Inevitably, one or two people with the blood of magical ancestors would be able to see them, and start screaming and pointing. Until security carted them out of the place.

"Val," Zav rumbled.

I still had a hand on his chest and felt the vibration of his voice. Though I might not admit it, it pleased me that he'd stopped calling me a mongrel and now used my name.

"Zav." I patted his chest and shifted to step back. With his sister flying away, we didn't have to pretend any longer.

His arm tightened around my shoulders, keeping me close. His gaze was locked on me again with that same intensity.

"We *are* just pretending, right?" I patted his chest again, though a wild, terrified part of me wondered what I would do if he didn't let go. If he pulled me closer and tried to *claim* me for real. "Because we both know I vex you as much as I vex your enemies. So you said those things just to fool your sister. Because if she reports back to your mother that you were lying, other dragons would come after me, right?"

He snorted softly, his grip loosening. "You *do* vex me."

"And the rest?"

He hesitated.

I glanced at Sindari, wondering if he would comment, but he was sitting patiently and not looking at us, as he had been since Zav showed up and we embraced.

"It is important," Zav said, "that all dragons believe you are mine. For your protection, until Dobsaurin's death is forgotten or something else has distracted all those with perches in the Dragon Justice Court."

"Would your sister happily turn me in if she figured out this isn't real? Or would it make sense to tell her the truth and bring her in as an ally?" I would have a hard time trusting Zondia, since she'd been clear she thought I was orc piss, but she did seem to care about Zav. Maybe she could be brought around. "I ask because she's been collecting my medical records and who knows what else. She's determined to find proof that I'm planning to betray you. Or that I'm unfit or something."

Was that a possibility? That if someone had medical issues, they would be disqualified from being claimed by a dragon? Sorry, no asthmatic mates for a high lord of dragondom. They're not worthy.

It was silly, but I'd always been careful not to use the inhaler in front of him. I hated this weakness that had only started plaguing me this last year, and I didn't want anyone other than my doctors to know about it. It was bad enough that Willard knew. But I'd seen her in a hospital bed almost dead, so it seemed fair that she know my problems too.

Zav raised his eyebrows. "Is there something she could find that would lend proof of that?"

"No. That's not the point. She's invading my privacy."

His eyebrows remained up, reminding me that, no matter what Zondia said, Zav hadn't forgotten his past experiences. As he'd already told me, he didn't fully trust me. He might like it when I vexed his enemies, but it bothered him that he couldn't read my thoughts the way he could most humans, and even though he'd never said it, I suspected it worried him that I had a weapon that could harm a dragon. Technically, Chopper had even *killed* a dragon, though that had been an extenuating circumstance.

"Whatever." I moved to step back again, and this time, he let me, his moment of pretending we were more than we were forgotten. "I guess it doesn't matter. I just don't appreciate someone diddling with the minds of people I know to gather information about me. I do have a lot of enemies, you know."

"My sister will not be an enemy to you as long as you are not an enemy to me, but I will instruct her to leave this world. There is no reason for her to be here."

"Good." I wasn't confident in his assessment of his sister's threat level to me. "Thank you."

"And later, we will discuss our plans for finding the two dark elves that I seek. And that I have instructed your employer to make you seek at my side."

"We were already seeking them. They're up to no good in our city." I didn't want Zav to believe he could order Willard to give me assignments that aligned with his interests.

"Your employer will obey my wishes." Zav nodded firmly and walked toward the edge of the rooftop. "She informed me that she sees the immense value of having a dragon in this city."

"That's because she's diplomatic." I noticed his colorful paint-spill sneakers again as he walked away and added, "And because you weren't wearing those shoes. Otherwise, she would have been too busy falling out of her chair laughing to acknowledge your immense value."

Zav gave me a hard-to-read look over his shoulder, then shifted into dragon form. He sprang into the air, flying off for that chat with his sister.

Why do you insist on goading him? Sindari asked.
It's called teasing, not goading. I tease you too.
But I cannot incinerate you with a thought.
You threaten to bite my foot off on a regular basis.
You can live without a foot. Incineration is forever.

Chapter 4

When Nin and Dimitri approached my table at Bitterroot BBQ in Ballard, I smiled warmly at them. I was relieved to have dinner with normal, non-threatening human beings instead of dealing with dragons, trolls, angry homeless people, or anyone else with ill-will toward me. Admittedly, one-quarter-gnome Nin and one-quarter-dwarf Dimitri weren't *entirely* normal, but their magical blood and enhanced crafting abilities meant they understood my world better than most.

"Thanks for coming." I had taken the bench seat against the wall so I could see the door and waved them into the chairs opposite. "Order anything you want. It's on me."

"Sweet." Dimitri plopped down, the chair creaking under his big frame.

"You do not need to pay for me, Val." Nin's tiny frame barely moved her chair. "I am a successful entrepreneur."

"I know you are."

"I'm not." Dimitri smiled, but as with most of his smiles, it had a glum cast. "Not yet."

"I asked you to join me so I can ask your opinions about something," I said. "Paying is the least I can do for your time."

"I actually want to ask you about something too. Both of you." Dimitri pointed at my chest and at Nin's. "I have an opportunity to improve my status as a successful entrepreneur, but I need to make sure

I don't screw it up."

"You're not going to try to talk me into putting on a dress and selling tinctures and yard art to innocent passersby again, are you?" I asked.

Nin's eyebrows flew up. This week, she'd dyed her hair a color that reminded me of cans of lemon-lime soda, but her slender eyebrows remained black.

"You didn't hear about my work at the farmers market?" I asked her.

"I did. Dimitri said you sell well. I didn't realize a dress had been involved. I've never seen you in a dress."

"It was a one-time occasion."

"You must be striking in a dress." Nin gave me an assessing look. Or was that a calculating look?

"You're not going to ask me to sell something for you, too, are you?"

"I don't know. Can you pronounce Sua Rong Hai yet?" That was Nin's signature—and only—dish at the food truck.

"I can say beef and rice."

"Hm." She looked me up and down again. "Maybe it would not matter if you were in a dress that showed your cleavage."

The waiter chose that moment to appear and, judging by his glance toward my chest, had caught the comment. He took drink orders, left menus, and departed.

"You're turning into a real American entrepreneur, Nin," I said.

"This is good. I have almost made enough to cover the repairs from the burning of my food truck last month. Soon I will have enough to buy a house and bring my family to America."

"Speaking of entrepreneurship…" Dimitri had been poking at something on his phone, and he leaned over to show it to Nin, and then to me.

"Commercial space for lease in Greenwood," I read aloud.

Dimitri swiped through photos of the interior and exterior of a 1960s avocado-green building with a cracked glass door opening toward a busy street. Next, he showed me a space in Fremont. Lastly, one up in Shoreline.

"That's the least expensive," he said. "Followed by Greenwood. Fremont is a fortune. I don't know if Zoltan will go for that. The leases on these commercial properties are all at least five years. That's a big commitment."

Elven Doom

Nin's forehead was wrinkled in confusion. Mine was too.

I wanted to ask the two of them if they could tell me anything about the orb shard before I took it to Willard's office for her people to examine—more specifically, I wanted to ask Dimitri if his vampire alchemist buddy Zoltan would take a look—but I felt obligated for the sake of friendship to show an interest in whatever he was doing. Life had been simpler when I'd been avoiding making friends or even long-term acquaintances of any kind, to ensure they would never be hurt by my work, but it had meant more dinners out alone too.

I waved at his phone. "Maybe you can unpack your plans for us if you want us to say something wise about them."

"Zoltan said he would become my business partner and help pay for the rent if I open a store to sell my yard art and include his formulas, tinctures, and lotions, and any other quirky stuff he wants to make. He's been thinking of ways to capitalize on his internet fame by starting an online store, but he can't go to the post office and ship things."

"Would mail services not pick up the packages from his place of business for an extra fee?" Nin asked. "I believe they will even pick up from a house if you do business out of your home."

"But not the carriage house in the back yard four hundred feet from the curb."

"Can't he leave the parcels by the mailbox?" I imagined a nefarious, cloaked vampire skulking through the shadows, a deadly threat to the necks of anyone he passed, carrying a stack of boxes of soaps that had been ordered from his Etsy shop.

"Not right now. The new homeowners moved in to the main house."

"I guess they would think it odd if a stack of parcels was sitting by their mailbox every morning."

"I believe so. Hence this solution." Dimitri smiled at Nin as he waved flamboyantly at the rentals. "I can run the store, pick up all the stuff he makes a couple of times a week, do all the stocking and selling things to customers, and he doesn't have to leave his secret underground chamber."

"That sounds like a good deal for Zoltan," I said.

Nin nodded gravely. "You have described your duties as those of an entry-level assistant."

"Guys, I live in a van. I am entry level."

"This is not the way an entrepreneur must think," Nin said.

"More importantly, wouldn't you have to move to Seattle for this?" I tapped his phone. "Aren't you paying my mom rent to live in her driveway in Oregon?"

"I gave her two weeks' notice a while ago. Bend is nice if you're into the outdoors. I injure myself when I go there."

"Your dwarven ancestors would be impressed by your heartiness," I said.

"I'm hearty indoors. Thoughts on these locations? Once I learn the ropes of running my own business, a *real* business, not a stand at a farmers market, I can hire other people to be entry level."

I thought he should master the farmers market before moving on to someplace where he was committed to a five-year lease, but Nin spoke up before I could quash his hopes and dreams.

"Let us look at each location, the demographics of who lives there, and the likelihood that your products would be of interest to the community." She looked at his information and plugged the addresses into her map. "The Greenwood location is right on Greenwood Avenue, so that is very good. A high-traffic thoroughfare. But it is far to the north in suburbia. There would be little foot traffic, so you would need to do a great deal of marketing to make people aware of the store. Is there parking? Hm, no parking lot. Forcing people to use street parking is not ideal for a business. Shoreline. This is a house that was converted into an office building and is now a retail space. The rent is low, but the traffic is not very good. This is also very much in a suburban area. The Fremont location is expensive, but there would be a good deal of foot traffic. I see there is also only street parking, but that it is more typical in that part of town. The building is another converted house, but this one is not a rectangular box. It has character. I believe this is in line with the brand you will establish."

Dimitri looked at me. "Have you ever noticed that she's a lot more articulate than we are?"

"You're surprised? She makes more money than either of us and doesn't live in a van."

Nin flashed a smile.

"So your vote is for Fremont?" Dimitri asked her.

"Yes. Look, it is next door to a psychic. And an ice cream shop."

"That'll bring the foot traffic racing to your door," I said.

"Do you think Fremont too?" Dimitri's expression was earnest, as if he truly valued my opinion.

I wanted to tell him this was a big jump for someone with little experience, but he looked so hopeful. I was reluctant to throw a bucket of ice water on his dreams. Besides, Zoltan had deep pockets. If he truly would be the backer, maybe things would work out. Going into business with a vampire alchemist. What could go wrong?

"Yeah," I said. "Fremont is quirky, and your, uhm, merchandise qualifies as quirky. People coming to see the psychic next door are definitely going to be susceptible to—open to buying enchanted yard art."

"Are psychics real?" he asked.

"Uh, maybe? If she had a magical ancestor, she might get some legitimate premonitions. Prescience is typical among gnomes and elves."

"So you and Nin might be psychic?"

"I am not," Nin said.

"I can tell when people are going to die right before I shoot them," I said.

Dimitri frowned. "You have… ghoulish moments, Val."

"Yup." We ordered our meals, and I pulled out the shard from the orb. "Now that we've masterminded your problem, I was wondering if either of you two enchanter types could tell me anything about this."

Dimitri took it first. "Is this from that orb you told me about under the shifters' house?"

"Another one like it." I was encouraged that he'd guessed that, especially since he hadn't seen the one under the house. Could he recognize the faint magical signature remaining in the shard as being dark elf? "The in-one-piece orb was in Rupert's bar a couple of weeks ago. Now the bar is closed and the orb is gone. Except for that."

"You found it left behind?" Dimitri asked.

"Kind of. I mugged an eight-year-old for it."

Their eyebrows flew up.

"I didn't mug him," I corrected. "I captured him and took it from him."

"That's what mugging is, Val," Dimitri said.

"I gave him forty bucks for it."

Nin poked him in the shoulder. "I do not believe either of us should hire her to sell our wares."

"I agree," Dimitri said. "She *is* a ghoul."

"Ha ha. Can you tell me anything about it?"

Dimitri closed his eyes and rubbed it between his thumbs and forefingers. He got so caught up in the examination that he didn't notice the waiter placing his bowl of pulled-pork-smothered macaroni and cheese down in front of him. That encouraged me. Dimitri *had* talent. Plenty of it. I'd seen it. Maybe his innate senses would tell me something.

Nin was also scrutinizing it. "I sense magic about it," she said when the waiter departed. "A strange magic with a sinister edge. I would not use it in my crafting."

"Sinister weapons aren't good?" I asked. "I would think people would pay more for them."

"This magic seems like it would be as dangerous to the owner as an enemy."

The orbs I had seen lured people into getting locked into worlds of such internal pleasure that they forgot to do anything else. I didn't know yet how the dark elves planned to use them, but in a vault in Willard's office building, there was a notebook I'd taken from their lair, and it was full of recipes on how to make the orbs and other artifacts.

Dimitri opened his eyes. "I agree with the assessment of sinister. I also wouldn't want to incorporate it into any of my work."

"Will you take it to Zoltan and see if he can figure out anything more concrete? I'm trying to learn where the dark elves went, what they're up to, and how I can find them and kick their asses."

"And you're expecting this to tell you?" Dimitri held up the shard.

"Not expecting. Hoping."

"Zoltan will charge you his hourly rate."

I grimaced. "Lawyers and prostitutes don't charge as much per hour as he does. What if you, his business partner who's going to do all the work in your collaboration, ask him about it without mentioning me?"

"Is this the reason you're buying me dinner?" Dimitri asked.

"I'm buying you dinner because I enjoy your wit and company." I pushed his macaroni and cheese toward him.

"I can't believe you can say that with a straight face. I have no wit."

Nin poked him again. "Do not be falsely self-effacing or you will begin to believe you are flawed. Entrepreneurs must be aware of their weaknesses but optimistic overall and able to rely on their strengths."

Dimitri opened his mouth, as if to protest, but he closed it, considered, then said, "Okay." He pocketed the shard. "I'll ask him about it."

"Thank you," I said. "I'll come and buy something for my apartment when you open your shop."

"What would you like? I'll make sure it's on the shelves when you come in."

"An electric fence and a giant attack dog."

"Does that mean you've had another break-in?" Dimitri asked.

"Not since I got back from Idaho and installed the doorbell alert camera, but it's only a matter of time." I'd checked the camera several times on my phone app that day, certain Zav's nosy sister would be by to snoop.

"Do freelance assassins also need to be optimistic overall?" Dimitri asked Nin.

"I am less familiar with that career," Nin said.

I sensed Zav flying in the area and sighed. "Trust me, pessimism is more typical for my line of work. It keeps you paranoid and alive."

Chapter 5

I chewed on my ribs, wondering if Zav would come into the restaurant or order me to meet him on a rooftop in the neighborhood. My apartment was nearby. Maybe he expected to find me there. I wasn't at his beck and call, which I would remind him if he demanded my presence, but I ate quickly anyway, in case he had compelling news about the dark elves and I voluntarily wanted to go.

But he didn't send any telepathic demands. A minute later, he strode through the front door, somehow dry despite the rain pouring down outside. He didn't make a sound, but every diner at every table turned to look uneasily at him.

Zav strode toward me, the hem of his black robe swishing around his ankles like the wardrobe of a badass wizard, the rainbow-colored shoes squeaking on the floor like the wardrobe of… a second-rate basketball star who couldn't afford to say no to a sponsorship deal.

Are you still experimenting with shoes because you're worried your usual slippers are effeminate? I asked silently.

You said high-tops are masculine. The purveyor of footwear where I acquired these assured me they are high-tops. And that I could pull off the look.

Ah. I decided not to argue that *nobody* could pull off that look and that it dropped his badassness rating from ten to a max of three.

Zav reached the table, met my eyes briefly, then looked at Dimitri and Nin. "Leave us."

"Okay." Dimitri stood, and Nin was right behind him.

Unlike most of the people in the restaurant, who vaguely grasped that Zav had an alien and dangerous presence, Nin and Dimitri could sense his dragon aura and *knew* he was alien and dangerous.

"No, no." I held up my hand to them. "Zav, these are my friends. I invited them to dinner. You may join us, if you wish." I waved to the open spot on the bench next to me and tried not to think about the last time we'd sat shoulder to shoulder. Fewer clothes had been involved then and more bubbles.

Dimitri and Nin were both out of their seats, though Dimitri was still bent over the table, shoveling in his mac and cheese now that he knew he would have to leave. But he *didn't* have to leave. I pointed to his chair, hoping he would sit again. Zav couldn't tell them what to do.

All right, he *could*, but he wouldn't if he wanted my cooperation.

"We will speak about the dark elves," Zav said. "This is a private matter. They must leave. You may have recreational time after the scientists are captured and taken to the Justice Court."

"May I? That's considerate of you to allot me free time."

"I am not a tyrant. My mate may pursue human friendships."

Dimitri choked on his food.

"*After* the dark elves have been removed from this world," Zav added.

"Did he call you his mate?" Nin whispered.

"No. You misheard."

"I have claimed Val as my *Tlavar'vareous sha*," Zav stated. "She is now my female and under my protection."

I swatted him on the chest. "Knock it off. There aren't any dragons here."

He gazed down at my hand without humor. *Their minds are simple and easy to read. If they believe a different truth than the one we have presented to my people, any dragon who encounters them will see it in their thoughts and question us.*

I sighed. "Fine. It's true. Zav and I are mates. Also, he's a thorough and attentive lover."

My sarcasm didn't go over well. Zav's stare was frosty, and I'd never seen Nin and Dimitri look so uncomfortable.

"Can we go now?" Nin whispered.

"Yeah." Maybe I should have shooed them away as soon as I'd sensed Zav.

"Come on, Nin." Dimitri patted her on the back. "Do you want to go to Tractor Tavern? I have tickets for the music tonight."

"Who is playing?" She hurried toward the door with him.

"Hobosexual."

"Homosexual?"

"No, Hobosexual. It's a band. And a trend. You need to watch out for men who live in their vans and try to woo you."

I didn't hear Nin's response to that, but I hoped it was suitably ironic.

Zav sat, not next to me but across from me, so he could continue giving me his cool disapproving glare. Usually, I would glare defiantly back at him, but I felt a little guilty so instead picked at the food on my plate. But I wasn't being unreasonable in not wanting to weird out my friends with this claiming stuff, was I?

"Let's not talk about it in front of people who can't guard their thoughts, okay?" I met his gaze. "Then it won't become an issue."

"Will they not find it suspicious that I am regularly in your presence?"

"I'll tell them you claimed my *boss* and she assigned me to work with you."

"Is that a joke?"

"Yeah. It was hilarious too. Feel free to laugh."

He did not. Though his eyes had lost their frosty edge.

I plucked the remaining ribs off my plate and handed them to him as an offering.

He eyed them, then eyed me, then eyed them.

"Do they smell offensive or are you suspicious of me because I might be poisoning you? I was just eating them myself. Look." I stuck my tongue out and licked the barbecue-sauce-slathered side.

"You have not offered me meat before."

"No, but I guess I should have. You don't like sweets, and you're a predator." I remembered discussing the unavailability of sheep-flavored ice cream with him in Idaho. "If the barbecue sauce doesn't bother you, then you might like this."

Did dragons cook their meat? Or prefer it raw and fresh off the carcass?

He sniffed and looked at the ribs again, then back at me. My shoulders sagged. He *was* suspicious. Was this why he'd been so reticent to take food from me? He'd only taken a lick of the ice cream cone I'd given him. Because he didn't like the taste, I'd assumed, but maybe he'd thought I'd sprinkled some poison on top before coming out with it.

"I'll finish them if you don't want them." I tried to sound like it didn't matter to me, but his suspicion stung. After the battles we'd been through, I wanted him to trust me. I trusted *him*. Not to be tactful or considerate but to be honorable and protect me.

As I was pulling the ribs back to eat, he caught my wrist. For a moment, he simply held it and gazed at me. No, he was gazing at the ribs again. Maybe they smelled appealing to him.

He took the ribs and raised the meatiest side to his mouth. Using the hand that was holding my wrist, he pressed my forearm to the table, pinning me there. What, was he afraid I would make a dash for the door now that I'd successfully foisted the supposedly poisoned ribs off on him?

I sighed dramatically, propped my other elbow on the table, and waited for him to eat. He chewed on a rib while watching me with that intense gaze of his. It was kind of… hot actually. Hell if I knew why. I was pretty sure I'd never gotten excited watching a guy eat. But being watched so intently by a predator—by him—was kind of flattering. Assuming he wasn't thinking about eating me too.

The ribs must have been acceptable to his picky palate. He cleaned the bones, leaving them in a pile on the tray. Then he wiped his fingers on a napkin and released my arm but only to capture my hand with both of his. His grip was gentle, and his gaze also grew gentler.

"I don't want to mistrust you, Val." He closed his eyes. "And you have not given me a reason to."

The admission surprised me, but I was glad to hear it.

"Even though I cannot read your thoughts, I believe you say exactly what you are thinking." His eyes opened, the first hint of humor crinkling the corners. "Even when it is clear you shouldn't."

"Diplomacy isn't my strength."

"Were you to travel to Xynar Sun Dhar as a greeter, the natives would cut your tongue out, roast it over a fire, and dice it for one of their soups."

"This sounds like a lovely place to vacation. Get me a brochure, will you?"

He grinned, and my breath caught. Why had he chosen to shape-shift into such a handsome human? Staying out of trouble with him would have been much easier if he turned into an orc or ogre.

"You have not given me a reason to mistrust you," he repeated, "but I have told you about my past."

"Yes, and I get it. It's fine."

"It is not, given that we have bonded, but... it is difficult for me to get around. And my sister has been reminding me of the many mistakes I made with Lyseera—the princess. I have forgotten none of them. I do not appreciate my sister lecturing me on this matter, but I believe she cares and her fears are genuine. I do not know how to assuage them or convince her to leave you alone. I asked her to depart from this world, but I do not believe she intends to listen. She is female."

"Problematic."

"She believes she knows better than all males, even older and wiser ones."

"She seemed a little uppity to me."

The grin flashed briefly again. "Yes. Perhaps in time, she will realize that you intend no ill-will toward me."

And will you, too, realize that? I wondered to myself.

"Yeah," was all I said.

Zav hadn't relinquished his grip, and his thumb rubbed the back of my hand. I couldn't quite feel my heart pounding in my chest, but I knew its beats had gone from a sedate plod to a sprint.

"Val," he said softly, his gaze holding mine.

For a wild moment, I thought he would ask if we could go back to my place and explore the limits of our trust for each other. Naked.

"Yes?" The word came out raspy.

"I require more meat." Zav let go of my hand and held up one of the bare bones.

"Oh." I laughed awkwardly and looked around for a waiter to wave over.

He had disappeared. The diners at the nearby tables had fled, either because they also had tickets to Hobosexual or because Zav was oozing his aura all over the place and making people uneasy. Was it strange that others fled his presence and I had to remind myself not to lean in too close?

I had to go back to the kitchen to find someone and place an order.

The food came out a lot more quickly than it had before Zav showed up. Three orders of ribs. It was just a hunch, but I assumed dragons had hearty appetites. When he had mentioned eating sheep, he hadn't referred to mutton chops or a rump steak. *Sheep* might mean everything but the wool.

Zav's eyes lit up as the trays were set down by the bewildered waiter. He hustled away without waiting to see who was going to eat all that food. Zav squinted back toward the kitchen, perhaps using his senses to check for dark elves or other suspicious people who might be waving vials of poison over the smokers, but he must not have detected anything alarming.

This time, when he ate, his focus was on the trays as he ravenously dug in.

I searched this city and all the nearby ones for signs of dark elves, Zav spoke telepathically as he devoured his meal. *I still have the pants-fastener you found that belonged to Baklinor-ten and have attempted to use it to locate him. If I am within ten miles of him, I should be able to tell, but I flew even into the wilderness to the far north and down to the area on the coast where we first met. Unfortunately, dark elves are good at hiding themselves and their lairs from even a dragon's senses.*

Maybe that was why I hadn't been able to find them either. The dark elves might have caught wind of Zav searching for them and were hunkering down now, waiting until he left to put their plans into place.

I didn't know what those plans were, beyond using their pleasure orbs on people, but since returning to Seattle, I'd been having nightmares of a dark-elf apocalypse that put the entire city in danger, including Thad and Amber. In addition to the dreams, the worry that I'd made a mistake in reuniting with them, and that they would be hurt because of their association with me, kept me up nights.

I also searched the remains of their lair underneath this city. Human workers walled off or filled in many of the tunnels, but I could tell that the dark elves themselves had removed their belongings and destroyed their laboratories and anything else they didn't take with them. Zav looked up, barbecue sauce smearing his jaw and conditioning his short beard. *You are able to use the technology in this world more aptly than I. Have you discovered any trace of them?*

I handed him a napkin and pulled out my phone. "I've checked the internet countless times, but I'll see if I can scrounge up anything new. So far, I've only found references to where they *were*."

Zav gazed at me, and I thought he might comment on how poor at researching I was. He always seemed to believe that a couple of hours should be enough to discover everything he wanted me to look up for him.

"I'm also questioning people that I know have dealt with the dark elves. I don't know where Rupert the troll disappeared to, but I have the address of the Northern Pride headquarters. That's next on my list. The shifter brothers are gone, but their allies may know where the suppliers of that now-defunct orb live."

Zav kept considering me. Judging me? Or waiting for me to say something more brilliant and useful? Why did I always feel like he was some aloof professor that I longed to impress?

"I require more meals," Zav said.

I sat back. Maybe he hadn't been judging me at all.

"*More?*" I wondered if I'd brought enough money along for this. "You didn't eat the cornbread. Or the coleslaw or collard greens." I pointed to the untouched sides next to the tidy piles of clean rib bones.

"You may eat those items if you wish. They are not meat."

Sighing, I flagged down the waiter. He was keeping an eye on our table.

"Can we get more ribs? *Just* the ribs? And a few boxes for these." I waved at the sides. I would be eating cornbread and sides for the rest of the week.

"We don't usually do the ribs à la carte," the waiter started, eyeing Zav warily.

Zav's eyes flared with inner light. "You will bring more meat."

The waiter stumbled back. I caught his arm to keep him from going down when he tripped over his own feet, then tried to pat it reassuringly when he recovered.

"More ribs and a couple of chickens, too, please." I gave him my best smile.

"Yes, ma'am."

When he left, I nudged Zav under the table with my boot. "Don't bully the waitstaff, please."

"Bully?" His eyebrows rose in indignation. "I am not a bully. I simply requested more food. A dragon should not have to ask twice to be served."

"You didn't ask twice. I asked and then you got grumpy."

"A dragon's mate should also not have to ask twice."

"He doesn't know about our relationship."

"Humans." Zav curled a lip not dissimilarly to the way his sister had. "They could not recognize a magical mark staking a claim if its wings beat them around the head."

"Maybe I should get my status as your mate printed on a T-shirt for those without magical senses."

He scrutinized me, probably looking for sarcasm; he must have missed it. "Yes. Do this."

I rubbed my face, imagining what the shirt would say. *I'm with* followed by a picture of a fire-breathing dragon holding a rack of ribs?

My phone buzzed.

"Hey, Willard. Is there any chance you know where a grumpy dragon can find some dark elves on a Friday night?"

"Does that mean you didn't find anything at the bar?" she asked.

I am not grumpy, Zav spoke into my mind. *I am pleased with this meal and not yet ready for it to end.*

Indeed, his eyes brightened—with interest, not with glowing magic—when the waiter brought three more trays out containing ribs and whole barbecued chickens. After depositing them, he gave me a wary look and slid the bill onto my corner of the table. I was afraid to check it.

Instead, I described the abandoned bar to Willard and told her I'd sent that shard off for Zoltan to look at. "Do you know anything about that health inspection sign?"

"I'll look into it. You should have brought the shard here. We have a doctor and a scientist that work with us."

"Yeah, but Zoltan has more than a hundred years' worth of knowledge in his head."

"Doesn't he charge you thousands of dollars for that knowledge?"

"Sometimes only hundreds."

"Bring it here after he examines it. And Val?" Willard's no-nonsense Southern accent took on a weird note. If Zav hadn't been sitting across from me, I would have thought he'd walked into her office. "Can you come to the office in the morning?" Maybe she remembered it was Friday night because she tacked on, "What are you doing this weekend?"

"Currently, I'm feeding Zav."

Not literally. He had no trouble feeding himself. But my hand could have disappeared into his mouth if it got caught between him and a rib.

"I'm imagining him on a couch and you dropping grapes into his mouth," Willard said.

"Close. It's a table and ribs." I took a picture of the mostly demolished pile of trays and sent it to her. "Grapes would have been a lot more affordable."

"You're paying?"

"Dragons don't have money."

"I didn't know you were so affluent. I must be paying you too much."

"I'm not and you're not. Trust me. What's at the office?"

"I want you to meet a new informant. She's asking about an internship."

"She doesn't have purple hair and nose rings, does she?"

"No. Should I ask you about that?"

"Let's just say that you may want to see if whatever records you have on me are still in the office."

"Care to expound?"

"I will in the morning. I'm about to visit the Northern Pride to see if the shifters there know anything about the dark elves."

I will also come. Zav had finished the meat—all of it—and leaned back in his chair with his hands folded across his stomach. Any normal human who'd eaten that much without exploding would have had a bulging gut, but shapeshifters didn't seem to bloat. Lucky them.

"That sounds like a bad idea," Willard said. "You killed some of their officers recently."

"I haven't forgotten."

"I doubt they've forgotten either. I'll send one of my people to question them."

"Your people won't get the answers I can get. Don't worry. I'm going to take backup." I smiled at Zav and leaned across the table to wipe barbecue sauce off his face. "Ferocious backup."

Zav's eyebrows drifted upward, but he tolerated this mothering. Maybe because I'd called him ferocious.

"I hope he's reliable," Willard muttered, not sounding pleased with my initiative.

"He is."

"If the shapeshifters don't maul you, be here at eight tomorrow to meet this intern."

"What if they do maul me?"

"You can have until eight-thirty."

"Generous." I hung up and paid the bill with my dwindling wad of cash. The money was for bribing informants, not feeding dragons. Hopefully, with Zav along, I wouldn't need to bribe the shifters to speak with me. "You said you're willing to come speak with the Northern Pride with me?"

"*Speak* with them?"

"We may need to speak *forcefully*." If we didn't end up in a fight. I stood up, leaving a nice tip for the waiter. "Feel free to bully them."

"Bullying feline shifters is permissible but not slow waitstaff?"

"Exactly."

His brow creased as he stood. "Are you doing what is referred to as sending mixed signals?"

"No. That would be if I told you I would never consider having a relationship with a dragon and then kissed you."

"Haven't you done that?"

"You kissed *me*." At least in the hot tub, he had. Dobsaurin had forced me to instigate our other kiss. But so far, I'd managed to keep from voluntarily planting my lips on Zav.

"You have *wished* to kiss me." Through some magic, he caused the door to open ahead of us.

"I thought you couldn't read my thoughts."

We stepped outside together, Zav sticking close to my side as we hurried down the street to a shop with an awning. Rain hammered down on the street with a stream flowing toward the nearest stormwater drain. I thought of the four blocks to where I'd parked my Jeep and wondered if Zav could magic us there or keep us dry for the walk.

"I do not need telepathy to know you wish to mate with me." Zav said it as if he were stating a simple fact, as if he'd been privy to the many lurid dreams I'd had about him since we'd met. And damn if my cheeks didn't flush with warmth.

"Is that so?" I wasn't sure I could lie to him, but I didn't want to admit he had any power over me beyond purely magical power. Even that, I resented. "I guess you think it's impossible for a female of any species to resist your allure. But I can. I have no desire to be your claimed Tlavar-thingy."

"Oh, I know this. You only wish me to join you in your bed."

I shook my head, though I couldn't meet his eyes as I made my silent denial.

"You wish to serve and obey no one." Zav smirked and touched my cheek. "I believe you vex even your own boss."

Why did that simple touch light a spark deep inside me? And make me think of him in my bed? I didn't want him to be right. It was much better when smugly arrogant people—and dragons—were proven wrong.

"I vex a lot of people."

"Yes." His smirk grew broader. "This is a foolish practice, since your human half is so weak and you haven't learned to tap into your elven ancestry. In truth, it should not please me."

"But you like feisty women, eh?"

"Yes."

Zav lowered his hand but only to slip it around my waist and pull me close.

I tried not to look at his lips. Those lips could get me in trouble. "I don't suppose *you'd* like to show me how to tap into that ancestry? Teach me some magic?"

"Each species uses magic in a way that relies on the natural aptitudes and abilities of their kind. Only a dragon may teach a dragon to use magic, and only an elf may teach an elf."

"That's disappointing."

"I would teach you if I could." He touched my cheek with his finger as his gaze locked with mine. Looking into his eyes was just as dangerous as looking at his lips. I found myself leaning against his chest as he added, "I do not wish to disappoint you."

He kissed me, and I stopped pretending I didn't want him to. His lips were not gentle and teasing but hungry and demanding. It startled me—he'd never been so straightforward about acting on his desires—but I didn't pull away. A lot more than a *spark* ignited in me, and before I could think better of it, my arms wrapped around him, sealing our bodies together. His hands roamed under my jacket, and that felt almost as good as his aura crackling over me. I leaned against his body, unable to think of resisting him.

I do not know if it is wise, Zav spoke telepathically as his mouth explored mine, *but I will claim you physically as well as magically. You will be mine in all senses.*

I don't belong to you or anyone else, I thought, though I knew I would go back to my apartment with him in a heartbeat, no matter what silly words he was saying into my mind.

I will take you in the carnal way of this species. When I am in this form, I think of it often. Since we fought together in the water plant, I have wanted you. I have not been honest with you because I've known it could be a mistake to act on these human urges, but even when I am in my native form, I want you next to me. Fighting at my side. Mine.

Magic flowed from his fingers, caressing me in places he wasn't even touching, and all coherent thoughts tumbled from my mind.

Take me to my apartment, I thought, tempted to wrap my legs around him right there, but... *We can't have sex in the middle of the sidewalk.*

No? He teased me with a lick of magic in a sensitive spot and shifted me against the wall. *Nobody will get between a dragon and his mate.*

It was true. A few people had walked our way, but they'd gone out in the rain to cross the street rather than disturb us.

I have a lot of enemies. And so do you. Dropping our pants in the open would make us both vulnerable.

I do not have pants.

I snorted. *I do. Let's go back to my place, so I can get out of them.*

For the first time, he withdrew his mouth from mine, pausing his tactile and magical explorations of my body. I gripped his shoulders in confused protest. We weren't going to stop *now,* were we?

Why do you want so much to mate at your domicile? Suspicion laced the words. He peered into my eyes, trying to read the story of my mind.

I groaned and dropped my forehead to his shoulder. I should have known. The seduction thing. His treacherous elf lover had probably lured him back to *her* room for the assassination attempt.

"Look, Zav," I murmured into his shoulder, not bothering to hide the sexual frustration in my voice. "If you don't trust me enough to get naked with me, fine, but you can't *start* something you don't intend to finish. It's..."

"Agonizing," he murmured, sounding frustrated himself.

I barely resisted the urge to grab him and kiss him again, to try to make him forget his concerns. Right then, aching all over with such longing as I'd never known, I would have sex against the building with him. But if I tried to push it, that might make him more mistrustful.

A nearby door opened and two people came out. They started, surprised to see us entwined against the wall, then put their umbrellas up and hurried away.

Zav stepped back from me, and I bit my lip on another protest. He half-turned, looking toward the cloudy night sky.

"I must go," he said.

"Go? But we were going to visit the shifters," I said, as if we hadn't been about to abandon that plan to shag like bunnies all night long.

"I've been told there is trouble at home. I must return to my world." Zav looked back to me. "Do not see the shifters until I get back. There would be too many for you to handle. I will join you to bully them." He nodded firmly. "And to protect you."

"Zav…" I started to tell him I didn't need a protector, except where dragons were involved, but whatever message he'd received must have been alarming.

He ran out into the street, changed forms, and sprang into the sky. A silver portal formed ahead of him, and he disappeared through it.

I let my head thunk back against the wall, trying to regain my equilibrium. I didn't pick up that many guys, especially not these days, but I wasn't used to them breaking things off in the middle and refusing to come home with me. Leave it to me to get hot and bothered over a dragon with trust issues.

Straightening my clothes, I resolutely walked out from under the awning. Cold rain pounded down on my head, but I didn't mind it now. I needed it.

You will not get your opportunity to betray my brother, a voice spoke into my mind.

I almost fell off the curb. Zondia.

Where was she? I hadn't sensed her presence. Granted, I'd been hugely distracted, but wouldn't Zav have sensed her?

Wait, maybe he had. Maybe that was who'd spoken to him.

Are you the one who told him to go home? I demanded.

He is needed there.

Is he really or were you just trying to get him away from me?

You fed him! Zondia said, not answering the question.

So? I fed my friends too. He showed up uninvited and demanded meat.

This is the act of a lesser species seeking to win favor with a dragon. Everyone knows that a belly full of food makes a dragon mellow and puts thoughts of mating in his or her mind.

Uh, not everyone.

Giving Zav ribs had made him horny? I'd wondered at the kiss and all that sudden honesty, but how would I have known?

Please. Do not pretend you did not know. You were trying to seduce him. And it was working because he's too damn noble and thinks everyone else is too. But you won't take advantage of him. While he is gone, I will find the proof to show him that you cannot be trusted.

I'm not going to betray him. Believe it or not, I like his cocky ass.

Even more now that he'd admitted he'd had feelings for me for weeks.

I do not believe it, Zondia said. *Humans are to be trusted even less than elves. If he cannot see that for himself, I will show him. And you will regret your choice to lure him into your web. Have you ever seen my brother angry? I promise you will regret your choice very much.*

I looked toward the rainy night sky, expecting to see her lilac form flying overhead, perhaps while cackling maniacally, but I didn't see anything but the clouds. And I still didn't sense her.

It was possible she was speaking to me from outside of my one-mile range, but I couldn't help but imagine her watching me from some rooftop—maybe she'd been watching both of us—masking her aura the way Zav had hidden his from the goblins in Idaho.

Thinking of her spying on me was creepy. What exactly did she plan to do to find the proof she sought? If she didn't find anything, would she stoop to manufacturing something?

And would Zav choose to believe his own sister over the mongrel Earthling he'd only known a few months?

Chapter 6

It was still raining when I drove into the empty parking lot of a plumbing fixtures warehouse across from the Northern Pride's headquarters. The sign on the outside of their brick and corrugated-metal building said it was a welding business. I double-checked the address—Willard had given it to me, along with all the information she had on the Pride, when I'd been researching the now-dead Pardus brothers.

Coming here without Zav might prove to be a mistake, but who knew how long he would be back home, on whatever wild goose chase that his sister had sent him? And who knew how long I had before Zondia gathered all the information out there on me and found some twisted way to act on it?

What if dragons showed up to drag me off to the Dragon Justice Court before I stopped the dark elves from deploying whatever vile plan they meant to put in place? What if I never saw Thad and Amber again?

A twinge of longing went through me as I sat in the driver's seat and thought of them. Amber had my phone number now. She hadn't called, but maybe one day she would. I wanted to be here for her if she did.

Maybe I should do my best to avoid Zav after we finished this mission—maybe I could even complete it myself while he was gone. Then Zondia wouldn't have anything to get uppity about, and Zav and I… wouldn't make any mistakes. When he wasn't around, I could think of plenty of reasons why getting involved with a dragon would be foolish.

When he was standing next to me, it was a lot harder to remember them.

Lightning flashed in the dark sky, and I focused on the present. Questioning the shifters and figuring out where the dark elves had gone was my starting point. Time to do it.

Rain hammered onto the windshield as I summoned Sindari. Silvery mist brightened the back of the Jeep, and he formed in a crouch, his head bumping the roof.

"Want to help me question some shifters, Sindari?"

Question? Have you not brought me forth to do battle with them?

"That will probably happen, but I'm going to try bribing them first." I patted the pocket with my much-diminished cash reserves and imagined them chortling at the meager amount. "Are you ready to go? That should be their headquarters across the street."

I didn't sense any magical beings inside it, but I might not be close enough. Or they might have some blocking material built into their walls.

It is raining. Sindari eyed the rivulets running down the back windows. He glowed a faint silver in the dim light.

"Yes, it is."

For future reference, you could wait to summon me until you are inside the enemy headquarters.

"Do you want me to send you back and call you again when I get there?"

Would you?

"No." I got out and opened the door for him, even though he was capable of opening it himself. "You won't melt."

My mother had always said that to me when I'd been a kid. I hoped my use of it didn't mean I was turning into her.

Sindari's ears flattened, and he showed me his fangs before he jumped out and galloped across the street, his paws splashing in the deep puddles.

Thinking of gnawing my foot off again? I jogged after him. At night, this industrial part of town was abandoned, so there was no need to worry about traffic.

Not if it's soggy.

My boots are waterproof.

We reached the front door where a small awning protected the entrance from the rain. Marginally. Some splashed off the pavement to the sides and hit us. The door was locked.

Do you sense anyone inside? I didn't.

No.

Any magical traps or other dangerous things I should be wary of? I touched a hand to the door and focused on my lock-picking charm.

Aside from my teeth around your foot?

Yes.

I weakly detect a few magical devices inside. I believe an enchantment on the building may be blocking my senses.

That's what I was afraid of. Be ready for trouble.

At your side? Always.

I grunted. *You'd be disappointed if you had a handler who never went into battle.*

This is true.

The lock clicked open more easily than I expected. Willard's research had dug up more than a hundred lion, jaguar, panther, leopard, and other feline shifters affiliated with the organization. Even if the headquarters was mostly a place where they held meetings, I had expected it to be highly secured and guarded around the clock.

The cavernous lobby area was dark, steel beams running across a corrugated ceiling high above. Rain pounded down on the roof, and lightning flashed again outside. I closed the door behind us.

Inside, empty couches and chairs were positioned against walls, and a receptionist's desk was empty. My nose wrinkled at the underlying smell of the place. It was like walking into the house of a long-time pet owner whose draperies and carpets were full of cat dander.

There were four doors leading away from the lobby, three normal-sized man doors and one roll-up garage door. They were all closed.

Where do you think they keep the boxes? I asked.

Boxes? Sindari's green eyes turned toward me.

Cats like to play in boxes. A headquarters full of feline shifters must have boxes.

Apex predators are regal creatures. I assure you that mature adult tigers do not play.

I've seen the videos on the internet. Tigers in refrigerator boxes. I'll show you later if you don't believe me.

Those are not regal tigers from Del'noth.

I'm going to get you a box one day, and we'll see if you can truly resist the allure. The internet suggests you'll succumb.

Sindari gave my foot a significant look.

I grinned and rubbed his head, then waved toward the roll-up door. *Let's check it out.*

There was a bank of light switches on the wall. I flipped them up, figuring the dark would be more of an advantage to feline shifters than to me. Nothing happened. This reminded me of Rupert's abandoned bar.

Think they forgot to pay the electric bill? I rested a hand on the door, listening and stretching out with my senses. As Sindari had suggested, some magic lay inside, but I couldn't detect living beings. The door was locked.

They may have moved their headquarters after they lost some of their officers.

Maybe, but that seems an extreme reaction to me killing a couple of their members. It's not as if I declared war on their whole pride. Not intentionally anyway. Who knew how the shifters felt about that incident? Witnesses had survived. I'd only been after the Pardus brothers and only because they'd tried to kill me first.

You're a known entity to them, but Lord Zavryd isn't. They might have worried he would come after more of them.

He was never there for them, just his dragon nemesis. And me.

The shifters don't know that.

Using my charm, I unlocked the door and pushed it up, careful not to expose myself to anyone inside. Just because I didn't sense anyone didn't mean someone couldn't be in there wearing a cloaking charm.

With that thought, I activated my own.

No sounds came from the vast open room inside. Sindari and I padded in on soundless feet.

I smell decomposing meat, he remarked.

Maybe someone left behind a bucket of chicken wings.

I don't think so.

Lead me to it, please. I couldn't smell it yet, but I trusted his superior nose.

We passed gaming tables, an indoor rifle range, and unmarked crates stacked in piles here and there, making room dividers of a sort. There were also desks with computers and a few bookcases and reading chairs. A streetlight glowed outside high windows on the far side. It was the only light.

Sindari led me toward a refrigerator and counter in a back corner behind a bar and stools. Maybe my guess about food having gone bad wasn't incorrect, after all.

A dark stain on the floor in front of the bar made me pause. A very *large* dark stain.

Sindari's gaze shifted upward. The same steel beams and corrugated ceiling ran above us, but a clump of bodies hung from a chain dangling from one of those beams. Some of them were in human form and some halfway shifted into tigers or lions, as if they'd been caught with their pants down and had died before they could fully prepare.

This no longer reminded me of Rupert's bar but of the water-treatment plant where Dobsaurin had eviscerated goblins and humans and strung them from the ceiling to die.

There are more dead behind the counter. Sindari walked around it and stopped. *These shifters had an opportunity to change fully. It did not matter.*

Three lions, an ocelot, and two cougars lay in more of a stack than a heap. Someone had arranged them back there, just as the bodies above had all been tidily turned to face inward, hip to hip.

This happened more than a day ago, Sindari said.

How could nobody have discovered them? This isn't the whole pride. You'd think others would have been by.

Maybe they were warned not to come. Maybe they were afraid to come.

I pulled the topmost cougar off the stack. The shifters were heavy. It would have taken the strength of an ogre or a troll to hoist the others up to the beam and arrange them tidily. Strength or magic.

Again, I thought of Dobsaurin, but his work had been more grisly. Messier.

The cougar's eyeballs were missing, and the tongue was slit down the center. A single hole had been cut in the chest with surgical precision, and the heart was missing. The others on the floor had been killed in the same way. Or mutilated in the same way. Something else could have killed them first. Poison? Tranquilizers? Magic? It was hard to imagine even a powerful magic user forcing the powerful shifters to hold still while this went on.

I can't tell from down here if the others suffered the same fate. Sindari gazed toward the batch dangling from the beam.

Me either. I don't want to climb up there or try to get them down to check.

I am a little disappointed that our enemies are already dead and we will not get to do battle with them.

I'm disappointed that we won't be able to question them.

Whoever took their hearts ensured they cannot be temporarily raised by a deadwaker for that purpose.

Does it? Interesting.

Whether that was the motivation, Sindari said, *I do not know, but these shifters will not speak again.*

Which meant we'd wasted our time coming up here. Another dead end.

I took a few photos, in case Willard or one of her researchers would recognize the significance of the mutilations.

A clatter came from the direction of the doorway. I whirled and drew Chopper.

Do you sense anyone, Sindari?

No.

Neither did I.

We will find out who has followed us in. Sindari strode in the direction of the noise.

If it was whoever had killed all those shifters, I wasn't sure I *wanted* to find out.

Chapter 7

Making sure my cloaking charm was active, I followed Sindari out of the kitchen area with Chopper at the ready. My ears and eyes were alert, but the noise hadn't repeated itself.

The roll-up door came into view, still open. The smell of rain drifted in, making me think the entrance door to the building, the one I'd closed, was also open.

Split up, I thought to Sindari, then headed one way along an exterior wall as he went the other way.

The crates impeded our view of all the big room's nooks and crannies, but I doubted whoever was here would be easy to spot anyway.

The faint smell of cat behind me was my only warning that someone had chanced close enough to see through my camouflage.

I whirled as an orange male tiger sprang toward my head. Reflexively, I slashed Chopper toward his belly and sprang to the side.

He twisted in the air to avoid my attack, the blade skimming his fur but not digging in. Claws slashed for my face, but I dodged too quickly for him. As he sailed past for his landing, I leaped in behind him, slicing into his flank.

Snarling, the tiger whirled and lunged for me, coming in low. I leaped straight up and thrust Chopper downward like a pole vaulter. The blade plunged into his neck, severing his spine.

A roar came from the other side of the room. Sindari had found another shifter, a man in human form with the tawny hair of a lion.

No sooner had I taken a step toward them to help than two shifters rushed close enough for me to see through whatever magic cloaked them. And they saw through *my* cloaking magic.

The big male in the lead was still in human form and carried a machine gun. The other shifter was a few steps behind, transforming into a black panther as he ran.

"You dare kill them and come back here to gloat!" the man roared, aiming the machine gun at me.

An instant before he opened fire, I dove under a nearby pool table. I rolled into a squat on the other side, keeping my head below the surface. His bullets rained down on the cement floor where I'd been and ricocheted in a dozen directions. Others pounded into the wood of the pool table.

Staying low, I switched from Chopper to Fezzik and fired under the table at his legs. One of my magical bullets left a crimson trail in the air as it cut through the dim lighting and slammed into his shin. He screeched and stopped firing, stumbling back.

His buddy, now fully formed into a panther, leaped over the table. He would have landed on me, but I scrambled under the table again and came up on the other side.

"I didn't kill your friends!" I yelled, though I doubted they cared.

The injured man roared and jerked the machine gun toward me again. Aware of the panther springing over the table at me again, I leaped behind a stack of crates for cover. Another hailstorm of bullets pounded from the gun, splinters flying as they hit the crates.

His gun jammed, and I leaned out to return fire. The panther came at me like a locomotive. I poured rounds into his chest, enough to kill him. Or so I thought.

He landed in front of me, yellow eyes enraged, claws slashing for my gut. I sprang back to the wall but clipped one of the crates, and pain blasted from my shoulder as those claws sliced through my duster and the flesh underneath. Back to the wall, I fired straight into his face.

I'm coming, Val, Sindari called, and I glimpsed him leaping over the pool table and tackling the machine-gun wielder.

My bullets finished off the panther before he could strike me again. His legs gave out, and he sank to the floor as I scooted away from him.

As I turned Fezzik toward the man Sindari was grappling with, I glimpsed his first foe across the room, groaning and grabbing his bleeding chest. He appeared out of the fight, but when he saw me, he snarled and reached into his jacket for something.

A gun? No. A grenade.

I tried to fire at him before he could throw it, but Sindari's fight shifted, putting him and the other shifter in the way. By the time I rushed into the clear, the grenade was hurtling toward us. I aimed, making myself take a half second to ensure my sights were tracking it precisely, and fired.

My bullet smashed into the grenade, knocking it from its trajectory. It exploded near a wall, tearing a hole to the outside. A gust of cool, damp air rushed in.

The machine-gun wielder screamed, then was cut off, Sindari's jaw sinking down onto his throat. His gun fell from his hands and clanked to the floor.

Trusting Sindari to finish off the man, I rushed to the wounded one, both to ensure he wouldn't throw more grenades, and because I wanted answers.

When I reached him, he was half transformed into his lion form, tawny hair rippling from human arms, claws extending from fingers. But blood puddled underneath him, his body torn in a dozen places by Sindari's claws, and he struggled to fully change.

"Change back." I switched Fezzik for Chopper and rested the sword against his throat.

He glared at me but slumped back to the ground, his human form returning fully. I doubted it had been my order so much as the extent of his injuries. Right now, he lacked the power to transform.

"I came to ask your people questions," I said, "not attack anyone. I would have paid for information."

"You… killed them all," he panted, glancing toward the bodies strung from the beam.

"I didn't kill anyone until you attacked us."

"You're in our headquarters! Again!" He spat the words in anger, and blood dribbled from the corner of his mouth.

"It's my first time here. Your people pissed off someone else."

"Lies."

"The truth. You flatter me if you think I could take out so many shifters at once. And what weapon do you even see on me that would have cut out eyeballs?" I showed him Fezzik and Chopper and spread my arms, so he could see that ammo pouches were the only things on my utility belt. "You'd need a damn serrated melon baller to do that precise a job on all those people."

He curled his bloody lip, but a hint of doubt crept into his eyes.

Sindari, his battle complete, padded over to join me.

"I bet the dark elves have such tools." It was just a guess, but it was hard for me to imagine who else, besides dragons, could have annihilated so many shifters in their own headquarters. "You know about the dark elves?"

He clamped his mouth shut.

What was I supposed to offer him? The guy was dying.

"The Pardus brothers had a deal with the dark elves," I said. "But I'm sure you know that. They're the ones who gave the brothers that orb, right? Or was it a loan? Did things go badly for your people after it was destroyed?"

I decided not to mention that *I* had been the one to destroy it. Not many witnesses had survived that fight. It was possible the other shifters thought the dragons had destroyed it.

"They said only… they were done working with us… not that they would *kill* us." His hand flexed to cover the gashes on his abdomen, as if he could stop the flow of blood.

I felt sorry for this guy—and those who'd already died—but they *could* have started with questions instead of trying to kill me. "Maybe you knew more than the dark elves wanted others to learn about. What are their plans? Why were they helping you and giving you tools?"

"Those who… worked with them… agreed to be… their test subjects." He coughed and spat up more blood. "I did not. I was glad… when they left."

"Any idea where they went?"

"No. I wouldn't tell you… even if I knew."

I doubt he knows, Sindari said. *Not if they all thought you were responsible for this. These minions weren't invited into the hunters' thicket with the leaders.*

I eyed the bodies again. *I don't think any of the shifters truly were.*

Likely not.

"Are there any of your buddies left who would tell me? I'm still willing to pay. Or help you find the dark elves that did that." I pulled Chopper away from his neck and pointed it at the bundle of the dead.

"Screw you." His voice was weaker now, the puddle of blood on the floor larger. "And screw those idiots… for working with those evil bastards…. Saw this coming. Why didn't they?"

I was debating if I should hunt for a first-aid kit and call an ambulance when he drew his last shuddering breath. I sighed, cleaned and sheathed Chopper, and wiped my face. My fingers came away damp with blood, and as my body cooled, I grew aware of the injuries I'd received.

"Guess I don't need to show up at Willard's office until 8:30," I muttered.

Chapter 8

It was 8:07 when I arrived at the unassuming brick three-story government building in South Seattle where Willard and ten full-time soldiers worked. Another dozen part-time specialists came and went, as Willard needed their expertise. There was no mention of the army on any of the signage, and I wondered if anyone ever thought it odd that uniformed soldiers strolled in and out of the building. The sign *did* mention an IRS office, which probably kept random people from wandering up to explore.

It had been several months since I'd been inside the building, and a few things had changed. Someone had painted the interior walls from white to beige, and a goblin was sitting on top of the secretary's desk in Willard's outer office. The last time I'd come, a lieutenant had been working there. Now…

"Willard, there's a goblin out here disassembling your stapler."

Her door was open, so I assumed she was inside.

"I know," her Southern drawl floated out.

"You know?"

Willard walked out, frowning at this unorthodox assistant. "I know about the goblin." She plucked the stapler from his grip. "*This* was news."

"Work Leader Willard," he protested, looking up. His face was familiar. Where had I seen him before? "I was repairing it."

"It was jammed?" Willard asked.

"No." His forehead crinkled, and he tilted his head. Two pointed green ears stuck out from his short mussy white hair. "It only dispensed one staple at a time."

"That's how it's supposed to work."

"That seems a poor design. What if you wish to fasten papers more earnestly and permanently? Or use this as a weapon to deter large enemies who are threatening your small but pleasing-to-you life?" He squinted at me.

"We have guns for that." Willard took the stapler from his hand and shoved it in a drawer.

"Gondo?" I asked, his face clicking for me.

The last time I'd seen him, he'd had longer hair. And he'd been squished under Sindari's paw.

"What are you doing here?" I asked him but looked to Willard for an explanation.

She sighed. "We have enough goblin communities in the area now that I thought it would be good to have a liaison. Preferably one that has moderately fond feelings for us."

"Are you sure Gondo qualifies? Sindari kept him pinned to the ground for an hour while I was negotiating with his boss."

"I hold no ill will." Gondo picked a drawing compass out of a cup full of pens. "You are the Goblin Speaker now."

"How'd you get that title?" I asked Willard. "Does it come with a plaque? Fringe benefits? Is there a clubhouse? A secret handshake?"

"If I'm understanding things correctly, that's *your* title." Willard smiled tightly. "You'll have to get the rest of the details from Gondo."

"Yes." He nodded toward me. "You kept the sheriff from arresting us and you helped us find a new home." He thrust the compass into the air as if it were a rapier.

All I'd done was throw the goblins into a U-Haul and tote them across the state.

"I spoke to the other work camps in the area. You also saved goblins from hunters. And you are the mate of a dragon. They saw this too!" His eyes gleamed. "Your status is extraordinary. Superb. Resplendent!"

"If that were true, a bunch of cat shifters wouldn't have tried to kick my ass last night. We need to talk, Willard."

"Oh? I kind of wanted to hear about how so many goblins witnessed you mating with your dragon."

"There hasn't been any mating."

"I did see you in the water box. You were entwined." Gondo stood on the desk and pantomimed embracing and kissing.

"That's not the same as mating. Willard, your office?" I pointed past her, not tickled by the gleam in her eye.

"I thought you just kissed," she said.

"We did."

"Vigorously. Ardently." Gondo thrust the compass up again. "Fervently."

"I told him I'd pay him more if he could fill out paperwork," Willard said. "He's been reading our dictionary to prepare for the task."

"The dictionary or the thesaurus?" I made a shooing motion, determined to get her into her office, with the door closed, before Gondo could pantomime anything else.

This time, she allowed herself to be guided inside, but not before pointing at the compass. "*Don't* disassemble that."

"I believe the implements on this desk could be turned into a trebuchet," Gondo said.

"That's not necessary." Willard closed the door after we were inside. "Nine out of ten times, I choose well when I select an informant."

"Is this not one of those times? Is he actually supposed to be an informant?"

"He doesn't know that he is. I noticed, when I talked to the new group from Idaho, that Gondo knew all the gossip for every goblin there as well as others in pockets in the wilderness I didn't know existed. I've already put together an extensive network of their outposts."

"Is it important to know where goblins live?"

"It's important to know where *everybody* lives. And people know their neighbors. If something goes on in those forests and the goblins can tell us about it, all the better."

A *twang-thump* came from the other room.

Willard groaned. "He can't have built it already, can he?"

"Goblins are hard workers. Did you get the pictures I sent from the Pride's headquarters last night?"

"Yeah." Willard went to a large tome open on her desk, the handwriting nothing I recognized. Sheets of translations were stuck between the pages. "This is a book on the various races' religious rituals, as recorded by the largely atheist gnomes, apparently out of scientific curiosity. We've referenced it before. There's a lot of good stuff in here."

"Stuff about slitted tongues and missing hearts?"

"The tongues and the eyes specifically. The hearts may have been removed to ensure the dead couldn't be raised."

"That's what Sindari said." I didn't know why hearts would matter. You would think removing the heads or even the tongues would be what would keep the dead from speaking, not that I'd ever been present for such a ceremony. "What species can raise the dead?"

"Dark elves. Occasionally vampires and those with enough power and a desire to learn from the dead will also master the ritual." Willard touched the page her book was open to. "This describes a dark-elf ritual of sacrificing those who have betrayed them to their bone goddess to receive favor and more power."

"Those who have betrayed them? Why would that include an entire warehouse of shifters?"

"They have rituals for all occasions." Willard selected a large clump of pages around the open one. "This entire chapter is on dark-elf rituals that involve enemies, betrayers, traitors, and lovers who weren't satisfying enough in bed."

"There's an actual ritual for them?"

"Apparently so. But gnomes have a sense of humor, so it's possible there's hyperbole in this resource."

I thought of the bodies hanging from the beam. "And it's possible there's not?"

"Yes."

"Could the dark elves be angry with the shifters because I destroyed their orb?" If they would sacrifice lovers to their goddess, shifters started to sound reasonable.

"That's what I'm thinking. There aren't too many species in the area that would take on that many shifters, especially on their own turf. They're dangerous."

"Tell me about it." I touched my sore shoulder and glanced toward the door. A magical being, someone with an aura much stronger than Gondo's, had joined him in the outer office. Some new informant?

"The shifters may have also known some of their plans or where they're staying now," Willard added.

"That's why I wanted to talk to them."

"I may have made a mistake in sending you to Idaho instead of putting you on this sooner."

Another thump-twang reverberated from the outer office.

"If you hadn't sent me, you wouldn't have a new assistant."

"Darn."

A light blinked on the phone on Willard's desk. "Work Leader? Your potential intern has returned." Gondo's voice took on an excited tone. "She's interested in my trebuchet project!"

"That's surprising," Willard murmured. "I want your opinion on this person, Thorvald."

"Opinions are free. I only charge for assassinations."

"You're a reasonable businesswoman." Willard opened the door.

A young blonde woman in an oversized blue button-down shirt, grease-stained overalls, and a gray beanie cap leaned over the desk Gondo was still sitting on. He was pointing and commenting on what was turning into a siege engine made from a tape dispenser and other office supplies, the compass now in place as the throwing arm.

The woman waved a pair of pliers at it and said something in goblin—I assumed that was the language, as I couldn't understand it, but Gondo reacted. He shook his head vehemently and waved away her pliers.

This was the person with the powerful aura. She reminded me of—

"Thorvald." Willard extended a hand toward the visitor. "This is our potential intern, Freysha. We don't usually hire outside of the service, but she speaks a number of non-Earth languages and is familiar with the politics of the Cosmic Realms. When I mentioned we had a book on the Dragon Justice Court's laws, she offered to go over it and see if our translations are correct."

Willard's tone was guarded. I doubted she trusted this potential intern.

Freysha turned to face us, smiling cheerfully. She had a beautiful face with impish green eyes that seemed as full of mischief as the goblin's, and she was even younger than I'd guessed. Maybe seventeen or eighteen?

No, I realized as Willard looked expectantly at me. She was *older* than I'd guessed. Her aura clicked into place as similar to that of the traveler in Greemaw's valley. An elf.

"Hello, Freysha. I'm Val."

"Val, the moon and stars shine upon you. I've heard of you." Freysha's English was almost as perfect and precise as Nin's but with a lyrical overtone that made the words sound more exotic than they were. She removed the cap, revealing ears as pointed as Gondo's, if less green, and flourished it with a gesture between a bow and a curtsy.

"That can't be good."

"It can't?" She cocked her head.

"Well, it usually isn't." I assumed she'd heard of me because of my reputation in the magical community, though I supposed she could be here *because* of me. Had the traveler—Syran Moonleaf had been his name—made it back to his world and reported my existence to my father? When last I'd seen him, he'd been lamenting the lack of portals on Earth, so I wasn't sure how he would have gotten home.

"No?" Freysha scratched the side of her head with the pliers. "Aren't you a hero here on Earth?"

"Uh, maybe to my people."

"You think we think you're a hero?" Willard murmured. "Really, Thorvald."

"Shush."

Gondo, only halfway paying attention to the conversation, fired his trebuchet. An eraser only made it halfway to the wall before plummeting to the floor.

"I told you." Freysha pointed the pliers at him. "You need a heavier counterweight."

"My creativity is stifled by the lack of suitable building materials in this room." Gondo hopped off the desk. "I must forage."

Willard caught him by the back of his shirt before he'd taken two steps. "You're not foraging in my building."

"What about *outside* of your building?"

"No. Sit down at the desk—in the chair—and finish your shift."

Gondo had a shift? Willard's office was getting stranger by the day.

Willard caught my gaze and jerked her chin at Freysha. Was I supposed to question her? Willard had said she wanted my opinion, but I had no idea what to make of the young elf.

"Have you been on Earth long?" I assumed she hadn't been born here—and also that Willard had asked this question.

"No. I came recently to explore."

"To explore? I didn't think elves or dwarves came here anymore for that."

"Oh, they don't. The air is terrible here. I'm thinking of making a *syshoral leniir* once I find a more permanent temporary home."

"Every home needs one." Whatever it was. I activated my translation charm so I wouldn't miss any more elven terms sprinkled in.

"On this world, they do." Freysha grinned. "I came because I'm a bit of a misfit at home." She set the pliers on the desk. "Elves are supposed to use magic to craft things, not tools. My aunt thinks a dwarf may have sneaked into my bloodline."

"Or a goblin," Gondo suggested.

"Yes, elf-goblin matings are very common." Freysha's eyes crinkled, which I took to mean they were as common as orcs with good attitudes. "Perhaps we look similar?" She pushed up a sleeve to reveal a pale arm and held it up to Gondo's arm.

"You have the same ears," I said. "Skin coloring aside."

"This is true. Then, yes, I could have a goblin ancestor. Whatever the reason, I've always found stories of this world and the technologies the humans create fascinating."

"She's the first visitor not to call our kind vermin," I pointed out to Willard.

"Is that because she's being diplomatic or buttering us up?" Willard asked.

"Well, if she wants a job here, she might be doing both."

Willard, squinting at Freysha, did not appear buttered.

"I am a stranger and must prove myself," Freysha informed me. "I first tried to get a job at the metal recycling plant near your railroads, but they said I need a green card." She spread her arms and shrugged. "I heard people here understand the magical community. And this building is close to a scrapyard and steel distributor." Her eyes lit.

So did Gondo's. "Precisely where I wanted to go to forage."

Willard raised her eyebrows toward me. Wanting that opinion?

"If you hire her, it will be easier to keep an eye on her," I pointed out.

And maybe I would have an opportunity to ask her about learning magic. Was she old enough to teach? Would she consider it or did I have to find a relative for that? Learning magic sounded like something that would take a lot of time. Maybe I could bring her a toolbox and she would value it so greatly that she would be eager to spend hours in tutelage with me.

"I'm already keeping an eye on Gondo," Willard said, "and it's giving me a headache."

"Maybe you can give her a desk less office-adjacent to yours. Don't you have a basement?"

"Yeah. That's the other reason I called you in." Willard left Freysha discussing the merits of scrapyards with Gondo and led me into the corridor. As we headed for the stairs to the basement, Willard spoke in a low voice. "Freysha specifically came here asking for employment. She would be a valuable asset, but I'm skeptical about trusting her. None of these magical beings *ask* me for a job. Every informant I've got today I've had to threaten, bribe, or blackmail into reluctantly agreeing to work with me."

"How much do you have to trust her to let her work for you?"

"She'd have access to everything in this office if she was here."

"Don't give her a key. Then she can only come when someone's on duty."

Willard's lips twisted into a sour expression. "If she has half the magic elves are reputed to have, it wouldn't matter if she had a key. She could get in any time she wanted." She flipped on the lights and trotted down the stairs. "I had a half-ogre wizard from Olympia put in a bunch of wards that are supposed to keep magical beings from forcing entry, but as you're about to see, it doesn't work on everybody."

She led me past more offices and storerooms, toward the vault door that secured the evidence room. There weren't any windows down here. It should have been difficult for someone to get in.

"I don't know if she's genuinely perky and innocent," Willard said, "or if that's an act."

"I don't know, either, from our brief chat, but if she were putting on an act, wouldn't she have chosen a persona that's more in line with our expectations? A bow? A quiver? Green and brown clothing with leaves sticking to it?"

"Maybe. But she doesn't add up for me. I think she's someone's spy."

"Whose? There aren't many elves—light elves—left on Earth. Unless that's changed recently."

"Who said she's working for elves?" Willard asked. "*Light* elves?"

A chill went through me as we stopped in front of the vault door. "The light elves and the dark elves are supposed to have been enemies throughout time. One shouldn't be working for the other."

"Times change. Maybe they need someone who can wander around in daylight." Willard reached for the fingerprint scanner lock. "And maybe she's not under her own control. That's what I was wondering if you could tell. You've been magically compelled to do things by dragons. Do dark elves have that power? And could some priestess or wizard among them be controlling her?"

"After all your research, you'd be more likely to know if they have that power than I. But..." I thought of the first compulsion I'd experienced, Zav commanding me to get that artifact for him. It had been subtle enough that I'd been able to go about my normal life and probably hadn't seemed any different to others. Only when I'd gotten close to that artifact had the urge to do something incredibly stupid come down on me like a freight elevator. I'd almost flung myself into the middle of hundreds of dark elves engaged in a ceremony to get the artifact. "It would be possible for her to be compelled about something and for it not to be apparent to outsiders. Dragons seem to be able to do this to people easily. I don't know if dark elves have that kind of power."

What if Zav's *sister* had been the one to find and send this elf? Was there a reason why she would? To gather information about me out of this office more easily than she could do it? All the records here were electronic. That could be an area she wasn't familiar with, but one where a tech-loving elf could thrive.

"According to the gnome book, they do," Willard said grimly. "I'll keep an eye on her and give her limited access to things. Like you said, I would rather keep possible enemies close than have them wandering the city where I can't watch them."

"Good idea. Let me know if you catch her pulling up my records."

Willard looked sharply at me. "You think this is about you?"

"Do you have anyone else working here who's as fascinating as I am?"

She snorted. "Corporal Clarke is pretty interesting."

"More in personality than his duties, I assume."

"True." The vault door had unlocked, and Willard pushed it open.

We walked into a metal-walled, windowless room filled with rows and rows of stark metal shelves, cabinets, and freezers. The shelves were packed with boxes, jars, and crates, everything labeled with a scannable code searchable by using software that only Willard and a couple of her trusted researchers had installed on their computers. She took me to a specific shelf and pointed at an empty spot.

"What was there?"

"The alchemy book you took from the dark elves."

"Oh. How long has it been missing?"

"Someone broke in Friday night. It's on the cameras, but we didn't get a face or a fingerprint, not that the dark elves are in the government databases. The person wore gloves and kept a mask and hood up the entire time. It looked like a woman, but it was hard to tell under the cloak. She waved her fingers at the front door of the building and walked in without triggering the alarms. *Or* the magical wards I paid handsomely to have installed. She paused a few times, like a hound sniffing the air, but eventually came straight down here. Another finger wave, and she walked into the vault and took the book. Nothing else. She walked back out again and disappeared from the view of the external security cameras before she should have." Willard snapped her fingers. "Gone like that before she was halfway back to the street."

"You have Zoltan's translations, at least, right?"

"Yes, though his original was found in ashes in the drawer where I'd put it. Fortunately, I'd scanned it and put it on the computer. The electronic file is still there."

"I don't think dark elves know much about our technology, despite having lived under our city for however long." I thought of how I'd found the vial that had held the substance that poisoned Willard in her garbage disposal. At the time, I'd thought the dark elf had intended to turn on the disposal to destroy it but been distracted. Now, I wondered if she'd even known it was there. She might have believed the vial would simply disappear down the drain.

"I agree. My concern here is that the dark elves have gone to such lengths to get their book back. They broke into your apartment looking for it first, right?"

"Yeah."

"I guess coming here wasn't that dangerous for them, other than having to worry about lights being turned on, but why take the risk unless they're still using the book and need the recipes?"

"You think they're making more pleasure orbs? At least two have been destroyed—I don't know who took out the one in Rupert's bar, but the shard I found suggests it's broken now."

"They could be," Willard said. "That was only one of many recipes in that book. There were also a bunch of numbers in the back that we never figured out the relevance for."

"It would be nice to capture and question one of these dark elves."

"No kidding." Willard slapped me on the shoulder. "I need you to make that happen."

I sighed. "I'm working on it."

"Work harder. It's just a hunch, but I have a feeling we may not have much time before they enact their plan."

"Wonderful."

Chapter 9

"Val!" My therapist, Mary Watanabe, met me in the waiting room as I walked in, coming forward to grip my arms, her face more animated than usual. "I'm glad you came. I worried you might be in trouble."

"I'm always in trouble."

"I also worried—" Mary lowered her voice and glanced at a couple of people waiting to see other therapists on the floor, "—that you wouldn't forgive us for the inexcusable loss of your file."

"No. That was a dragon in human form that came to get it. You couldn't have kept her from what she wanted. If you'd tried, she might have torched the place."

Judging by the uncertain wrinkle to Mary's brow, she didn't know if I was joking. I wished I were.

"Don't worry about it." I waved toward her office, but as I started to follow her, I paused. "Wait, what was actually in my record? Anything that might..." I groped for a way to explain Zav and the sister, but it would be difficult to do so without explaining *everything*.

Maybe I should. Thus far, Mary had been willing to take my stories about slaying magical criminals at face value, but I wasn't sure she'd ever met any in person or truly believed everything I said. Maybe she did. If not, she would have been trying to medicate me or put me in a straightjacket, right?

"We can talk about it during your session." Mary led me inside and waved me toward the chair.

The first day I'd come, she'd placed it with the back toward the door, but each time since then, she'd had it with the back against a wall and facing the door and her desk. I was convinced that was the normal position and that she'd been testing my paranoia during our first meeting.

I surprised myself by telling her everything about my trip to Idaho and what had happened since my return. Maybe my frustrations about the dark elves, Zav's sister, and dragons in general were bubbling over and I needed more than a magical tiger to vent to. Or maybe I was tired of holding things back and trying to get help based on partial truths. Either way, I spent most of our session blabbing.

If the uncharacteristic outflow surprised Mary, she didn't show it. I wondered if she would consider this a breakthrough or a breakdown. Either way, she typed notes into her computer instead of scribbling them into a notepad, as had been her previous habit. Zondia had those scribbles now. I wished I'd asked Mary to see them before so I could better guess what kinds of conclusions Zondia was drawing about me. Not that she'd been subtle about sharing them thus far.

"I'm pleased that you've spoken to Thad and Amber." Mary always named them, never referring to them as the ex-husband or my daughter. "And that it went reasonably well, given the circumstances."

"The circumstances of a dragon trying to kidnap Amber twice? Yes."

"And you're now referring to your crafting acquaintances as friends." Mary smiled. "Have you decided that they're capable of taking care of themselves and won't be in too much danger from knowing you?"

I paused. Had I? I hadn't realized I'd consciously started considering Nin and Dimitri friends. "They're both kind of… in the biz."

"The assassination biz?"

"No, the business of dealing with magical beings or at least making magical things. I guess they're more capable of taking care of themselves than most mundane people."

Nin was anyway. I smiled, remembering her blowing a hole in Rupert's ceiling because she'd wanted to protect *me*.

"Good. I suggest you continue to develop those friendships. Let's discuss Zav."

"Uh, all right." Why did I suddenly feel wary? Because I'd told her about the claiming bit and she might not understand?

"During our first meeting," Mary said, "you mentioned that you weren't seeking a romantic relationship."

"That's right. I'm still not."

"No?" Her face remained neutral, but I sensed skepticism in the word.

"I'd have sex with him if the opportunity arose, but it's not like we're going to get married. He's not even from this planet. You know what they say about long-distance relationships."

I'd hoped for a smile—and her being willing to move to another topic—but she only regarded me gravely, then typed something into her computer.

"Are you going to get judgy about me having casual sex with people I don't want to get involved with long-term?" I asked.

"No. It does sound like it would be a problematic relationship."

"Right. We're working together right now, and even that's problematic. Even if the sister weren't around, it wouldn't be a good idea."

"Though he *would*, if everything you've told me about dragons is true, be able to take care of himself around your enemies." Mary smiled slightly.

"It's his own enemies he has to watch out for." But I knew what she meant. That was the reason I'd given her for my avoidance of Thad and Amber and my unwillingness to gather new friends. In the past, people had died because they'd gotten close to me and my enemies had found out about it. I'd lost one of my best friends that way, and I was terrified of having that happen again. "But yes, I wouldn't have to worry about an orc gunning him down in the street. The problem is, the sister aside, I'm not sure he gets that *claiming* me doesn't mean he owns me and can control me. Sometimes, I think he gets it, but sometimes, he gets all huffy and *dragon* on me." I thought of his threatening words and glares to other men who came close to me. Like a possessive boyfriend. Only Dimitri hadn't received that, but if Zav could read minds as easily as he said, he knew Dimitri had no attraction toward me, or any other woman, apparently.

"Dragon?" Mary prompted.

"Yeah. Like, in their society, if the dragon claims you, they're basically taking ownership of you and will have a loyal slave girl, or at least that's what it sounds like. Or a slave boy. I gather it can go the other way and doesn't have to do with gender, just with who's the dragon and who's the lesser species. Lesser species are supposed to be so enthralled by the dragon that they fall over themselves in their eagerness to please him or her."

"Hm." Mary typed a few notes.

I wondered what she was getting at with these questions about Zav. She admitted it wouldn't be a good idea for me to have a relationship with him. A part of me wished she hadn't. What if she'd said you only live once and if you get the opportunity, you should definitely let him push you up against a wall and have his way with you? That had *almost* happened. Where might that have gone if I hadn't mentioned my apartment and if his sister hadn't shown up? To explosive levels of pleasure and passion, I gathered from how things had started out.

Mary was studying me. I wiped the stupid, speculative grin off my face.

"What do you think?" I waved my hand casually. "Workplace romances are always a bad idea, right?"

"Romances with men who think they own you are a bad idea."

"Oh, I know that. I just wasn't sure about the rest."

She gave me a hard-to-read look. "As I said, I'm not here to tell you what to do, but you do seem less glum since you've started associating with more people." One of her eyebrows twitched. "And you get a goofy grin and touch yourself when you talk about Zav."

"I do not *touch* myself."

She looked at my hand. Hell, it was on my chest. I snapped it down to the armrest and glared at her.

"And how's your health? Have you been doing yoga and your breathing exercises?"

Uh, no. "I've been kind of busy."

"I would love for you to take relaxation more seriously."

"Me too. I just need life to slow down a bit." I considered the last couple of weeks. "I actually needed my inhaler less than usual while I was over in Idaho."

"Ah? Perhaps you subconsciously were more relaxed being engaged in an assignment where you didn't have to kill anyone."

"I don't mind that. I only kill people who deserve it."

Her eyebrow twitched again.

"Honestly, I found it more stressful than assignments where I just have a target to get rid of. I'm not a P.I. And I'm not… Well, I'm not dumb, but I'm not a genius. I know my limitations. Willard's the one out of Intel. She does the brain stuff."

"Maybe you found it relaxing to reconnect with Thad and Amber again."

"I'm glad now that I did it, but that was stressful too. It's probably that the air was less polluted over there. I've noticed my lungs tighten up when things get emotional and I'm frustrated, but they're also majorly affected by environmental stuff. Mold kicks my ass. I'm annoyed at how many of my enemies live in underground lairs marinating in mold and mildew."

"I see." She sounded dry. Did she think I was in denial? "Then perhaps you should get an air purifier for your apartment and see if that helps."

My phone dinged. That wasn't my usual text or phone-call buzz.

"Hang on." I frowned as I pulled out the phone and saw an alert from the app for the doorbell-camera I'd installed.

At a tap, the video popped up. Someone had stood in front of the doorbell for long enough to trigger the alarm. My frown turned into a groan as a familiar black-leather-wearing and lilac-haired woman was displayed. I showed it to Mary.

"The person who took my record, right?"

Mary squinted at the display. "She does appear to match my receptionist's description. Is that your apartment?"

"Yes." I turned the phone back to me in time to see Zondia lift a hand and blow my door inward. The camera blacked out. "Damn it. I have to go."

"Will you confront her?" Mary asked. "Didn't you say she was a dragon?"

"Yes and yes."

Confronting her might not be a good idea, especially if Zav wasn't around to stop her from surfing in my mind again, but what else was I supposed to do? Let her ransack my apartment and keep screwing with my life?

Chapter 10

On the way back to my apartment, I decided that if Zondia was still inside, I would volunteer to let her read my thoughts.

The main secret Zav and I had been trying to hide was that I'd been the one to kill Dobsaurin, but all those dragons knew that now. The only other thing we were worried about was that they would find out Zav hadn't truly claimed me. But, in the eyes of his people and his law, *hadn't* he? What did it matter what *I* believed? I was the lowly lesser species that he'd claimed. Maybe my wishes or beliefs didn't matter. Besides, if Zondia saw into my thoughts and saw that I had no intention of betraying Zav, she ought to leave me alone.

As I pulled into my parking garage, I wondered why it hadn't occurred to me to let *Zav* read my thoughts. Or why he hadn't asked if he could do a scouring or a probe—whatever the dragons called it. He'd said he couldn't read my surface thoughts the way he could with most species, but Shaygorthian and Dobsaurin had been able to dig deep into my brain and pull out information. It had hurt like hell, but they'd been able to do it.

Maybe that was why Zav hadn't suggested it. Maybe there was no way to do it without causing pain. But if I could let him see without a doubt that I didn't plan to betray him, wouldn't that be worth enduring some pain?

Yes, I decided, but I would rather he do it than Zondia. Even as I jogged toward the elevator, prepared to walk in and volunteer myself for this, I hoped I was too late and that she was already gone.

But she wasn't. I'd sensed her aura as I'd driven closer and, as the elevator rose, I could tell she was still on my floor, still in my apartment.

It had taken me twenty minutes to fight traffic and get over here. What was she doing in there? I didn't have a diary to read. Maybe she was watching Netflix or perusing my *Lord of the Rings* books. How offended would she be if I asked if she had a job back in her world that she should be doing?

When I stepped off the elevator, a neighbor was eyeing the shards of wood littering the floor in front of my blasted-open door. Her arms were full of canvas grocery bags from the store on the first level, and she continued past, only glancing inside. Thankfully, no gouts of fire streamed out at her.

As I approached, I drew Chopper. I considered summoning Sindari, but he hadn't had any more luck fighting dragons than I had. At least Chopper could cut into them—if they let their guard down.

You will not succeed at harming me with your dwarven toothpick, Zondia spoke into my mind.

I don't want to harm you. I want to pry your scaly butt out of my apartment.

I stepped into the doorway, ready to spring aside if a gout of fire roiled my way.

It did not. Zondia was in the open kitchen scowling at something on the counter. Other than the broken-down door, she hadn't destroyed my apartment, at least not to the extent that the dark elves looking for their book of alchemical recipes had. Drawers were open, and the files on my desk had been strewn around, but it was a relatively modest ransacking.

"My butt is smooth and sleek." Zondia looked at me over the counter, her violet eyes ice cold.

"I'm sure whatever mates you've claimed will appreciate that."

"I assume you have not shown this to Zavryd'nokquetal?" She raised the poster he had given me shortly after we met, one of himself posing in human form with his leg up on a chair. There was a hole through the face, courtesy of the dark elves.

"I think I told him about it." I couldn't remember. "He hasn't been in here for a while."

"You *told* him that you created a likeness of him to pin on the wall and put holes in? What did you do? Throw your sword at his face?"

"*He* had the poster made for *me*, and it was a dark elf's bone knife,

Elven Doom

not a sword." I crossed the living room, realizing how that poster could look to the suspicious Zondia, and opened the drawer where I'd stuck the blade. "This is it."

I showed her, but if she recognized it as dark elven or the object that had pierced the poster, she didn't show it.

"I never did find out which ones did it," I said, "but they also stabbed a hole in one of my bras and pinned it to the door with a note. Did you see that while you were illegally trespassing and rummaging through everything in here?"

"No."

I tossed the knife onto the desk. "What will it take to get you to leave me alone? If you find proof that I don't have any bad intentions toward Zav, will you return to your world and let us capture the dark elves who are threatening my people and who killed a bunch of shifters in another world? Your mother ordered him to find them."

"I know this."

"You're interfering with that by playing tricks on him and getting him to leave Earth."

"To leave *you*. For his own safety."

As I stared at her, not sure what to try next to deal with her, I had the sense that I was dealing with someone young. Someone young but very powerful. Much as Zav did, she radiated that dangerous aura of a predator. She could kill me easily without even trying.

"If I had proof," Zondia said, "that you are genuinely smitten with him and not plotting against him, I would leave."

The reasonable statement surprised me. I hoped she meant it, since I was about to volunteer my innermost thoughts to her.

"Do I have to be smitten with him? Can't I just think he's okay and not plan anything nefarious toward him?"

Her eyes narrowed. "Your lust for him suggests more than feelings of *okay*."

"Humans can lust after people without being enamored with them."

Her lip curled. Maybe that hadn't been the best argument.

I lifted my hands. "Listen. I'm willing to let you read my mind without fighting so you can see for yourself. Will that satisfy you?"

Her eyes stayed narrowed. "Some elves are gifted enough telepaths to trick even a dragon into failing to see truths that are there."

"I've never met my elven family or been off Earth. I have no training in magic. Do you really think I'm one of those people?"

She looked me up and down and seemed reluctant to admit, "No."

"Right. Let's get this over with. What should I do?"

Another neighbor with grocery bags walked past, gaped in at Zondia for a long moment, then scurried away. I wondered if someone would call the police. My break-ins had become famous in the building, and it had been a while since anyone had reported one. Admittedly, they were usually done in the middle of the night and didn't involve my door being entirely removed from the frame.

"Cover the door so we will not be interrupted," Zondia said.

"You're the one who broke it. Can't you put it back up?"

She glared at me.

I sighed, walked through shards from the frame, and picked up the door, my locks still secure. Too bad the jamb had been destroyed right around them. The doorbell camera dangled from wires on the hallway wall. I examined it, amused that it was still working—it looked like the only reason I'd lost the signal was because it had been facing the wall. I stuck the camera back on the wall and shifted the door so that it leaned over to cover the entrance. That would have to do until I could get to the hardware store. Lenny, the superintendent, had said months ago that I'd surpassed the maintenance money allotted for any one apartment, so I was on my own for repairs.

Zondia sat on one end of the couch.

"Oh, good. We get to be comfortable for this." I sat on the opposite end.

She frowned at me and pointed at the floor in front of her feet. "Put your sword aside and kneel."

"*Kneel?*"

Was she joking?

"Kneel here where I can touch your temple."

"You were going to do this on that rooftop. You didn't need me to kneel there." I was certain she only wanted to show her power over me.

"You may also lie at my feet if you wish. The scouring is painful. You may black out. Would you not prefer it if you did not fall and hurt yourself?"

"I'm willing to take that chance. And why can't I keep my sword?" It occurred to me that I had no reason to trust her. I trusted Zav, but for all I knew, everyone in his family was a dick. His mother had threatened me before leaving this world, and it wasn't as if Zondia had been cuddly so far.

"I will be somewhat distracted by reading your thoughts. You could see it as an opportunity to strike at me."

I rolled my eyes. "You're *all* paranoid. How can people so powerful be so paranoid?"

"Because the lesser species have sought to kill us and dethrone us for countless millennia." She squinted at me. "Do you not know what it is like to be hunted?"

I sighed. "Yes, I do."

Reluctantly, I set Chopper and Fezzik on the coffee table and sat cross-legged in front of her. That seemed less obsequious than kneeling, but it still made me feel vulnerable and uncomfortable. This close, her power battered me like off-key bagpipe music. There was no pleasing aspect to the sensations crawling along my nerves, not like when I got close to Zav. I felt vulnerable because I *was* vulnerable.

"Go ahead." I stared at her knee instead of looking up at her.

Already, I had second thoughts. If I'd wanted to do this, it should have been with Zav. He could have sifted through my brain and told her what he found. But he might not have been willing if it would hurt me. He'd made himself my protector, whether I wanted one or not, and I wagered he wouldn't approve of this.

Zondia pressed her cool fingers to my temple, her nails painted black to match her leather. At least she didn't turn her nails into claws and dig them into my head. Dobsaurin had done that. Maybe this wouldn't be so bad. It was voluntary.

"This will hurt," she said.

"I gathered." I was surprised she'd bothered warning me.

For the first time for one of these telepathic intrusions, I tried to relax and open my mind instead of walling it off. I also tried not to think about the cool touch of those fingers and the fact that they could turn into claws and rip my head off.

Power wrapped around me, locking me to the floor. Fear trampled on my attempt at relaxation. This wasn't necessary. The other dragons had also used their power to hold me in place, but I'd been trying to escape. I was voluntarily here for this.

I tried to say as much, but I couldn't open my mouth to speak.

Another type of power flowed from Zondia's fingers, drilling down into my brain, eliciting the pain she'd promised. Unwanted tears sprang to my eyes, and I was glad I wasn't looking at her. I didn't want her to see them.

Memories of Zav were wrenched from my mind. Our first meeting—she lingered on that, digging through all the feelings of anger and fear and defiance I'd experienced as he'd destroyed my Jeep and *almost* destroyed me. Zondia didn't say anything, but I could guess what she was thinking. That, after that introduction, I had a reason to hate Zav.

She surfed through our following meetings, and I relived them along with her. Not only did she dig through memories of things that had happened, but she found my dreams, nightmares of being attacked or losing my family and friends.

What did any of that have to do with Zav? Did she think I thought killing him would change something about my nightmares? Or how the magical community reacted to me?

They would fear you if they knew you killed a dragon, she purred into my mind. *Do not pretend you have not thought about this. Such a reputation would make you safe.*

Before I could rebut, she drilled deeper.

My back would have stiffened from the pain if I'd been able to move a muscle. She scoured through my erotic dreams of Zav, embarrassing me. I hadn't dreamed of harming him in any of them, but the lurid fantasies were filled with carnal desires. More than a few had me ordering Zav to do what I wished in bed, rather than the mindless devotion she might expect from a lesser species honored to have been chosen as a dragon's mate.

A high-pitched squeal came from somewhere in the building, and Zondia broke the contact. Her sharp withdrawal hurt like a serrated knife being yanked out of my brain.

I gasped, wanting to roll onto my side, grab my head with both hands, and cry. But Zondia sprang to her feet, and I worried some threat was approaching. Wincing, I scrambled to the end of the coffee table and grabbed Chopper and Fezzik.

The squeal came again, like a dog whistle but worse. It pierced my ears hard enough that I worried my drums would rupture and bleed.

The rolling of the balcony door sounded. Zondia rushed outside, sprang to the railing, and leaped off. Turning into her dragon form, I assumed, and not jumping to her death.

I sensed someone with magical blood in the hallway, heading in this direction. It wasn't anyone I recognized.

The horrible whistle stopped. I rounded the couch, so my furniture wouldn't be in the way, and faced the door with Chopper.

The magical being halted outside. I crouched, muscles aquiver, waiting for him or her to batter the door down. Not that force was required. If someone breathed hard, the door would fall inward.

The person knocked. Softly and politely.

"Uh, come in?"

"Are you sure?" a woman asked in accented English. An accent from where, I didn't know, but I thought I'd heard something similar recently.

"Not really."

After a hesitant moment, long pale fingers slipped into view, grasping the door and moving it aside. A dark elf? My grip tightened on Chopper. If it was, this would be someone I could question.

With the door out of the way, I was looking at a slender figure about my height, a green cloak and hood shadowing her face. Through a gap in the cloak, a cream tunic tied with leather laces was visible, the hem fringed. She wore brown trousers and… I decided to call those *moccasins* to complete the outfit. She also wore a magical sword in a back scabbard, a slit in the cloak allowing access to the hilt.

The pale fingers—not albino like a dark elf's—lifted, showing me a bone flute. My senses found it as magical and notable as the sword. When her sleeves slipped back, they revealed bracelets with charms on them. None of them were the same as the ones on my necklace, but they were also magical.

"The dragon fled," she said, and I finally remembered where I'd heard a similar accent. Willard's new helper, Freysha. "Was I in time to keep you from being hurt? When I was assigned to come find you, I didn't expect you to be—" her voice changed from pleasant and curious to cool and hard, "—on the floor of your own home, in a *dragon's* clutches."

"It's not how I imagined spending my evening either."

"I assumed not. Dragons are arrogant and presumptuous. They

believe they have the right to steal the thoughts of others, no matter how much pain they inflict."

"I've noticed that. You said you were assigned to find me? By whom?"

She tucked the flute into her belt and stepped farther into my apartment. She slowly lifted her hands to the hood and pushed it back, revealing silver-blonde hair in a braid, pointed ears, and blue-green eyes.

"I am your cousin, Lirena. Your father sent me."

Chapter 11

"My father sent you?"

And she was my cousin?

I couldn't help but stare at her. I'd always thought I mostly looked like my Norwegian mother, but both this woman—this female elf—and the quirky one visiting Willard seemed like they could share blood with me. They had finer features than I did, but our skin coloring and the shapes of our faces were similar. Did I look more like an elf than I'd realized?

Maybe my mother also had similar features to them, and that was why my father had fallen in love with her all those years ago. Or at least had a relationship with her. Since I didn't know his side of the story, I had no idea if she'd been a true love or some exotic Earth chick he'd bagged for fun. I knew nothing about him at all, save what tidbits my mother had shared. I'd only recently learned he was some elven king.

For most of my life, I'd told myself I didn't care that I was an only child and had never met my father or any of his family, but deep down, I sometimes felt that I'd missed out on something. Even at forty-odd years of age, I was intrigued by the idea of possibly meeting a family I'd never known. *If* she was who she said she was. Was she?

"He did," she said.

"I didn't know he knew I existed."

"I do not believe he did until recently."

"Did Syran Moonleaf get back to your people and say something?"

She—Lirena, she'd called herself—frowned slightly. "I don't know who that is."

"He's the only elf—light elf—I've ever met. He seemed to recognize me. I thought he might have made his way home and mentioned me to my father." Was it arrogant to believe the elves would care about some half-blood mongrel and talk about me in their own world?

"The family learned of your existence from the Dragon Justice Court," Lirena said.

I groaned. "Those guys."

"Indeed. I see you do not care for them." Lirena sounded like she approved.

"Most of the dragons I've met have been assholes."

"Only most?" She smiled slightly.

I almost said something about Zav, but I didn't know who this lady truly was. If she *was* my cousin and if my father *had* sent her, I wanted to trust her, but for all I knew, King Eireth was a bastard who was embarrassed that I existed, and he'd ordered Lirena to come assassinate me. Admittedly, I would be surprised if my mother had fallen for someone like that, but their romance had been more than forty-two years ago. Time changed people.

"Yeah, most of them." I waved to her belt. "What's that whistle you used on Zondia?"

"Zondia? She gave you her name before she tried to rip your thoughts from your mind? How polite."

I tried to decide if it was weird that Lirena had figured out almost exactly what was going on in my apartment from the hallway, or wherever she'd been when she started blowing that thing. Maybe it wasn't. Zav had always been able to tell what I was up to from a distance. Elves weren't as powerful as dragons, but some of them were reputedly up there.

"Actually, she gave me a much longer name, but I don't remember what it was. Something unpronounceable."

"Dragons do have pretentious names." Lirena removed the flute. "I will show you if you lower your sword."

"I can do that."

I'd been holding the point between us. A safety precaution.

As I sheathed Chopper, Lirena stepped forward, the flute resting on her open palms. Despite her elegant features and slender build, there were sword callouses between her thumb and forefinger on both hands. I assumed she knew well how to use the blade she carried. The magic emanating from it, the flute, and all the other items she carried jangled at my senses. Her gear was far more powerful than any of mine, with the possible exception of Chopper.

"There is not a word for the instrument in your language, but it was made by a bard who is a crafter. She's very powerful. It can play music that's passable to listen to, but that is not its purpose. The different notes contain magic and were chosen because the auditory range is displeasing to the beings they target. I played the dragon note. It is difficult to hit for all but trained musicians, but it disrupts their concentration so they struggle to draw upon their magic when it's assailing their ears."

"It assailed my ears too."

"Yes, mine as well. You found it unpleasant, but the dragon-specific note would not be a detriment to you using your magic."

"I don't have magic to use."

Her eyebrows rose. "I wondered if anyone had ever taught you."

"There aren't any elves on Earth, or at least there weren't until this summer, as far as I know."

"That is true. This world became inhospitable to our kind. I will only be able to stay for a short time." Lirena returned the flute to her belt.

"It takes a musician to play that? No chance I could learn?" I wondered if she would be willing to sell it. Or trade it. Our money wouldn't mean anything to an elf from another world. What would? I had some nice souvenir Alki Beach magnets on the fridge.

"With time, I'm certain you could," Lirena said, "if you have an interest in music."

I didn't, but even if I couldn't play the flute, a musician in the city might be able to learn. I could start dragging a mariachi band along on my dragon encounters.

"You would have to come to one of the elven worlds to find an instructor," she added.

Ah, the mariachi band was out. But was she extending an invitation to *me*? I almost asked, but I had work to do here.

"Maybe someday I can. I have a mission to complete here and a lavender dragon who keeps getting in my way. I don't suppose you have anything else that you would be willing to sell, trade, or lend to me that would be useful in driving dragons away?" I didn't truly expect her to part with any of her goodies—I knew full well how hard it was to acquire powerful artifacts—but it couldn't hurt to ask. She had a veritable armory of magical items.

Lirena hesitated. "I am only supposed to observe you, not give you things."

"If I die on this mission, you'll have come a long way to observe a corpse."

She frowned.

"Never mind." I waved to dismiss the request. I'd always made do with what I had, and I would do so again.

"Do you believe that dragons will keep pestering you?"

"Probably. They seem to be my destiny these days." I wondered how much she knew of my story. Had Zav's mother, or whoever had blabbed, filled the elves in completely? Or only told the king that he had a half-breed daughter wandering a forgotten planet?

"An unfortunate destiny."

"Tell me about it."

Lirena nodded. "I see we feel similarly on this matter."

"At least your people have effective ways to fight dragons."

"To some extent, yes, but dragons are so powerful. It is rare we can do anything more than temporarily drive them away. If their numbers were greater, they would have enslaved or destroyed all who opposed them eons ago. As it is, we are under their rule. They pretend that we are allowed to govern ourselves and maintain our independence, reporting only infrequently to them, but if you break one of their laws, you find out exactly who the supreme rulers in the Cosmic Realms are."

"So I've heard."

Mankind had no idea how lucky it was that dragons had never shown an interest in Earth.

"I do not think your father would object if I gave you something to help protect you against dragons. That is not truly interfering, right?" Lirena pursed her lips and twisted one of her charm bracelets around her wrist. Since she seemed to be leaning in favor of helping, I kept my mouth shut while she finished debating. "And I already assisted you with that dragon, so what is done is done. I might be able to lend you something… small."

I didn't point out that she hadn't *truly* helped me with Zondia, though I could see why she wouldn't know that. She believed the dragon had barged in here and forced me to give up my thoughts. Understandable. But I feared Lirena might have inadvertently made matters worse. What if Zondia believed that Lirena and I were allies? She might think I'd faked being willing to reveal my thoughts, knowing all along that Lirena would show up and stop her. That could make her *more* suspicious of me.

"Elves help other elves." Lirena nodded, as if she had convinced herself.

I decided not to remind her that I was a half-elf mongrel. Instead, I leaned forward with curiosity, not quite managing to keep the whatcha-got-for-me? expression off my face.

"And we are cousins." Lirena unfastened one of her bracelets, the charms tinkling together.

"Do I have a lot of elven cousins? I don't have any human ones. My mother was also an only child."

"Nine. Five females and four males. One of our uncles has been prolific by elven standards. The longer-lived species usually only have a couple of offspring."

"Nine? Do half-elves ever get invited for family dinners?" I imagined ten cousins fighting over drumsticks at Thanksgiving.

"Whether or not you're invited to visit your elven family will depend on your behavior when I am observing you and what I report back to your father. No matter what, you would always have the right to come to the elven court and request *shyserasha*—the right to have your grievances heard by one of the three kings."

"Huh."

"I see you're overwhelmed with emotion at this honor."

"Yeah, it completes something in my life."

She smiled. "I was warned that humans trend toward sarcastic."

"You seem to have tendencies toward dryness yourself."

"This is possible. I'm not a favorite in the elven court. You're not allowed to be irreverent there until you're at least five hundred years old."

"How old are you?"

"Only a hundred."

"Such a young pup."

"Yes."

I almost asked if she knew Freysha and how old she was, but something made me decide not to reveal more than necessary about my life, or who had wandered into it of late. It wasn't as if Lirena had shown me her passport. Just because she said we were cousins didn't mean it was true. What if she was a dark elf in disguise and only pretending to be my relative?

"How long are you going to be observing me, and what does my father want to know?"

"Not long. I do not wish to intrude in your life. I would not have even come into your dwelling if I hadn't sensed the dragon. Your father, as one of the elven kings, is very busy. That is why he sent me to see if you are well and also to see *who* you are. What kind of person are you? Are you someone who should be invited to visit our world—and *him*—or not? He is married to another and has a child with her, so it's a delicate matter."

"Because he's had a kid with another woman?" An unappealing thought occurred to me. "He wasn't married to his wife when he came to Earth and shagged my mother, was he?"

"Shagged?"

"Had sex with and whispered sweet nothings in her ear. I assume that was done. I wasn't there."

Lirena worked out the slang and shook her head. "Not married, no, but he would have known he was, as a warrior from a favored family, expected to marry an elven female also from a favored family."

"Like he knew he'd be king one day and was expected to marry someone suitable to become queen? Not some human chick?"

"He would not have known at that time that his family would become royal, but… that is a long story. Another time, I can tell you more, but I am not yet supposed to expose you too much to our world and ways."

Lirena had been unfastening one of the trinkets from her bracelet, but she paused, as if reconsidering. I had no idea what the charm did, but now that she'd started to give it to me, I would be disappointed not to get it. Especially if it could help protect against dragons.

The charm looked like a large diamond, though it did not sparkle in the light. There was a matching one dangling on her other wrist—if she had two, then parting with one wouldn't be a big deal, right?

"I have heard from the magical beings here that you are an assassin," Lirena admitted.

"Of magical beings who commit crimes, yes."

"I will refrain from passing judgment until I see what this entails."

"Gee, thanks."

It was so nice that I had so *many* observers these days. I almost suggested that she track Zondia down to get my files so they could peruse them together.

Lirena ignored my sarcasm and held out the diamond charm.

"What does it do?"

"It will make you lucky." Lirena placed it in my palm.

"That's it? Lucky?" I curbed an urge to let that word come out laced with sarcasm. Magic emanated from the item, and it was slightly warm against my skin. Maybe it was better than it sounded.

"It is a desirable charm among many species and more valuable than you might guess, but it will have to prove itself to you over time. It will make you less likely to get sick, more likely to evade a deadly blow in battle, and more likely to land on your feet if you are knocked out of a tree."

"So basically, it keeps me from rolling a one?" I waved toward the D&D books on my shelf. I hadn't had anyone to play with since I'd gotten out of the army, but I still had my dice and a few old manuals.

"Is a one bad?"

"Yeah. A fumble, critical failure, whatever you want to call it."

"It may not prevent you from *ever* rolling a one, but you should notice that it makes you luckier in battle and in life."

"And in avoiding dragons?"

"I shall hope so for your sake. Nobody wants to deal with dragons."

"Very true." I wondered what Zav would think of the charm. That I'd been snookered? It *was* magical. It had to do *something*, but this wasn't the epic dragon-repelling artifact I'd hoped for.

"We will meet again, Val. I will let you know when I finish my observations and am ready to leave your world." Lirena gave me the same bow mixed with a curtsy that Freysha had offered, then walked to the door. "Do you want me to replace this behind me? It appears somewhat broken."

"Don't worry about it. I have a frequent-shopper card at the hardware store."

She gave me a blank look before she walked out.

I'd been tempted to ask what kind of *observing* she would be doing, but did it matter when a dragon was already prying into my life? What was one more stalker? Maybe I should publish my autobiography and put it on the coffee table to make things easier on everyone who broke into my apartment.

It was too late to go to the hardware store for wood and new hinges, so I did my best to shove the door back into the broken frame and plopped my heavy change jug down in front of it to keep it from falling inward. After that, I flopped down on my bed and contemplated moving to a new apartment building. I'd done this annually in the past, but it never seemed to make a difference. My enemies could always find me. So, it seemed, could elven spies and overly protective dragon siblings.

Chapter 12

The next night, I was driving up the dark winding roads of Woodinville toward Zoltan's carriage house when I sensed Zav for the first time since someone had called him back to his world.

My day hadn't turned up anything relevant to the mission, so I hoped he'd found a dark-elf lair or two on his way back from his portal. Doubtful, but the time I'd spent hunting for Rupert and bribing anyone who'd ever gone to his establishment for information had amounted to nothing.

At least I'd gotten my door repaired that morning and another lock installed. On a whim, I'd purchased a scratch lottery ticket to test the luck of my new charm. I'd won a hundred dollars. Maybe Lirena hadn't been exaggerating the usefulness of the charm.

Even better, Zav's sister hadn't returned. That surprised me. I'd kept expecting her. If all Lirena's flute had done was hurt her ears while she'd been in range, why wouldn't she have returned as soon as the elf left?

I didn't *want* to relive the mind-scouring experience, but I didn't think she'd gotten deep enough to learn all that she needed. I kept worrying that she thought I'd set up a trap with Lirena, that I'd known her and invited her to come attack Zondia while she'd been busy reading my mind. If so, that may be why Zondia was staying away. And she would never believe I had no ill intent toward Zav.

He was flying right over my Jeep now—it was too dark to see him, but I sensed him.

Do you want me to stop so you can get in? I asked.

We were still a couple of miles from Zoltan's place. Dimitri had called on his behalf right after dark, saying he had some information on the shard.

My passenger-side door opened, startling me. Zav, in his human form, pulled himself inside as a huge gust of wind flung the hem of his robe up. There was something amusing about the fact that these shapeshifters got their human bodies correct all the way down to the wavy dark leg hair. At least his lack of underwear wasn't apparent this time. I knew from our hot tub interaction that he didn't wear any.

"Not necessary." Zav settled in and closed the door.

I reached over and pushed his hem down so his bare knee and shin hair weren't visible. They weren't offensive so much as they made me think about Zav nude, and I didn't need to do that. It was bad enough that his magnetic aura was noticeable when we were this close.

"You must have missed me," he said. "Already you are fondling my leg. Is this not considered foreplay among humans?"

"If I had foreplay in mind, I'd be uncovering you, not the other way around."

He took that in stride. "You are going to visit the vampire?"

"Yes. I've been scouring Seattle for clues about the dark elves, but I haven't found much. Zoltan has information about that shard."

"Excellent. Due to matters at home, I have been unable to further my investigation here. Earlier, my mother ordered me not to leave this world until I finished capturing all of the criminals here, but then she ordered me home to glare menacingly at her political enemies." He spread a hand, as if this wasn't surprising.

"She's the one who called you home? I assumed it was your sister."

"No. Why would my sister have called me?"

"To get you away from my vile clutches."

Zav looked over at me. In confusion?

"Because we were about to have sex against the wall of a building in Ballard," I said. "Also, she was pissed that I fed you."

"Ah." He drew out the single syllable, infusing it with understanding. "She spoke to you?"

"We've had several conversations now." I turned down the road that led toward Zoltan's subdivision.

"I instructed her to leave you alone."

"Does she usually obey you?"

"No," he admitted. "My mother's political enemies are more likely to wilt under my stare than my little sister is."

"I think that's typical among most siblings. How'd you make her enemies wilt?"

"Word has gotten out that I defeated Dobsaurin and almost single-handedly defeated Shaygorthian and his two kin as well. There are also rumors that I killed Dobsaurin despite the Justice Court's official statement to the contrary. I think my sister may have been behind them. Whether she acted of her own accord or was carrying out our mother's wishes, I do not know, but many dragons now believe me to be unbalanced, unpredictable, extremely dangerous, and capable of killing our own kind."

I couldn't tell how he felt about that. Did he sound slightly dazed?

"My mother is using that to her advantage," he said.

"Will having such a reputation harm you?"

"It's too soon to tell. Some dragons may fear to battle me because of it. Others will seek me out and challenge me, thus to defeat me and better their own status."

If that was a typical dragon thing, that might explain why Zondia believed I wanted to kill Zav to improve my own reputation.

"Already, I was forced to engage in one such fight. It is why I did not return earlier. I was injured, but I am healing quickly. If you wish to go to the shapeshifter headquarters tonight, I will accompany you."

"What do you mean you were injured? Some dumbass dragon challenged you to a duel? And you fought him?" Realizing I'd driven past the house, I turned the Jeep around and headed back.

"I had no choice. But do not worry for me. I was victorious." His smile was smug as he looked over at me. "You have allowed yourself to be claimed by a powerful dragon. I will protect you, and no other dragon will take you from me." He was back to wearing his usual slippers. Maybe he'd decided that the flamboyantly colored high-tops were not the footwear of a powerful dragon.

"You're the only dragon crazy enough to want me, but I'm glad you can handle yourself against others of your kind." I tried not to think about what would happen if more than one dragon ganged up on him.

Despite the rumors his sister had started, he hadn't been winning that fight against three of them. Not even with my help, though I hadn't done more than keep one of the dragons distracted for a minute.

I parked in front of the bushes across the street from the house and looked Zav over, wondering where he'd been hurt. In the past, injuries he'd received in his dragon form had shown up on his human body.

Perhaps guessing at my silent question, he pulled up the hem of his robe, this time all the way to his hip. "He got in a lucky blow to my flank that was very deep."

The light of the dash revealed three deep gouges—talon marks—on the outside of his thigh.

"Ouch. I'm sorry." I was glad I hadn't inadvertently touched that spot when I'd tugged his hem down. It had to hurt. A lot.

"It will heal," Zav said, as if it were a hangnail. He pushed the hem back down. "I am a powerful warrior."

He gazed at me. Was he trying to impress me by giving me this information and showing off his war wound? Well, he'd helped me enough times that I knew he was badass, so I didn't bother attempting to deflate his ego. It wasn't as if it would work.

"I never doubted that." I met his gaze, thoughts of that molten kiss flashing into my mind, and looked away.

The last thing I wanted was to prompt his sister to show up and start yammering in his mind about how my elven cousin had attacked her.

"Let's go see Zoltan." I reached for the door handle.

"Val." Zav rested a hand on my other arm. Even though my duster covered my skin, a little zing danced along my nerves. Damn dragon magic. "First, I must explain something."

"You've already covered your magnificence and battle prowess."

"That is not it." He lifted his hand but held me in place with his gaze. "I wish to explain my actions the other night."

"You don't have to explain anything. We're…" I turned my palm up, not sure of the word I wanted. Dating? Flirting? Hot for each other? We hadn't admitted to any of that. The other night after dinner had been the first time he'd actually said he wanted me. Before that, he'd been assuring me he didn't. Though I'd been close enough to him a couple of times to know that at least his human parts were interested in me.

Zav raised his eyebrows, maybe as curious as I was about how I would define us.

"Allies," I finished.

"Do human allies frequently engage in precoital acts in public?" He didn't point out that the precoital acts had been well on their way to becoming coital when his sister had shown up.

"I believe the definition of the word involves people cooperating with or assisting each other to achieve a particular outcome. Sex isn't explicitly excluded. The word is nicely vague."

He snorted softly. "Very well. But I wish to explain that dragons experience strong feelings when they are hunting and eating. We are predators, after all."

"Your sister said feeding you gets you horny."

He blinked. "I wouldn't put it exactly like that, but... it can cause something of a euphoric state. When a male and female feed together, mating often happens after that. It can also lower one's inhibitions. Similar to the way alcohol acts in the systems of your species."

"So when you said you'd been into me since the water-treatment plant, that wasn't true?"

"It is true. I had not intended to say it. Or to act on it."

"Because you don't trust me."

"Because my past has made me wary, yes, and because I claimed you as a means to protect you, but I am realizing I may not have achieved that. It is true that you are no longer in danger of being brought before the Justice Court, but you may be a target for others because of the link between us." Zav's hand strayed to his thigh. Had his enemy brought *me* up during that fight? "Your life is now more dangerous because I am in it. I will do everything I can to protect you from dragons and all others, but you should never have been brought into our world."

"I'm not going to disagree with that, but my life was already dangerous. It comes with the job I picked."

"You can handle most of your enemies. Dragons are another matter."

"I can't deny that."

"It would be for the best if we can figure out a way to cause all dragons to forget you exist and to forget your world exists, or at least lose all interest in visiting it."

"Earth would be a safer place without dragons," I admitted, but

I didn't like the implication that *all dragons* might include him. My life would be simpler and maybe safer if he were gone, but did I truly want that? He wasn't an appropriate match for a relationship—my therapist agreed—but I would miss him if I never saw him again. "Does that mean you're planning to leave and not come back once you've collected all your criminals?"

His gaze shifted toward the windshield, though the dark street was empty. "That would be the wisest course of action. Dobsaurin would never have come here if he hadn't been looking for me. The others wouldn't have come if we hadn't killed him."

"*You* didn't kill him. Don't blame yourself for that."

"And my *sister* wouldn't now be here harassing you if not for me."

"Did she tell you about the mind-scouring?"

His gaze jerked back to my face, his eyes sharp. "She tried to steal your thoughts again?"

"I told her she could. She broke into my apartment and saw that poster of you, the one the dark elves stabbed the face of, and she was convinced I'd done it. I thought that if I let her see my memories and opened everything up, maybe she would realize I'm not your enemy."

He radiated anger and displeasure, and I wasn't sure he'd even heard my response. Even though I knew the anger was for his sister and not me, a shiver ran down my spine, and I grew more aware of the dangerous power coiled within him.

"She hurt you?" he asked harshly, his voice almost a growl. He lifted his hand to the side of my face, his thumb touching my lips, his fingers brushing my temple where Zondia had touched me.

"It's fine, Zav."

My heart was pounding. In part because I didn't want to put a rift between him and his sister, and in part because I didn't know what he would do. My body tightened in response to his touch. I longed to lean closer, but I was also wary. Nothing good had come of dragons touching my temple.

Was he just reassuring me? Or did he mean to do something to my mind?

"I said she could do it," I repeated, my mouth dry.

"She will know my wrath, that she cannot defy me in this."

"It really wasn't a big deal. I know she's looking out for you."

A pleasant warmth flowed from his fingers, a magical caress that soothed my scalp like a good massage, then flowed downward through the rest of my body. What exactly he was doing, I didn't know, but it invigorated as it soothed me, relaxing my nerves and my muscles, and the week's tension seeped out of my body. I slumped forward, resting my forehead against his shoulder, basking in the healing magic like a cat in a sunbeam.

His fingers shifted into my hair, winding under my braid and rubbing my scalp. That stirred up new sensations that had less to do with healing and more with bedroom thoughts. I told myself to lean back and get out of the Jeep, even if crawling over into his lap sounded more appealing. He'd just given a very good reason why we shouldn't be together. It was somewhat hypocritical of him to start touching me. But I didn't pull away.

"When I am finished here on Earth," Zav murmured, his lips not far from my ear, "there will be no reason for dragons to come back, nor for my kin to bother you."

"No dragons to massage the back of my head and send magical tingles through my body," I muttered into his shoulder.

"It is for the best." He withdrew his fingers and leaned back, the magic slowly fading. "You will be safe and not used as a lever against me."

The cold of disappointment came in where the warmth of his magic had been.

A sudden suspicion crept into me. "Did your mother talk to you about me while she was using you for politics?"

His lips twisted ruefully. "We did speak about you."

"About how foolish it was for you to claim a mongrel?" I turned away from him and stared out the windshield. The last thing I'd wanted was for him to claim me, like some prize with no rights, but now that he was withdrawing, I resented that someone else might have caused it.

"She did call me foolish. For many reasons. But it was the encounters with my family's enemies that made me realize my act was not entirely altruistic. I *wanted* to claim you."

His gaze grew intent again as he studied my profile. I could see him out of the corner of my eye, but I kept looking straight ahead, afraid I would be drawn to him again if I met that gaze.

"I'd been thinking about it as a possible solution to the problem with the Justice Court since before Shaygorthian showed up," Zav continued. "I *wanted* it to be a solution, so you would be mine, and I could take you whenever and wherever I wished."

This hypothetical presumptuousness and stealing of my freedom should have affronted me, and I would have been furious if he'd ever tried to make this a reality without my consent, but these admissions, after the numerous times he'd told me he *didn't* want me, got me hot instead of disgruntled.

Zav, who hated this vermin-infested planet and had reasons to hate anything even vaguely elven, wanted *me*. A mongrel who hadn't a clue how to use her power.

He looked away from me. "When I am in my native form and not as affected by human sexual desires, my thoughts are clearer. I know you would not want to be my property, and even if you did, as I said, this link between us places you in harm's way. When I have successfully captured all the criminals on my list, I will remove my magical mark and free you."

I was supposed to feel relieved, not disappointed that I'd been cast aside, and I understood that he wanted to protect me. Still, my words came out bitter when I spoke. "Good. You're right. Humans don't like being other people's property. In this country, when you get married, you're equals."

"That is not the dragon way."

"That's because dragons are assholes."

He was the one who looked disappointed when his gaze shifted back toward me. But before he said anything, headlights appeared on the street ahead and glared in our eyes. Dimitri pulled up in his van.

I got out of the Jeep. It was time to forget about disappointments and dragons and see what Zoltan had for us.

Chapter 13

We had to sneak in through a different yard since the new owners of the main house had not only moved in but were throwing a party. A dozen cars were jammed in the driveway and along the curb out front, and laughter flowed out through open windows.

The old haunted carriage house at the back of the property was shrouded in its usual darkness, the landscaping lights not daring to stray too close. The playhouse that dark elves and I had collaborated to partially blow up had been removed.

A dog barked as Zav, Dimitri, and I hopped the fence, but it was in the house. I wondered if it knew about the vampire in residence in its back yard.

Dimitri didn't comment on the dog, simply leading us through the root-cellar entrance and under the carriage house. Red eyes glowed in the secret tunnel we entered, and he paused.

"It is a mechanical sentry." Zav lifted a hand. "I will destroy it."

"No!" Dimitri flung up his own hand.

I grabbed Zav's arm and stepped in front of him. "Dimitri made it. It's Zoltan's guard tarantula."

"If it does not let us pass, I will destroy it," Zav said matter-of-factly.

"Dimitri?" I waved him forward. "Does it have an off switch?"

"It's controlled by remote. Let me text Zoltan. Distract your aggro dragon, will you?"

"I'm doing my best." I patted Zav's arm. Too bad I was pretty sure I couldn't make him tingle the way he could me. Maybe I ought to carry ribs in my pocket for distracting purposes.

"Aggro?" Zav asked. "What is this? Your dictionary does not have this word."

"Kind of like aggressive."

"It's from MMORPGs," Dimitri said, speed-texting Zoltan. "When you wander too close to a hostile mob, and it attacks your party, it's because it's aggro."

Zav looked at me. "M-what?"

"Don't worry about it."

"He's calling it back," Dimitri said.

Clanks sounded as the glowing red eyes retreated. The mechanical sentry hid itself in a large alcove as we passed, the six-foot-plus metal spider impressively large and also impressively well fanged. With luck, I could avoid having to fight this one.

The door to the lab opened, and the glow of infrared lights spilled into the corridor. Like a good host, Zoltan stood on the threshold, wearing a perfectly tailored white suit with a red cummerbund and red bow tie.

"Greetings, my fine business partner. And my dear robber. And my dear robber's recently acquired mate."

The word *mate* made me think of our conversation in the Jeep, and I grimaced.

"Hey, Zoltan." Dimitri strode in without acknowledging the rest.

As I walked in ahead of Zav, he said, "Is this vampire attempting to be witty?"

"He's probably burbling because he's nervous about hosting a dragon," I said. "But you've met before, haven't you? I seem to remember you coming here before we were working together."

"He has indeed visited my humble abode before," Zoltan said. "He was frosty and aloof. Unpleasant all around."

"Aggro," Zav said.

Dimitri wrinkled his forehead at this dubious use of his word.

"Did you find out anything about that shard, Zoltan?" Social norms probably suggested we should banter for another fifteen minutes, but I would prefer to get to business.

Elven Doom

"The shard that my business partner was oddly interested in and requested I investigate?" Zoltan quirked his eyebrows at me and then at Dimitri.

"Yeah," I said. "Dimitri is into dark-elf artifacts."

"Who isn't?" Zoltan waved me toward one of his lab benches, then pointed at Dimitri. "Have some brandy, my young business partner. And when you've relaxed, do check out those crates of tinctures and lotions that I put together. Do you think they will work well in the store? I labeled them as aptly as I could, but I didn't know where to place those barcode stickers you suggested. Maybe you can apply them as needed."

"I can, yes."

"Barcode stickers?" I asked.

"Nin insisted we have them made to facilitate scanning for the retail point-of-sale system we'll need to get," Dimitri said. "I'm learning a lot about business."

"Like how to put stickers on bars of soap?"

"Among other things."

Zav wandered around the lab, peering in cabinets and opening books while Zoltan showed me his work station. It was clear Zoltan didn't believe Dimitri had been the one behind the request for research. I suspected a bill would find its way to me soon.

"I melted the shard down and analyzed it here." Zoltan waved to an electric crucible and data on a computer screen.

"You *melted* it?" I pressed a hand to my cheek.

"Of course. It would have been impossible to identify the constituent materials without doing that. Is that a problem?"

"I guess not. I was supposed to bring the shard to Willard to examine after you looked at it."

Technically, Willard had wanted it first.

"Your lowly government officers can't discover anything I can't, but I can let it harden, so you can take it with you if you wish. The melting point was quite low. There's a lot of gallium in it."

"Gallium? Is that a metal?"

"Yes, my dear robber," he said patiently, as if speaking to a slow three-year-old.

"What's it used for?" I debated looking it up on my phone, so I wouldn't have to deal with a pedantic vampire, but the reception wasn't that great in his underground lair.

"Occasionally as a non-toxic substitute for mercury in thermometers. Gallium arsenide is used to make laser diodes, LEDS, solar panels, and mirrors."

"That's it? I was hoping for something more nefarious."

"It also holds magic well," Zav said from across the lab.

"Yes, I was getting to that." Zoltan frowned over at him.

"You meander, vampire."

"I have a name," Zoltan said.

"Don't bother," I told him. "It took me ages to get him to stop calling me mongrel and use Val."

"What did you do to prompt a change of such magnitude?"

"I'm not sure. It may have been when I kissed him."

"I refuse to engage in such a practice."

"I don't think he wants your fangs near him anyway."

"Unfortunate. Drinking dragon blood would give me enhanced vitality for centuries." Zoltan pushed a printout over to me. "Here are the rest of the physical ingredients. They are interesting only for their ability to hold shape and magic. They are typical favorites of the dark elves. Bone is one of their preferred substances for religious ceremonies, but it is a poor conduit of magic and even worse for a store of power."

The list of metals didn't enlighten me in any way. "Got anything else? Like maybe where this stuff would have come from? I'm trying to locate their new lair. They've disappeared from the city, and Zav has been flying all over the Pacific Northwest, but they're well hidden."

"You could order these supplies online easily," Zoltan said.

"Do dark elves do that?"

"I haven't quizzed them on their shopping practices." Zoltan pushed another printout over to me. "Magic is more difficult to analyze, but I have alchemical formulas that do help. I can say with a high probability that the shard was from one of the pleasure orbs you described and that I read about in the journal that you, my dear robber, stole from their lair."

"They stole it back if that pleases your sense of morality."

"From your apartment?"

"From my boss's secured vault in the basement of a secured building.

She said her people did a fingerprint dusting but didn't find anything."

"Naturally not. Dark elves are professionals at skulking about and not being found."

Which frustrated me immensely. If I believed they had gone into hiding and had no plans to bother humanity again for a few centuries, I wouldn't have cared if we never found them, but... that wasn't what Willard's intelligence gathering suggested, and that alchemist had told me straight up they'd been trying to get rid of me because I was a threat to their big plans. Whatever they were.

"Do you have any idea what those orbs do besides getting people so addicted to pleasure fantasies that they forget to eat and drink and sometimes die?" I asked.

"I believe that is all they do."

"Unless they intended to put one in every house, they couldn't have taken over the world or even Seattle like that." I eyed the list of ingredients. "You don't think that's their plan, do you? How much gallium is there in the world?"

"It's moderately abundant in the Earth's crust at five parts per million. But, my dear robber, there were numerous recipes and other data in that book. To think their entire plan, if there truly is one, relies on one simple type of artifact seems shortsighted."

"Other data," I murmured, my mind sticking on that. "Willard said something about numbers in the back and that her team hadn't figured out their significance. You did the original translation. Did you think anything of them?"

"I recorded them but did not consider them deeply. The alchemical recipes, as you might imagine, interested me more, and the directions for building magical devices were also of interest."

"What sorts of things caught your eye specifically?" I'd skimmed through the headers after Dimitri had given me the translation but given it all to Willard without reading everything line by line. Most of it had been confusing gibberish to me. Like reading advanced chemistry papers without a background in the sciences.

"I've already made their susceptibility formula, the wrath reflector, and a couple of their poisons. One never knows when one might have to defend oneself. I have new neighbors."

"By neighbors, do you mean the new owners of this property?"

"Indeed. The ten-year-old girl was already sucked into the haunted carriage house for attempting to take a puzzle off a shelf. The house is quite possessive about its belongings."

From across the room, Dimitri grunted in agreement.

"I assume she got out?" I asked.

"The house spit her out the next day. She had a wild story for her parents. They didn't believe her, but they also forbade her to go in there again. Excellent for my privacy. One doesn't want to listen to footsteps thundering around overhead while one is working."

"Have you drunk any of your neighbors' blood yet?" I wondered how long it would be until this family also moved out and put the house up for sale.

"Their guests' actually. They host card-game parties regularly that get quite boozy. This prompts guests to stay overnight with their throats available to anyone who climbs up the drainpipe and through the window."

"I'm sure that's a lot of people."

"Myself and the occasional burglar."

Zav came over and stood next to me to look down at the analyses. He had never seen the dark-elf notebook.

Realizing he might be the best resource we had on all things magical, I asked Zoltan, "Do you have a copy of your translation that we can see?"

Zoltan pulled a three-ring notebook off a shelf and slid it over to me without getting too close. He did glance at Zav's neck, but I highly doubted he would make that move.

"How familiar are you with dark-elf alchemy and artifact creation?" I asked quietly.

"Not very." But Zav flipped through the notebook and mentioned that he'd seen a couple of the formulas and artifacts before. "This is what they used to kill the thirty thousand shifters."

The sketch managed to be both vague and menacing. I shivered, imagining such artifacts placed around a town and oozing power that slowly killed people.

Zav turned to the pages in the back. More than ten were filled with numbers in a long series without breaks but with numerous decimal points.

"There was no white space between any of these digits, Zoltan?" I touched a page.

"No."

"But these have to be a lot of numbers, not one long one, right? You'd never have more than one decimal in a value, unless dark-elf math is special."

"Math is the same everywhere," Zav said. "The different species have different methods for recording and solving numerical problems, and some don't use base-ten math—not everybody has a pair of hands with five digits—but the elves and dark elves have developed similar systems."

Zoltan nodded. "The problem is that since they didn't put white space into this book, we would only be guessing." He pointed. "Is that 3.458 and 2.72 or is it 3.4 and 582.7 and 2?"

I gazed down at the rows and rows of numbers, trying to see a pattern. "I suppose Willard's people would have dumped everything into internet searches, and probably searches in other databases, to see if any matches came up."

"It would be difficult to do such a search without context."

"Don't we have context?" I asked. "It's a book full of chemistry and magic. And they're dark elves. What kinds of data would be of interest to them? These numbers couldn't represent people who died in their experiments, not with decimals. Pints of blood poisoned?"

Zoltan snorted.

"Perhaps they were recording data from the world around them that could affect their experiments," Zav said.

"If this is data that is publicly available out there somewhere, it should match up with a search."

I grabbed a pen and paper and started writing out the first couple of rows, taking guesses at where the splits would be.

"If I had the original," Zav said, "I could determine if all the numbers had been entered at once or if they were recorded over time."

The original that had been taken out of Willard's vault. I plugged my number guesses into my phone and waited while it did a slow internet search, limited by the poor reception.

"I *had* the original," Zoltan said, "and I could not determine that."

"You are not a dragon," Zav said.

"I fail to see how your ability to fly and incinerate buildings makes you more astute at analyzing data." Zoltan sounded miffed.

"I also have the ability to detect magic and smell and sense details about the world around me. Including ink on a page."

Plugging a mass of numbers into a search engine didn't return anything useful. I flipped to the very first page of data. The first entry was a single digit followed by a decimal point and more digits. How big were dark elves on zeroes? I didn't see that many of them. Using the first entry as a pattern setter, I assumed each number set started with one digit, using zero through nine, followed by a decimal point and the subsequent digits.

"I already have a headache," I muttered, tapping my possible numbers into another internet search. "This is why I give the intel stuff to Willard. She *likes* numbers. She likes problems of all kinds."

"Willard is the grumpy colonel with all the weight equipment in her apartment, right?" Dimitri asked. "Who told me to get out of her way because she was as busy as a one-legged cat in a sandbox?"

"That's her. Don't let the Southern accent or the country idioms fool you." I glanced at the time and wondered if it was too late to call her for something non-dire.

I still didn't get a match from the new figures I searched, but adding the white space started getting me partial matches on some of the sets of numbers. None of the hits seemed relevant as I skimmed along, and I was about to give up when something on the seventh or eighth page made me pause.

"Earthquake in Thailand, 5.1," I read a webpage title. I doubted our dark elves had anything to do with events in Thailand, but the report made me reconsider what the lists of numbers might signify. "If you lived underground, earthquakes might be a concern, right? What if all this data represents numbers on the Richter scale?"

"What is the Richter scale?" Zav asked.

"Our way of measuring the severity of earthquakes. It's logarithmic." I ran a finger along the lines I'd copied. "These would all be fairly low indicators of seismic activity. That 5.1 is the highest in this batch."

"Would other data not have to be included for the list to be useful?" Zoltan asked. "Such as dates?"

"You would think." I shrugged. "This is just a guess."

If the dark elves were recording seismic activity… that put a chill down my spine. What if they were working on some artifact that could cause earthquakes? Seattle wasn't the hotbed of activity that California was, but every now and then, the newspapers reported on the possibility of The Really Big One and talked about the destruction and tsunami that had occurred the last time one had happened in the area. Some three hundred years ago, if I remembered correctly.

I decided to risk Willard's ire and call her.

"It's almost midnight, Thorvald," she answered, almost a growl. Her words broke up, and I was tempted to go outside, but they were understandable. "Did you find the dark elves or something worth waking me up for?"

"No, but there's a card-game party on Zoltan's property. I know you're into euchre. I thought you might want to join in."

"Report to the office at eight a.m. for an ass kicking. And tell me why you *really* called."

"I'm looking at the numbers translated from the back of the dark-elf notebook. Did you guys try searching for them as Richter scale entries?"

"Yes."

"Oh." Here I'd thought I'd been brilliant.

"There weren't any matches on the internet. We also pulled data from the Pacific Northwest Seismic Network."

"From all the locations where activity is recorded?"

"No, from the monitors around Seattle, since that's where the dark-elf lair is. *Was*. There's a *lot* of data out there, so we had to make some assumptions. Primarily that they were interested in earthquakes around population centers. Everything we've deduced from their book and our informants is that they want to get rid of humans."

"You have volcanos," Zav said, having no trouble hearing both sides of the conversation. "I have flown over them."

It took me a moment to get the connection. Right, seismic activity could be caused by magma moving underground, not only by movement along fault lines. "Did you hear that, Willard? Did you check the stations by Mount Rainier and Mt. St. Helens? What if it's not earthquakes they care about but predicting volcanic eruptions?"

Or *causing* them? I rubbed my face. It was easier to imagine magic diddling with magma underground than moving entire continental shelves along fault lines.

"Willard?" I asked. She'd gone silent. "What do you think?"

She sighed. "That your dragon is smarter than he looks. I'll get the data. Come by the office in the morning."

"For an ass-kicking?"

"To retrieve staples from the walls of my outer office." She hung up.

"I do not look smart?" Zav touched his jaw.

"You look pretty." I patted his chest.

"These traits are mutually exclusive in humans?"

"Not necessarily, but people like to make assumptions based on looks. Be glad you're not blonde."

His gaze drifted toward my hair. Then he rested a hand on the back of my neck and narrowed his eyes at Zoltan on the other side of me. He had been eyeing my neck.

"Can you read vampire minds, Zav?" I assumed Zoltan was having fantasies about my veins, not about taking me to bed.

"This one is simple to read, yes. He was a human."

Zoltan lifted a hand. "Forgive my straying thoughts. I have not had a meal yet tonight, and you know how the dragon aura that marks you tempts me. It would make your blood even tastier than usual. And there is even more of him on you now. He has claimed you as a mate, yes?"

I thought Zav might say *No* or *Not for long*, since we'd discussed him removing his mark when he finished his work on Earth, but Zav eased closer, and his hand moved to stroke the back of my head.

"She is mine," he growled at Zoltan.

I refused to let that growl give me a shiver. Or at least, I refused to acknowledge that it did.

"Excellent," Zoltan said. "My dear robber, in the future, when you have work for me and realize you cannot pretend to run it through my business partner, I may ask for payment in your blood. Unless I can get you to collect some of his for me." He looked hopefully toward Zav.

"You will have blood from neither of us." Zav's eyes flared with violet light.

"I am entitled to payment for my services," Zoltan said.

"This is America," I told him. "We use dollars for monetary exchange here, legal tender for all debts public and private."

"Hm."

"Dimitri, you're going to have to start letting me use your cervical collar when I come here." I closed the notebook, since Willard had her own copy of the data, and pushed it back to Zoltan. Then I picked up the analyses of the melted shard. "Mind if I take these with me?"

"You may. I'll have my business partner deliver an invoice for my time."

"Wonderful." I imagined the payment options broken down into dollars or blood.

My phone buzzed. Expecting Willard, I started to answer it, but Thad's name popped up.

Fear zapped me like a wet fork in an electrical outlet. He wouldn't call this late just to say hi.

Chapter 14

I ran through Zoltan's tunnel and outside to take Thad's call. I didn't want poor reception to interfere, nor did I want the others to be able to listen in.

"Hey," I answered, striving for casualness, though I had a bad feeling about this. "What's up?"

Wet grass batted at my jeans as I stepped away from the carriage house and into the unkempt lawn at the edge of the property. A quick check ensured nobody was around. The party in the main house had ended.

"Sorry to call you so late," Thad said, "but I got home from work late, and I just got Amber to talk to me. I mean, it wasn't that late, but she didn't say anything earlier. She seemed quiet and withdrawn at dinner. I thought she'd had a fight with a friend and didn't think much of it, but…"

My grip tightened on the phone. "What happened?"

"She said someone came by the house today, asking her about you."

I kicked the grass and swore to myself before managing to calm down enough to ask, "Blonde hair or purple?"

Thad paused. "You knew this would happen?"

"No. I would have warned you if I'd known someone would show up there. I would have camped out on your driveway with all my weapons."

"That… would have alarmed the neighbors."

"Which one was it, Thad?"

I wouldn't be that worried if Lirena had been the one to visit and ask a few questions about me. Oh, I would worry about what conclusions she would draw from my ten-year absence as a mother, but I doubted she would have threatened Amber. Zav's sister on the other hand…

"Purple hair."

"Damn it. Did she just ask questions?" My grip tightened even further. The phone bleeped a protest.

"Amber said it was weird, and she's not quite sure what happened. The woman… Amber said it wasn't a woman, Val."

"It's another dragon."

"I thought you said they left."

"I thought they had. Is she okay? What did she do to Amber?" I ground my teeth. If Zondia had done that mental scouring and hurt her, I would find a way to put a fist through her skull. Or Chopper through her skull. I didn't care if she *was* Zav's sister.

"Just asked questions about you, Amber said, but she also admitted she barely remembered it. She isn't sure what happened exactly, but she remembers bringing the woman in to show her her room." A hint of anger replaced the concern in Thad's voice. "She says she didn't want to do it, but something made her. It all sounded creepy as hell to me."

"That's because it is." I was shaking and in danger of hurling my phone a hundred feet. "I'm sorry this intruded on your life. I'll figure out some way to deal with it, to stop this from happening."

How? There was no way I could truly kill Zondia. Zav was right. The only way to fix everything was to get all dragons off Earth. Including him.

"Thank you," Thad said. "I reported her to the police, but I'm sure that won't do anything."

"It won't, but *I'll* do something."

Zav was coming out of the carriage house. I hung up and spun to face him, rage clenching every muscle in my body.

"Your *sister* was interrogating my daughter about me."

I expected him to react with surprise or indignation and denial, but he did neither. He merely stood there, digesting the information, then said, "I did not expect that."

"I want her off this planet and out of my fucking life."

"I will tell her to leave."

"You told her to leave before, and that didn't do anything. You said she doesn't listen to you."

"I will deal with her," he said, calm but firm.

"By opening a portal and shoving her through it? I mean it, Zav. If the problem is you having a relationship with me, then it has to stop. *Today*, not whenever you finish hunting down criminals. Un-claim me. Whatever it takes. I've had enough of my family being endangered by you asshole dragons." If I hadn't been so angry, I wouldn't have included him in that group, but my fear for Amber, for what *could* have happened, both today and back in Idaho, kept me from thinking rationally.

"If I leave Earth, neither my family nor their political enemies should come here again any time soon."

"Good. Then go."

"You do not wish to see me again?" He gazed at me without any magic making his eyes glow. If not for his aura, he would have seemed to be just a man standing with me in the wet grass.

I sensed that my request stung him, but what could I do? I couldn't choose him over the safety of Thad and Amber. What if Zondia had hurt Amber, digging through her thoughts, and made it so she didn't remember it? The idea made me seethe.

"If that's what it takes to get rid of dragons on Earth, yes. This was your idea anyway. You said you had to leave Earth."

"After I collect all the criminals here."

"That could take years. This has to stop *now*." Still shaking, I turned my back on Zav and brought my fist to my mouth.

"You will have to deal with the dark elves yourself."

"I can handle it."

After a long, silent pause, he said quietly, "Very well."

A silver portal appeared in the sky over the trail behind the house.

Before shifting into dragon form, Zav walked up to me and placed a hand on my rigid shoulder. In no mood to be touched, I almost jerked away from him. But through my anger, I knew he was saying goodbye and that I would regret it later if I didn't let him.

Once I am gone, my sister should not care about you. But this time, I will do more than speak with her to make sure she leaves you alone. He shifted his hand from my shoulder to the side of my neck, brushing me gently with his fingers, then kissed my cheek.

I didn't react or say anything. I didn't know what I *would* say.

Zav walked away, shifted into his dragon form, and flew through the portal.

Realizing I had tears running down my cheeks, I wiped my face. Great. Zav had kissed a cheek smothered with salty tears. It bothered me that he would remember me as someone who cried. I didn't cry.

Chapter 15

The next morning, I pulled up to Willard's office before eight. After parking the Jeep, I tried calling Amber again. The night before, right after Zav left, I'd tried, and she hadn't answered. It wasn't surprising. She'd barely wanted to talk to me at the end of our Idaho adventures—*misadventures*. That had been before some weird purple dragon had come along and done who knew what to her.

This time, I left a message in her voice mail.

"Hey, Amber. Your dad told me a dragon came and bugged you. I'm sorry she found you and came to the house." I wanted to demand that Amber call me, to tell her she needed to explain everything that had happened—and let me know if she'd been hurt, physically or mentally. I couldn't do much if she had, but at least I could let her know I understood what it was like to be a victim to dragons. Would that help her at all? I didn't know. But I was afraid if I pushed, she would *never* call me. "If you want to talk about it, I'm here. Bye."

After hanging up, I glowered at the phone in frustration. This was unacceptable. Zav was gone, but I had no idea if Zondia was. What if he'd assumed she would follow him through a portal but hadn't actually ordered her to leave me and my family alone? I believed he cared about me and would do what I'd asked, but I worried the sister wouldn't cooperate.

If he was gone and she was still here, that would be a double whammy. I hadn't even wanted to send *him* away. But he'd been right. It was the only way to get rid of Earth's dragon problem. To get rid of *my* dragon problem.

Minutes ticked past on my phone's clock, and Amber didn't call back. Rivulets of rain ran down the windshield, and the sky was so dark and gray, it barely seemed like morning. Reluctantly, I jogged inside.

It was too soon for Willard to have gotten the data from the volcano-monitoring stations, but I hadn't wanted to stay home. Alone. Angry. Frustrated. I needed a lead to follow, some bad guys to hunt down. I didn't even care that going into a dark-elf lair without Zav would be suicidal. I'd told him I'd handle it, and I would find a way. As soon as we located them.

Rain sloughed off my duster as I crossed the hard tile floors inside. I kept glancing at my phone, hoping to see Amber's name pop up.

Willard was waiting for me outside her outer office with a giant cup of coffee from the drive-through stand on the corner. I hated the stuff, but this morning, I would be tempted to try it if she offered me some. I hadn't slept well. As usual.

She looked me up and down, taking in my wet braid and dripping clothing. "You look like you've been through three wars and a goat-roping."

"More like a dragon-roping."

"You and Zav have a tiff?"

"No." I didn't want to talk about it. "Any new data from the seismic network yet?"

"Not yet. They're grabbing it for me. I had to guess at the date range."

A cackle came from the outer office. Willard sighed and lifted her eyes toward the ceiling.

"Is that your goblin helper?"

"Yes. He comes in early and stays late. Except for yesterday. He and my new elf intern went to the Pacific Science Center."

"They let goblins in?"

"He wore a hood, goggles, and black leather gloves. Because he was short, he got the children's rate." Willard sipped her coffee. "I understand they went to the railroad exhibit and got to design and test bridges. Competitively."

"Who won?"

I wouldn't have cared, but I was mildly curious if Freysha was the tinkerer she appeared to be. If she showed up today, maybe I would ask her if she knew Lirena. This might be an opportunity. I could question them about each other and see if any discrepancies came up in their stories. Though I supposed they might be from different worlds and have never met. Also, if Lirena had truly been sent by my father, she wasn't here as a refugee, like most of the magical beings who came to Earth. Freysha might be in hiding from the elven court because of some crime she'd committed.

"Gondo told me he built the superior bridge," Willard said. "Later, Freysha told me she won the competition and also got the phone number of the college kid volunteering there."

"Did she want that?"

"I don't think so. She asked me what she was supposed to do with it. Most magical beings don't have phones unless they're pre-paid flip phones." Willard's own phone rang, and she pulled it out. "This looks like our data."

"Good." I followed her through the outer office, pausing to gape at a mountain range of shredded paper along the wall. Gondo sat on the floor with the shredding machine, gleefully inserting documents. Strips of paper dangled from his pointed ears and scattered the tiles around him. He seemed to be munching on a small pile of blue shreds next to his thigh. Did blue paper taste better than white? "He's supposed to be doing that, right?"

"Yes." Judging by the baleful look Willard cast at Gondo before turning into her office, he was taking liberties with the assignment.

"Is he actually useful to you?" I asked once we were inside with the door shut.

"Amazingly, yes. He's an incredible gossip. He's lived in our world for a year, and he knows everything about every goblin in the Pacific Northwest, and even into California and Canada. He knows more than you would expect about the species that goblins trade with too. That includes trolls, ogres, gnolls, kobolds, canine but not feline shifters, and a clan of dwarves we didn't know had returned to Earth."

"Are wolf shifters more accommodating to goblins than lions and tigers?"

"They don't try to eat them."

"I guess that's one way to accommodate."

Willard stepped behind her desk, leaning her weight on her hands and eyeing the big screen of her Mac. "We've got a match."

A lead? *Finally*? Hope filled my chest for the first time in days.

"One of the volcanos?"

"One of the monitoring stations at Mount Rainier. Located at Observation Rock," Willard read from a report that had come in along with the numbers, "it's approximately eight kilometers northwest of Mount Rainier's summit. The numbers we sent over match activity recorded from June of last year to June of this year."

"June is when I took their notebook."

Willard nodded. "In an average month, the station detects three to four earthquakes of up to 3.9 in magnitude, but there was a period of four days in May when a *swarm* of over a thousand earthquakes was detected."

"Swarm sounds ominous."

The numbers recorded indicated earthquakes small enough that hikers probably hadn't noticed them, but it still struck me as ominous.

"Swarms are rare," Willard read—maybe whoever had put together the report had anticipated our concern, "—but they do occur on occasion and do not necessarily precipitate an eruption. However, another swarm occurred in July. Scientists from the USGS have deployed additional instruments on and around Mount Rainier to monitor the situation. Thus far, it's believed that these are not tectonic in nature, that the quakes are a result of hydrothermal fluids lubricating existing faults inside the basement rock underlying the Rainier edifice."

"Is lubricating a code word for dark elves experimenting on them with magic?"

Willard leaned back, her face grim. "It could all be natural, but the fact that the dark elves were recording the data from the station... They must have had at least one person going up there during this time period, intercepting the readings on their way from the monitoring equipment to the base computers."

"Ominous was the right word, I think."

"I'm inclined to agree. Were you alive when Mt. St. Helens erupted?" Willard squinted at me. "I keep forgetting how old you are."

"We're almost the same age, remember? My ancientness just isn't that apparent."

"Not like mine."

"You don't look a day over fifty."

"I'm forty-four."

"I know." I flashed a grin, though I was joking more to break the tension than because I was in a good mood. The more I thought about this, the more scared I was getting.

Willard didn't rise to my bait. She had to be concerned too. "I lived on the other side of the country when Mt. St. Helens erupted. I remember it being in the news but not much else." She smiled fleetingly. "I think the news interrupted *Sesame Street*."

"We lived in Snohomish County then, Mom and me." I waved to the north. "I was a toddler. I remember some ash fall in Seattle, but I think it was a lot worse to the east. The wind blew it out over Yakima. Still, we wore dust masks for days." I grimaced, imagining how my lungs of today would handle ash-choked air. I tapped my pocket, making sure I had my inhaler with me. "Portland wasn't in the line of fire, or whatever you would call it, and relatively few people died overall, but some logging crews and campers didn't make it. I've seen articles that say Mount Rainier erupting could be a lot more devastating."

"I know. I've seen projections for lava flows and lahars."

"Remind me what lahars are?"

Willard tapped it into the computer for a precise definition. "Lahars are destructive mudflows from the slopes of volcanos that can be as much as a hundred feet thick and travel forty-five to fifty miles per hour."

"Shit." I imagined an entire population center trying to evacuate and outrun such things.

"On Mount Rainier, the risk from lahars is more than from lava flows and volcanic ash fall," she read on. "Their projected pathways go through densely populated areas and important infrastructure such as highways, pipelines, bridges, and ports. Approximately eighty thousand people and their homes are in lahar-hazard zones."

Eighty thousand? My gut tightened.

"Was this the dark elves' plan all along? Decimate Puget Sound so… What do they want? To take it for themselves?" I thought of the goblins in Harrison, Idaho, that had hoped to scare away the population of two hundred people so they could claim the town for themselves. That plot was almost innocent compared to this, but maybe it demonstrated how many of the refugees who had come to Earth thought. Our people hadn't made a place for them. Maybe the dark elves intended to *take* a place. "And if that *is* their plan, how do the pleasure orbs tie in?"

"I suppose it depends on where they've been placed and how many there are. The ones in Seattle are gone. Maybe they were just here for testing, and now they've been moved down south." Willard waved toward a map showing the lahar zones. "All of this is speculation at this point, but wouldn't you agree that if people were attached to one of those things, they wouldn't pay attention to an eruption? They wouldn't evacuate."

"Oh, I agree. Humans and shifters can't keep their paws off them. *I* barely could."

Willard pulled out her phone. "I'll make some calls. Like the report said, the government will have more people monitoring the volcano with the increase in activity, but I'll tell anyone who'll listen that, for the first time in human history, magic could play a role in the eruption of a volcano."

"How many people will listen?"

"My superiors know that magic is real and refugees from other planets are on Earth. World leaders know too. The problem is that few of them have practical experience. People like you and me are the ones who've battled these magical beings and dealt with their otherworldly powers. You especially. Out of ignorance, those in charge may make idiotic choices."

"How shocking for our world leaders."

"I want you to go up to Rainier, see if you can find proof that dark elves are there, and if they are, keep them from dropping bombs on the glaciers or whatever their plan is." Willard shook her head. "Probably something more sophisticated than that. It looks like they've been researching this for a long time. They could do a lot of damage."

"No kidding. The goblins in Idaho nearly brought a town to its knees, and they're a lot less menacing than dark elves."

A delighted cackle came through the door. Maybe Gondo had found another tasty flavor of paper.

"A lot less menacing than *anyone*," I corrected.

Willard pointed at my chest. "You had cold-weather training in the army, right?"

"Almost twenty years ago and aimed at pilots who might crash, yeah. I got to practice building snow forts in Fort Wainwright."

She didn't look impressed.

"It's not going to be *that* cold up there in August." I shivered, remembering Fairbanks in November and sticking MREs under my jacket for an hour before eating to try to thaw the contents.

"At the summit, there are glaciers and ice caves all year around, and, yes, there are blizzards in August. Rainier is a tough climb."

Ice caves? Ugh, that was probably exactly where a bunch of dark elves would hang out too.

"Before we start prepping, why don't you send your dragon to look around the mountain to see if he can sense the dark elves up there and how many we're dealing with?" Willard suggested. "Maybe he could even bring back proof that they're there. It'll be easier for me to make calls and convince people if I have more than a list of numbers stolen from a monitoring station."

"My dragon isn't on Earth."

"When's he coming back?"

I closed my eyes, an unexpected lump of emotion swelling in my throat. "He's not."

"*Val.*" Willard sounded more disgusted than sympathetic. "What happened?"

"It's a long story."

"Give me the CliffsNotes version."

I did. I hadn't wanted to talk about it, and I still didn't, but I also didn't want her to think some lovers' spat was what had prompted me to send Zav away.

At the end, Willard groaned. "He finally becomes a somewhat reliable ally, and when we need him most, he's gone. This is as much *his* mission as ours. I thought he was supposed to get the two dark-elf leaders and all those other criminals."

"He was. He is." I shrugged helplessly. "I don't know what will happen."

Zav would probably tell his mother why he'd failed to complete his mission, and she would end up hating me—more. And what would happen if she tried to send some other dragon to finish Zav's duties? A less reasonable dragon?

"All right," Willard said. "Then it's back to the way it was. Just us."

"Yeah."

"I'll gather a team of reliable people to go with you. If you have any personnel requests, let me know. I saw the pictures of the remains of the dark-elf lair in Seattle. You can't handle them alone, not if there are more than a few. They're all warriors and wizards, right?"

"Even the scientists."

"Brilliant. I wish I could send you up there right this minute, but it'll take time to gather a team and appropriate gear. You need a favorable weather forecast too." She looked toward the rain outside the window. "It's probably snowing up there right now. I'll do my best to get everything together today and check for openings in the weather. The earliest you'll leave will be tomorrow. I'll get a helicopter pilot on standby."

"I could drive up to Rainier in two hours."

Willard gave me a scathing look. "You could drive to the *parking lot*. The trail to the summit involves a nine-thousand-foot elevation gain. It's as much as from the Everest base camps to its peak. Your Jeep isn't driving you there. You *do* have climbing experience, right?"

"Not in snow, but yes." I preferred city work, but a lot of the magical races were far more likely to take up residence in the wilderness, and wyverns and rocs loved mountain caves. Beach caves, too, as I'd learned on the mission where I'd met Zav. "I have climbing gear in my storage locker if someone hasn't stolen it."

"That's something anyway."

I eyed her. "You haven't by chance climbed our volcano, have you?"

"When I was first stationed at Fort Lewis, yes. A few months before I got moved up to this office. I've never done any of the epic climbs around the world, but I've done Denali in Alaska."

That sounded plenty epic to me.

"Then, my friend—" I put a hand on her shoulder, "—my personnel request is you."

Willard stared at me. "I can't leave for however long this will take. The whole place would be filled with shredded paper and siege engines made from office supplies." She waved in the direction of the occasionally-cackling Gondo.

"Didn't that Major Cecil just get assigned up here? I'm sure he's ready to prove himself capable of running things. He can wrangle goblins and answer phones for a couple of days."

"What about my cat?"

"You can board her."

"I can't board Maggie." Willard sounded as indignant as if I wanted the cat sent to a slaughterhouse and made into tiny steaks to feed my tiger.

"Because she'll be emotionally scarred or because she complains the whole time and the boarding facility has blackballed her?"

"Ah, I remember, you've spent time with my cat."

"Two six-hour car trips, yes. My eardrums are still recovering. Don't you have a new neighbor who can watch her? This is kind of important."

Willard chewed on the inside of her mouth. She hadn't rejected the idea outright. That was something.

She had soldiers in the office with experience fighting magical beings, but I bet the list of people who also had experience climbing glacier-covered mountains was a shorter one. I'd only been vaguely aware that snow-capped Mount Rainier was that big of a deal. For me, it was something I admired in the skyline on a clear day, nothing more.

"Remember the adventures we had when you first got put in charge of this place?" I asked. "And you thought I was a sarcastic blonde smartass that you didn't want to work with?"

"You *are* a sarcastic blonde smartass."

"True, but you like working with me now."

"No, I like the results you get. You're a pain in the ass and every supervisor's nightmare."

I grinned at her. "I get warm fuzzies thinking about you, too, Colonel."

She looked contemplatively out the window. "Yeah," she said finally. "If you go without someone experienced, I'm terrified you'll fall into a crevasse before you even see a dark elf."

"Excellent."

Willard had combat experience and knew as much about dark elves as I did. More. And I had Sindari, Chopper, and my new lucky charm. Maybe that would be enough for us to succeed.

"While you're finding us a ride," I said, "I'll go visit Nin and put in an order. And I'll get you a gun. What's your preference? Rifle? Handgun? Howitzer?"

Willard snorted. "I'm not carrying that nine thousand feet up a trail."

"I thought we were taking a helicopter so we don't have to do that trail."

"Ah, that's right."

"Don't sound so disappointed."

"Just get me whatever she has that will pierce dark-elf armor. And plenty of ammo."

"Will do."

A knock sounded at the door. I'd been engrossed in planning and hadn't noticed the approach of an elven aura.

"Expecting Freysha?" I asked.

Willard glanced at the time. "Yeah. It's nine. Everybody should be at the office now."

She opened her door.

Freysha, still in overalls, her hair in two braids today, walked in carrying a stack of books almost as tall as she was. "Good morning, Colonel. I've finished going over the translations from these tomes. Your translator was largely accurate. I found a few corrections to make. I apologize for the dampness of the books. I don't yet have a domicile that is completely waterproof, but I did my best to keep the rain off them."

Willard took the books and put them on her desk. "You're sleeping outside?"

"Yes." Freysha's eyebrows drew together. "The weather has been mostly quite acceptable, but these last few days have been very wet. It has, however, meant there was no need to bathe in the fountain."

The fountain?

"Gondo, where are you sleeping?" Willard peered out—the goblin was half-buried in a new pile of shredded paper. Was Willard getting rid of all sensitive material because the dark elves had proven themselves capable of getting in? "Do you have room for an elf?"

Gondo's pointed ears swiveled toward us. "I sleep under a bridge. I showed Freysha the fountain. I'm a good host."

"Willard, your interns are homeless. How many bedrooms does that apartment of yours have?"

"One." She gave me a dark look. "How many does *yours* have?"

"One. And it's broken into regularly. Clearly your lodgings are superior." I almost pointed out that she wouldn't need them while she was on our adventure, but she could say the same to me. And these two characters weren't trustworthy enough to leave in my apartment.

Freysha looked at me curiously, her gaze shifting to my neck. "You acquired a new charm?"

"Yeah." I shrugged, pretending it wasn't odd that she'd paid enough attention to me during our first meeting to spot a new charm. I was pretty sure Zav hadn't noticed it, though the power of my trinkets had to be inconsequential to a dragon. Chopper was the only one of my magical tools he'd ever shown interest in. "Know anything about it?"

Her eyebrows rose. "Don't you?"

"A little."

"I thought you knew what all that crap does, Thorvald." Willard gave me the same frown as when I'd suggested I would simply drive up to find the dark elves.

"I know what *most* of them do. Someone gave me this one recently. She told me what it does, but I don't know her that well, so it could have been a story."

I realized how stupid that sounded. That I'd met someone once for twenty minutes and accepted a magical trinket from her. But it hadn't done anything bad yet, and I'd won that hundred dollars.

"It looks like an elven luck charm," Freysha said. "What did she say it is?"

"An elven luck charm."

"It's probably fine then. They're actually considered quite valuable. You say a stranger gave it to you?"

A relative, apparently, but that wasn't any of Freysha's business.

"Don't take this the wrong way," I said, "but I'm not going to open up to you. I don't know who you are or why you're here. And I'm positive you're not as young and innocent as you look."

Gondo plucked long shreds of paper off his ears.

"*He* might be as young and innocent as he looks," I said.

Freysha spread her hands. "I am thirty-seven of your years. That actually is young for an elf, but I am well educated and can be useful. I wish to earn a place here." She turned shining eyes toward Willard. "I found a catalog for one of your city's universities. They have many engineering programs. Is it very expensive to attend? How much will you pay me to work here if I earn a human degree and prove myself a reliable employee?"

"Uh." Willard wiggled her fingers. "Let's talk about that after you've been here for more than three days. I want to find you somewhere to sleep first."

"Of course."

"Let's go see Lieutenant Reed."

"Wait." I held up a hand. If Freysha had been able to tell the diamond trinket was a luck charm, what else might she know? "Freysha, you said this is of elven make?" I touched the charm.

"It is. I would be able to sense something made from our people's magic even if I hadn't seen others like it."

"What about this?" I touched Sindari's figurine.

"Dragon magic."

That matched what Sindari had told me about how some of his people had come to be linked to the charms.

"And my sword?" I tapped Chopper's hilt.

"Dwarven."

"*I* could have told you that," Gondo said.

I ignored him and asked her, "Do you know words of power that might activate it?"

"You don't?" Freysha's brows rose again. Surprised that I was wandering around with stuff I didn't have a pedigree for? Well, that was how Earth worked. We didn't have full-blooded master crafters walking around. You took what you could find and were happy to get it.

"I know one word." Because Zav had told me.

"There are often as many as ten or twelve linked to a high-quality blade crafted by a master. I could look that one up if I were back home, but…" She was stuck here. Bathing in a fountain.

I feared I would need to search elsewhere for a resource. Too bad Lirena hadn't given me a way to contact her.

"Go shop for munitions, Thorvald." Willard waved me toward the door. "You can research your treasure chest of goodies when we get back."

"Yeah, yeah. I'm going."

"Yes, Colonel," she corrected me. "Right away, Colonel."

I smirked back at her. "You said I was a smartass."

"And a pain in the ass. Don't forget that part."

As I walked out, Willard was asking Freysha if she knew anything about feeding cats and tending litter boxes. Maybe she would have a place to stay this week, after all.

Chapter 16

"You are cleaning me out, Val," Nin said, stepping into the little armory in her food truck where she made merchandise far different from her signature beef and rice dish. Outside, the rain had stopped, and her two assistants in the kitchen were busy serving meals to customers.

"I need enough for me and Willard to blow up a hundred dark elves if we need to." I put another case of ammo on the counter for her to tally up.

I'd selected a rifle for Willard. It wasn't automatic, but Nin, who usually only took custom orders, didn't keep a lot of extra merchandise on hand, so it would have to do. Realizing we would be tramping around on foot, at least for part of this adventure, I kept myself to one case of grenades instead of two, but I was taking enough flashbangs to outfit an army. They were usually for distraction, but they might be effective weapons against the light-sensitive dark elves.

"Are you paying for all this today?" Nin pulled out her tablet to tally everything up.

"Yes, but put the rifle and its ammo on a separate invoice that I can give to Willard. And the flashbangs too. She's feeling generous today."

"As you wish. Val?" Nin lowered the tablet. "Did Dimitri ask you to co-sign on his lease?"

"Lease? Is he getting an apartment?"

"No. For his Fremont shop."

"He didn't, no. He knows I'd tell him he's a nutcase and Zoltan can co-sign."

"Zoltan does not have a credit record. I asked."

"Did he ask *you* to co-sign?" I frowned at her.

"Yes. I like him, but I have concerns. I have worked very hard to become a citizen and establish credit for myself and my business."

"Don't risk your credit record on their start-up. Zoltan has the money to make something happen if they can't go through the normal channels."

"That is what I was thinking. But I did not want to be a bad friend."

"You're not. You're a good friend for telling him that he's being irresponsible by trying to drag you into his scheme."

"Oh, I do not believe it is a scheme. I made him do a business plan. I think he can be profitable, but it would be risky for me to invest or co-sign on a lease at this juncture."

"Damn straight. Tell him that. Or I will." I patted the case of ammo. "Send him to me if you need to, and I'll shoot down his idiocy."

"I can do it. I just was not sure if that was right." Nin nodded. "Thank you. You are also a good friend, Val."

"Does that mean you'll give me ten percent off on these flashbangs?"

"No. Those are magically enhanced, and this is business."

A soft rap sounded at the inner door. Nin slid it aside.

"There is someone here to see your client." Her assistant pointed at me.

Maybe Willard had come down to select her gun personally. No. As I focused on the square outside, I detected someone with a familiar magical aura.

"Oh, good. I was hoping to ask her some more questions. Nin, will you bag all that stuff up for me? I brought a canvas tote."

"Excellent. I will give you ten cents off for bringing your own shopping bag."

"The crazy good deals you give me are the reason I keep coming back."

"And the excellent merchandise." She winked at me as I let myself out the back door.

Lirena faced it, as if she'd known where I would come out. Once again, she wore a cloak, but her hood was down, her blonde hair wrapped into buns almost as impressive as Princess Leia's. They were higher on the head and hid the points of her ears. They also made her look like she was wearing cinnamon rolls, but judging by the guys in line trying to catch her eye, nobody was worried about her hairstyle.

"Greetings, cousin." Lirena offered the bow-curtsy. "I am glad I was able to find you."

"You seem to be able to find me wherever I am." We were miles from my apartment, and I was positive I hadn't mentioned Nin's food truck.

"Of course. We share blood, remember."

"I'm here shopping for munitions for a mission. I don't suppose you'd like to lend me that flute and teach me how to use it? Is there a special note to hurt the ears of dark elves?"

"Yes, but you would need to spend many years studying music in order to play it. Also, it is a valuable family artifact, so I cannot part with it."

I'd figured as much.

"There is something I wish to speak with you about." Lirena glanced at the line of people watching us. "Will you walk with me?"

"Yes." I doubted we would find more privacy on the busy streets of Seattle, but I extended a hand for her to lead the way.

We hadn't walked far when she asked, "Do you know what happened to the dragons?"

"Dragons?"

Did she mean Zav and Zondia? Or was something going on at the Dragon Justice Court?

"Two were here in this world only yesterday."

"Ah. I'm glad to hear they're gone. How can you tell?"

Lirena frowned at me as we turned a corner on the sidewalk, busy men and women streaming past us toward a crosswalk. "I can sense that they left. You cannot?"

I hated being reminded of how poor my magical abilities were. "I can only sense them when they're within a mile or so of me."

"They are nowhere near this city, nor this ocean and coast."

"Your range is a lot larger than mine."

"I can show you how to improve that, but tell me why the dragons left." Lirena squinted at me. "You do not seem surprised."

Her interest in this topic made me wary—hadn't she supposedly come to observe me and see if I was elfy enough to meet my father?—but her offer to teach me something that would be incredibly useful kept me from saying something sarcastic.

"I asked Zav to leave and take his nosy sister with him." I didn't intend to share my life with this near stranger, but I found myself explaining what I knew of the incident with Zondia and Amber.

"Dragons *always* presume they can read the thoughts of others without their permission. That is one of the reasons their kind are so infuriating." Lirena spread a hand across her chest. "Elves would consider that a crime, akin to rape. To force yourself into another's mind is a heinous offense, especially if someone is weaker and has no way to fight back."

"I agree."

"I should also teach you better mental defenses. I assume they have difficulty reading your surface thoughts? Your father's line is known for their mind powers. Even a half-elf should have inherited some of that natural aptitude."

"I've been told dragons have trouble reading my thoughts, yes. But they can force their way in if I can't figure out how to prong them with my sword and convince them to go away."

Lirena glanced at Chopper's hilt over my shoulder. "Even with tools that can breach their barriers, it is difficult to do substantial damage to a dragon. Our kind—all of the other species—have always had to use trickery to have a chance against dragons."

I remembered Zav's story of the elven seductress-assassin. Trickery, indeed.

We'd crossed busy Alaskan Way and were in front of the ferry terminal.

Lirena pointed to the large car- and passenger-ferry loading up. "You will pay for passage across the water? This vehicle traffic noise makes it difficult to hear."

"Elves don't have money either, huh?"

"Not that spends on your world."

"I'll pay if you show me how to extend my range while we're on board." I expected her to say such a thing would take years to master, not a half-hour ferry ride, but she nodded.

"Yes, I will show you the basics. And you will tell me when the dragons will return."

"They *shouldn't* return. I told Zav to take his sister and get out of here."

"You told him? That means little. Dragons do not obey the wishes of humans or elves. They will return." Again, she nodded. Firmly and to herself.

"Do you consider that good or bad?" I was still trying to work out why she cared about the dragons if she was here for me.

"Their presence anywhere our species exists is bad. Did you not say they were a threat to your daughter?"

"Yes. I don't disagree with you. That's why I don't want them to come back."

As pedestrians, we bypassed all the cars waiting to board the ferry, and walked on. I led Lirena up the interior stairs and out to one of the observation decks. The rain had stopped, but the sky was still gray, and wind blew across the Sound, tugging at our hair. What would Lirena do if her big buns tumbled down and revealed those ears?

"We will practice here." She pointed to the railing at the front of the ferry, a spot devoid of people. The weather was sketchy enough that most of the passengers were seating themselves inside. "What do you know of how elves use magic?"

"Nothing."

She frowned at me. "That cannot be true. You have some ability to sense magic, yes?"

"Within that mile range I mentioned. I can sense artifacts and people with magical blood." I pointed at her. "But I don't know how it works."

"A natural aptitude, then. Long ago, the various intelligent species found different ways to access magic and focus its power as they evolved, each in line with their natural aptitudes. Some use songs and spells, some artifacts like wands or stones of power."

I nodded, having seen trolls chanting and goblins wielding wands.

"Elves are similar to dragons in that we need no tools other than our minds." Lirena sounded supercilious as she said that, but all I cared about was that she was teaching me. "But it is difficult to will things to happen outside of our own bodies, so we use mental tricks to help. It is simpler to access our own inner power, which you may have done by accident before, but there is much more power outside of us, at least in most places. Some worlds have more magic than others, as you'll learn if you travel. Your Earth is a poor source of magic. It is only desperation that drives the magical races to this place. When they are here, they lose much of the power they are accustomed to being able to access. That is why few species truly care what goes on in this world. It is resource-poor by our definition of the word."

"But dragons aren't affected?"

"All species are affected. Dragons are simply so powerful that, to you, they seem unaffected. But in their magic-rich native world, their powers are even greater. The shifter world is also full of magic—you know that shifters were originally humans taken from your world for an experiment?"

"I've heard that."

"Over time, they evolved and became a stronger race, one infused with magic. But their world has a lot of chaotic magic, so it is also unpopular with most of the races. The three elven worlds—" she touched her chest again, "—have a large amount of even and predictable magic, which makes them very desirable. Our people have had to grow strong in the ways of using magic to keep other species from conquering it—and us."

Willard would find this fascinating, but I struggled not to grab Lirena's arm and force her back to the topic of concern to me. How I could increase my range.

The ferry engines thrummed under the deck as we departed from dock.

"You said something about tricks?" I prompted.

"Yes. We use patterns as foci. For example, the *syi'i* leaf is often pictured in the mind for levitation. You see the leaf floating on the breeze, the intricate silver veins along its spine, and your body will become like the leaf, rising in a breeze or drifting slowly to the ground."

"I imagine a leaf and I can levitate?" I didn't manage to keep the skepticism out of my voice.

"With much practice, essentially. The leaf is simply a pattern, a trick that makes it easier to access what is all around us."

If I was going mountain climbing, knowing how to levitate would be handy, but I didn't have years to learn a new skill. Since I could already sense magical beings, maybe extending my range would be a simpler matter.

"What's the pattern for sensing magic at a distance?"

Lirena raised her hand, her palm open toward me, and a spider web appeared in the air between us, several feet wide but anchored by nothing. It didn't look like a holographic projection; it appeared perfectly real, so much so that I had to touch it to check. My finger passed through it to tap her palm.

"Huh."

"You will imagine the *azailee* web when you wish to check for magical beings, spreading it out around you for miles or even hundreds of miles." She tilted the illusion so that it was horizontal with the ferry deck. "The information you seek will flow along its strands to you."

I attempted to do what she suggested, though I didn't expect to sense magical beings in the water around us. My senses told me she was the only non-human on the ferry. The rest was a void. I tried to extend my senses back to the shoreline we'd left, but it was more than a mile away now, and if anyone magical was near the water, I couldn't tell. I realized I'd lost the image of the web in my mind and grunted in annoyance.

"It will take time," Lirena said.

"I wish I had time. I have a mission that I may be leaving on as soon as tomorrow." I eyed the dark clouds, trying to decide if the sun might break out later.

"What mission?"

I opened my mouth, almost giving her the details, but I still didn't know that much about her. "My people are fighting dark elves," was all I said. "I don't suppose you would like to help?"

Her face grew hard. "Our kind have warred throughout the eons with our dark-elven kin. We drove them from our worlds after they attempted to take them over. It must have been with reluctance that they settled here. Rumors say they've found ways to more fully access the limited magic of this planet. Watch out, or they will try to drive your people from this place and keep it for themselves."

"That's our concern. Want to come help fight them with me?" I tried again.

Lirena might not be as powerful as Zav, but I wouldn't reject a magical ally of any kind.

"Our people currently have a truce with the dark elves. If I were to fight, it would be considered an act of war." A glint entered her eyes. "But I will help you practice how better to access the magic of this world, and you will be a more powerful foe against them."

"I'll take what I can get."

A strong ally would have been nice, but I always preferred relying on myself, so learning more about my own power was good too. I only hoped Lirena would stay long enough to make a difference.

"Good. Let us consider again the *azailee* web." She held up her illusion again.

I tamped down my skepticism and opened my mind, hoping to absorb as much as I could.

❖❖❖❖

The sun came out in time to see it set over the Olympics as I walked from the ferry terminal back toward Occidental Square where I'd parked. After helping me practice extending my range for sensing the magical, Lirena had stayed on Bainbridge Island. Whether she wanted to visit Frog Rock or preferred the lesser population density, I didn't know, but since she could levitate—she'd shown me—it didn't matter if she had money for the ferry.

I wish *I'd* learned to levitate, but I wasn't even sure I'd figured out the web thing. Everything took years of training, according to Lirena. No wonder elves lived so long. They had to in order to have time to learn anything.

As I headed to Nin's food truck to pick up my munitions order, I sensed a full-blooded magical being crouched behind it. The line out front had dwindled, but a few people sat around, eating their meals. Nobody seemed alarmed.

I casually walked around to the back of the truck, my fingers tapping Fezzik's hilt.

A familiar blue-skinned troll crouched there, frowning at me. It was the eight-year-old boy I'd caught outside of Rupert's.

"What's up, kid?" I hoped he hadn't come for his shard—the one Zoltan had melted. We hadn't exactly agreed on the forty dollars as payment for it before he'd been scared away by Zondia's arrival.

He licked his lips and looked me up and down, his gaze lingering on Chopper's hilt. His white hair was matted to his head in greasy clumps, a bruise swelled under one eye, and his clothes were torn. Had he looked that rough the other day? I didn't think so.

"I want to hire you." He held up two twenty-dollar bills, clenched in his fist.

I politely did not point out that was the money I'd given him. "To do what?"

"Avenge my father's murder."

Ugh, I didn't have time for extracurricular assignments this week. "Who's your father?"

"He owned the bar. They threatened him, and then he broke their orb, and then they killed him!" He blinked rapidly, moisture filming his eyes.

"Your father is—was—Rupert?"

The boy nodded.

"And the dark elves were the ones who killed him?"

Another nod.

"I'm sorry, kid. That's horrible." Now I felt worse for chasing him. "When did it happen?"

"Last week. He... They left him not quite dead, and I thought... I thought he would get better. That he would heal. I went out and gathered food and brought it back and took care of him." He sniffed. "If there had been a shaman, I would have brought him for healing, but our own people wouldn't help. They were too afraid. They're *cowards*. Dark elves aren't that scary. Cowards."

"So he just passed away?"

"Yeah."

Had he still been alive when I'd caught up with the boy on the rooftop? I wished I'd known all this. I could have gotten Rupert help—and asked him for all the details about the dark elves.

"Who did it?" I asked. "A male and a female?"

Rupert had told me the same two scientists that Zav sought had been the dark elves to install that orb.

The boy nodded and dug out a limp napkin from a bar. "I wrote down their names for you."

He shuffled forward warily, glancing at Chopper again.

Careful not to make any threatening moves, I crouched down and held out my hand. He deposited the napkin in it.

The writing was barely legible, but I recognized the names, so they were easy enough to read. Yemeli-lor and Baklinor-ten. Zav's criminals.

"Here." The boy tried to thrust the forty dollars at me.

I held up my hand. "I'm already after these guys. You don't have to pay me."

"You'll kill them and avenge my father's death?"

I started to hesitate—Zav would want them taken back to his Justice Court for punishment and rehabilitation. But Zav wasn't here. And despite what Lirena believed, I doubted he would defy my wishes and come back. This was my problem to deal with now.

"I will."

"*Good*," the boy said savagely.

"What's your name, kid? Do you have a place to stay? Relatives who will take you in?"

He hesitated again. Was he being shunned because his father had been singled out by the dark elves?

"If not, I know this goblin with ties to the local goblin community... How are your tool skills?"

The boy scowled. "I am Reb. I will be a great troll warrior, not a wimpy goblin worker."

"You have to survive to grow up first."

The scowl deepened.

"Wait here. I'll get you some food."

Nin didn't ask questions or charge me when I said I needed five meals. Maybe she'd known about the troll boy lurking behind her truck. Or maybe she didn't want to charge me when I was spending thousands of dollars on weapons and ammo.

Either way, Reb's eyes brightened when I deposited the bundles of food in his hands. "Come find Nin—she can get in touch with me—if you change your mind about needing a place to stay."

I wanted to *make* him change his mind, but it wasn't as if the goblins, should they be willing to take him in, could keep him from escaping if he saw himself as a prisoner. He would have to voluntarily stay. And maybe his own people would take him in once the dark elves were out of the picture.

Which would be soon, I vowed.

My phone buzzed. Willard.

"When do we leave?" I answered without preamble.

"The weather is clearing and the report is good for the next couple of days," Willard said. "We leave in the morning." She ran down the time, where to meet, and reminded me to bring my climbing gear as well as clothes for all seasons.

"Got it. I'll be there."

I hung up. The boy hadn't left. He crouched in the shadows, watching me.

"I'm going to get them tomorrow," I said.

"To kill them."

"That's the plan."

Because if I didn't succeed in killing them up there… they would kill me.

Chapter 17

The noise-canceling headset dulled the thrum of the engine and the whop-whop-whop of the helicopter blades, but the familiar sounds stirred nostalgia in me. During my piloting days, I'd flown a similar craft. That had been my job, not shooting hostile ogres and orcs. Only a near-death experience had resulted in the army figuring out I had elven blood and pulling me aside to be trained as an assassin.

Today, if we found dark elves on Mount Rainier, I might get to put all that training to use again. For now, I was sitting in the back of the helicopter with Willard, Corporal Clarke, and Sergeant Banderas, a shaven-headed Puerto Rican I'd seen around the office but hadn't worked with before. The strong, silent type, he wore an Army Ranger patch on his uniform, and I trusted he had experience fighting the magical as well as the mundane. I was less certain about the young and smooth-talking Clarke, who was a courier, not a warrior. But he'd been chosen because he had some magical blood and would be able to, like me, detect dark elves from a distance.

A second helicopter held four more soldiers Willard had picked, people with combat and climbing experience. One of them, Lieutenant Sabo, was a quarter elven. Clarke had never said what species his magical ancestor was, but I suspected fae. Neither of them would have my range, but having more people who could sense our enemies could only help. With their magic, dark elves could sneak up on even elite soldiers.

"Look at the sun," Clarke drawled in his Jamaican accent, the words clear over the intercom. "It's a pretty day to climb a mountain. Or have your helicopter set you down right on top of it."

True to the weather report, the day had dawned sunny. Summer had returned to the Pacific Northwest. We'd left the city early and were flying south along the Cascades, lush green forests below us interspersed with clearcut logged areas, brown scabs on the mountainsides waiting to be replanted.

"There's no way any dark elves will be out there today," Clarke added. "We are assuming they're in caves somewhere, I take it?"

Banderas, who hadn't spoken more than two words since we'd gathered before dawn, glared at him.

"Is this a no-talking mission, Sergeant? I didn't know."

Banderas looked to Willard.

"I know," she said. "We shouldn't have given him a headset with a mouthpiece."

Clarke was never overtly disrespectful, but I'd also never seen him intimidated into silence by someone of senior rank. If he'd made it through Basic without being assigned a lot of extra push-ups and floor-buffing duty, I would be shocked.

"We'll fly a couple of laps around the mountain," I said, though the pilots had already been instructed. "See if we can sense any special tourists down there."

"Special tourists in caves?" Clarke asked.

"They would have to be, yes. Dark nooks and crannies underground. Or under the ice. I looked up Rainier last night. The Paradise Ice Caves melted a while back, but there are all kinds of grottos and caves under the glaciers. Scientists like to explore them. Hopefully, nobody's up there now."

"There *is* a team up there," Willard said grimly. "They haven't been heard from for a couple of days."

"Is that normal?"

"No. The scientists usually explore during the day and sleep in tents outside at night. They're supposed to keep in radio contact with their base camp. There are carbon monoxide, hydrogen sulfide, and other dangerous gases under the ice. Rainier hasn't erupted since 1894, but it *is* an active volcano with discharge."

That made me grimace. I'd been thinking of how my lungs would do if the volcano erupted and flung ash everywhere. I hadn't considered that the air in the caves would be deadly. Even if it wasn't deadly, fumes floating up from magma chambers couldn't be good for asthmatic lungs. Strange to think that, with all my fighting experience, I might be the weakest link on this team, at least when it came to surviving hostile air.

"We also received a message," Willard said, "that the seismic-monitoring station that's had readings that match the numbers in that notebook went silent last night."

"Could some climbers have knocked it out?" Clarke asked as we flew closer to the white-capped, fourteen-thousand-foot peak. "There are a lot of people up here in the summers, right? Have they reported anything funny?"

Willard shook her head. "No, but the last few days have been too stormy for climbers. If people start up today, we shouldn't see anyone near the summit until tomorrow."

Missing scientists and a possibly damaged monitoring station. It didn't sound like a coincidence or anything that normally should have happened. My gut told me what my senses couldn't yet confirm. That we would find company up here, and not mountain climbers.

"We're heading past Camp Muir and up to the summit for our first circuit around the top," the pilot announced.

We were in forest-service choppers with forest-service pilots. Willard hadn't wanted to use military craft and risk alarming civilians until we knew there truly *was* a reason to alarm them.

Banderas put his rifle scope up to his eye and scanned the mountain below. As Clarke had suggested, he shouldn't see anything, unless our enemies had been tramping around on the glacier at night and left some obvious signs. Dark elves could barely stand bright nights. Coming out in the sun would never happen.

"I watched a documentary on the eruption of Mt. St. Helens last night." Willard looked at me.

"Riveting stuff?"

"Let's just say I'm convinced we don't want to let pointy-eared terrorists make Rainier erupt. It's a much bigger volcano than St. Helens, has a lot more glacial ice locked up on it that would melt in a hurry, and the flows would dump into much more heavily populated areas."

"If they're planning mayhem," I said, "we'll stop them."

Then, like Banderas, I turned my attention to the mountain below. This time of year, it wasn't completely blanketed in snow and ice but was a mixture of white in depressions and bare rock in more exposed areas. Farther down the slopes, evergreens and grass grew, but above the tree line, it was stark, either white or gray or black. My untrained eye couldn't pick out the glaciers from the snow. Wherever the caves were, I couldn't see them from the air.

Willard took out a pair of binoculars. I closed my eyes and focused on the ice and rock below with my senses, practicing the pattern Lirena had shown me to extend my range.

"Saw a cougar," Banderas said.

"A nemesis most foul," Clarke said. "Prepare your rifle, Sergeant."

I didn't have to open my eyes to know Banderas gave him another dark look.

Minutes passed, with sightings of nothing more nefarious than marmots. Then the pilot said, "I'm swinging by the scientists' camp, per a request from the USGS."

"What were they doing up here during the bad weather?" Willard asked.

"They were supposed to pull out three days ago, but they didn't show up at the pickup point."

"How many people?"

"Six. Geologists and a couple of microbiologists looking for interesting life near steam vents and lakes under the ice."

"They may have found it," I muttered.

We flew over the remains of a camp, tents under inches of snow or torn half-free of their stakes and flapping in the wind. There were no people.

I stretched my senses as far as I could, trying to probe under the glaciers themselves. Would the thick ice limit my range? I wasn't sure. Even though I hunted outside of urban areas often, the Pacific Northwest was known for its rain, not substantial amounts of snow, and I'd spent little time tramping around on glaciers.

"There must be a cave entrance nearby." The pilot took us low, almost skimming over the ice. "The other chopper is checking on the seismic monitor, Colonel. The pilot says… it's gone."

"Destroyed?" Willard asked.

"Removed."

"Maybe the cougar ate it," Clarke said.

Nobody paid attention to him.

"Lieutenant Sabo wants Thorvald over by the monitor's location," the pilot relayed a message. "Nobody's seen anything, but he thought he detected something magical for a second."

Nobody here scoffed or made a comment about our abilities to detect magical beings and items. These soldiers all worked, at least part-time, out of Willard's office. They might not have all seen dark elves—I suspected I was the only one here who had—but they'd all seen plenty of magical beings.

The other helicopter came into view as we sailed around the mountain. They were hovering over what looked like a random bare spot on a ridge.

"Wait." Banderas still had his scope to his eye. "Go lower. Right here."

The pilot glanced back at Willard.

"Go ahead," she said. "Val, you sense anything?"

"Not yet." I tried not to feel useless.

"This is as low as I can get without landing," the pilot said, hovering above the snow.

"Look at those prints, ma'am." Banderas pointed the spot out to Willard, and she focused her binoculars on the snow. "Too big to be a bear."

"They're too large to have been made by a dark elf." Willard took a long look, then handed the binoculars to me. "You've seen real sasquatch now. What do you think?"

The helicopter hovered relatively still long enough for me to peruse several trails of tracks across fresh snow. Very large tracks. Banderas was right. There was no way a bear had made those. Or bears. A whole pack of the large-footed creatures had passed through. At least six.

"They do remind me of sasquatch prints, but they're not quite the same. The sasquatch had feet very similar to humans. Large but human. Those prints have marks that were made by digits with claws, not toenails." I moved the binoculars aside and rubbed my eyes. Between the sun and the snow, it was too bright outside to look at the white ground for long.

"So, what made them?" Willard asked.

I dug my sunglasses out of my pocket. Willard had reminded me to bring them.

As I pushed my headset around to loop them over my ears, a whisper of something tickled my senses. A dark elf? I didn't think so. But it was something living and magical. It came from farther up the mountain.

When I lifted a finger to point, the presence disappeared. Had it moved out of my range? Or had my imagination been playing tricks on me? Conjuring some beast to go with the prints?

No, I was too experienced for that. Something was out there. *Six* somethings.

"Follow the tracks," Banderas told the pilot.

"The other chopper wants to know where we're going."

"Follow the tracks," Willard said. "Tell them we'll be there soon. We're tracking something else."

Flying low, the pilot took us up the slope. Between the snow and the rock, the mountain seemed too bare to hide much, but then we flew over a glacier, and numerous cracks and crevasses grew visible. One of the mountain-climbing trails crossed over a deep gap in the ice, a meager bridge without handrails stretching over it.

Something tickled my senses again, and I leaned forward as much as my harness would let me.

"The footprints disappear into that crevasse," Banderas said. "All six sets. It looks too deep for them to jump down but..."

"They don't pick up again on the other side," the pilot said.

He took the chopper in circles, trying to pick up the trail.

"It looks like they went down into that crevasse," Willard said.

"They couldn't have," Banderas said. "Look at that thing. It's wicked. You'd need climbing equipment to go down there without dying."

"If you're *human*, you would," I murmured, my gaze locked on the shady depths of that wide crack in the blue and white ice. The contours of the sleek walls hid the bottom from view. It could have been fifty feet down. It could have been five hundred.

"Is it possible it's not the dark elves up here enacting their plan?" Willard asked. "But something or someone working for them?"

"Working for, ma'am?" Clarke asked. "Do dark elves have employees? Give them benefits and a 401(k)?"

"Think enslavement rather than benefits," I said. "I didn't see any other species while I was in their lair, but I wasn't there long. It wasn't a cozy place to hang out." I shivered, thinking of that massive statue of bones and the vat of blood. And the sacrifice of that girl they'd been about to make…

Willard was looking expectantly at me. Waiting for an identification?

I wished I had one. "From the size of the prints, ogres would be a possibility. They don't have the strongest of minds and would be susceptible to mental compulsions." But ogres didn't quite match up. The ones I'd met wore footwear and also had something closer to toenails than claws. "We could also be looking at some creatures the dark elves made with magic. Guardians or slaves to come out into the daylight, since they can't. Uhm." A new thought occurred to me. "How many scientists are on the missing team?"

"Six," Willard said.

And six sets of prints. Even though I'd never heard of magic that could turn human beings into giant monsters, my mind ruminated on the possibility. If that had happened, would there be any hope of turning them back? Or would we have to kill them?

"I've circled the area five times, Colonel," the pilot said. "The trail's gone."

"Right." Willard waved him away from the crevasse. "Make a note of this spot, but take us to the other chopper."

I watched the crevasse as we retreated, uneasy as I considered what kinds of allies the powerful dark elves could have enslaved or conjured out of thin air. Last time, I'd managed to get the best of them, but only because I'd had Zav with me and because they hadn't been prepared for him. This time, I didn't have a dragon… and the dark elves would be ready for us.

Chapter 18

The helicopter landed next to the other one on a snow-covered shelf looking up at the summit. Once the blades stopped whirring, the mountaintop grew very quiet, save for the rustles and clanks of soldiers gathering gear and putting crampons onto their boots. I was the only one not wearing a Kevlar helmet, tactical vest, and carrying a rifle, but I had traded my usual jeans and duster for layers of lightweight waterproof hiking pants, shirts, and a jacket that promised to keep me warm if it dropped below freezing. Under the shirts, I wore Nin's magical armored vest, and Chopper had its usual spot across my back, Fezzik in the thigh holster.

With the sun beating down on me, I was already warm and would shed the jacket if we ended up trekking from here. It had to be in the sixties, so worrying about cold-climate survival tactics seemed strange, but I trusted Willard's promise that the weather could change rapidly up here. The fresh snow was a testament to how cold it got, even in August.

"That's where the seismic-monitoring station *was*," someone said dryly, pointing to an empty spot on the shelf.

As Willard and Banderas walked over to take a look, I summoned my ally who didn't rely only on his eyes or his ability to sense magic to hunt prey. Silver mist formed at my side, with Sindari soon following.

Clarke looked over at him, offered his cocky smile, and Sindari's first words were: *Why is that one here?*

We're on a mission with the Army. He's in the Army.

He talks too much to be a warrior. And he has presumptuous hands.

As far as I could remember, Sindari had only met Clarke once, when we'd been helping Willard move into her new apartment. Clarke had petted Sindari, something he allowed from friends—Dimitri apparently had excellent hands—but had hissy fits about if others did it without asking.

He's here because he can sense magical beings. Just like you. I patted Sindari on the back. *We need to find out if the dark elves are up here. They would most likely be in caves formed by ice melting under the glaciers.*

Why would ice melt under a glacier?

It's a volcano, and hot gases ooze out of the ground.

Sindari lifted a paw and looked at it, as if expecting to see these oozing gases tainting his pads.

We also saw tracks as large as but different from sasquatch, I added. *Only a few miles from here. How are tigers at walking on snow and ice?*

Unless the snow is deep, it should not be problematic. I am a magnificent stalker from the Tangled Tundra and have hunted and downed prey in all weather conditions.

Good, because I couldn't find booties with cleats for tigers.

Booties? No predator would wear such a thing.

Dogs wear them in poor weather. I'm sure Rocket has a set.

Sindari sniffed. *Your* dogs *are not real predators. They chase their own tails. I bet Rocket would have found the dark elves by now.*

Sindari glared at me and then gave my foot a significant look.

If you chew it off now, you'll find the experience unpleasant. I'm wearing little metal spikes on the soles of my boots.

Armor for your feet?

Armor to keep my ass from sliding off the mountain.

"Get that tiger up here," Willard called.

She may not pet me either, Sindari informed me, then stalked up to the empty patch of ground Willard and Banderas were examining.

Her cat will appreciate a lack of tiger scent on her hands when she returns home.

I pulled my pack out of the helicopter and arranged it on my back so I could still access Chopper. Even though we ought to be safe from dark elves during the day, the prints of those mystery creatures ensured I wouldn't set my weapons aside, even to pee.

As I walked up to join Willard—Sindari was already sniffing the ground—the ice axes, carabiners, and other climbing gear jangled. There wouldn't be much point in activating my cloaking charm as long as I carried all this.

"I don't see a monitoring station," I said.

Sindari, already finished sniffing, headed off up the mountain.

Willard kicked aside some snow and pointed to four metal legs with the tops melted off, leaving only nubs bolted to a boulder embedded in the earth. "It *was* here. You're sure there aren't any dragons on Earth right now?"

The melted and re-hardened nubs *did* look like they had been blasted by fire—extremely hot fire.

"Reasonably sure," I said. "Dark elves would be able to conjure heat with magic."

Off to the left, Banderas pushed aside more snow, revealing the warped and melted husk of what must have been the equipment's metal housing.

Dark elves were here, Sindari spoke into my mind. *Not dragons. This happened last night. I am following their trail.*

I don't see any prints here except ours.

It snowed after they walked this way, but I can smell them. There were four.

Four isn't so bad.

I'm sure there are more at their destination. Are you coming?

Yeah.

"Sindari has the trail of dark elves." I waved to where his silver form was already a quarter of a mile up the slope. "Are we going in now if he finds a cave?"

"Better by day than by night." Willard had the men set up and test radios and gave orders to the helicopter pilots to wait until we figured out if we would be setting up a camp and staying in the area.

I pulled out my phone and wasn't surprised to see reception that fluctuated between one bar and *no signal*. No ordering pizza delivery up here.

We tramped up the mountain after Sindari, maneuvering over the snow and slick rock much more slowly than he did. Soon, the rock disappeared as we trekked onto a glacier. Since we were well above the tree line, it was easy to see the route ahead. It grew steeper, so we would have to dig out ropes and ice screws and slow down even further.

Sindari reached the last relatively flat spot and sat, gazing up a rocky slope that would be challenging for us to climb. Blue ice gleamed in the sun, making me squint even with sunglasses on.

The trail disappears here. His nostrils twitched as he tested the air.

Disappears? I don't see any caves they could have gone into.

My guess is that they levitated over the glacier. Wait here. I will find a route to the top and attempt to locate where they came down. Perhaps an entrance to their lair is close.

I trusted that he, much closer to a mountain goat than a human, could find a path safe for him. If he fell off a cliff, he could return to his own realm, and I could summon him again to my side. If only the rest of us had that luxury.

"We're climbing that?" Clarke asked as Sindari trekked up the mountainside. "I didn't realize the dangerous mountain-scaling portion of this adventure would start right away."

"Sindari is checking it out first," I said, "to see if he can pick up the trail again."

"He lost it?" Willard frowned.

"He thinks the dark elves started levitating at this point."

"Handy. When do you learn to do that?"

I thought about mentioning Lirena's leaf. The night before, I'd spent a couple of hours trying to form the patterns in my mind that she had shown me, and succeeded only in giving myself a headache.

"I'll let you know," was all I said.

I smell fainter traces of other people who were up here. Sindari was no longer in view, and his words had grown fainter in my mind. *Humans.*

There's a missing team of scientists up here somewhere.

A long silent minute passed before he spoke again. *You better come up here.*

Did you find the trail?

Yes. I also found your scientists.

Chapter 19

It took us an hour to traverse what Sindari had goated up—I decided that was a legitimate word for it—in scant minutes. The glacier was slick under the fresh snow, and the slope grew steeper, so we had to rope together and drill in ice screws to set anchors along the way.

Our progress felt as glacial as the glacier itself, and I looked wistfully back at the area where we'd left the helicopters, but there wouldn't have been anywhere for them to land up here, nor would it have been easy to find a safe place to rappel down from them.

I didn't sense anyone magical around, other than Clarke, Lieutenant Sabo, and Sindari, but the mountain itself was dangerous, and who knew what had happened to the scientists? From the ominous way Sindari had spoken, I assumed we would find them dead. I doubted he was up there, sitting in the middle of a cheerful group and getting petted.

Behind me, Clarke grunted as his foot slipped, even with the crampons. "A bunch of scientists came this way?"

"I'm sure any scientists who come up here have mountain-climbing experience," I said.

They probably knew Rainier a lot better than we did and had picked an easier path to their destination.

The ground shuddered faintly, and we all paused. Snaps came from the glacier, some right under us.

"Earthquake?" someone called.

"There's volcanic activity up here all the time," Willard replied.

A hint of brimstone entered the air from some nearby vent.

I didn't point out that the numbers we'd pored over from the now-defunct monitoring station had rarely registered high enough on the Richter scale for the ground shaking to be noticeable to people. At least, they hadn't in the last year. The last couple of weeks were another matter.

The snaps faded, and we pressed on until we reached the edge of a gully. The ice we'd been walking on sloped steeply downward to scree and a stream of meltwater running along the bottom. A hundred meters up the gully was the source of the water, a large ice cave almost twenty feet high at the mouth. I sensed Sindari in that direction.

We climbed down the slope to reach the scree and water. A couple of food wrappers that had blown away from someone's pack proved that others had been here, even to those of us who couldn't sniff out trails.

Sindari appeared out of the darkness of the cave and waited in its mouth. Steam fogged the air around him, creating a surreal mist in the air, and the brimstone smell returned, more intense than before.

"Better than a hound," Clarke said when we reached our furry guide.

Sindari didn't comment, merely turning to face into the shadows. The cave entrance was in shade, the sun behind the mountain, but it still took a moment for our eyes to adjust to the dim interior. And to pick out the bodies. Mutilated bodies.

If I'd been skeptical that Sindari had truly smelled dark elves, this would have removed all doubt. There weren't any beams that the bodies could have been hung from, but they were staked to posts driven into the hard, frozen ground—nothing short of a gas-powered fence-post driver or magic could have accomplished that. As with the dead in the Northern Pride headquarters, their eyes were gouged out, their tongues slit, and their hearts carved from their chests.

There were four men and two women, the entire research team. This ended my notion that the scientists might have somehow been turned into the creatures tramping across the mountainside. Finding them dead wasn't any better, but I was a little relieved we wouldn't have to battle monsters with human souls trapped inside.

Willard bowed her head and mumbled a prayer for the dead, then ordered Banderas and another man to scout the area to try to figure out what had happened. She had the rest of the soldiers take the bodies off

"They probably know what lithostatic means without having to Google it too." I eyed my phone and the lack of reception. I couldn't even pretend to be smart without the internet at hand.

"Probably."

"Did you know? Before talking to Einhorn?"

"Of course."

I squinted at her. "I'm debating if I believe you."

"Try opening a book now and then that doesn't have dragons in it."

"Trust me, I've sworn off dragon books. I'm reading a romantic comedy now. All of the characters are human."

"Sounds unimaginative."

Sindari left the cave, and bounded up the slope to sit next to me. *For the briefest moment, I thought I detected some magic behind those boulders.*

A dark elf? I rested a hand on his back.

It seemed inanimate, like one of your charms, but it had even less of a magical signature.

Maybe a beacon or alarm to let them know if someone disturbs their rocks?

That is a possibility, Sindari said, *but I suspect they already know we're here and what we're doing.*

You don't think they're busy sleeping? I assume they do that during the day.

We'll find out.

"The charge is set, Colonel," sounded over Willard's radio.

"At your leisure, Sergeant."

Brace yourself, Sindari, I thought.

Parekh trotted out of the cave and climbed up to join the group. The detonator was clipped to his belt.

"Whenever you're ready, Sergeant," Willard said.

"Yes, ma'am. Ten seconds."

Everyone hunkered down on the ice. We were all out of the gully and clear of the blast area, but this was a strange situation set up by a strange enemy, so we expected the unexpected.

When it came, the boom was muffled and not as impressive as I'd imagined. Chunks of ice thudded down inside the cave, while smaller debris shot out on a surge of meltwater.

A magical presence appeared to my senses so rapidly that I gasped. Willard glanced at me.

"Trouble." It wasn't a dark elf. I didn't know what it was, but its

He spent an hour on the phone conferring with a volcanologist. I was hoping the answer would be nothing, that the dark elves are deluding themselves."

"I take it the answer is that they aren't?"

"We don't think so," Willard said. "We're all fuzzy on what exactly they can do with magic and what kinds of devices they can make, but we've seen a lot of magical goblin devices, so we can make guesses about what's possible."

"*Goblins* are the demo species? Gondo with his stapler trebuchet?"

Willard snorted. "Some of them make more serious inventions. For the dark-elf plan to work, our guys said it would take a volcano that's already primed to erupt, one with a lot of magma and pressure built up down there over decades. It's been more than a hundred and twenty years since Rainier has done anything significant. There was an eruption recorded in the first half of the nineteenth century and volcanic activity all through the last half, but it's been quiet since 1894."

As we climbed out of the gully together, I thought of the vents melting the ice, promising a great deal of geothermal activity in the area. But those little vents probably weren't enough to let off the serious pressure that built up in a volcano.

"So it's primed to erupt even if the dark elves do nothing?" I hunkered down beside Willard.

"We can't predict when it would happen naturally, but there's a reason there are seismic monitors all over the mountain. And then there are the glaciers. Einhorn says Hollywood movies of dropping nukes into calderas aside, the most likely way to trigger an explosion would be to weaken the top of the mountain—the cork on the champagne bottle essentially—and release the lithostatic pressure keeping all that rock in place, then dump a bunch of cold water on the molten magma and let the fireworks start." Her voice was absolutely humorless as she spoke.

"So all they have to do is make some holes in the roof and melt the ice?"

"Basically."

"Shit."

"Yeah. It wouldn't be easy for us to do with explosives—which is probably why you don't see a lot of terrorist plots to blow up Yellowstone—but your dragon could do it, I'm sure. And we know the dark elves are powerful and that they like to build magical artifacts."

That's true. Let's see what Willard wants to do. I had grenades, but I'd seen her team pack explosives specifically designed for clearing rock.

"Anything back there?" Willard asked when I rejoined the group.

"They blocked the passage with boulders. Sindari doesn't sense them anywhere behind it. If this was the entrance to their new underground lair, they've moved it."

"They were here last night." Banderas rose, wiping ash off his hand. "There's still a hint of heat within the embers."

"They may have come specifically to deal with the scientists," Willard said, "to make sure nobody stumbled across them and could report their existence to the world."

One of the other soldiers brought over something he'd found. A smashed cell phone.

"Definitely no reporting back," I murmured, then raised my voice and shared Sindari's thoughts on the blockage.

"He speaks to you?" Clarke asked.

"Telepathically."

The men regarded Sindari curiously, but again, nobody questioned it beyond Clarke's query.

The helicopters arrived while Willard and Banderas were checking the back of the cave. I helped the others carry the dead scientists outside and carefully wrap them up to be airlifted out. Not that their comfort mattered much now. They'd been killed and their bodies maimed. What would their families think? What had *they* thought? They'd thought the dangers of the mountain would be the worst thing they would face and had probably only stayed in that cave for protection from the storm.

"We can blow up those boulders," Willard said after the helicopters departed and we reconvened in the cave mouth, "but I have to have a good reason. This is a national park." She looked at the posts where the dead scientists had hung. "I think that's reason enough. Sergeant Parekh, set up the charge."

"Yes, ma'am."

As the rest of the team climbed the gully slope back up to our anchors and ropes, I quietly asked Willard, "Is there any chance an explosion up here will set off the volcano?"

"No. I had Einhorn—our physicist—do a big analysis yesterday of what dark elves could possibly be planning to do to make Rainier erupt.

the posts. While they worked, she radioed a report back to the helicopter pilots, saying that we had proof that hostiles were in the area and needed the choppers to come pick up the bodies.

I wasn't sure who her reports went back to, but someone higher up her chain of command must have given permission for the outing. She would have to keep them in the loop.

The dark elves were here for several hours. Sindari walked past a spot where a campfire—or *sacrifice* fire—had recently burned, then headed deeper into the cave. *But there is no access to deeper tunnels. At least not now.*

As I followed him, we passed a vent spitting sulfuric smoke into the air. The ceiling grew lower after that. When we reached a spot where I could reach up and touch it, Sindari stopped. The way ahead was blocked, not with ice but with boulders. The way those boulders had been precisely packed to form a wall made me doubt Mother Nature had arranged them so.

Sindari nosed the ground. I pulled out a flashlight and fanned the beam over the area. There was more dirt than rock, and I could make out footprints. Human—or elf—sized footprints made by shoes, not bare feet.

I believe they closed this off recently, Sindari said, *because there are old trails as well as fresh here. They may have been using this entrance for some time.*

Can you tell if a tunnel continues on the other side of the blockage? Would there be any point in blowing up the boulders and trying to get back there? I looked over my shoulder to where Banderas had his hand in the ashes while Willard took photos of the bodies.

I cannot tell if there are tunnels back there, but I do not sense anyone with magical blood within my range.

And your range is larger than mine. So there's not a dark elf for miles.

Correct, he said.

We should look for another access point then.

Even if there were miles of tunnels back there—I assumed the promise of something expansive to study had drawn the scientists to this place—they would probably be even harder to traverse than the glacier outside. These passages, formed by warm gases from vents, wouldn't be as spacious and open as something like an old lava tube.

It is possible the dark elves are there and cloaking their auras, Sindari pointed out.

aura was almost as powerful as a dragon's. "Sindari, that's more than a beacon."

Rumbles and scrapes emanated from the cave. They didn't sound like ice falling.

It blossomed into something more. Sindari trotted to the edge of the glacier to look toward the cave.

Blossomed? Try erupted.

Staying low, I hurried after him. Ominous thumps came from the cave, the ice under us reverberating with each one.

A cloud of dust obscured the entrance, the fine powder wafting out into the clear sky. Something stirred inside that cloud. A huge blocky shape that looked more like a mountain itself than a living being crawled out of the cave on vaguely human-like hands and knees. When the creature rose to its full height on legs made from pillars of rock, it stood almost thirty feet tall and twenty wide.

"Rock golem," I breathed. "They must have put it back there to guard that entrance."

"You didn't *sense* that behind the boulders?" Willard asked.

It was inert until we triggered the equivalent of a tripwire, Sindari said, *with only the slightest magical signature.*

"Sorry," I said to Willard. "It wasn't activated until we disturbed its resting spot."

Willard groaned and pulled her rifle off her shoulder.

The massive stone head and its even more massive neck and shoulders swiveled to look up at our team. Red eyes flared with inner light, and the rock golem strode down the gully toward our position.

Chapter 20

I shrugged off my backpack and dug out grenades. Even if the rock golem somehow *hadn't* been magical, I doubted bullets would have done anything to it, but it oozed power in the same way Zav did. I worried that even Chopper and Nin's enhanced grenades would not be enough.

"I'm throwing some explosives!" I warned the soldiers readying their weapons.

Only Willard, Banderas, and Sabo had magical weapons, but everyone was taking aim.

Willard gave calm orders to back up, fan out, and stay out of each other's line of fire. "Thorvald, any chance we can negotiate with this thing?"

Something akin to red laser beams shot out of the golem's eyes and struck the closest soldier—Clarke—in the shoulder. He cried out in pain and tumbled onto the ice, only his carabiner hooked to a rope keeping him from skidding down into the gully.

"No." I pulled the tab, counted, and threw a grenade.

It exploded as it struck the golem in the chest. At Willard's order, the soldiers opened fire.

It may not be able to climb the ice to get to us. Sindari crouched on the rim overlooking the gully, poised to spring.

The boom of my grenade echoed from the mountainside, smoke swallowing the top half of the golem. But it soon moved out of it, walking up the slick valley wall, using its huge hands to help maneuver its body up the ice. A hairline crack in its chest appeared where the grenade had hit it, but there was no greater sign of damage.

Gravity and physics shouldn't have allowed that huge thing to climb up the ice, but magic defied both and propelled the golem toward our group. Bullets pinged off the rock monster's face and chest. The soldiers' aim was impeccable, but it didn't matter. Even Willard's magical bullets did little to stop it.

"Aim high!" I barked, spotting Sindari running in.

He snapped his jaws at the golem's legs as it stood straight, having made it to the top. The soldiers backed away, unhooking from the ropes—they dared not remain anchored in place with that thing stomping toward them.

Clacks sounded as Sindari's teeth struck the rocky pillar of the golem's left leg. If his powerful fangs did any damage, I couldn't see it. The golem slammed a fist down at him.

He sprang to the side, escaping the blow by scant inches. The golem pounded a crater in the ice where he'd been.

Even with his sure feet, Sindari slipped on the treacherous ice and almost ended up falling. Snarling, he whirled around to face his assailant again.

"Stay back for now, Sindari!" I hurled another grenade.

Even though he was magical, Sindari was flesh and blood and could be hurt by weapons and claws. And friendly fire.

The grenade struck, followed by grenades from two other soldiers. I didn't think theirs were magical.

Beside me, Willard fired a series of shots at the golem's eyes. My grenade exploded, the glacier trembling under our feet.

Once again, the golem walked on, barely damaged. Clarke had scrambled out of its way, but it was almost to Lieutenant Sabo, who was firing determinedly at it, believing the magical bullets streaking out of his gun would be enough to save him.

"Fall back!" Willard yelled at him, then growled, "Should have had you get the Howitzer for me." She shook her rifle. "Thorvald, this isn't doing shit."

"Here." I thrust Fezzik at her, drew Chopper, and snatched another grenade out of my pack. "I'm going in. Tell everyone to hold fire, but if you see an opportunity, go for it."

Elven Doom

I ran across the ice, more agile than the full-blooded humans but still feeling awkward, even with the crampons—or *because* of them. The golem saw me coming and turned away from Sabo. Its eyes lit, and I read the warning in that and dove to the side.

Beams shot out, instantly boring holes in the ice, vapor steaming up. I turned my dive into a roll and sprang up, running toward the golem again. Before it could swivel its head to target my new spot, I rushed between its legs. Behind it, I turned and jumped up, driving Chopper toward its lower back like one of the ice axes we'd brought.

With the mighty swing I took, I expected the blade to sink in several feet. It gouged only a couple of inches into the golem. The thing was nearly indestructible.

It lumbered around, trying to face me, but I stayed behind it. Visions of pulling myself up the golem-mountain using Chopper as a pick washed out of my mind. Instead, I stuffed my grenade in my pocket and sheathed the blade long enough to leap up, catching its arm and swinging my body up on top of it.

The head swiveled toward me, and beams shot out of its eyes as it shook its arm. Dropping flat on the huge limb, I hung on tight. The beams shot over my head, hot enough and close enough that my scalp prickled.

Hanging on with one arm, I drew Chopper again with the other. When the beams disappeared, I lunged up to the shoulder and swung at those eyes.

A crack sounded as the edge of the blade connected. One crimson orb shattered like glass. I didn't know if the golem needed its eyes to find its enemies, but hoped it wouldn't be able to shoot more lasers out of them if it lost them.

It didn't shriek or growl; it simply swung its opposite arm toward me like a club. I scrambled across its shoulder and around the back of its head to avoid the grasping sausage-like digits. The thing was nearly indestructible, but at least it wasn't fast.

When I reached its other shoulder, I swung Chopper at the remaining eye. It burst, tiny red shards tinkling down to the ice.

The golem grabbed for me again, but I evaded the grip once more, leaping atop its head. Using my legs to hold on, I drove my blade down into its skull.

Once again, the sword didn't penetrate nearly as far as I'd hoped. Two fists swung toward me at once. Chopper almost didn't come free, and one rock hand clipped my shoulder. I cursed at the pain—it was like being hit by a boulder tumbling down a mountainside—but managed to keep from falling off. I caught the golem around the neck, hanging on by one arm as I hacked at the side of its head with my sword.

I *was* doing damage—shards of rock flew off—but not enough, and I snarled with impatience, worried it would trample on the soldiers while I was working like molasses.

A roar sounded and Sindari, springing more than twenty feet from the ground, landed on its other shoulder. His claws didn't do damage, but when he bit into the other side of the golem's head, more shards of rock peeled off.

Dangling by my arm, I tugged the grenade out of my pocket. I pulled the pin with my teeth, grimacing at the taste of metal, then counted and reached around. It clunked against rock teeth.

Bite it! I mentally yelled to Sindari.

He'd been tearing gouges from the creature's head and face, but he chomped on the amorphous stone ear sticking out of the side of its head. The golem probably didn't have pain receptors, but it was startled enough to open its mouth. I stuffed the grenade in.

Get down, Sindari!

I flung myself backward, twisting and hoping to land on my feet. But the ice had softened—maybe I landed on a spot hit by one of those laser beams—and it gave way under my boots. One foot plunged into a hole.

The grenade blew, tearing the golem's head off. The soldiers let out whoops.

But the creature didn't fall. It spun around, raising its arms to chop down onto me.

Swearing, I yanked on my boot, but the ice had my foot caught.

Automatic fire opened up behind the golem. A hail of bullets slammed into its back, and it paused. I hacked at the ice with Chopper. It gave, and I yanked my foot free. Bullets slammed into the headless golem's back. It resumed its downward chop at me, but I was free now and dove to the side. The fists struck only ice.

More bullets rained into it, all of the soldiers opening fire. I jumped up, intending to run out of the way, but the golem and I were close to the edge of the gully. Ice crumbled and gave way. I tumbled down the slope to the bottom, meltwater still rushing past, and landed hard on my back. The golem pitched down right after me.

Again, I rolled to the side. Most of the golem missed me, but an arm landed across my waist like a tree trunk, pinning me. Pain blasted me, but I wasn't sure if the thing was still animated and attacking or had simply fallen on me. Even while stuck under its arm, I hacked at it with Chopper, chiseling off more pieces from its hulking rock body.

The golem didn't fight back. It didn't move at all. Slowly, it dawned on me that the magic of its aura was fading.

I let myself collapse back in the mud and snow. Maybe in a minute, I would try to get out, but the arm had to weigh hundreds of pounds. After having it land on me, walking would not be fun.

Val? Sindari asked. *Are you all right?*

I hope so. Thanks for the appropriately timed bite.

You are welcome. I was chagrined that my claws and fangs did so little against the golem. It was a pleasure to be of assistance. He looks better without a head.

I concur.

Willard came into view, looking down at me, her dark skin and green-and-brown camo helmet contrasting with the pale blue sky and the white ice rising up all around me. "You always end up pinned under your enemies after a fight, Thorvald?"

"Never more than two or three times out of ten."

"Those odds don't seem conducive to good health."

"It's why it's good that I heal fast." With luck, my pelvis wasn't shattered, because even my elven blood wouldn't help me heal from that fast enough to be useful.

"Do you need help up?"

"Possibly. I'd estimate this arm weighs about as much as Dorothy's house."

"Looks like it." Willard waved for a couple of her uninjured men to come help.

While they heaved the arm upward a few inches, I squirmed out from under it. My pelvis did indeed hurt, but I didn't think any of the bones were broken.

"Is there anything else magical nearby that you'd like to warn us about?" Willard asked. "Preferably more than three seconds before it attacks us?"

"No?" *Sindari? I asked silently. Nothing else?*

Nothing. Not even a hint of magic.

"No," I repeated more firmly.

"Good." Willard gave me a hand up and returned Fezzik. "*Next* time you order me a magical weapon, get me something automatic. Preferably in a caliber suitable for taking down a paraceratherium."

"A what?" Even if I'd known what that was, I wouldn't have been able to pronounce it.

"The paraceratherium is an extinct species of hornless rhinoceros—it's believed to be the largest land mammal that ever lived." Willard raised her eyebrows. "Books, Thorvald. Books without dragons in them."

"Yeah, yeah. You intel people are insufferable. I was just a pilot, remember. As for weapons, I'll keep your preferences in mind. Thanks for saving my butt." I liked to think that I could have rolled to the side quickly enough to avoid that blow, but it seemed like a good idea to show gratitude to people who helped out, thus to encourage repeat performances.

With my first step, my pelvis let me know it hadn't appreciated being hurled down a glacier or having a golem land on it. I stifled a gasp of pain, not wanting anyone to think I would be a liability going forward. We hadn't even seen a dark elf yet.

I would walk it off. It would be fine.

"You're welcome," Willard said. "It was my turn."

"To save my butt? I don't think I've saved yours recently. You're not out in the field much."

Willard raised her eyebrows.

Oh, the magical cancer thing.

"Technically," I said, "you were only in danger from that because the dark elves wanted me out of the way."

"I thought they wanted my office out of the way."

"Because your office sends me out after dark elves."

"You're kind of self-centered, you know."

"I've been hanging out with a lot of dragons."

"That'll do it." Willard got on the radio and called for one of the helicopters to return to pick up Clarke, who tried to bravely protest that he could go on, but he had a laser-beam hole straight through his shoulder.

I walked gingerly along the bottom of the gully as I cleaned Chopper and reloaded Fezzik while hoping the pain pulsing between my spine and hip would go away. Willard sent a couple people into the cave to see if the explosion had cleared a route—and to make sure no other enemies were back there.

You are injured? Sindari was watching me.

No.

There's no need to lie to me about such things.

I thought you might feel pity for me if you knew and insist on letting me ride on your back instead of walking.

Predators don't feel pity, but I would allow you to lean some of your weight on me while we maneuver across the ice. Tigers do not permit themselves to be ridden like one of your horses. How degrading.

Are there any animals on this planet that you don't believe you're much better than?

None that have permitted themselves to be domesticated. A tiger would never allow this. Even a tiger on this backward planet.

I once saw a tiger with a saddle and a rider. I rotated my hips in a slow circle. A sharp pain stabbed me. That was worse than walking. Where was a dragon with healing hands when I needed him?

Now I know you're lying.

It might have been in a cartoon. I decided not to explain *He-Man* to Sindari.

As the whir of chopper blades reached my ears, a shadow fell across the gully. Clouds that hadn't been in the sky earlier were drifting across the sun. Darker, grayer clouds had formed on the northern horizon, hiding distant Mount Baker from view. Below our lofty elevation, clouds had also drifted in over the lower peaks of the Cascades. Hopefully, if any precipitation came, it would fall below us.

"Colonel?" Banderas's voice came over Willard's radio. "There's nothing back here. No cave that continues on. Just a nook that the golem must have been waiting in. Behind it, the ice goes all the way down to the ground. It looks like it was deliberately knocked down, so we could try blowing another hole, but…"

Lieutenant Sabo spoke next. "I think they sealed this off completely and left that present for us."

"Us specifically?" Willard looked at me.

"I don't see how they could have anticipated *us*," I said slowly, though I wasn't confident of that. I'd invaded their Seattle lair, so maybe they had assumed I would eventually show up here. "But they would have expected *someone* to come looking for the missing scientists."

"Why would they have bothered the scientists at all? Until now, the dark elves were circumspect and didn't do anything to let anyone find out about their presence here. Now, we've got dead scientists and a blasted monitoring device in one night."

"Maybe they found out we were coming and wanted to get rid of anything that could point to them."

Her eyes narrowed. "How would they have found out? A spy in the office?"

"You think Gondo or Freysha?"

"I'd be shocked if it was Gondo."

And I had a hard time imagining the tool-loving elf colluding with dark elves—or *any* elves colluding with dark elves—but that could all be an act. Just because she was young didn't mean she was innocent or to be trusted.

"Are those the only new people?" I asked.

"Yes. And the only people in the office who aren't at least partially human. That doesn't necessarily mean others couldn't betray us, but ninety percent of the staff are in the service and have been for years. The civilians are part-time advisors, like you, and don't know that much."

"Oh? Are they ignorant on extinct hippos too?"

This time, Willard's narrowed eyes were for me. "You know what I mean. They don't know that much about our operation or what we're investigating at any given time."

"So Freysha or Gondo could be a plant from the dark elves. Or there's another possibility." My phone buzzed, and I pulled it out, surprised a message had come through.

"That they're very close to enacting their plan and don't *care* if we find out about them?" Willard asked.

Amber's name popped up on my phone. I started to answer before realizing it was a voice mail. The message had come in while I'd been fighting, or at some random point when there'd been enough reception for it to get through. I'd never heard it ring, so it had probably gone straight to voice mail.

"Either that, or the scientists stumbled onto their lair and had to be taken care of," I said.

"That seems a grim thing to hope for, but it would mean we have more time. If they're planning to mess with the volcano *tonight*... I'd hate it if the only thing we can do is start disaster mitigation procedures." Willard clenched her fist. "I want to *prevent* the disaster. Before innocent civilians get hurt."

When I tried to access my voice mail, the reception flipped from one bar to *no service*. I hadn't even moved.

I hoped Amber had decided she was ready to talk, not that something more dire was happening. Unfortunately, I had no trouble imagining the dark elves, having learned of my daughter's existence, sending some magical minion to kidnap her.

"That had better not happen," I growled.

"I agree," Willard said, though we were talking about two different things.

Chapter 21

The injured Corporal Clarke had been picked up, the helicopter pilot promising to return in two hours, but as the clouds grew thicker, wreathing the peak of Rainier and detracting from visibility, I wondered if that would happen.

My right hip and pelvic area throbbed with each step as I waited for the ibuprofen I'd taken to kick in. Hopefully, if we went into battle again, adrenaline would keep me from noticing the injury. All we were doing now was trekking across the glacier toward the crevasse we'd seen earlier, doing our best to keep from sweating and getting our clothes damp. The temperature had dropped noticeably with the sun blotted out.

After poking around and agreeing that whatever cave system had existed had been too thoroughly collapsed to reopen, no matter how many explosives we used, Banderas had suggested going to the point where those tracks had disappeared and seeing if I could sense anything from the rim of the crevasse.

It was the only other lead we had, so it made sense to follow it, but I didn't like the idea of fighting six more enemies, enemies that could be nearly as large as that golem. *They* weren't the ones threatening the people of Puget Sound. I wanted to find the dark elves, capture or kill the two scientists, and destroy whatever device they had concocted to make the volcano erupt.

Willard, who was walking ahead of me, cleats digging into the ice with each step, kept eyeing those clouds. "The forecast was for clear skies this morning and partial cloud cover in the afternoon and tomorrow. Nothing about rain, snow, or fog that would make helicopter landings difficult."

"A weather report that wasn't correct? In Seattle? How odd."

She glowered over her shoulder at me. "They can usually get the *short*-range forecast right." She stopped, waiting for me to catch up, and lowered her voice. "Do you think dark elves can control weather?"

"You know more about their abilities and lore than I do, I think."

"There's not that much about them. Even the other magical species don't know them that well, at least those I can count on as informants. Elves—surface elves—are intimately familiar with them, or were at one time."

"You should have asked Freysha for the scoop on them."

"You think I should have asked the person we were accusing of being a spy a half hour ago for mission-critical information?" Willard asked.

"*I* haven't accused her of being a spy. I could have asked her."

"Feel free to reach out telepathically."

"I haven't learned how to do that yet, and I think she would be out of range anyway." A raindrop splashed onto my cheek. "My guess would be a no on weather manipulation. Zav hasn't mentioned dragons being able to do that—not that I've asked—and they're more powerful than elves. Also, why would dark elves care about the weather if they live underground? Even if it could be manipulated, would they have bothered to learn how?"

"A good point."

"I bet this is just bad luck. And it might clear up in an hour."

"True. I do wish I'd had the choppers take us to the crevasse, then go back for the dead, instead of volunteering to march over there on foot."

"I do too." I kept myself from touching my injury, but since we were standing still, I did lean my weight onto the other side. "But Clarke needed medical attention."

"He would have been all right. I looked at his injury. That beam burned straight through, cauterizing as it went."

"He was writhing and complaining that he was too young to die, having only slept with—what was it?—sixty-eight people."

"Eighty-six," Willard said dryly.

"I knew it was a large and likely bullshit number."

"Yes. As if anything greater than, say, eleven isn't ridiculous."

"I would have said twenty-five, but go on."

"Since these are politically correct times, I won't insinuate that you're a slut."

"Thank you. Can we insinuate that Clarke is?"

"No, I don't think that's allowed either."

"The world has become a weird and unfamiliar place."

"Tell me about it." Willard continued onward.

At least we had come across one of the regularly maintained trails for climbers, so the walking wasn't as onerous as it had been earlier. But dealing with the injury still had me sweating—and worried people would catch up with me. I hated being the weak link.

When Banderas thumped me on the shoulder, I thought it would be to tell me I was going too slowly.

"Good fighting back there, Thorvald," he said instead. "How can I get one of those swords?"

"I had to kill a zombie lord for mine."

"Where do you find one? A graveyard?"

"Mine was in a church in Anacortes, munching on the congregation."

"So they like islands, do they?"

"Who doesn't? If you're going to eat brains, you should do it with a view."

"How about the gun? Reminds me of an Uzi."

As we kept walking, I gave Banderas the details on Fezzik and told him about Nin and where he could find her in town. It amused but didn't surprise me that talk of weapons had brought out the silent sergeant's chatty side.

The rain picked up, hammering down in time with the throbbing of my pelvis, so I let Banderas take over the talking. It kept me from glancing repeatedly at my phone, hoping the reception would improve long enough for me to check my voice mail. Banderas went on to explain that he had three kids he was raising on his own, so he didn't have money to spend on personal weapons; he had to make do with what the army issued him.

"Maybe after this, Willard will make sure everyone in the office has automatic weapons with magical bullets."

"I'd like that."

"Say, Banderas, Willard and I were discussing terminology. What would you call a guy who'd slept with eighty-six women?" I supposed some of them could have been men. Dimitri had suggested Clarke had leanings both ways, and he was more in tune with that stuff than I.

"Lucky?" Banderas offered.

"Hm, we had other words in mind."

A voice spoke into my mind, almost startling me into tripping.

One of the dragons has returned. It was Lirena.

Where are you? I glanced around, half-expecting to see her standing off to the side of the glacier, but even if she had been, I wouldn't have seen her. The visibility had dropped to half a mile, maybe less.

Near your domicile in the city. Have you been practicing the patterns I showed you? Your telepathy range has improved.

I think that's your range that's letting us talk. I shouldn't have been surprised that she could send her thoughts a hundred miles. Zav had spoken to me from Seattle when I'd been in Idaho. *Have you changed your mind about coming to help us battle dark elves?*

If she was here to observe me, shouldn't she observe me battling enemies? Even if she didn't join in, she could be useful up here. Did she have healing abilities? I drooled a little thinking of the time Zav had incinerated a bullet in my hip and healed me to a hundred percent in seconds.

I cannot raise my hand against them without creating consequences for my people. They are the only species in your world powerful enough to open portals, portals that could take them to one of the elven homelands.

She wouldn't appreciate it if I followed up with, *Better there than here.* Instead, I asked, *A dragon, you said? Is it Zav?*

The male who claimed you?

Uh, yeah.

I assume he forced you into that and his attentions are unwanted.

His healing attentions weren't unwanted. And… I could no longer say without lying that the rest of his attention was entirely displeasing. Something told me that Lirena, who'd made it clear that she didn't like dragons, wouldn't want to hear that.

He didn't ask me if I was willing, no. He assumed.

As dragons do. They're monsters. The female is the one I sense.

I stifled a groan. I'd thought that if Zav left, Zondia would also stay off Earth. He had also believed that. And he'd promised to speak with her.

Had she pretended to cooperate with him, but then come back here at the first opportunity? And if so, *why*? If Zav wasn't here with me, what did it matter if I had some magical mark that let others believe I was his mate? It wasn't as if I could open a portal and go complain to him if someone pestered me.

The lilac dragon? I asked. *Is she the only one here on Earth?*

Currently, yes.

Is she in the city? Would Zondia have a reason to go bother Amber again? My fist clenched.

She was. Now, she is flying southeast.

Toward us? I didn't manage to stifle the second groan.

She may change course, but for now, she is flying toward the mountain you are on.

I tried not to find it disconcerting that Lirena could tell exactly where I was. *Are you sure you don't want to come up here? There may be a dragon to fight, not only dark elves.*

I will consider it. Is there any more instruction I can offer to help prepare you for your battle?

"We're not far from the crevasse," Willard called back.

I don't think I have time for instruction. Maybe we can set up a tutoring schedule when I get back. If I survived the mission. *Wait, do you know anything about dwarven swords? Like common magical words that are used to activate their powers? I only know one for Chopper.*

Chopper is the name of your sword?

It's not the original name. I assume the dwarf master who made it—Dondethor, I was told—called it something else.

Undoubtedly. The dwarven-made blade that King Eireth—your father—wields has a name that translates to Resplendent Alloy Crafted from the Fire of My Heart. The elven name for it is Moonbeam Gatherer.

I'll stick with Chopper.

If Dondethor was truly the craftsman, try krundark *for fire or heat. And* keyk *for ice. It likely has some specific greater power embedded deep within it, but less generic things are associated with longer and more descriptive terms.*

Like Resplendent Alloy Crafted from the Fire of My Heart? I imagined yelling all that out as I ran into battle.

Along those lines, yes. Keyk *may be particularly helpful if you're battling a dragon.*

Can you repeat those? I dug out my phone and tapped in the words, spelling them with best guesses. From what I'd learned of activation words, the spelling didn't matter, but you had to say them precisely, or nothing happened.

Lirena repeated them, then added, *Make sure to memorize* keyk. *Even though dragons are impervious to almost everything when they have their magical shields up, their scales are weak in general against ice. They are creatures of fire and magma, since volcanos erupt frequently in their native world. They do not like cold climates, and a cold blade will slide into their flesh more easily than one at normal temperature. Dwarves know that and most of the swords they make have an ability to become like ice.*

I wrote down both words to memorize—and try out ahead of time. Enemies rarely paused in battle for one to check one's notes before attacking.

Thank you, Lirena. I meant it.

Certainly. I wish you to be victorious.

Will I be more likely to be accepted and allowed to visit your world if I am? I had no intention of breaking my neck trying to prove myself to some father I'd never met nor a cousin who'd only recently appeared in my life, but I was curious.

Our people do admire great warriors who are capable of protecting our citizens and our way of life.

Think my sword has any special commands that would help against dark elves? I was concerned that Zav's sister was heading in my direction, but unless she'd grown more hostile since our last meeting—which *was* possible—the dark elves were a bigger threat.

It's possible, but you would have to research that particular blade to find out.

Where could I do that?

Taron Morak, the dwarven home world.

I suppose I can't take an Uber there.

What?

Never mind.

A hint of something magical brushed my awareness, and I lifted a hand to stop the column behind me. "Willard? Hold up."

I closed my eyes, stretching out as far as I could with my senses.

Right now, that was farther than I could see with my eyes—the visibility continued to drop as thick clouds rolled in.

The magic, a tiny hint of it, was under us.

"You sense something?" Willard asked.

I pointed downward.

"A dark elf? A device?" Willard grimaced. "Another golem?"

"An artifact of some kind, I think. It's stationary and doesn't have an aura like a living being. Let me get Sindari back." I'd dismissed him, wanting to save him for when we truly needed him. This looked like the time.

As I summoned him, Willard radioed one of the pilots, asking about weather conditions, how far out they were, and if they thought they'd be able to return for us tonight. We'd brought gear enough to spend a couple of nights up here, but the idea of camping out next to a bunch of dark elves who might get active once the sun went down was more chilling than the pervasive ice.

I sense magic, Sindari reported as soon as he formed.

Me too. Can you tell what it is? And where *it is? I sense that it's below us, but I'm not sure how far below.*

On the ground under the ice.

And how thick is the ice? Thick, I feared, but I hoped his superior senses would have a less vague idea.

Five hundred feet? Perhaps more.

"Thorvald?" Willard had finished the radio call and was looking at me.

"Are the glaciers five hundred feet thick here?" I asked, hoping that geologist she'd spoken to had told her differently.

Standard climbing ropes were shy of two hundred feet. We could go down in stages, but I'd been envisioning an easy rappel to the bottom of that crevasse to see if there were any cave entrances. I don't know *why* I'd been envisioning that. Nothing about this mission had been easy yet.

"Here?" Willard pointed down. "I don't know about this precise location, but Emmons Glacier is supposed to be close to a thousand feet thick near the White River Campground." She waved, presumably toward wherever that campground was on the mountain.

"Well, we sense magic, and Sindari thinks it's under the ice, five hundred feet down."

Perhaps more, he corrected.

"*At least* five hundred feet."

"Let's take a look at this crevasse. We can rappel down five hundred feet if it goes all the way to the ground, but we'll need to consider it carefully and the possibility of being attacked in the middle of a descent. We'll also have to climb back up afterward." Willard pulled out her phone to check the time. "It's gotten dark with the clouds, but it's still only one. Sunset isn't until almost 8:30 today. Can we assume they won't attack us before dark?"

"If it's dark down there, the sun won't bother them. And even if they're sleeping, we've already seen that their minions have no trouble operating in daylight."

It is possible that's another golem, Sindari added, *not yet activated and emitting its full magical signature.*

"Sindari thinks we might be sensing another golem." I glanced back. The rest of the soldiers had caught up and were listening.

"At least we know how to fight those now," Willard said.

"Yeah, point Thorvald and her sword at it," Banderas said.

Lucky me.

While we were all together, I gave Willard and the others the information Lirena had shared—that Zondia was on her way. Willard swore, but then shook her head and said it wouldn't change what we had to do. I hoped she was right and that Zondia didn't intend to interfere.

"Thorvald," Lieutenant Sabo said, "if you have more of those grenades and want to distribute them equally among us, that could help."

"We're not throwing grenades under a glacier," someone else said. "Not if *we're* all down under it too."

Willard lifted a hand. "Let's scout the crevasse first. If we do send a team down, we're not all going. Some of us have to stay back."

"To mount a rescue?" I worried that another golem was the least of the trouble we would face down there. "Or to point the helicopter crew toward where the next batch of bodies will be?"

"To cover our backs and rescue us if needed, yes." Willard didn't mention bodies. Maybe mission commanders were required to employ positive thinking.

It was a good thing I wasn't in charge.

Chapter 22

The rain turned to freezing rain and pelted the backs of our jackets as we peered down into the crevasse. It was about fifteen feet wide where we were, but ledges and bulges made it impossible to see how far down it went.

Lieutenant Sabo flipped a coin over the edge, perhaps thinking it would bounce off the walls all the way down and we would hear it land, but this wasn't a well. It hit one icy blue ledge and bounced into a shelf of snow and disappeared.

"What was that supposed to accomplish?" I asked.

"Not quite what I imagined," he said wryly, "but now you have something to aim for on your descent. A quick and easy way to earn ten cents."

"Such riches. You don't think you're going too?"

"I've never climbed anything like that." Sabo looked to Willard.

She shook her head. "Thorvald and I will go down and scout. Banderas will lead a rescue team if needed."

Sergeant Banderas was about a quarter mile away, investigating the footprints we'd seen from the helicopter. He seemed a natural choice to take along, but...

"*You're* going down?" I asked Willard. "This isn't Hollywood. The senior officer doesn't go on the away missions. You send the red shirts."

Sabo snorted. Willard gave me a blank look. Now that I thought about it, there hadn't been any *Star Trek* mugs among the *Garfield* and

Smurfs collection in her kitchen cabinets.

"I know more about dark elves than you do," Willard said, "and if it's possible to negotiate with them, you need a senior officer."

"If they're interested in that, I'll let them know the address of your tent and your office hours."

Willard thumped me on the shoulder. "You're not in charge here. You just let me know if you sense a platoon of elves with magical bows down there waiting to shoot up at us."

"No, I can't even sense the magic that Sindari and I detected over there." I pointed my thumb back the way we had come.

"Did you put him away?" She glanced around.

"Yeah. His time on Earth each day is limited. We'll want him when we get to the bottom." There wouldn't have been a way for him to climb down, regardless. Even a goat wouldn't be nuts enough to go down the slick vertical walls.

"Agreed. Sabo, get a camp set up over there." Willard waved to a relatively flat area on our side of the crevasse. "If anything crazy happens, that's the way out." She pointed up the slope toward the path we'd been following earlier, to where a temporary bridge had been laid across a narrow section of the crevasse by whoever maintained the mountain trails for climbers. Wind had kept it largely swept free of snow, but it was little more than a metal plank laid across the gap. "The trail continues down the mountain and will eventually get you to Camp Muir."

"Does that mean the choppers won't be back today?" Sabo asked.

"Not unless the weather gets better." Willard waved toward the clouds socking us in. "It won't hurt us to set up and be ready if they don't."

"Yes, ma'am."

"We could *all* just set up camp and hang out up here," I said. "Maybe they'll come up to visit us tonight, and we wouldn't have to fight in territory they know and have likely booby-trapped."

Willard considered the argument. "Why would they come out?"

"To kill us? It's a fun hobby for dark elves. You saw the scientists."

Her grim expression and head shake suggested she wasn't in the mood for humor, and I silently apologized to the dead for any disrespect.

"They can probably levitate in and out of there without climbing,"

I said, "so it wouldn't be as epic a feat for them to visit us. With all their weapons."

Wind gusted, tugging at our jackets. The freezing rain had stopped, at least for the moment. If we were going to rappel down, this might be our best time for it.

"Levitation sounds handy," Willard said. "We'll go down, set the anchors, and scout the bottom today, and that's it. It makes sense to see if there really is a cave system down there. For all we know, the creatures that made those tracks turned Disney-lemming and fell to their deaths."

I highly doubted that, but I didn't argue further. Willard was right that the dark elves might ignore us if we stayed on top of the glacier, especially if they were already in the middle of implementing their plan. Up here, five hundred feet above the ice, we were no threat to them.

If I made it down there and learned they *were* already implementing their plan... I would have to go in, not climb back up to spend the night. It sounded about as appealing as wandering out onto a live firing range. But this was the job I'd signed up for, and tens of thousands of lives were at stake. I had no choice.

As I stared down into the icy depths, past layers of white, gray, and pale blue, I wondered if I would ever make it out again.

Chapter 23

Banderas protested when Willard announced I was going down with her. He kept protesting as we screwed in anchors at the top to make future descents—and the climb back up—more manageable. Only when we started rappelling into the crevasse did he subside.

Willard had agreed that Banderas had more experience than I did—this was my first time climbing ice, and I didn't hide it—and would have been the logical choice under most circumstances. But these weren't most circumstances. She wanted me and my sword beside her in case of an ambush.

The inside of the crevasse was breathtaking, swirls of dark and light ice all around us, with places where the frozen walls had melted and then hardened into epic icicles. After seeing those, and hearing things crack and break free as we descended, I was glad Willard had made one of the soldiers lend me a helmet.

The ice was softer than I expected, though maybe that was typical in the summer. Our picks and the screws for creating anchor points went in without too much trouble. Hopefully, that meant the climb back up wouldn't be too onerous, but I doubted it. Five hundred feet, creeping up a foot at a time, would be hard work. At least on the way down, gravity was with us.

My injury ached as the rappel seat dug into my thighs, my full weight cradled by the meager straps, but the pain didn't impede me too much.

The climb back up would be a different matter, when I had to use my legs to push myself up the ice walls, and I wondered if the dark elves would mind if I camped outside the door to their lair instead.

We reached the bottom in one piece, clumps of hard snow and shards of fallen icicles crunching under our boots. The air was much cooler down here, as if we'd stepped into a walk-in freezer, and I zipped my jacket up to my chin.

As Willard radioed up to give a status report to the rest of the team, I turned a slow three-sixty. There weren't any caves in sight, but those footprints were down here. The massive creatures had left numerous tracks as they came and went, but the main trail led up the slope.

I sniffed a few times, wondering if an animal scent might linger in the area. Instead, I caught the first hint of brimstone wafting along the air currents.

A carbon monoxide detector was clipped to each of our packs, giving me some reassurance against us wandering into toxic air, but my lungs might react to gases that wouldn't bother others. Wouldn't that be fun.

Willard finished her report, the radio spitting static as often as issuing words. If we left the crevasse and entered a cave system with hundreds of feet of ice above us, we would lose our ability to communicate with the team.

"I sense the magic we felt from above," I realized. It was faint and somewhere beyond the wall of ice to my left. "Let me get a second opinion."

I touched my feline charm, calling Sindari back for his superior nose and superior senses.

As soon as he formed, he looked up, an uncharacteristic hunch to his shoulders.

The walls go up and up, and you can't see the sky, Sindari thought into my mind.

He was right. Some gray daylight made its way down to us, but it was dim down here. From no point along the bottom could we see the sky above.

How will I climb out to escape? he asked.

By stuffing yourself in my charm and riding up on my neck.

How will you *climb out to escape?*

Right up the wall like a spider. I showed him my ice axes and the crampons on my boots. The ground was as slick as a skating rink, so I needed the metal teeth to keep from slipping. I'd expected to find bare ground at the bottom of the glacier, but maybe it was under a layer of ice. *Do you sense the magic, Sindari?*

Yes. About a quarter of a mile away and down here with us.

Can you tell if it's another golem? Or something else?

I believe it is something else.

I'm not sure whether that's good or bad.

Neither am I.

"What's he think?" Willard asked.

"He doesn't think it's another golem."

"That's non-specific."

"He's a non-specific kind of tiger."

Sindari squinted at me, perhaps trying to decide if I was teasing him. I ruffled the fur on the top of his head.

Since the slope didn't look too challenging to navigate, I traded my ice axes for Chopper.

"*Eravekt,*" I said.

The blade glowed a soft but strong blue, highlighting the slick frozen walls to either side of us.

During the earlier trek, I had tried the new dwarven commands Lirena had given me and found that both worked. The results were less dramatic than the sword's illumination, but I'd touched Chopper's blade and had indeed felt that it heated or grew cold at the words.

Whether that icy metal could better penetrate dragon scales remained to be seen. Even though Lirena had warned me about Zondia, I hadn't yet sensed her. I hoped she wouldn't harass the soldiers up there making camp.

Willard started up the slope, carabiners and ice screws jangling on her belt. I left behind anything that could jangle and caught up with her. So far, I didn't sense any magical beings, but if I had to activate my cloaking charm, I didn't want to worry about noise giving away its camouflage.

"Any sign of dark elves?" Willard asked as we walked side by side, the crevasse wide enough for two. "It's hard to see anything but the prints of these giant creatures."

"No."

I smell that creatures neither human nor elven have traveled this way, Sindari said.

"Do you recognize them?"

Willard opened her mouth but must have realized the question wasn't for her.

We do not have a word for them—they do not exist in our realm—but they are great two-legged creatures, protected from the cold by magic. They thrive in it and cannot abide heat. They are larger than ogres. They must barely fit down here.

"The jötnar?" I mused, thinking of legends from my mother's ancestors.

"Frost giants?" Willard asked.

"Essentially."

"If dark elves exist, I suppose giants can." She eyed the walls rising above us. "It's hard to imagine them fitting down here. Or anyone levitating something that large up and down that far."

"Size matters not," I said, not expecting her to get the reference, since the *Star Trek* comment hadn't rung a bell.

Willard's eyebrow twitched. "When your ally is the Force?"

"Yup. Or magic."

This way. Sindari had gone ahead and reached a section of the crevasse that was blocked at some point above so no daylight filtered down. This was where we might encounter our light-hating enemies. And their frost-giant pets.

I walked up to join him, my crampons clicking on the ice. Stealth would be difficult down here, even without clanking gear. "Let's see if we can find that magical signature, Sindari."

Before we'd gone far, the ice under our feet turned to rock. Warm sulfur-laden air whispered past our cheeks.

To one side, a crack ran up the ice wall, and visible steam wafted out of a vent. It fogged the blue-tinted air, my sword's light mingling with that of our headlamps.

A few steps farther on, Sindari turned, facing an ice cave, the ceiling rounded about fifteen feet overhead. It led back into absolute darkness.

The magic we sensed is in that direction, Sindari told me. *And there is more magic beyond it. Many, many devices. Also, I can now sense the auras of dark elves.*

How far away are they?

Another half mile beyond the first device. It is placed away from their other devices and encampment. It may be an alarm or another type of magical sentry.

I gave the information to Willard, then stepped into the cave with Sindari at my side. "If we can get closer, Sindari and I might be able to count how many dark elves are down here by their auras."

"They'll sense us, too, I assume. And maybe come visit."

"Visit, right."

I paused, considering our options if a horde of dark elves streamed out at us. We couldn't levitate, and that climb out would take a long time, even without enemies shooting at us. We'd both left our rappel harnesses on, so all we had to do was clip in and go, but it wouldn't matter if we were being chased.

"I have the flashbangs, which might slow them down, but... maybe you should wait here. Sindari has magical stealth, and I can activate my cloaking charm. I'm sure they know our group is here, but at least they wouldn't sense me coming in to scout."

"I don't like the idea of you going in alone." Willard's tone turned dry. "Even if there weren't enemies with a fondness for killing humans inside, you're not supposed to explore caves by yourself."

"I'm not alone." I patted Sindari on the back. "We won't be gone long. Maybe you could get Banderas and one of the others with a magical gun down here, in case I'm not as stealthy as I think and the dark elves try to follow me out."

Willard clenched her jaw. I could tell she wasn't pleased with this proposition, but she also couldn't argue against it. None of the soldiers had an equivalent to my cloaking charm.

"Get a head count and take pictures if you can," she said. "Even better if you can make a map. If there are alternative tunnels that lead into their lair, so we don't have to make a straight-on attack along a route they've had plenty of time to booby-trap, that would be ideal."

I had a feeling that other cave we'd seen might have *been* an alternative tunnel—and that was why the dark elves had blocked it off.

"I'll do my best." I waved her back into the crevasse, activated my charm, then turned off my headlamp and proceeded by Chopper's glow.

As dark as it was in the cave, I could have used my night-vision charm, but I wasn't ready to continue in pitch-blackness. It was creepy down here, knowing thousands of tons of ice were over my head and could drop on me, either through magic or nature's whims, at any second.

Once we were closer to our enemies, I would have to extinguish the blade, so its light wouldn't give away my position, but not yet.

As Sindari led me deeper, cracks and snaps, ice shifting above and to the sides, made me twitchy. Glaciers moved, I reminded myself. Slowly, yes, but they did advance and recede. This wasn't anything unusual.

A tremor shook the ground, and more snaps sounded, one right over my head.

That was less usual.

I licked my lips and glanced back, but the wide passage had bent enough that Willard was no longer in view. Neither was any of the natural light filtering down from above.

I checked the time. Not wanting to climb out in the dark, I gave myself an hour to explore. If I took longer than that, Willard would worry.

Not without cause.

Chapter 24

Sindari nosed at the ground as we walked deeper into the cave. The bare rock did not hold tracks, but they held smell. He'd informed me that the giants had come this way many times. He didn't know if they were inside now or out on the mountain somewhere.

I didn't know which to hope for. Inside, I would have to deal with them. Outside, the soldiers would.

Water dribbled down the rounded walls, and a drop splashed on my gloved hand. Steamy sulfurous air caressed my cheeks.

Was my chest growing tighter? Or was that my imagination? I'd felt constriction before purely due to my own emotions stressing me out, so I tried to breathe evenly and maintain a calm state of mind.

The tunnel widened, opening into an underground chamber with a lake in the middle. Water dripped into it from above, and pungent wisps of steam rose from the surface.

Sindari trotted to a great alcove in one side where pine needles had been scattered all over the floor. A few furs were piled among them, and the scent of an animal den mingled with the volcanic gases.

Sindari nosed one of the furs. *They sleep here.*

So, we found the kennel for the guard dogs?

Essentially.

I can't help but notice that they're not home.

No.

We won't go much farther. I'd thought I was leaving the soldiers in a safe spot up on the glacier, but they might be in more danger than we were. *We're almost to that device. We'll check it out and then go back.*

As we skirted the lake toward a passage opposite the one we'd entered, I thought about taking the photos that Willard had requested, but I couldn't do that without using the flash on my phone. This looked like a place where dark elves might be standing guard, dark elves with cloaking magic that hid them from our senses. Afraid of being spotted, I'd already extinguished my sword and switched to my night-vision charm.

A few other low-ceilinged tunnels led away from the lake chamber, and I tried to make a mental note, so I could sketch a map later. A part of me wanted to explore them while I was here, but I would have to crawl on my hands and knees to do so. That could take a lot of time. From here, it was impossible to tell if they ended after a few meters or went farther back and rejoined the main tunnel, or led somewhere else altogether.

Sindari stopped in front of the large tunnel on the far side of the lake. *The device we've been sensing is just ahead.*

As I joined him, I sensed it and, for the first time, the auras of dark elves. A *lot* of dark elves.

Some were in groups straight ahead, and others were in singles or pairs ahead and to the sides. Even though I couldn't sense the layout of the tunnels or anything non-magical, the arrangement of their auras suggested a vast complex.

My chest had grown tighter. I would have been curious to see the air quality and composition of it, but I didn't have any equipment for taking such readings.

Letting Sindari go ahead, I dug out my inhaler and used it. Once, I'd promised myself I wouldn't wait, not if the threat of danger lay ahead. As I put it away, I tried not to think of the dark-elf alchemist who'd seen my inhaler and known to exploit my weakness. She was dead, and I had survived.

There it is. Sindari stopped, his head lowering to peer at something. *Not a golem.*

That's good. I'd been bracing myself to battle another one. *Unless it's something worse.*

I believe it's an alarm. If we enter this tunnel, it will alert the dark elves that we are here.

I crouched beside him to look at a cylindrical device attached to the wall a foot above ground level. The ice had been melted and allowed to re-harden to embed it. The device glowed faintly, a dim red that didn't do much to brighten the area around it, but my senses detected filigrees of magic spreading from it. They ran down to the floor and up the wall to the ceiling and around.

No chance that our stealth will keep it from going off? I asked.

Doubtful.

Is it possible that we could destroy it without them knowing it? I rubbed Chopper's hilt with my thumb.

I'm certain you can destroy it and also certain that whoever set it will be alerted. I also suspect... He inched closer, sniffing and examining the device while being careful not to cross the filigrees. *The canister contains a fluid. It may shoot it out and mark whoever attempts to pass.*

So they'd be able to find us even through our stealth magic?

That is my guess.

Let's go back and check the side passages by the lake. A part of me wondered if it mattered if we tripped the alarm, since the odds of us sneaking up on the dark elves were low anyway, but the idea of being marked with some beacon that would lead the entire lair right to me was disturbing. Zav's magical marking of me was bad enough—I was crossing my fingers that it didn't ooze out when I had my charm activated, but I hadn't had a chance to test that yet.

I believe they would have also warded or booby-trapped those tunnels if they led anywhere, Sindari said.

You may be right, but let's check anyway.

I picked the one near the main tunnel that seemed most likely, at least from the location of the entrance, to lead back toward the lair. When I dropped to my hands and knees to crawl into it, the ground shuddered again.

Are there always earthquakes up here? Sindari asked.

Not this significant.

So they may be doing something to cause them?

Unfortunately, yes.

Sindari followed me into the tunnel, also forced to crawl. The ceiling rose and fell, never high enough above for me to stand, but the ground—fine rock ground down by eons of glacial movement—was relatively flat.

We wound back farther than I expected and didn't encounter any magical devices in the tunnel. I continued to sense the dark elves in their lair. We were getting close to it.

Dare I hope this was a back way in?

Faint red light grew visible—infrared light, I wagered, thinking of Zoltan's laboratory. He'd once said that his vampiric night vision wasn't good enough to read in the dark, so he needed some form of light, and infrared did not bother him the way regular light or sun did. Was it the same with dark elves? There had been infrared light at their big ceremony too.

A flutter of excitement teased my belly. Maybe this tunnel led somewhere important. I could now sense more magical devices up ahead. Two dark elves were in that direction, as well, but Sindari and I might be able to handle two of them, especially if we caught them by surprise.

Before I could grow too enamored with the idea, the route ahead grew more constricted. The ceiling dipped to within a few inches of the ground. The infrared light seeped under that gap, suggesting the passage continued on the other side, but the route was effectively blocked. Unless Sindari and I could shrink ourselves, we couldn't continue forward.

Steamy sulfuric air whispered out from under the ice, but it wasn't doing enough to melt that low ceiling. How long did it stay that low before the tunnel got larger again? I dropped to my belly to peer under, but I couldn't tell.

Val, that is not passable. And this ice could tumble down and crush us any second.

Sindari hunkered behind me, his head pressed against the low claustrophobic ceiling, and looked miserable. And maybe a little afraid.

I'd never seen him afraid of anything. He was understandably wary with dragons, but he'd never balked at going into battle with them or anything else we'd fought. But this was something different, something he'd likely never dealt with on the open tundra of his homeland.

We won't stay much longer. Willard will be worrying about us.

Us? Or you? Her feline would be joyous if she returned home and told it I had been crushed by a glacier.

Maggie probably would be joyous, but Willard knows your value. I turned back to the ice, shifting Chopper into a position where I could poke at it.

Wait, Sindari said before I could jab at the ice and make any noise.

I sense two dark elves in an area directly ahead of us, wherever that light is coming from.

Yes, I sense them too. I even thought I could hear voices now.

Were we that close? What if all I had to do was find a way through here and into their laboratory, and I could find whatever they planned to use on the volcano and destroy it?

But I couldn't chink at the ice if the dark elves were close enough for me to hear them speaking. I activated my translation charm in case words reached my ears, but the ice and distance muffled the voices too much.

I rested a gloved hand on the ice wall blocking us. If only I could melt it. That wouldn't be that noisy.

My new commands, I blurted mentally.

What? Sindari asked.

The elf Lirena gave me two new commands for Chopper. One of them heats the blade.

I pressed the tip into the ice and mouthed, "*Krundark,*" hoping the magic didn't require me to say it loudly. The dark elves' ears would be keener than mine, and I could still hear them talking.

A soft *thwomp* came from up ahead along with a flare of magic that lit up my senses. Whatever they were doing, I hoped it was related to their plans and they weren't making some poison or device to flush me out of the tunnels.

Chopper's blade warmed, the heat it radiated feeling good against my chilled cheeks.

Are you sure it's wise to make heat when the ceiling above us is made out of ice? Sindari asked.

No.

Just making sure you know you're being foolish.

If this ice is the only thing blocking us from sneaking into their lair, we have to try melting it.

Water dripped down the sword and onto the ground. It was working. But how long would it take?

As I shifted Chopper, laying its length against the ice, hoping it would melt upward faster, a pungent scent wafted back to us, something different from the sulfur. What were the dark elves doing in there?

The sword heated to its fullest, and the ice melted faster and faster. It was working. This would work. We—

A beeping came from my pack.

Sindari jerked his head up. *Val! They'll hear that!*

I know. I know. I set Chopper down and struggled to get to my pack in the confining space. It was the carbon monoxide detector beeping. So much for the cursed luck charm Lirena had given me.

Trying not to make any *more* noise, I clawed off my pack and unhooked the detector. I yanked my glove off and stabbed the buttons, trying to find an off switch. It kept flashing and displaying "dangerous levels of carbon monoxide detected."

Even if that was true, I didn't care at that moment. I was more worried about the dangerous levels of dark elves.

Especially since I couldn't get the detector to turn off.

Sindari lunged in, grabbed the device in his mouth, and crunched down on it. A final weak beep came out, and it fell silent.

Everything fell silent. I still sensed the dark elves up ahead, but they weren't talking anymore. They'd heard that noise, and they knew someone was here.

Chapter 25

If the way ahead had melted enough to let us pass, I would have considered continuing on, bursting in on the two dark elves, and hoping I could overcome them before they alerted the whole lair to our presence.

But that wasn't an option. I pulled my pack on and scooted backward as rapidly as I could. Sindari did the same. We had to crawl a hundred feet before there was room to turn around. Despite being larger than I, he scrambled faster than I did, and he soon disappeared in the dark.

If they are in the lake chamber when we get there, Sindari told me, *I will attempt to distract them while you run to rejoin your comrades.*

Thanks, but I'm hoping they're not there.

Maybe that was a vain thing to hope for. Even though we crawled as fast as we could, we'd followed that low tunnel for hundreds of feet. I tried not to think about the climb out of the crevasse that awaited me.

Sindari reached the lake first. *They're not here yet, but I sense some of them coming this direction.*

I'm almost there. There hadn't been time to put my glove back on, and the cold earth scraped my palm raw. My pelvis hadn't objected that much when we'd been crawling along slowly, but now, it blasted pain through my body with every rapid move.

Six of them. No, eight now. I think they're stopping to gather allies along the way.

The brimstone scent of the lake chamber grew stronger, and I had to fight not to cough. Almost there. Almost there…

The water came into view, and the ceiling rose. I lunged to my feet.

Sindari faced the tunnel with the magical alarm, the tunnel the dark elves would come from.

Run, I silently ordered him. *We're both getting out of here.*

With Chopper in hand, I sprinted for the tunnel leading back to the crevasse—and gritted my teeth to keep from crying out from the pain of my injury. Now, I wished I'd asked the soldier with the medical kit for something stronger than ibuprofen. And I wished I'd been able to call Amber back. What if I died down here without getting a chance to say goodbye? Or at least answer her call and share any wisdom I could.

"Just worry... about getting... out of here," I grunted to myself as I ran, my breathing labored. I didn't know if that was because of the gases affecting my lungs or simply the altitude I was unaccustomed to. Maybe both.

Sindari loped after me, but didn't catch up. He was deliberately staying behind, watching my back.

My senses told me those eight were running after us—after me. The other dark elves in the lair that had been still—probably sleeping—were up and milling about now. I might be bringing Armageddon back to Willard.

No, I decided as the first hint of daylight brightened the tunnel ahead. The dark elves wouldn't come out until after dark.

I hoped.

Down! Sindari barked into my mind as the hair on the back of my neck rose.

I flung myself belly-first to the ground. A crackling sphere of roiling black power sailed over my head. It slammed into a wall and blew ice everywhere, shards pelting my exposed skin.

Up! was Sindari's next order as he drew even with me. *They're still coming.*

I jumped up, my injury making me gasp with pain, and returned to sprinting. "Of course they are."

My crampons crunched on the fresh ice blown all over the ground, but it wasn't slippery enough that I had to slow down. Not that I would have anyway. When I risked glancing back, I saw the glints of red eyes in the dark depths behind me.

"Thorvald?" came Willard's query from up ahead.

"Incoming with company. Start climbing!"

She swore. So did I as my senses shouted a warning into my brain.

Jump sideways, Sindari ordered, even as I was about to fling myself to the ground.

Twisting mid-fling, I plastered myself against the icy wall.

Another black energy ball blew past, this one skipping along the ground like a flat rock on a lake. It blew up pieces of rock every time it touched down, and I turned my back to the flying shrapnel.

As soon as the ball of magic passed, I sprinted on, rounding a bend. More light came into view and so did Willard. She leaned around the corner of the cave mouth, her modified magical rifle pointed past my shoulder.

The dark elves were still coming—did they have masks or goggles to protect their eyes? If they didn't stop, we were screwed.

As I sprang around the opposite corner of the cave mouth from Willard, I dug out my flashbangs. She opened fire on the shadowy figures rounding the bend.

Sindari stopped before reaching the cave mouth. He spun to face our enemies, crouching low to spring.

"Brace yourself," I yelled to both of them, arming and throwing two flashbangs over Sindari toward the dark elves.

Another black ball of energy sped straight toward me. I lunged to the side, and it shot past and into the far side of the crevasse.

Before my flashbangs went off, their attack slammed into the ice wall behind us. Huge shards broke off and flew toward us.

I yelled a, "Look out!" as I turned away again. Pieces slammed into my pack and torso, making me glad for Nin's armor. Unfortunately, it didn't cover my arms, and a shard like a dagger gouged through my jacket and into my triceps.

My flashbangs went off, the light of a sun filling the tunnel as thunderous booms hammered our ears. Ice tumbled down from the ceiling, and the ground shook.

Willard glanced upward, as conscious as I was of all the ice that could potentially break away and bury us forever. The walls above us quivered as the ground under our feet trembled. A rockfall—no, an *ice* fall—slammed down, but it happened inside the tunnel.

Sindari backed out and joined me. I sensed the dark elves backing in the opposite direction. Two were helping one that had been pinned under the ice. I hadn't realized the flashbangs might bring down some of that tunnel, but I was relieved.

"We have to go," I said. "They're distracted for the moment."

"You don't have to tell me." Willard shouldered her rifle and pulled out her two ice axes.

We rushed back toward our ropes. The ground switched from rock to slick ice, and we had to slow down to maneuver down the crevasse.

Sindari, will you watch our backs? I asked as we clipped ourselves to the ropes we'd left anchored above.

Of course. I am certainly not going to sit in your backpack while you climb that cliff.

That's good, because you would be one humungous deadweight.

I'm a live weight, thank you.

Let us know if they're coming, but don't fight them. Go back to your realm if they rush out.

I will delay them if possible before returning to my realm.

That's not what I said. I grimaced, imagining Sindari being blown apart by those energy balls. *Don't let yourself be wounded. We'll need you later—there are still frost giants out here somewhere to battle.*

I wished I hadn't thought of that. We had enough problems to worry about.

Hurry, he urged. *They are melting the ice that is blocking the way.*

Shit.

Had I assumed incorrectly? That the dark elves would leave us alone as long as it wasn't night yet?

"Don't let yourself rush," Willard ordered, pushing off with her legs and using the pick sides of her two ice axes to calmly and methodically start up. "Make sure you maintain three points of contact, even if you're going to turn to shoot. *Especially* if you're going to turn to shoot."

"Got it." Reluctantly, I sheathed Chopper. If I had to use a weapon while dangling from the side of the cliff, it would be Fezzik.

Forcing myself to take a few calming breaths, I started up next to Willard, keeping space between us in case one of us fell. Before we'd gone fifty feet up, my entire lower back and hip hurt so much that involuntary tears sprang to my eyes. Sweat ran down the sides of my face, and I almost laughed at all that cold-weather survival training advice about not letting yourself get damp.

Elven Doom

They've almost cleared the ice, Sindari reported.

Do they know you're there?

I do not believe so. I am using my natural stealth. They're complaining that their eyes hurt from the blinding light bombs you threw and debating how to destroy you before you reach the top without coming out themselves.

I hope that's a conundrum they can't figure out. But I had no problem imagining them hurling more of those energy balls at us. If they could bend their trajectories around obstacles, they could easily pick us off.

"How'd they detect you?" Willard asked as we slogged upward.

"My carbon monoxide detector went off at an inopportune moment. Wish I'd thought not to bring one."

"Yeah, better to keel over and die from poisonous gases."

"*They're* down there. I'm sure the air is fine." That wasn't entirely true. The sulfur had been stinging my eyes, and I'd already used my inhaler.

"*They've* been living underground for thousands of years. They may have evolved to be able to handle poor air. Dwarves reputedly have, and elves—surface elves—are supposed to be more susceptible to such things."

"I didn't realize representatives of those species had signed up for scientific studies." My forearms ached as we continued up, and I struggled to push my weight up the ice wall with my injured leg.

"The evidence is anecdotal at this point, largely gathered from my informants and old books from when dwarves and surface elves still visited Earth." Willard glanced over her shoulder. We couldn't see the floor of the crevasse anymore. "Is your tiger still down there?"

"Yes. He's spying on the dark elves and will let us know—"

They have pulled hoods and masks over their faces and are coming out into the crevasse, Sindari reported.

All eight of them?

Six are here. Two went back to meet with others near that lake. Many others. The entire community must know about our intrusion now.

I wished I still had the carbon monoxide detector so I could break it again.

They're preparing to launch an attack. I will go up the crevasse in the opposite direction and make noise to attempt to distract them.

Thank you.

"Let us know?" Willard prompted.

205

"Keep climbing. It sounds like they have a way to attack us."

She looked up and sighed.

The gray sky came into view as we maneuvered around a shelf—it had been protecting us from icy rain that now pelted our helmets and shoulders. I placed my picks and my crampons very carefully, worried the ice would be even worse when slick with moisture. More than once, my feet slipped. My agility wasn't much help with this feat.

A roar echoed up from below and farther up the crevasse.

"Is he fighting them?" Willard asked.

"Just distracting them." I hoped.

It is working. They are firing weapons at me.

Don't let them hit you, I replied.

That is my goal.

We climbed past another shelf, and the ends of the last ropes came into view, the ones attached to anchors on the surface, outside of the crevasse.

"We're coming up!" Willard bellowed.

"Waiting for you, Colonel!" Banderas's head came into view, poking over the edge.

Seeing that we were close renewed my energy, and I urged my aching forearms to move faster. Another roar came from the depths below, but it was cut short in the middle, as if Sindari had been struck.

Did they get you? I asked. *Are you okay?*

Sindari didn't answer. My charms were under my shirt, so I had no trouble feeling it when the cat figurine heated, then went ice cold. It had done that before when he'd been forcibly evicted from our world—when *dark elves* had forcibly evicted him.

I hoped that was all it was, that they hadn't managed to destroy him.

Willard, not as tired as I, surged ahead as we neared the end. My forearms were shaking so badly that I feared I'd drop my ice axes. Twenty feet from the rim, I paused, willing the remaining energy I had to flow into my arms and legs. I could do this.

My neck hairs rose as a surge of magic registered to my senses. Swearing, I gave up my rest and hurried upward. There was no way to dodge up here.

"Look out, Val!" Willard shouted from the top.

I looked down only to see one of those huge black balls of energy crackling toward me at a hundred miles an hour. Hoping my carabiner was secured to the rope, I pushed off the ice, trying to fling myself sideways more than away from the wall.

The blast of energy slammed into the spot where I'd been, power blowing in all directions. It struck me like a hurricane, hurling me farther to the side than my legs ever could have, and my shoulder struck the ice wall. I bounced off, twisting on the rope, my heart in my throat.

"Get her up, get her up!" Willard shouted from above.

Thankfully, my knots held, and I didn't plummet, but it was like being on a pendulum in a windstorm. I struck several more times before I managed to turn back to face the wall, my crampons dug into the ice.

My rope started moving as the soldiers above pulled me up. By the time they dragged me over the rim, my entire body throbbed with pain. They carried me away from the edge, as if worried more magical attacks would come flying up. Maybe they would.

"Are you all right, Val?" Willard crouched, gripping my shoulder.

I stared up at the gray sky, rain falling, and realized the visibility up here was still horrible. We would be stuck spending the night in the little camp the soldiers had erected. And hoping the dark elves didn't come to visit.

I sighed. "I'm going to have to be."

Chapter 26

I'd heard that camping above the clouds at fourteen thousand feet was surreal, with the stars above magnificent, but we were socked in with the clouds wrapped around us like a dense fog. The rain had turned to snow, it had dropped into the twenties, and it was hard for me to appreciate the nature as I sat outside and night closed around me.

The only thing I could appreciate was that I was drugged enough that my body didn't hurt as much as it had—though a delightful headache had blossomed a couple of hours ago to add insult to injury—and the dark elves hadn't sent up any magic to utterly destroy the camp.

Whether wise or not, our tents were set up near the crevasse. The soldiers had done that while Willard and I had been down below, before they'd known that my carbon monoxide detector and I would alert the entire enemy camp to our existence. I still couldn't believe I hadn't foreseen that possibility. All evening, I'd been mentally kicking myself and wondering if we'd lost any opportunity to get back down there, overcome them, and destroy their volcano-diddling artifact. If so, it would be my fault. The one person with a camouflage charm who should have been able to sneak in...

I groaned and flopped onto my back. The glacier wasn't overly comfortable. My sleeping bag was spread in a nearby tent with Willard's, but there was no way my mind would quiet down enough to allow rest. Another soldier and I had volunteered for watch. He was patrolling the perimeter doing a professional job of it while I sat and bemoaned my mistakes.

From on top of the glacier, I could no longer sense the dark elves. They must have retreated to the depths of the lair. I could still sense that magical alarm in the tunnel near the lake. Nobody would sneak in that way, and I wagered they would set a second alarm at the spot where I'd been melting the ice.

Even if we took the whole team down there, could we shoot our way in? I had sensed dozens of dark elves down there at the edge of my range, and there could have been dozens more of them deeper in their lair. Right now, we didn't even have Sindari to help. I'd tried summoning him earlier, but the charm was still ice cold against my skin, and he hadn't responded.

That worried me, but I kept telling myself he'd likely been injured and needed time to recover. He wasn't dead. It would take more than some dark-elf energy blast to destroy him. I hoped.

Closing my eyes did not alleviate my headache. Since my skull was one of the few things I hadn't injured that day, I blamed the thin air. Earlier, the altitude hadn't bothered me that much, but now that my body had quieted down and had time to think about it, I was experiencing a number of symptoms of altitude sickness. My lungs were okay, for the moment, but in addition to the headache, my thoughts were scattered and my brain foggy.

I rummaged in my pack for one of the canisters of pure oxygen Willard had thought to bring along. It was peppermint flavored. Peppermint air in a can. When had the world gotten so strange?

For the tenth time, I checked to see if I had enough reception to call Amber. I'd managed to retrieve her voice mail earlier, but all she had said was, "Never mind."

If I'd been able to answer, I was sure she would have spoken to me, but she hadn't wanted to leave a message. It distressed me that I hadn't been there for her when she'd finally called.

"Thorvald?" Willard called softly from our tent. She'd zipped up the flap earlier, saying she would try to sleep, but it was open now.

"We're going to be sleeping together. I think you can call me Val."

"Sleeping in the same tent isn't *together*."

"Are you sure? It's tight in there. Our sleeping bags are touching."

"Women bunk with women and men bunk with men. It's a rule." Willard waved toward the other tents, dark bumps against the foggy white and gray landscape. It amused me that the tents were "woodland camo" colored. I couldn't imagine anything less camouflaging on a glacier.

"Right. You wouldn't want any of these unmarried soldiers hitting on you."

"I think you're in more danger of that than I am."

"Are you sure? Haven't they seen the squat rack in your bedroom? I thought that got guys excited."

"Clarke was the only one here who'd seen it, and he's gone."

"Then I guess you're safe. He would have tried to make you eighty-seven."

She snorted. "He's not dumb enough to try."

I wasn't sure I agreed, but it didn't seem right to take digs at someone who wasn't there to defend himself, so I kept the thought to myself.

Willard squinted in my direction. "Are you using your charm? I can hear your voice but barely make you out."

"I am. So I can ambush anyone who tries to attack the camp tonight."

"You think they'll come up here?"

"With the cloud cover, I think it's dark enough that they could."

"Is there any way we could lure them up if they don't?" she asked.

"You *want* them to come up?"

"We'd have a better chance of fighting them up here than down in their lair."

I *had* noticed that someone had taken a stab at digging a couple of shallow foxholes in the glacier around the camp.

"Can I be honest?" I asked.

"Are you ever not honest?"

"Rarely."

"Go ahead."

"Us succeeding at this mission with this small team and only a handful of magical weapons was always going to be predicated on us sneaking in, catching them off-guard, and only having to face a few of them at a time." I tried not to dwell on how close I had been to accomplishing that before my failure. Besides, I didn't truly know that. Maybe that hadn't been a laboratory I'd been crawling toward but some random stockroom the dark elves had set up.

"I always assumed it was doubtful that we'd be able to sneak up on them," Willard said. "I should have brought more people. But until you actually got chased out of there by dark elves, we hadn't actually seen any of them and only had hypotheses about what we were dealing with."

Sindari and I, with our magical senses, had known earlier, but it would have been hard for her to sell that as proof to her superiors.

"Now we know without a doubt," was all I said.

"I'll radio in more help as soon as the weather clears enough that the choppers can come in. Fort Lewis was getting teams ready the last I heard."

"Teams with magical weapons?"

Willard hesitated. "They should have a few that they've acquired over the years. Same as us."

"If we survive this, I think you should have the army put in a big order with Nin."

"I wish I already had. It's hard to get funding approval for magical weapons."

"She might be open to trade."

"What kind of trade items would a chef-turned-weapons-manufacturer want?"

I almost said a house for her family, but if the army wouldn't pay for magical weapons, it definitely wouldn't pay for a house in one of the most expensive metro areas in the country.

"New deep fryers," I said. "Fuel for her truck. A few thousand pounds of beef."

"I'll keep that in mind. While I'm lying here not sleeping."

"You too?"

"I'm tired as hell. I thought I'd crash. It used to be that I could sleep anywhere."

"It's probably the altitude, not that you're a less virile sleeper these days."

She grunted and muttered, "Virile sleeper," but didn't otherwise comment on my creative vocabulary.

I sat up and waved the oxygen can. "Want to try some peppermint air?"

"Maybe later. It's too bad the choppers couldn't come in and take us down to Camp Muir to sleep. Ten thousand feet wouldn't have been as noticeable."

"Zero feet in Ballard would have been even nicer."

"In your apartment that's as likely to be broken into as this tent?"

"I'd take the chance." I looked upward, disappointed at the heavy cloud cover. "We don't even get a view of the night sky. I bet the stars up here are great. You can't see much from the city most nights. No Big Dipper, Little Dipper, Orion, Draco."

"Draco? The constellation or your dragon?"

"He's not up there." I wondered what had happened to Zondia. She must not have been heading this way, after all. But if she hadn't returned to Earth for me, then for what?

"Too bad. A dragon would even the odds a lot."

"Tell me about it."

I did wish Zav was with us. Both because I would feel safer going in to face the dark elves with him at my side and because... I'd rather my sleeping bag was touching his than Willard's. What would he think of a sleeping bag? Master it easily or find the zipper befuddling? I hadn't seen much that mystified him yet. Even using my phone, once I'd unlocked it, hadn't seemed to faze him. If he put his mind to mastering our technology, he could probably do it easily. Mostly, it was only words that had altered meanings in the last century or two that confused him.

Remembering the incident at the ice cream shop in Idaho made me smile. At the time, I'd been flustered and angry that he'd overreacted to someone hitting on me. But, looking back, it had been a mild offense. He seemed to be getting better, understanding me and humans more, and maybe even losing a tiny bit of his arrogance. Or maybe I'd started to see through it to the person underneath. The person who had been, ever since we fought Dobsaurin in the water-treatment plant, going out of his way to protect me. Even though I was, as he'd pointed out often, sarcastic and sharp-tongued with him. Now, I wished I could take back some of the snippy comments I'd made. Teasing him was fun, and I didn't think he minded it, but he didn't deserve my cranky moments when I lashed out in anger, not humor.

I wished he were here so I could tell him. And also because we had been getting to the point where he'd been closer to trusting me. If his nosy sister hadn't shown up, where might we be now? Fighting dark elves up here together? Camping out next to this very crevasse and necking in two sleeping bags zipped into one big one?

"Damn it." I dropped my face into my hand.

I wasn't going to cry again, but something about this place, the quiet of the wilderness and being on top of the world, gave me too much time to think, too much time to fill my mind with regrets. I didn't regret taking action to make sure Amber wouldn't be hurt or used as a pawn again, but I did regret reacting so hastily. Zondia was the one I'd wanted to get rid of, not Zav. I should have calmly talked things through with him and figured out a way we could convince her to leave while he stayed and continued his mission. Continued to spend time with me.

"You all right?" Willard must have heard my soft curse.

"Yeah." I could feel her looking in my direction, wondering what was wrong with me. "You ever been married, Willard?"

She hesitated, and I was sure she hadn't expected the question. She looked out at the other tents, maybe making sure nobody else was close enough to hear us.

"I kind of missed my chance," she said quietly. "By the time I got serious about looking, I was used to being in charge. That works fine if you're an officer in the military. Less fine in domestic situations. I had a hard time… not being the boss."

"I think the modern and evolved man is okay with a strong-willed partner with equal say in things."

"I don't want to be equal," she said dryly. "I want to be in charge."

"Then you need to find yourself a nice beta male who doesn't mind your pushy nature."

"I'm not pushy; I'm assertive."

"And a hundred percent in charge."

"I might settle for ninety percent."

"Uh huh. Better find someone who will have dinner ready when you get home and massage your feet after a hard day on the job."

"Those aren't the guys I'm attracted to. I usually end up in relationships where there's a lot of head-butting and muscle flexing."

"From both of you?"

"Yes. I haven't given up hope, but the older you get, the slimmer the pickings become. And the more rank you get, the more complicated things are in regard to work relationships because of the fraternization policies."

"You can date outside of the service, can't you?" I asked. "Seattle is full of single guys."

"Who has time to look for them?" Willard flopped back onto her sleeping bag. "You should have stuck with the dragon. Then you could have had him introduce me to a sibling. Does he have brothers?"

"I believe so. I think you're more broken up about the end of our relationship—which was never truly a relationship, since we didn't even date—than I am."

"Is that true?"

I took another hit from the oxygen canister. Was it? How frank did I want to be out here?

"No," I admitted. "I think I screwed up."

"I think you did too."

"Thanks so much for your honesty. Just for that, if he comes back, I'm *not* going to set you up with one of his brothers."

The ice cracked deep within the glacier, loud enough to wake up anyone who had been sleeping, and Willard didn't respond to my remark. Not that it had been witty or worthy of a response.

"Besides," I said, "dragons are pains in the ass. You only met him once, so you don't know."

"Oh, I got the gist," Willard said, dry again, "when he visited my office and *commanded* me to order you to assist him with the dark elves."

"And told you he'd claimed me as his mate?"

"Yup. You'd talked about him a lot even before that. I could tell you were into him. And I can see why. All that sexy dragon aura."

"He's arrogant and exasperating."

"Yeah, and you like that. If he comes back, you better tell him you want him in your bed and that's that."

"Thanks for the tip." I didn't feel like going into Zav's hang-up about trusting elves—and half-elves.

"Don't forget to invite me to the wedding."

"I don't think dragons do weddings. They just magically brand you so other dragons know you're theirs."

"You should insist on a wedding. Attended by his equally sexy brothers."

"You're hilarious, Willard."

"I am. That'll be on my tombstone."

Another crack sounded, this time from down in the crevasse. Even though I didn't think the dark elves would announce an attack by tinkering loudly with the ice, I checked the area with my senses, listening and straining them to their fullest.

I sensed something. Not from the crevasse itself, but somewhere on the other side of it.

"Get your weapons." I rolled to my feet.

"Dark elves?"

"No, something else magical. I think it's the frost giants coming from across the glacier." I pointed beyond the crevasse, though I couldn't see anything yet.

"How many?"

"All of them."

Willard swore and bellowed, "Incoming!"

As the soldiers scrambled to grab their weapons and get into the shallow foxholes, I tapped my charm and tried to summon Sindari. It was still cold and unresponsive.

I'd never fought a single frost giant, much less six, and I didn't have my most loyal ally at my side. This was not going to go well.

Chapter 27

The frost giants, massive blue-gray-skinned creatures that stood more than twenty feet tall, came in two groups, thundering out of the night and toward our camp. The snow and fog shrouded them, but as they ran closer, they grew more distinct.

Unlike the rock golem, they were made of flesh and blood. That ought to make them more vulnerable, but their stout legs were as thick as cedars. They wore thick furs over sturdy chain mail, and they carried clubs the size of logs and shields bigger than doors. Some of them also carried slings. Their armor and clubs emanated magic, no doubt enchanted by their dark-elf allies. Or dark-elf masters, more likely.

"Regular bullets may not hurt them!" I called to the rest of the soldiers. "Use whatever magical weapons you've got."

I dropped to my belly in a natural dip in the ice and aimed Fezzik at the two in the lead. The giants were coming from the other side of the crevasse, and I didn't sense any dark elves around to levitate them, but with those long legs, they might be able to jump over the fifteen-foot gap.

"Not if I shoot you first," I muttered.

"Any chance of negotiating with them?" Willard called from the shallow foxhole she'd claimed. She always wanted to negotiate. Maybe it was written up as standard operating procedure for the office.

One of the lead giants twirled his sling and loosed a projectile the size of a bowling ball. It slammed into a tent behind Willard, tearing it from its stakes and sending the material skidding across the glacier. That would have killed any one of us if it had struck human flesh.

"I don't think so." I shot at the slinger's face, avoiding targets that his mail covered.

The soldiers also opened fire. Bullets slammed into the giants, many clinking against chain and being deflected, but others striking their bare arms and fur-clad legs. The ammunition from regular guns didn't pierce their thick flesh, but Willard's magical rifle was effective. Our rounds thudded into our targets. One of mine hit a giant in the eye, the orb bursting with a splash of gore.

Either impervious to the bullets, or magically compelled to ignore them, the two lead giants sprang across the crevasse as if it were a crack in a sidewalk. The four coming in the second group weren't far behind.

I was on the verge of yelling an order to retreat—though there was nowhere to retreat *to*—when I sensed the auras of two dragons. Zondia—I groaned—and Zav—I mentally cheered.

The giant whose eye I'd shot out charged straight at me. I rolled to the side a second before his big foot slammed down into the depression I'd been firing from.

Scrambling to my feet, my injury sending pain lancing through my body, I rushed away from him until I could once again see his head from twenty feet below. I opened fire again. My bullets slammed into his ear and the side of his skull.

The giant roared and spun toward me. Willard, now behind him, also fired at his head. The hulking creature stomped toward me, the ground quivering under his pounding weight, and slammed his club downward.

Again, I dodged out of the way, my crampons letting me keep my footing on the slick glacier. The ground trembled once more as the club struck down, spraying snow and ice.

The winged form of a black dragon grew visible against the cloudy sky. Zav.

The side of the giant's head looked like hamburger, but he hefted the club for another swing. Even though my bullets were hitting him, they weren't doing enough. I was tempted to switch to Chopper, but what would I target? His knee? With my injuries, I doubted I could duplicate my earlier feat of climbing my enemy's back. Just dodging the attacks had me panting with pain.

Two more giants made it to the crevasse and leaped over it. The back two paused, looking to the sky.

Shouts came from the camp—half of the tents now smashed—as the soldiers had to scatter. Like me, they were finding that their bullets weren't strong enough to halt the giants, not easily.

My attacker was slower with his next swipe of the club. I backed away, firing again, aiming for his remaining good eye. If he couldn't see, he wouldn't be as much of a threat.

Zav swooped down, opened his great maw, and clamped onto the head of a frost giant stamping through the camp. His powerful wings flapped, and he lifted the twenty-foot-tall creature from the glacier.

I gaped, forgetting to shoot my target as this magnificent scene played out. Zav didn't struggle as he toted the giant a hundred feet—he had to be using his magic to enhance how much he could lift—even though the giant fought back, pounding at Zav's sides with his club. The blows were deflected inches from Zav's black scales. His magical shield protected him as he whipped his neck to hurl the giant from his maw.

The creature dropped his club and flailed as he soared toward the crevasse. Zav's neck whipped around in time for him to spew a gout of fire at our foe. The giant screamed as flames roasted him, even as he tumbled hundreds of feet. I didn't check, but I doubted the dark elves were down there to slow his descent with a levitation spell.

Out over the glacier, the second dragon—Zondia—was now visible. She flew low toward the two giants that hadn't leaped the crevasse. They turned and ran in the opposite direction, but she was faster. Like Zav, she poured flames from the depths of her throat, the brilliant yellow-orange lighting up the dark foggy air. The gout struck one of the giants in the butt, and he squawked and threw his club over his shoulder at her. It burst into flames before it reached her.

As their chase continued away from our camp, I lost sight of the two giants and Zondia and focused on the enemies on our side of the crevasse. The soldiers, some still in foxholes and some scattered across the glacier, hadn't ceased firing. By now, all of the giants were riddled with bullets. I took careful aim at the eye of my personal nemesis—he kept stomping after me with that damn club—and pounded Fezzik's rounds into his head.

Finally, through attrition or a good shot, the giant halted. He wobbled on his massive legs, then toppled like a redwood. Snow flew up on all sides.

The two most recent giants to cross the crevasse were using their slings to hurl projectiles at Zav. The head-sized boulders emanated magic. Enough to hurt a dragon?

Somehow, Zav sensed the attacks and twisted in the air to avoid them. He banked and arrowed at the two giants. One of them turned and ran for the crevasse. The hulking behemoth bellowed in his own language—a cry to be levitated down?

The ice at the edge crumbled, and he tumbled into the crevasse. Zav landed behind the last one alive on our side.

"Hold fire!" Willard shouted.

Zav towered on his hind legs behind the giant, opened his maw, and snapped his jaws down, completely covering our foe's head. The giant screamed, beating at Zav's face with his club, but again, the weapon didn't breach Zav's magical barriers.

With a flick of his neck, Zav tore his foe's head from his body and flung it into the crevasse. The body collapsed, limbs twitching a few times before growing still.

Willard swore, alarmed or impressed. I wasn't sure which.

"That's some boyfriend you've got, Thorvald," she said.

Zav, his violet eyes glowing like torches in the fog, looked toward us, his gaze locking on mine. Even when he was in human form, I had trouble reading his expressions. I had no idea what he was thinking, but there seemed to be a question in his blazing eyes.

You will send me away? he asked telepathically.

What? No. I'm happy to see you.

Are you? Excellent. Zav sprang into the air and flew across the crevasse. *I will help my sister defeat the last two giants.*

Defeat or rip the heads off?

Usually, Zav arrested miscreants for punishment and rehabilitation, but maybe the giants weren't on his list of criminals. Or maybe, in the eyes of dragons, they didn't count as intelligent species and fall under the same laws.

Whatever satisfies my predatory urges. These giants were attempting to slay you. This is not *permissible.* He glanced back as he flew off into the fog, piercing me with that glowing violet gaze. I shivered a little. Maybe he put aside his laws when it came to protecting me.

"What was that look about?" Willard sounded like she couldn't tell if it had been good or bad.

"Zav was explaining his predatory urges to me."

"Hopefully, to be demonstrated only on giants and dark elves and not humans, right?"

"I believe that's his intent." I realized it was the first time Willard had seen Zav in battle. After watching him rip a giant's head off, it would be hard to see him as anything other than the incredible force of nature and dealer of death that he was. "Do you still think I should get him in bed?"

"Not in *that* form."

"No, I think that's illegal in this country."

"He'd also crush your bed."

"This is true. You should see what he does to deck chairs."

Banderas trotted up. "What now, Colonel?"

"Have everyone hold steady until we're sure they're all dead." Willard looked at me. "Can you tell if the dark elves have crept out of their lair?"

"I don't think they have." I didn't sense anything magical and living at the bottom of the crevasse. "Also, the flaming giant that Zav dropped down there is dead. Along with the one that fell after it." I would have sensed them if they had survived.

"I don't suppose he would care to come back and move that one out of our camp?" Willard pointed her rifle at the headless giant next to a flattened tent.

"I can ask when he comes back."

Which, my senses told me, would be soon. Zondia and Zav were both heading this way, flying side by side. What would she say when they arrived? She'd helped with the giants, but could we trust her? I didn't know. When I thought of her showing up at Thad's house to question Amber, it made me clench my teeth—and my weapon.

I walked out of what was left of the camp, assuming I was in charge of liaising with the dragons.

Zondia landed on the far side of the crevasse, her lilac scales barely discernible in the foggy night. She glanced my way, then turned her back and gazed out at the glacier. Did that mean she was irritated with me and wouldn't help further? Or was she assigning herself a guard position in case more threats showed up?

Zav landed ten feet in front of me, his back to Zondia and the crevasse, his eyes glowing a little less fiercely now that the battle was over. He spread his wings, his muscled chest thrust out, as if to show off his magnificence. As usual, he radiated power that made me want to gaze enraptured at him and do whatever he wished. Judging by the soldiers gaping at him, they felt similarly.

Willard says I can't sleep with you in that form, I thought.

He pulled in his wings and lowered his neck and head to gaze levelly into my eyes. *She is correct. I do not feel sexual urges in this form, nor is dragon genitalia compatible with human genitalia.*

I figured. Why don't you change into your human form so I can give you a hug?

Are these men with weapons your allies? They are considering me with wariness and wondering if they will have to battle me.

If I hug you, they'll figure out that you're not an enemy. I glanced toward Zondia's shadowy form, wondering if she was listening in on our telepathic conversation.

Zav transformed immediately and strode toward me, the hem of his black robe stirring the fresh powdery snow. His eyes continued to glow softly, the same striking violet as when he was a dragon. A hint of humor gleamed in them. *What will they think if you* kiss *me?*

Is that a good idea with your sister watching?

Yes.

Really? Had something changed drastically?

No.

Zav flashed that grin that would have melted any girl's heart and wrapped his arms around me, lips brushing my cheek, one of the few spots where I had skin exposed.

I would have preferred having him nuzzling my neck, but Zondia looked over her shoulder, and I hesitated to even return the hug with too much enthusiasm.

Zav grasped the back of my head lightly, turning my face toward his, a tingle of warm magic flowing from his fingers. That was amazing, especially here in the cold with snow spitting on my face, and I had to resist the urge to lean into his hand and thump my leg like my mother's golden retriever.

There are things I must discuss with you, he spoke into my mind, *but first, I will show you that I am pleased you still wear my mark.*

Your magical mark?

Yes. The mark that shows all with magical blood that you are mine. There wasn't any humor in his eyes now. He was utterly serious.

I didn't know removing it was an option. I've tried loofahs...

You will not *remove it.* He brought his lips to mine, fiercely demanding as his power wrapped around me, flowing over me and waking up every nerve in my body. Before I could think to object to this talk of being his, or remind him that he'd said back in my Jeep that he meant to free me from his claim, I found myself returning the kiss. I lifted my hands to push through his short hair and lean into him. My injuries twinged at the contact, but I barely noticed. The electricity crackling around us felt too good for me to be bothered by minor discomforts. I would have forgotten all about our enemies, about the camp, and about the soldiers gaping at us, but someone coughed and spoke.

"Is that allowed on a mission, ma'am?"

"I'm going to allow thirty more seconds," came Willard's dry response. "The dragon *did* help us. He should be rewarded."

I knew I should be embarrassed—or at least professional—and pull back, but it was hard. Both because my body longed for this after the day of abuse—after a lifetime of abuse—and because I'd missed him. When I'd thought he might never come back, I'd berated myself for that impulsive choice. I didn't know why he'd returned, but I gripped him tighter, so he would know I wanted him to stay, no matter what I might say in some fit of anger in the future.

The tighter grip caused another twinge to my lower back, this one surprising me, and I didn't quite manage to keep from flinching in pain.

Zav drew back, and I was disappointed that I'd let a little injury stop a good kiss. All right, an *amazing* kiss. I wouldn't admit it to him—dragon egos were already gargantuan—but all that magic was nothing to scoff at, especially when it woke up nerves that human hands alone couldn't have roused.

You are injured. His eyes narrowed with concern that touched me, though his eyebrow quirked upward as he added, *Again.*

Yes. A golem fell on me.

Had I been there, I could have prevented this. He must have been able to scan my body with his magic, for he slipped his hand into my jacket and around to my backside, resting it precisely above the internal injury.

I believe you. But I unwisely told my strongest ally to get off my planet.

You agree this was unwise?

Yes.

Good. You are correct. Healing warmth flowed into my body, and I couldn't manage to issue a snarky comeback. A few strands curled up to my shoulders, soothing the bruises I'd received crashing against the wall of ice. Even my headache faded, replaced by a feeling of energy and almost euphoria.

You are an excellent ally, Zav.

Yes. Why has it taken you so long to realize this?

Well, you did try to kill me when we first met.

I did not. I was merely expressing my disgruntlement.

Uh huh. Look me in the eye and tell me you weren't contemplating killing me.

He did look me in the eye, but he paused before admitting, *I was having a bad month. And I believed you were a villain.*

What changed your mind? I wondered at what moment he'd decided I was okay. After I'd risked myself to help him in the first dark-elf lair and retrieved his precious dragon artifact?

I still believe your methods are vigilante at best and possibly criminal, but now that I have claimed you as my mate, it is my duty to instruct you in better behavior.

Oh, that'll be fun.

His expression grew a little smug as he touched the side of my face and said, *I will ensure that your compliance and good behavior are rewarded by pleasure.*

This time, snarky words leaped right to my tongue, but another tendril of magic flowed from his fingers, a hint of the pleasure he could deliver, and I almost forgot my objections. But not quite.

I stepped back, clasping his hands so he couldn't ooze any more magic into me, no matter how good it felt. *I'm not a recalcitrant hound to be trained with treats. Maybe* you're *the one who needs to learn good behavior. You don't exactly* get *Earth customs. If you fit in adequately, and treat me like an equal instead of some object that you now believe you own, I'll reward* you.

His eyes glowed—that was a warning, he'd once explained. But curiosity seemed to win out over indignation, because he asked, *With what will you reward me?*

I could feed you again. The next time I get paid. More ribs. I wriggled my eyebrows at him.

"Thorvald," Willard said quietly, "that other dragon is glaring daggers at you two from across the crevasse. Is it going to be a problem?"

"No," Zav answered firmly. "She is going to assist us in obtaining the two dark-elf criminals. That is all she will do."

Did you and she have a chat? I asked. *You didn't fight over this—us—did you?*

We did fight. We even drew blood, but I was victorious. I pinned her to the ground and demanded she stay out of my life and never bother you or your kin again.

And that worked?

He hesitated. *Not as well as I'd hoped. She is quite determined to out you as an assassin and protect me from my unmanageable lust.*

I rubbed my face. *So nothing has changed?*

It has. She has agreed to leave you alone, to not bother your comrades or kin, and to assist me in collecting these dark elves.

She promised that to you?

She promised it to our mother. His lips twisted wryly. *She interrupted our battle, said we were embarrassing the family during a time when we most need to show we have the right to rule and maintain order, and shamed my sister into returning here to help me complete this mission. She was sent back first to look for the dark elves, but she did not realize that you had already found them.* He beamed a smile at me. *As I knew you would.*

The praise tickled me, especially since I'd felt like a failure most of the day, but I didn't let myself bask in it.

I patted his arm. *Yes, but we have a problem. They're trying to set off that volcano, which could kill a lot of my people. And I think they may be close to accomplishing it. What are the chances that you can arrest those two tonight? And take the rest of the dark elves with you when you go?*

The latter is unlikely. As to the rest... His eyes grew distant as he used his magic. *They are in caves under the ice. Far under the ice. Let us make a plan before we charge recklessly down there.*

Uh, yeah. Good idea. Only an idiot would recklessly charge into a dark-elf lair. Or recklessly sneak in with an alarm that might start beeping in the middle of the incursion.

He gave me a puzzled look.

Never mind. "Willard? Can we use your tent?"

"For snogging? No."

"For planning an incursion so Zav can arrest dark elves while I find all their artifacts and destroy them."

"You mind if I come to this meeting in my own tent?" Her words dripped sarcasm, which Zav missed or ignored.

"I will permit this," he told her.

"Thank you so much."

Willard stalked toward the tent, hopefully to shove stuff around and make room for three. I doubted she wanted to play footsies with Zav.

"Your leader has a tongue similar to yours," he said.

"We're kind of like sisters."

"Sisters can be problematic."

"Yes, they can."

"I heard that," Willard said over her shoulder.

Chapter 28

"I can sense the dark elves down there." Zav sat on my sleeping bag, facing Willard and me, a small lantern throwing our faces into light and shadow. His sister remained on guard near the crevasse, not communicating with me or anyone else in the camp. "They are quite active. They may be implementing this volcano plan you spoke of."

Willard swore. "Then we need to go back down there tonight. I'd planned to wait until morning, hoping they would be sleeping during the day, but..." She opened her palm toward the low dome-ceiling.

"I'm willing to go back down tonight," I said. "Zav, what can you do down there? I remember you taking the brunt of the attack from dozens of dark elves at once in their lair under the city. You used your shields to keep them from hurting you."

"Yes, until your explosion caused the street above to fall onto me. As well as several large metal conveyances." He rubbed his head.

"Cars, yes, and I'm sorry, but I had to get that kid. And, as you may recall, I also got your platter."

Willard snapped her fingers. "Focus on *these* dark elves."

Zav's eyelids drooped as he regarded her, and I suspected he was thinking of letting her know that the dragon was always in charge, not the lowly human military officer. Willard wouldn't likely find a relationship with one of his brothers as appealing as she thought.

"Are you as powerful in human form as in dragon form?" I asked, in part to distract him from whatever ire he felt for Willard, and in part because I'd wondered for a while, and it would be useful to know.

He lifted his chin, his head brushing the ceiling, then gave it a baleful look for presuming to impede him. It had started snowing again, so I hoped he didn't incinerate the tent.

"I would prefer to battle them in my dragon form."

"So, that's a no?" I asked. "You're not quite as strong?"

His chin remained up, and he didn't speak. I thought he would refuse to answer the question, but he switched to telepathy.

I am not as powerful in human form. You are correct. It is more difficult to access the shakorath. *I am still capable of facing many dark elves, but I cannot defend myself and attack them at the same time.* "I would prefer to face them in my dragon form," he repeated aloud. "How large are the tunnels down there? Have you seen them?"

"I've seen them." I closed my eyes and imagined that chamber with the lake. It might be large enough for him to stand up with his wings spread, but that was the only spot. "You might be able to fold in your wings and get to the bottom of the crevasse, but not the tunnels or even the entrance. As a dragon, you'd be too big to fit in the hole."

Willard lifted a finger, her dark eyes twinkling as her focus was momentarily derailed.

"Don't say it," I told her.

"What would I say?" Her lips twitched in a barely restrained smirk. "Him being too big for the hole is more a problem for you to deal with than me."

"Unless I get you that brother."

"True."

"*I* am focused," Zav said.

"Right." Willard dropped her fledgling smirk. "What are you able and willing to do, and how can my team help get Val in to find the artifacts? Can you distract the dark elves?"

"If he went in through the main tunnel and kept them busy, maybe we could sneak in another route." I explained the side passage and that it seemed to be a possible back way in.

"I sense approximately a hundred and fifty dark elves down there. They are among the most powerful of the lesser species, and they've had time to hunker in and place defenses." Zav lowered his chin to his chest as he spoke. "I sense numerous magical artifacts. You will need time to find the one that is applicable to your problem."

"I thought I'd just shoot the crap out of any that I came across," I said.

"That will still take time. If I go straight in, they will find it difficult to deal with a dragon, but they have likely made plans for this eventuality. Yemeli-lor and Baklinor-ten know I have been after them. As powerful and great as a dragon is, it would be foolish of me to walk into the mouth of their cave and invite them to use me for target practice."

"I suppose your sister wouldn't be willing to do that either."

"No. And my mother would be displeased if she were killed when this is my assignment."

"What's *her* job?"

"Being young and learning from her elders."

"Oh God, is she a teenager?" I looked at Willard. "Doesn't that sound like a teenager to you?"

"I will think of a use for her," Zav said. "Perhaps I will send her up to breathe fire on the glaciers and melt them."

"Uh, to what end?" I imagined floodwaters gushing down the sides of the mountain.

"To concern the dark elves that we are removing the water source they need to cause an eruption of this volcano. I assume they plan to funnel glacier meltwater down to the magma to cause a reaction? Is this what you believe?"

"That was our physicist's guess, yes." Willard thumped me on the shoulder. "Your dragon is smarter than I guessed."

"He's not just a pretty face."

"Dragons know all about fire and volcanos." Zav's brows drew together. "*Her* dragon? I have claimed Val as *my* mate."

"Yes," Willard said. "I know."

"She does not have ownership over me. That is not how it works."

"No? I thought females were in charge on your world."

"Female *dragons*. Val is…" He extended a hand toward me.

"A mongrel," I supplied.

"A half-elf." He had apparently decided to stop calling me derogatory names. Progress.

"She's smoking hot here on Earth, so you had better treat her right,"

Willard said, "or she'll go back to her programmer."

Was she trying to help me? I was more horrified than honored.

"She will not." Zav's eyes blazed.

I lifted my hands. "Hey, we're focusing here, right?"

"Yes," they said, glaring at each other.

"Zav," I said. "You don't have to be a target, but if you and your sister can keep the dark elves looking the other way, I'll hunt for their artifacts. And if I can find the two scientists, I'll knock them out, tie them up, and drag them out with me."

He nodded. "I will consider how I can best draw their attention. It is likely they will send their greatest mages and priestesses to face me, so you may have room to maneuver. But remember that Yemeli-lor is also a priestess—she will have magic—and Baklinor-ten is also a warrior. They will not be easy to defeat."

"Trust me. I'm not expecting anything to be easy." Nothing had been yet.

"What do you want us to do?" Willard pointed at her chest and waved toward the rest of the camp.

"There is little mere humans can do," Zav said.

"They have flashbangs, magical grenades, and a couple of magical weapons," I said.

Zav looked blankly at me, as if this changed nothing.

"I'm *positive* they can help."

"They may assist you then," Zav said imperiously. "They would only be in my way when I'm hurling fire and magic at my enemies."

I lifted a hand to stave off a protest from Willard. "He's right. He'd have to worry about frying you guys—or the dark elves frying you. You can sneak in with me if you're dying to go back down there."

"I'm not, but I refuse to sit up here and knit a sweater for my cat while you're risking your life."

"I'm sure Maggie is relieved."

"Maggie likes sweaters."

"Wearing them or nesting in yours?"

Willard wriggled her fingers to dismiss this. "I'm going. We all are. Also, your dragon isn't calling the shots here, and neither are you." She frowned at me.

Zav frowned at *her*.

I rubbed my face.

"I am called Lord Zavryd'nokquetal," Zav stated, "not dragon or *your* dragon."

Willard opened her mouth, but Zav had gone from amiable—his version of it—to irritated, and his face was stony as he glared at her. Stony and dangerous. He always had that powerful predator aura about him that made people cross to the other side of the street when they saw him, but when he grew annoyed, it was stronger.

Willard kept whatever she'd intended to say to herself and shared her exasperated glare only with me. "Fine, he can be the distraction—" she pointed to Zav, "—and you'll go in the back door while he hurls things at them. I'll talk to Banderas and the others about putting together a couple of teams, one to assist you, and the other to search in another direction. If their lair is as sprawling as we think, it would be better to have multiple teams looking for those artifacts."

She crawled out of the tent and left without waiting for a response. Since she'd made her decision, little would be gained by pointing out that the rest of the soldiers would be unlikely to recognize the magical artifacts or tools we needed to destroy.

I leaned over and zipped up the flap, though there wasn't much heat inside to escape. Only what we'd created with our breath.

"It would be better if you and I went in without them," Zav stated quietly. "Humans will only be a liability against dark elves."

"They can help. They're well-trained fighters."

I shifted over to sit next to Zav, though only to drop my face in my hand. The others *could* help, but this was also skirting close to one of my nightmares, of friends being killed because I'd failed to protect them. If Willard died down there, I would lose my boss as well as a friend, and it would be my fault. She hadn't been planning on coming on this mission before I'd suggested it. Zav's presence on our team would bring the odds closer to even, but he would also be like a tornado down there, hurling his magic at the dark elves, who would be hurling their own magic back at him. It would be easy for someone without armor against magic to be flattened by accident. It would be easy for *me*, even with my armor and charms, to be flattened.

"You know I am right," he said.

"I thought you couldn't read my thoughts," I muttered into my hand.

My headache was creeping back. Even dragons couldn't permanently cure the symptoms of altitude sickness. What a time to go into battle. Though once we got it over with, I could get off the mountain and go back to my sea-level home. If I survived.

"I am getting better at reading your body language." Zav wrapped an arm around my shoulders.

We were already sitting cross-legged, knee to knee, so it was easy to lean into him and accept the embrace.

"What happens if you fail to bring these rogue scientists home?" I asked.

"I will not fail. It is already intolerable that it has taken me so long to locate them." He opened his palm to show me the cufflink-like button Sindari had found in Rupert's pub back before it had closed, the button we believed belonged to the male scientist, Baklinor-ten. "The owner of this is down there. I can sense him. This time, I will not fail to retrieve him."

"They've probably been up here for weeks. That's why you couldn't find them in the city. It's not your fault."

"My people do not accept excuses. I must capture these two and then continue to collect all the criminals on my list. Only then will the members of the Dragon Justice Court know that my family is still strong and powerful and has the ability and right to enforce our laws, no matter that our numbers have diminished."

"How come all of this is on you?"

"It is not. I have three brothers who are collecting criminals on other worlds. Worlds less savage and infested with fewer vermin than this." Distaste had crept into his tone. It seemed the delicious barbecue ribs hadn't convinced him yet that humans had redeeming qualities. "But your world has come to particular attention among our kind because a dragon was slain here, so I am being closely observed."

Ugh, because of me.

Zav didn't put any blame on me, simply continued on with his story. "It was because of the rogue faction of elves—those who tried to assassinate several of us—and who, in the case of one of my brothers, succeeded—that many of these criminals are out in the Crimson Realms causing havoc. One of those elves invented an artifact that could reverse the effects of the magic we use to rehabilitate criminals into acceptable members of society. Their new personalities were torn away, reviving the old ones. We hadn't thought this possible and were caught unprepared."

So that was why Zav—or his mother—felt personally responsible for collecting the criminals. This had happened on their watch.

"I hadn't realized those elves were still a problem for your people. From what you said before, it sounded like you defeated them and replaced them with new rulers." It made me wonder if that was how my father had become a king.

"We did, but some members of their resistance survived and continue to plot against dragons."

I thought of Freysha mysteriously showing up to apply for an internship in Willard's office—Freysha, who had made buddies with the goblin gossip who knew everything about the magical species of the Pacific Northwest. We'd already considered that she might have warned the dark elves we were coming, but what if she was even more dangerous than we thought? To dragons as well as humanity?

"I'm sorry those elves are making your life difficult." I patted Zav's knee. Had I been a part of the politics of the Cosmic Realms and born on an elven world instead of Earth, maybe I would have joined them in fighting against dragons, but I didn't know them, and I did know Zav. The rest of the dragons I'd met could go chase their own tails, but I didn't want him to be a target for assassination plots or anything else.

"It is not your fault. We will go into battle together and capture Yemeli-lor and Baklinor-ten. All will be made right. This is my duty."

"Let's stop a volcanic eruption along the way, all right? My duty includes that."

I expected him to say that volcanos weren't on his list, so that part wasn't his problem—that had been his response when I'd hinted that help against the panther-shifter brothers terrorizing Nin would have been appreciated.

"Yes," he said, surprising me. "I will assist you with that. Even a dragon cannot stop a volcano once it is erupting, so we must ensure they do not have the ability to start it. As we have discussed, you will seek the device and the scientists while I keep the rest of the dark elves busy. When you locate the scientists, call to me. I will find a way to get to you to help. They will be too powerful for you to fight alone." Zav lowered his arm. "But we must go now. The humans are completing their talk of plans. We will go before they know we have left."

"Uh, Willard is my employer. She's going to be pissed if I take off against her wishes."

"Is it not better for her to be angry than to be dead?"

Yes. But...

"I will fly us to the bottom," Zav said. "By the time they climb down on ropes, we will have succeeded at this mission."

Or failed spectacularly. But if Willard and the others didn't come with us, they would still be alive to try something else. Or at least warn everyone that an eruption was coming.

"Are you prepared for battle?" Zav shifted toward the tent flap. He had already assumed I agreed with him and we would leave without the others.

I wasn't sure I believed that he was reading my body language rather than my mind, but it didn't matter. I gathered my weapons, extra ammo, and grenades and flashbangs, then touched a finger to Sindari's cat charm. It was no longer ice cold. Did that mean he'd recovered enough that I could call him back? I hoped so. Both because he was my friend and because I needed someone to watch my back while Zav was busy with the dark elves.

"I'm ready. One thing before we go."

He tilted his head.

"Are you still planning to remove your mark and, uh, un-claim me when you've completed your mission on Earth?"

Several seconds passed, and he only gazed at me. Was he contemplating an answer or refusing to answer?

"Remember when we discussed mixed signals? Telling me we're breaking up and then kissing me a few days later would be an example of that."

I half-expected him to ask for a definition of *breaking up*, and I didn't know what I would tell him since we hadn't ever dated, but he looked like he knew exactly what I meant.

"It would be best if I removed my mark and left forever," he finally said. "But every time I return to find you in danger, I want to protect you and fight at your side to defeat your enemies, and the thought of letting anyone else have you for a mate disturbs me. Even though I've known you only a short time, you have... made an impression on me. That is the correct saying, yes?"

"Yes. You've made an impression on me too."

"Good." Zav waved his hand, and the tent flap unzipped, a few snowflakes swirling inside. "We will discuss marks and claiming after we defeat our enemies in battle together. Come."

He hadn't given me a concrete answer, but I nodded and followed him. We had more important matters to face first.

I engaged my stealth charm as I crawled out and glanced toward the light and voices coming from the closest tent. Willard would be furious when she came to get us and we weren't here, but Zav was right. Better for her to be angry and alive than the alternative.

Chapter 29

Zav and I walked to the edge of the crevasse, and Zondia, still standing guard on the opposite side, turned to look at us. Zav turned into his dragon form.

We are going into the lair, he said telepathically, the words for both of us, though he looked at his sister. *We will go through the direct route down below. I want you to search for another way in so they will have to split their forces. I would suggest burning through the glacier, but it is very thick.*

"There may be another way." I glanced back at the camp, worried Willard would finish her meeting and see us if we lingered. "We found a golem in a cave two miles that way." I pointed. "Its body is still there. You should be able to find it. The dark elves had collapsed too much ice for us to enter there, but maybe it would be easy for a dragon to melt the blockage out of the way."

Zondia gazed at me with her eyes that matched Zav's in color but were nothing like his in temperament. I wanted to ask her what she'd done to Amber, but this wasn't the time. I lifted my chin and braced myself, expecting a snide comment, but she merely shifted her gaze to Zav's and held it for a long moment. Then she launched into the air and took off in the direction I'd pointed.

She still does not trust you and believes you are sending her nowhere important, but she will not interfere with this mission or go against our mother's wishes. Zav lowered himself so that his belly rested on the ice. *I will carry you down.*

I don't know if that entrance is important or not, but she'll see the dead golem and the cave.

Yes. She senses it. Zav levitated me onto his back.

I held on the best I could with nothing but smooth scales to grip, and he sprang into the air. He flew up and circled before diving into the crevasse.

In most places, it was too narrow for him to spread his wings, and my heart tried to claw its way up and out of my throat as we picked up speed. A wing twitched here and there, and he twisted or shifted to avoid shelves and bumps in the walls, but it was hard not to feel like we were plummeting to our deaths. What if there wasn't room at the bottom for him to spread his wings and stop without crashing?

There wasn't, but somehow we slowed down anyway. Zav employed the same type of magic the elves used for levitation. A skill I needed to learn.

After I slid off his back, Zav looked up the crevasse and seemed to sigh as he shifted into a human. He'd been evasive about how much power he lost when he abandoned his native form, but I tried not to dwell on it. I'd seen him do plenty as a human; he was still more powerful than any elf.

Any *singular* elf. Too bad he'd said there were dozens in there. No, a hundred and fifty, he'd said. I tried vainly not to feel daunted.

It was pitch-black at the bottom of the crevasse. Later, I might use Chopper for light, but for now, I activated my night-vision charm. As we walked toward the cave—somehow Zav didn't slip on the ice, despite wearing his slippers—I also touched my cat charm and called Sindari's name softly. Relief came over me as the silver mist appeared, and he formed inside.

I paused to hug him. *I thought they got you.*

Not completely, but I stayed longer than was wise, and they succeeded in injuring me with their magic. I thought you would need as much time as I could give you to escape. Sindari turned his green eyes toward me and leaned into the hug.

I almost toppled over. Having a seven-hundred-pound tiger lean against you is a little different from a seventy-pound dog doing the same.

We did need it. Thank you. I patted him, then hurried to catch up to Zav.

He'd reached the tunnel entrance, mounds of ice from my previous incursion littering the ground, and was looking back, but he didn't comment on my reunion taking time. There weren't any enemies waiting for us, not here. My senses picked up dark elves deeper inside. I couldn't tell how far back they were, but hopefully, they weren't at that lake. It would be hard to sneak into the side tunnel if they were watching.

I removed my climbing gear. This time, none of my equipment would betray me with clanks, beeps, or other noises.

I had hoped not to return to this place, Sindari commented as we walked in, letting Zav take the lead.

Sindari and I had our camouflage magic activated, but Zav didn't muffle his aura the way I'd seen him do before. He strode straight in, letting them know he was coming. But I could no longer sense Zondia. That might mean she'd flown out of my range, but she might also be trying to be sneaky.

We didn't get to battle anyone last time, I replied to Sindari. *I thought that would disappoint you and you'd want another chance.*

Not in this place. He eyed the exotically textured glacier overhead, the shell-like pattern of melted ice comprising the ceiling surprisingly even.

I can release you back to your realm if you want. I did not wish to, but if he feared the claustrophobic tunnels, it was cruel to make him stay.

No. Sindari looked forward again. *I will remain at your side.*

Thank you.

If there had been time, I would have hugged him again, but we'd almost reached the chamber with the lake, and I sensed dark elves waiting inside. Four, at least, though others could be hidden with cloaking magic like mine. An entire army might be waiting, and I wouldn't know it.

Zav paused, glancing back at me. *It will begin soon. I will do what I can to defeat as many as possible. Stay camouflaged as long as you can. You will find them strong foes.*

I had no doubt. Zav would never admit that he was worried the dark elves could, with their combined might, kick his ass, but I had no trouble reading between the lines.

I'm ready. I drew Chopper, but right away, something happened to belie my words. Intense hatred flooded into me, along with an urge to drive my sword between Zav's shoulder blades and into his heart. It was so powerful that Chopper moved several inches before I caught myself and jerked it back. The blade fought me, as if it longed to be free to make the killing blow.

What the hell?

Zav, his back turned, hadn't seen it, but Sindari looked curiously at me.

I gritted my teeth and stepped back, telling the sword to knock it off, even as the implications of the magical urge hammered home. The dark elves had to know I was here. One of them was using his power to try to compel me to take out Zav. Terror clutched me at the thought that it might have worked. He was expecting an attack from ahead, not from the ally behind him.

No. I pushed my blade down, pointing the tip at the ground. No, it wouldn't have worked. I was too strong to be manipulated that way.

I hoped.

I'm going in. Zav walked toward the lake without looking back. *You are cloaked, but wait a minute for me to engage them, so they are too distracted to search for my allies.*

But I wasn't as cloaked as I wished, not if one of them had detected me. I thought about saying something to Zav, but he was focused and already disappearing around the bend ahead.

Since we were splitting up, this would be a non-issue. I just had to get into that side tunnel—and hope he happened to take out whichever dark elf had tried to control me.

It's fine, I told Sindari.

He was still looking at me. Concerned. *Are you sure?*

I hope so.

Chapter 30

Nobody shouted or roared a war cry as Zav strode into the chamber. The battle began with a flare of fiery orange light and an explosion of magic that registered on my senses, not to my ears.

Sindari and I, crouched in the tunnel a hundred meters from the lake chamber, took this as the sign to start our mission. I jogged forward as quickly as I could without making noise. One dark elf might know I was there, but hopefully, he hadn't told all of his buddies.

When we reached the lake, we saw Zav on the far side, a sword he'd magically produced in one hand and a fist-sized orb I hadn't seen before in the other. They both glowed, as did the spherical barrier of energy around him, a shield that protected him as the dark elves—there were indeed more than four—crouched in the tunnel ahead of him casting attacks. Some were bolts of energy and black spheres like they'd hurled at me. Others were devices that they rolled out to explode against Zav's shield.

From behind him, I couldn't see his face or tell how much of a strain this was putting on him, but I assumed he couldn't withstand that forever.

I had an impulse to rush forward and throw flashbangs and grenades at the dark elves to help him. But then that nefarious urge to attack him returned to my mind. I swore silently. I had to leave him to handle this on his own. As we'd planned.

Skirting the outside of the chamber, I hurried past two small tunnels to the side passage I'd entered before. None of the dark elves glanced at me as I dropped to my hands and knees and crawled into it. Sindari, down on his belly, followed me. I wanted to think something to Zav, to let him know we were in, but I worried the dark elves would be able to sense my meager attempt at telepathy. No, I would wait for Zav to contact me.

Going much more quickly than before, I scrambled down the tunnel. We came to a spot where I could run, my head ducked to avoid the ceiling, and I went faster. Thinking of Zav standing there, his energy being drawn down by all those attacks, I felt like a time bomb was ticking down to zero.

Be wary of traps, Sindari warned. *They may have booby-trapped this in anticipation that you would return.*

Good point. I made myself slow down.

Soon, I sensed something magical up ahead. It was hard to pinpoint with all the other magical devices scattered throughout the lair, but there was definitely something in our path.

I smell dark elves, Sindari added. *They have been back here since we were.*

Checking out the hole in their security, I'm sure.

We reached the spot where I had started melting the blockage earlier. Something dented was stuck to the bottom of the low ice ceiling. The night-vision charm made it hard to pick out the details, so I pulled out Chopper and whispered the illumination word. Then snorted. It was my carbon monoxide detector that Sindari had mangled with his teeth.

That is the source of the magic, he said. *It has been modified.*

He was right. I didn't sense the filigrees of magic, as with the alarm device in the main tunnel, but it had a noticeable signature. Would it explode if we touched the ice? Or tried to cross that point?

I inched closer and examined it by Chopper's light. *That looks like a tiny speaker fused to it. Something to amplify the beeps it can make? Maybe it'll start wailing if we touch it. And then explode.*

I am not an expert on dark-elf artifacts, but it feels more like an alarm than explosive magic to me.

There's not enough room to go under it without melting more of the ice. And it's in the way. I dropped to my belly to double-check. I'd made some progress melting the low-hanging ceiling before but not enough to pass through. *So we have to figure out how to disarm it. Or destroy it before it can go off.*

Elven Doom

I envisioned slashing it with Chopper, but if the device was like the original detector—or any of those incessant fire alarms that went off when the batteries needed changing—a dozen strikes might not slay it.

I'm going to try to unlock it with my lock-picking charm. I reached up to my leather thong.

It's not a door or a lock, Sindari said dryly.

I know, but the charm was originally made to remove enchantments on doors and gates. This is blocking a doorway… of a sort.

That seems like a stretch.

What are our other options? Zav won't be able to keep those guys busy forever. I rose to my knees in front of the device and touched my charm, starting to will it to unravel the magic, but an idea popped into my head. *Sindari, have you ever carried anything back to your realm with you when you've left?*

Like a pack or weapon? No. If I'm wearing anything, it will not come along on the journey with me.

Ah, darn. I thought you might be able to bite it off and then jump back to your realm before it went off. If it goes off there, well, I assume there aren't many dark elves on your tundra to talk about it.

No. My chieftain might talk about it if the noise was audible from the den. Sindari crept forward and sniffed the device. *If I took it in my mouth, it might* make the journey with me.

Let me try disarming it first. Normally, I would have rested my hand on a door—or, in this case, the ice next to the device—but I worried that getting too close would trigger it. Instead, I stared intently at it as I willed the magic of the lock-pick charm to work, not opening anything but deactivating the device.

This charm required no strange foreign words to work, only my own will. And maybe, as I'd started to believe, some of my own power.

Magic flowed from me to it, but magic also seemed to be building up inside of the device. Was it humming faintly? I backed away mentally and physically. The magic in it kept increasing, an audible hum reaching my ears.

Damn. I think I triggered it.

Sindari lunged forward, ripped the device from the ice with his fangs, and faded before my eyes. I scrambled back, lifting Chopper in case it went off before he disappeared. It kept building in intensity, but it didn't start shrieking or whatever it was supposed to do. It might be sending out a silent alert to whoever had placed it.

Sindari disappeared before anything substantial happened, leaving me kneeling in the passage with my sword raised toward empty air.

A distant boom reached my ears, and the ground trembled. Zav? Or the dark elves throwing explosives *at* Zav?

Or—I grimaced as a new possibility reached my mind—had Willard brought her two teams down?

The ground shivered again, even though no boom accompanied it this time. The tremor continued, and snaps emanated from deep in the glacier above me. I tried not to think about how much the hundreds of feet of ice above me would weigh as it crashed down onto me. It didn't work.

"At least you'll die instantly," I muttered as I pressed Chopper against the ice blocking my way. I said, "*Krundark,*" to activate its heat power.

The pervasive smell of brimstone that lingered down here became stronger, mixed with other gases I couldn't identify. Water dribbled from the ice as Chopper slowly melted it.

The low-grade headache that had been with me for most of the night grew more intense. Maybe it was from the noxious air, not only the altitude. This was the spot where the carbon monoxide detector had originally gone off, not as a dark-elf alarm but to let me know it wasn't safe for humans to be down here. And it wasn't as if my lungs were better than a full-blooded human's. If anything, they were a weakness.

Zoltan's charm. I would have snapped my fingers if I hadn't been holding my sword with both hands.

The vampire alchemist had made a trinket for me to help against a gas he'd concocted to offend the noses of feline shifters. I still wore it on my leather thong with my other charms. It might not do anything against volcanic gases, but I tapped it twice to activate it. As with the previous time I'd used it, I didn't feel anything. It had proven helpful against the shifters when I'd gassed them, but these gases were different. At the least, it couldn't hurt.

A large puddle formed as the ceiling melted upward. A few more inches, and I would be able to squeeze through on my belly.

The infrared light we had seen on the other side before wasn't visible now. Hopefully, the dark elves had turned it off, and that was all. But what if they had blocked the passage farther on? As I stared at the ice, glumness descended over me. That seemed such a distinct possibility that I couldn't imagine otherwise.

As the ground kept shaking off and on, I worried about more than ice falling. What if the dark elves had started the process for making the volcano erupt?

I dried off and sheathed Chopper, then scooted under the ceiling, low-crawling like I'd once done in Basic Training. My belly had been in the mud then with concertina wire over my head. That sounded blessedly divine compared to wading through this puddle with a trembling glacier scraping at my helmet.

After several meters, the ceiling rose higher again. For the first time, I could stand fully. But it was only to walk a dozen more meters to stare at caved-in chunks of ice that fully blocked the tunnel. This had been done recently.

I leaned Chopper into them, hoping I could melt through once more but worried it would take too long.

Val, Zav spoke into my mind.

Yes?

You need to hurry. He didn't say why, but his telepathic voice was strained, tense.

Droplets of melted ice languidly ran down the blockage. This would take days.

I'm doing my best. I patted down my gear, considering my other options, and reluctantly settled on two grenades. *If I get buried down here, will you do me a favor?*

You do not believe I will also be buried?

You're a dragon. You're practically indestructible. I didn't have a way to set the charges and rig a delayed trigger, so I scooted back to the low-ceilinged portion of the tunnel. I would have to throw them and hope for the best.

I wish that were true. What favor do you seek?

Tell my daughter I'm sorry I got her wrapped up in my life and that I didn't get a chance to talk to her.

I waited for him to scoff and tell me something like I wouldn't die and I could tell her myself.

Very well, was what he said. *I will do this.*

I swallowed, my throat tight. *Thanks.*

Once I was under the low ceiling and had some protection, I pulled the pins on both grenades at once and rolled them so they would nestle against the ice. Then, scooting farther back, I hoped I wasn't about to bring the glacier down on my head.

Chapter 31

I managed to get to the other end of the low ceiling and the puddle of melted ice before the grenades blew. The noise was thunderous in the tunnel, and I climbed partway up the side out of some vague notion of avoiding the shockwave that would blast back.

But the tunnel quaked so badly that I tumbled down, barely managing to get my feet under me. Snaps and cracks and a booming crash battered my eardrums. Shards of ice broke away from the ceiling and hammered my helmet.

"Stupid, stupid," I groaned, even though I hadn't had a choice.

The ice fall dwindled, but head-sized chunks littered the ground all around me, and larger pieces had fallen from the ceiling I'd carefully melted back. That allowed me to see through to the blockage. It hadn't been fully demolished, but there was a gap now at the top and red light flowed through.

Another snap came from above and behind me, and more ice crashed down. I had a feeling I wouldn't be able to get back out the way I had come in.

"So be it." I clambered over the piles of ice and drew Chopper again as I squeezed through the gap between the top of the blockage and the ceiling.

As I scrambled down the back side, a chamber as large as the one with the lake came into view. I'd expected some kind of laboratory, but I realized that would have been silly. It wasn't as if the dark elves had brought construction crews up here to install cabinets and counters under the ice.

I didn't sense anyone in the chamber, but I summoned Sindari again before inching out of the tunnel, listening as I scanned the place.

Crates and packs and toolboxes were stacked against the ice wall where I'd exited, the magic of dozens of devices emanating from them. An infrared light panel resting next to the gear was the source of the red glow, either powered by battery or powered by magic.

Other alcoves and tunnel entrances opened up along the walls of the oval chamber. Most were too small and low to the ground to enter, but I could have walked straight into a few of them. Water gleamed on the textured ice of the expansive ceiling, and cracks in it made me uneasy. But it was the two strange vertical pipes in the center of the chamber, about thirty feet apart and rising out of the ground to waist height, that held my attention.

I was incorrect, Sindari said when he'd formed and determined that there weren't any enemies in the chamber with us. *It was an explosive.*

I spun toward him, afraid he'd been horribly injured, but he appeared no different than usual.

I flung it away in time, and nobody was hurt. But my chieftain had words for me.
Did I bring you back before the lecture was complete?
Yes. Thank you.

Will you start checking those packs and crates? As I pointed him toward them, I spotted a binder underneath a bag. *No, look in that first. Can you read Dark Elven?*

No. Can you?

No. My charm only translated spoken words. I'd tried before to read a foreign language with it and hadn't had any luck. *Maybe there are pictures to look at. I'm going to check out those pipes, and then I'll join you. Zav said we need to hurry.*

The ground trembled, and the ice groaned.

Yes, I can see that.

I ran to the first pipe. There was a hint of magic about it, though it appeared simple, not like one of their devices or tools. The pipes were metal and there were metal caps on them. They reminded me of a well dug on a rural property before a pump house was built up around it.

Do these go down to magma? I wondered. *Is this how they plan to deliver water?*

I have no idea what you're talking about. Sindari pawed the bag aside and used a claw to flip the binder open. Another time, I would have laughed at the sight of a tiger reading a notebook, but not now.

It took both hands, and the metal was almost too warm to grip, but I was able to unscrew one of the caps. A blast of noxious hot air flowed out. I stumbled back, waving ineffectively and trying not to choke on the fumes. I rushed to screw the cap back on.

Could I break the pipes somehow? Deny the dark elves access when they were ready? I was surprised they hadn't already started their deadly experiment.

A drop of water landed on my helmet. I looked up, startled to find a huge framework of metal embedded in the ice. It included a massive funnel with the spout lined up with the pipe. None of that had been visible from the tunnel. I could feel magic up there too, something that hadn't been noticeable because of all the devices crammed into their packs and crates.

"They've got it all set up," I whispered. They would use magic to melt the ice at whatever rate they needed and funnel the water down below. I drew Chopper. "How hot can you get with that magical word, my friend? *Krundark.*"

I laid the blade against the seam between the cap and the pipe, hoping I could weld it shut. That would only be a small delay for the dark elves, but maybe it would be enough for Zav and me to find the scientists and get rid of them.

Unfortunately, whatever the melt point was for the alloy they'd used for their pipes was high. Or maybe Chopper could only warm up to a few hundred degrees. I needed a furnace, not a sword, to melt the metal.

I've found pictures that may be helpful, Sindari told me, the binder open on the ground, *but two dark elves are on their way here from that tunnel.*

The two scientists? Dealing with them would be a challenge, but if we could manage it, maybe the rest of the dark elves were less schooled on how to cause an eruption. I tapped my translation charm, so I would understand if they said anything useful when they came in.

Two males.

So at most, one of the scientists. The male, Baklinor-ten.

Or maybe two random dark elves who had been sent to investigate the noise from my explosion. Unfortunately, that seemed most likely. But we could question them if we captured them.

We're stealthed, I added. *Let's try to ambush them as they come in.*

Careful not to make any noise, I trotted toward the tunnel Sindari had indicated. It was one of four that were large enough for people to walk through. I paused to put the binder on the packs so it would be less noticeable and glanced at a map he'd found of the cave system. It showed the chamber with the lake as well as our chamber, with two circles marking the spots where those pipes were.

I barely held back a groan. According to the map, there were three more chambers with pipes around the complex.

They're almost here. Sindari was crouching to one side of the entrance.

I glimpsed movement in the tunnel and almost grabbed Fezzik and opened fire before catching myself. Sindari could see me because of our link, but the dark elves shouldn't be able to see through the magic of my charm.

Or so I thought. As I hurried to take up a position opposite Sindari, one of the dark elves shouted and pointed right at me.

I leaped to the side and out of their view. A crossbow quarrel zipped past, missing my sleeve by a hair.

The dark elves rushed into the tunnel as I reached the ice wall, putting my back to it. They didn't see Sindari, and he leaped onto the back of the male with the twin-barreled crossbow, another bolt already loaded. It launched as Sindari bore him to the ground. The bolt embedded in the ceiling.

The second dark elf unsheathed a sword and whispered a word in his tongue. His weapon flared with a strange red glow, and powerful magic emanated from the blade. He rushed me, not giving me time to draw Fezzik, so I met his attack with Chopper.

At the first parry, my blade flared with blue light. The dark elf stumbled back squinting but only for a split second. He whispered something else, maybe something that diminished the light, and came after me again.

He was fast—as fast as I would expect from a full-blooded elf—and well-trained. Right away, he put me on the defensive, parrying and giving ground to avoid being cut by that wicked red blade. I swore and wished I'd shot them both when they'd been in the tunnel. Not that it would have worked. They likely had armor under their flowing black robes.

To the side, a burst of magic lit up my senses. Sindari flew twenty feet, and the dark elf he'd attacked snarled and leaped up.

Sindari landed on his feet, facing his opponent. The dark elf's clothing was shredded, and blood streaked from claw marks on his face, but he flung a second attack on the wave of the first, throwing Sindari back again. He almost struck one of the pipes.

My opponent feinted twice and lunged in, committed to an attack. His blade glided past my defense and nicked me on the jaw. Fiery pain stabbed into my skull as whatever that magic was amplified the intensity of the blow.

"It is not wise to get in a sword fight with a four-hundred-year-old master of the blade," he said in accented English.

"*Now* you tell me." Concentrating fully on him, I blocked his next three combinations of attacks, but he was right. I was outmatched. And he wasn't giving me the time to try anything else. Like drawing Fezzik and blowing his head off.

Worse, I was already gasping for air. The dark elves had been up here long enough to get used to the altitude. I had not.

"Warriors of this world are weak and poorly trained." He pressed me back again, his blade blurring before my eyes, it taking all of my focus to read his attacks in time to deflect them. "On our world, someone like you would have been culled from society in childhood."

"It would've been tragic... if the cosmos... missed out on my wit."

"Your stamina is pathetic. On our world, warriors battle from dawn to dusk to hone their bodies."

Distant shouts came from somewhere beyond the tunnel they'd used. Concern flashed across his face.

His buddy shouted something to him in their language, my charm translating: "There's a second dragon!"

For an instant, my assailant's attacks slowed, and he glanced toward the tunnel.

I flicked my sword at his face to distract him, then hammered a kick into his groin. He stumbled back, though he whipped his blade into place to defend right away. But I wasn't coming in with my sword. I used the second I'd gained to spring out of his reach and draw Fezzik.

He saw the danger and rushed toward me, but I had time to fire.

Three rounds slammed into his chest. A faint metallic clank told me he wore armor under his robe. As he lifted his blade to cut me, I jerked my gun up and fired multiple rounds into his face. He had no armor there. The bullets slammed into both eyeballs and his mouth. His attack never landed.

"That's how we do it on *this* world, motherfucker."

I kept my gloat to a minimum. Sindari was still battling his foe—or trying. The dark elf had recovered from the surprise of the ambush and kept casting magical attacks at Sindari, pushing him back so he couldn't spring and use fang or claw.

Focused on my tiger ally, the dark elf hadn't yet realized his buddy was down. Nor did he see me raising Fezzik until it was too late. His head wasn't armored either, and two bullets blasted into the side of his skull with finality.

Sindari, enraged after being pummeled ruthlessly with magic, sprang at the dark elf before he fell. He bore our adversary to the ground and shredded him to pieces.

I glanced down the tunnel to make sure more dark elves weren't coming—between my shooting and the grenades, they couldn't have missed our arrival.

Though I sensed more enemies in the complex—*many* more—they were busy. Zondia must have found a way through that other blocked tunnel. Good.

Once the second dark elf was dead—very dead—Sindari turned toward me. He recovered his equanimity and sounded calm and regal when he said, *Thank you for your assistance, Val.*

No problem. It was my turn to help you. Watch the tunnel again, please. I sheathed Chopper, keeping Fezzik in hand, and picked up the binder. *We're going to have to figure out how to break those pipes and then break the ones in the other chambers too.*

How we would do that... I didn't yet know.

Chapter 32

The ground shuddered again as I poked through the crates, hoping to find something that would let me plug or melt the pipes. My lungs felt like they had cotton in them, the gaseous air worse in this chamber than it had been in the tunnels. I didn't need a special detector to tell me that I needed to hurry and finish up before I passed out—forever.

Several of the crates held more pipe, shorter pieces. The dark elves must have welded many of them together and drilled them into the ground. There had to be tools somewhere. Wouldn't they have used blowtorches or something similar when they'd originally strung them together?

My knuckles brushed the binder—it was still open to the map Sindari had found—and I glanced at a few of the pages behind it. One held a diagram of what looked like their pleasure orbs. I grunted, wondering how many the dark elves had placed out there to distract people while ash rained down and lahars destroyed their houses.

I was about to push the binder aside—there was no time now to contemplate the dark elves' plans, but a newspaper clipping in English caught my eye. It wasn't about Mount Rainier but about Yellowstone. There were diagrams and photographs and columns of text speculating what would happen if the mega volcano ever erupted. Someone had highlighted chilling words like *volcanic winter* and *ash encompassing the entire planet*.

For a moment, I couldn't move as horror swept over me. Was Mount Rainier only Step One for them? A *practice* volcano?

"Shit, shit," I whispered and removed the most damning pages. I folded them and stuffed them in a pocket.

Though terrified by the possibilities, I made myself go back to looking for tools. All I could worry about tonight was stopping them here.

Finally, I found a crate full of tools and snatched out two blowtorches.

Val, Zav spoke into my mind. *Our battle is weakening the ice. It will not be safe to be down here much longer.*

It's not safe now. I hurried to the closest pipe and ignited one of the blowtorches.

My sister has gained entrance and is searching for the two scientists. I have pushed into the lair but have not encountered them yet. The other dark elves know I seek them and are impeding me.

We've killed two males, but I don't think either of them was Baklinor-ten. I wanted him to know that Sindari and I had been doing things, not wasting time while Zav risked his life, but we'd accomplished so little. *We found a map. There are four chambers where they've drilled access points down into the volcano. The scientists may be hanging out in one of the chambers.*

Find them. There's not much time. Already the way out may be compromised.

I hadn't wanted to hear that.

Working on it. Except I wasn't. I felt guilty being evasive with Zav, but stopping this eruption was the priority for me.

I applied the blowtorch flame to the seam between cap and pipe, hoping to melt them together so the access point couldn't be opened again. Not easily. With the dark elves' magic, what if they could simply blow the tops off?

A resounding *ker-thunk* came from above me. I almost sprang away from my work, anticipating the ceiling would drop, but stubbornness kept me in place. The pipe had started to melt.

The cap flew open, flecks of molten metal striking me. I was wearing gloves, but a bit sizzled on to my bare wrist, and I almost dropped the blowtorch.

The cap on the other pipe had also opened. Drops of meltwater trickled down from the funnels overhead.

"It's starting," I whispered.

And if it was starting here, it had to be starting in the other chambers too.

Growling, I pushed at the cap to shove it back into place. Water droplets bounced off the top and spattered my face. Some magic made the cap push back against me, wanting to spring open.

I cursed and climbed atop it. My weight held it in place. I bent awkwardly, applying the blowtorch to the seam where I'd been making progress before. My boots were perilously close to the flame.

Is there something I can do to help? Sindari asked.

Not unless you can grab the second blowtorch and weld the other pipe shut.

My paws will not hold it. He held up his foreleg. *Do you know how long it took me to figure out how to open your car doors to let myself out?*

I know. Just keep guarding the tunnel. Thanks.

The drips of water turned to rivulets and splashed on my back. Soon, they would be waterfalls. Something up there was heating the ice, but I could neither reach the ceiling nor guess how to destroy the sprawling framework embedded in it. The heater was probably buried ten or twenty feet up there. The dark elves had had weeks to set all this up.

Another rumble went through the ground, seemingly originating from right under us.

Will there be time to close all of those pipes? Sindari asked.

I don't know.

I doubted it. Water streamed onto my back now. It was taking forever to weld one cap shut, and we had no idea if the other chambers would be empty of dark elves. What if we had to fight our way through hordes of them to reach the pipes?

Zav? I knew he would prefer I was hunting the scientists over doing this, but we would all be screwed if the volcano erupted while we were standing on it. *Can you see what I'm doing? Is there any chance that you or your sister could find the other chambers like this one and destroy the pipes or the funnel framework above them to stop water from dumping down to the magma?*

I'd finished melting the seam all the way around, the metal now gooey and molten from the blowtorch, and willed it to harden quickly. I tried to lean to the side as I kept my weight on the cap, so the water would hit the cherry metal and cool it.

Zav? A thrum of fear went through me.

I could still sense him—and Zondia was farther away but within range now too—but there was no way to tell if he was injured. Or unconscious.

I tapped part of the seam. It had hardened. I sprang off and ran to the second pipe, grimacing at all the water rushing into it. The dark elves had been precise in lining up their funnels and little was wasted spattering to the ground.

Once again, I had to lean my weight against the cap to get it to budge. Clenching my jaw, I pushed it down and clambered atop it. I set to work with the blowtorch as icy meltwater rained down on my back.

Yes, I see what you are doing, Zav finally said. *The dark elves are focused on me, and I cannot get free to search for those chambers, but I will relay this to my sister.*

The sister who hated me and had interrogated my daughter. Just who I trusted to save the day.

Thanks, I made myself think. Aloud I said, "I think we're on our own for this, Sindari."

How much water must flow down there to cause an eruption? he asked.

"I don't know. Hopefully a *lot*."

At least right now, none was making it down in this chamber. Aside from what had already descended through this pipe.

Another rumble shook the floor, and a snap echoed over my head. I made myself keep welding, but visions of that framework breaking and collapsing on top of me came to mind.

A shriek came from somewhere down the tunnel that Sindari guarded. Was that a dark elf? Some animal familiar? Or one of the dragons? Whoever it was had been in pain.

When the seam under me melted, I leaned back, again trying to let the water cool it. The other cap was still shut. Good. I'd half-expected the magic to thwart my welding attempts and for it to have popped open again.

I wiped my face, sweat mingling with the water. Given how wet I was now, I shouldn't have been hot, but the air temperature had increased and hazy moisture clouded the chamber. It felt like a steam room in here, a steam room with horrible air quality. My throat and lungs were raw, my chest rising and falling with big breaths that didn't do nearly enough to make my body happy.

The idea of dying while alone in one of these chambers, not even battling enemies, filled me with angst. I tried not to think about how much worse the air would be in the other chambers where the pipes had been open this whole time.

I jumped off the cap, relieved when it stayed in place. For now, this chamber wasn't contributing to the problem.

"Which way to the next spot?" I took two puffs from my inhaler, hoping they would keep my airways open—and hoping the stimulating medication wouldn't make my hands shake in battle.

The route appears to be through that back tunnel. Sindari had spent more time studying the map than I, and he pointed his nose with confidence toward a passage we had thus far ignored.

As I took a step toward the tunnel, another inhuman shriek came from the main part of the lair. I pulled out one of my grenades, armed it, and threw it into the tunnel the two dark elves had come out of. Maybe if I could block that route with ice, it would keep them from getting in here to fix my sabotage.

"Run," I ordered, my throat raspy.

Sindari and I reached the back tunnel as the grenade exploded. The cracks and thunks of ice falling reached our ears, but I didn't hang around to see if I'd caused the blockage I hoped for. It wasn't as if we could spend more time to fix it if it hadn't worked.

Our new tunnel wound through the glacier, meltwater flowing in a shallow stream along the ground. It was a miracle this place hadn't already collapsed.

It should be about a hundred meters ahead, Sindari told me as he led the way. *But I sense dark elves in there.*

So did I. Four of them. Damn it. We'd barely survived fighting two.

I tapped my cloaking charm to make sure I was as hidden as possible and hoped we could surprise our enemies. A vain hope, I feared. The first two had seen through my magic without trouble. Advancing with Chopper in my right hand and Fezzik in my left, I tried not to think about that.

A slow and measured incursion into the new chamber would have been ideal, but there wasn't time. I paused only long enough to peek inside and see where the dark elves were and what they were doing before I opened fire.

A guard faced our tunnel, a second guard was placed at another tunnel on the other side of the chamber, and two dark elves with clipboards—

freaking *clipboards*—stood around one of the two vertical pipes, taking notes and measurements as water gushed into them from above.

The dark elf facing us didn't see through our camouflage—maybe he wasn't as powerful as those other two had been—and I got off a couple of shots before everyone in the chamber spun toward me.

As my rounds thudded into our closest enemy's chest, Sindari raced toward the second guard.

The scientists, a male and a female—had I stumbled across Zav's criminals and the masterminds behind all this?—lifted their hands. It wasn't a gesture of surrender but of attack, and magic crackled in the air around them.

Though I didn't hesitate to shift targets and spray rounds at them, it was too late. My bullets bounced off invisible shields they'd raised. A wrecking ball of power slammed into me, hurling me down the dark tunnel. Stunned by the blast, I landed hard on my back, my air whooshing out.

You will not stop us, mongrel, a female voice spoke into my mind as I struggled to get to my feet. *Soon this land will belong to our people. We will no longer have to hide. One day, this entire world will be ours.*

This ash-choked world that will get no sunlight once you're done?

As we prefer it. Our magic allows us to breathe the air. You are the one who will die in it.

I wished I had a witty comeback for that, but her words rang with truth. Snarling, I used the wall to stand up again.

Jaws snapped and growls sounded as Sindari battled the second guard. I willed energy into my legs and ran back to the chamber. I had nothing to defend myself against the dark elves' magic, but I couldn't leave Sindari in there alone with all three.

I grabbed a flashbang as I ran, pausing in the entrance to throw it into the middle of the chamber. For an instant, I contemplated using the deadly grenades, but if I blew up those pipes, the water would flow even more easily down to the magma.

As my flashbang sailed into the chamber, one of those black balls of energy sped toward me. I dropped to my belly, flattening my cheek to the gritty earth. It sailed past an inch above my head, searing my back with strange painful energy even though it didn't strike.

The boom of the flashbang echoed from the chamber, brilliant light illuminating the place like a sun. I sprang to my feet and rushed inside, hoping I'd blinded and discombobulated them for a few seconds.

The dark elves' hands were still up, and I sensed magic in the air about them—they radiated power almost as strongly as Zav did—but their eyes were closed. They were still shielded. Only Chopper would have a chance of cutting through that.

Blade raised, I sprang for the two scientists.

Sindari roared, but it was cut off, ending in a pained grunt. Two more male dark elves had rushed into the chamber with swords and crossbows, all of the weapons glowing with magic. They were ganging up on him, and blood already ran from a deep gash in his side. He snapped at one of his foes, biting down on an arm too slow to retract, but the other dark elves leaped for him, weapons darting in with impossible speed.

"Get back!" I yelled at him as I swept Chopper toward the female scientist.

My blade bounced off a shield. She'd known it would. She didn't even flinch, merely glared at me with crimson eyes.

You will fail, she spoke silently into my mind. *Already, you are too late to stop us.*

Refusing to be daunted, I swung again, willing all the power inside of me to aid the blade, to cut through her barrier.

But my attack halted in midair, not getting close enough to stir a single strand of her white hair. My body stopped moving, and the familiar helplessness of being in a dragon's magical grasp came over me. I couldn't even swear, though I dearly wanted to. I hadn't guessed the dark elves could also do this.

"She damaged the pipes in Chamber B," the male scientist said. Baklinor-ten. It had to be.

Was he getting the information out of my mind? Or did his magic allow him to see what I'd done?

I wished I could ask him if he had a safety pin holding up his pants under his robe. A growl stuck in my throat, my frozen muscles unable to spit it out. I tried vainly to finish my swing and lop her head off, but brute force wasn't available to me.

Instead, I tried the mental power Lirena had confirmed I had. I looked straight into the female's eyes, willing her to fall over backward and land in the stream of water, her mouth open so she promptly drowned.

"They will be simple enough to fix," the female—Yemeli-lor—said, unaffected by my attempts to use my power.

"Kill her, so she can't be any more trouble."

"I will. But she is magically marked as the mate of that dragon."

"So?" Baklinor-ten asked. "The dragon is proving himself an enemy to us."

"There may be repercussions if we kill his female."

Sindari snarled, springing in and out of reach of his foes, trying to down the three dark elves as they fired crossbow quarrels into him and cut his sides and chest with sword strikes. He moved more slowly than usual—one of the quarrels sticking out of his hide had to be a tranquilizer or some kind of poison.

Go back to your realm, I silently ordered him. *Don't die here for this.*

I won't leave you to die here.

I feared he couldn't save me from that fate.

"The dragon is attacking our people right *now*," Baklinor-ten said. "What further repercussions could there be? *Kill* her."

"Very well."

Magical energy like a huge vise clamped around my throat, squeezing my already beleaguered airway shut. Again, I tried to break the hold, but Yemeli-lor continued to hold me rigid and helpless with her power. My lungs spasmed, and my legs would have given out if her magic hadn't been holding me up.

Panic stampeded into me as blackness crept into my vision. All I could do was glare at the dark elves. It wasn't enough.

Chapter 33

My vision blacked out, I stopped hearing things, and my ability to sense magic disappeared. My brain was too fogged from lack of oxygen for anything to work. I tried to summon some strength to fight my attackers, but my body needed air, and I couldn't get it past the magical hold closing my airway.

The ground spasmed, and what was likely my last thought popped into my mind. I'd failed. The volcano would erupt, killing countless people, and it wasn't even the end of their plans. It was only a test. After this, they'd go on to the next volcano, and the next, sheathing Earth in ash that would block out the sun and keep anything from growing for who knew how long. All of humanity could be utterly screwed by this band of dark elves.

Abruptly, the hold on my throat disappeared. So did the magic pinning me in place. I pitched to the ground, my muscles barely working, barely able to gasp in air.

That air, thick with steam and volcanic gases, wasn't as quenching and refreshing as I wanted, but it was all there was. It was enough to bring feeling back to my fingers, and slowly, my vision and hearing returned.

I grew aware of my cheek pressed into a puddle and magical attacks flying through the air over my head. A tiger's roar echoed through the chamber. Sindari was still here.

Someone ran through my view, someone with slippers and a silver-trimmed black robe. Only then did my senses recover enough for me to pick out Zav.

He rushed to me, pressed a hand against my back long enough to send a brief burst of healing energy through me, then turned to face our nemeses. He and Sindari had flattened the armed guards, but Yemeli-lor and Baklinor-ten faced Zav, blasting him with magical attacks. Those black balls of energy bounced off Zav's shields and slammed into the ice walls, blowing holes in them.

Zav stood between me and the dark elves, extending his shield over me. Somewhat recovered from his magic, I struggled to my hands and knees. I had to help, not be a liability.

Where were Chopper and Fezzik? Stacked more than twenty feet away with the blowtorch. Damn it.

Zav dropped his shields long enough to hurl raw power at the two dark elves. It battered their defenses and flung them against one of the icy walls. But the female fired an attack at him, one that struck before he had time to raise his shields again. The edge of it hit me like a punch to the nose, and it hurled Zav over me. He levitated instead of landing on his back and recovered, his shields up again.

Yemeli-lor's gaze fell on me, no longer within Zav's protection.

I snatched the only weapons I had left on me. A grenade and a flashbang.

Zav flung an attack, giving me the second I needed to pull the pins. They hadn't done much before, but maybe with Zav keeping the dark elves busy…

I hurled the projectiles and mentally shouted, *Light and an explosion coming!* to Zav, hoping he was monitoring my thoughts.

Then I lunged to my feet, almost blacking out again, and rushed away from the elves—and the explosives. Yemeli-lor batted the projectiles aside with a burst of telekinetic power. That didn't keep them from going off.

Zav grabbed me as the grenade boomed. He pulled me in front of him and put his back to the explosion. Huge chunks of ice smashed to the ground, and tremors wracked the chamber. Shards of ice would have pummeled Zav and me, but his barrier wrapped around us, deflecting debris.

Then the flashbang went off, another brilliant burst of light blinding anyone with their eyes open. Two elves near the tunnel cursed and staggered back. Sindari tore into them. His movements weren't as fast as usual, but he was still effective, still deadly.

Zav spun back toward the scientists and poured a tsunami of magic at them. Even from behind him, the power staggered me, and I fought to stay on my feet. It didn't help that the ground kept quaking, the movements growing stronger instead of fading away.

Had I thrown the grenade that would finally bring this place down? Or was that the volcano getting ready to erupt?

Under Zav's assault, waves and waves of magic crashing into the two scientists, they staggered back to the wall. Their hands were up, and they combined their power to try to keep a protective barrier up, but it wasn't enough against him.

As soon as their barrier was down, I ran to my weapons and grabbed Fezzik. Making sure Zav wasn't anywhere near my sights, I fired at the dark elves. He probably wanted them captured, but I wanted them dead, so they would never do this again. They'd already killed humans with their artifacts, killed thousands of shifters on another world, and killed Rupert the troll, leaving that poor kid homeless.

But I only got two rounds off—one taking the female in the shoulder and one the male in the chest—before an intense urge to turn my gun on Zav came over me.

Damn it, I'd forgotten about that. But hadn't it been one of the elves in the lake chamber that had been responsible? Who in here could be doing it? Yemeli-lor or Baklinor-ten? The two dark elves Sindari was attacking were on the ground, barely stirring. They weren't looking in my direction. I sensed others in the tunnels beyond, but they were distracted. Zondia was out there too, not far from us.

Shoot him! a female voice screeched in my mind. *He is not guarding his back.*

The voice sounded familiar, but it wasn't Yemeli-lor. My befuddled mind struggled to place it.

I glowered at the scientists, willing my hands to steady Fezzik and aim at them. To finish them off.

They weren't looking at me either. All of their attention was on Zav, on defending against the barrage of magic he was unleashing on them.

Yemeli-lor gripped her shoulder where I'd shot her but still had one albino hand splayed toward Zav. She continued to battle him. Beside her, Baklinor-ten dropped to his knees, blood spattering the ice-covered ground. If he'd been human, my shot would have taken him in the heart, but I remembered that dark-elf anatomy wasn't the same as ours. He was still badly wounded, if not mortally wounded.

Confusion swamped me. The scientists didn't look like they had any extra energy for anything, much less coercing me to hurt Zav. It couldn't be one of them.

Another intense urge rushed into me, and like a marionette on strings, I spun toward Zav, my arms straight out and Fezzik pointing at him. Before my finger tightened on the trigger, I jerked my hands farther to the side. Against my will, my finger squeezed the trigger.

Thankfully, I'd moved the gun enough. The bullet slammed into the chest of a dark elf rushing into the chamber. One coming behind him aimed a crossbow at me, but Sindari pounced on him, bearing him to the ground.

These will be my prisoners, Zav spoke silently to me. *Do not kill them.*

He had no idea about the struggle I was dealing with. I had to overcome this. What the hell was it? Who was *coercing* me?

Kill him! Now's your chance. Kill these dragons before the glacier collapses, and nobody will know you were responsible. I'll help you get the female next.

With sudden and startling certainty, I realized who was speaking to me. Lirena!

How was she controlling me from Seattle? Or had she lied and she was here on the mountain?

My gun jerked back toward Zav. It didn't matter where she was, just that she was trying to get me to shoot my strongest ally, someone who'd just saved my life.

Hands shaking, I forced the sights away from his back again. Sweat slithered down the sides of my face. My lungs struggled to find breathable air in the miasma of steam and gases.

Zav, unaware of my struggle, had taken several steps away from me and closer to the dark elves. He was wrapping golden coils of energy around the two scientists, preparing to transport them back to his world.

Do not defy your roots, Lirena snarled into my mind. *Stop fighting this. Kill him. He's a dragon!*

"He's my ally!" I roared aloud, wanting to warn Zav of the problem, even though I was ashamed that I couldn't simply flick the mind manipulation aside.

This was an elf, not another dragon. I should be able to fight her off.

Zav turned to face me as I struggled to shift my gun away from him again. Behind him, the two scientists were wrapped in those golden coils, forced back-to-back, bleeding and gasping in pain.

"Someone is... manipulating me," I gasped. "Take my weapons."

Once more, my finger threatened to pull the trigger.

Zav stared at me. I couldn't tell if he was stunned at this betrayal or trying to figure out who was controlling me.

"Take them," I panted, hoping he had his defenses up in case I couldn't keep from shooting.

Dizziness made the chamber seem to spin as the ground undulated under my feet.

Someone shouted in the tunnel outside. "The other dragon is coming!"

Take out the female if you won't kill the male, Lirena ordered. *You want to kill that one!*

My finger tightened on the trigger. With a heave of strength and willpower, I pointed Fezzik at the ceiling just before the gun went off.

What are you doing? Sindari had finished off the other dark elves and was staring at me.

That elf—Lirena—is controlling me. My shaking hands jerked back down, the gun aiming at Zav's chest. *Come tackle me. Sit on me. Please!*

Zav was the one to stride toward me, lifting a hand toward me. As Zondia sprang into the chamber in her human form, I lost the battle of wills and fired at Zav.

"No!" I screamed.

He incinerated the bullet before it struck. With a flick of his power, he tore the gun from my grip.

I slumped, horrified but thankful he'd defended himself.

Use the sword! Lirena cried.

"Get out of my head!" I roared, locking my knees as some power tried to drive me to grab Chopper.

What is she doing? Zondia demanded, the telepathic words booming painfully in my mind.

Finish destroying the pipes, Zav ordered her, not looking away from me.

He looked me up and down with greater intensity than he'd ever studied me before. His gaze locked on my thong of charms, and he seemed to study each one, but my oxygen-starved brain struggled to recognize the significance.

When he reached for my neck, fear stampeded into my body. What if he didn't realize I was being manipulated? What if he believed I'd been biding my time until I could turn on him? Would he choke me? *Kill* me?

Zav grabbed my leather thong of charms, not my neck. Heat flashed as he incinerated the knot and pulled it off me.

The compulsion to fight and kill the dragons disappeared, and I had to lock my knees again to keep from collapsing at the relief. Control of my muscles returned to me.

Zav held up all of my charms, but only one caught my eye. I swore like a sailor being chased down by a hurricane. The diamond charm, the one Lirena had given to me. For luck, my ass. It let her control me.

"This *looks* like an elven luck charm," he said, "but another spell has been laid onto it. It now contains compulsion magic."

"I'm sorry, Zav," I whispered, feeling like an idiot.

He didn't respond, but he looked disgusted. I could only guess that he felt disappointed or angry or betrayed. Or all of those things.

Fire flared, driving all the shadows from the chamber. Zondia had transformed into the lilac dragon, her body squished even in the large chamber. She was breathing fire onto the two pipes, doing in ten seconds what I had struggled to do slowly and methodically with the blowtorch. The caps didn't just melt; the entire visible portion of the pipes warped and slumped, turning to molten puddles and then hardening as the water raining from the ceiling funnels quenched the metal. Once they hardened, they sealed the access to the magma far below.

While Zondia was doing that, Zav removed the diamond charm from my thong and handed the rest back to me.

Who gave that to you? Zondia boomed into my mind.

"An elf who claimed to be my cousin." The ground was still shaking, boulders of ice dropping down, and I feared we'd be trapped in here. "Can we talk about it later? I sealed the first chamber, and that looks good for this one, but there are two more chambers like this."

More dark elves rushed into our chamber. They gaped as they spotted the huge lilac dragon. They looked like they would flee, but Zav smashed them to the ground with magical power and created more golden ropes of magic to bind them. Before he finished, two more elves, their auras as great as the scientists' had been, charged in and attacked him.

He grunted in surprise but recovered and returned the attack. He hadn't given Fezzik back to me, so I grabbed Chopper in case I needed to help. We had to get out of here. The cracks and rumblings kept growing more intense.

Zondia shifted back to human form—she wouldn't have fit through the exit as a dragon.

I expected her to help Zav, but she rushed up and grabbed my arm. *Do not raise a weapon at him again,* she snarled into my mind.

I wasn't going to. He took the charm that was controlling me. I'm going to help.

I tried to pull out of her grasp using a move that would have worked on a normal human, but magic gave her grip more power. She growled and whipped her other hand up to my face. I thought she would strike me and ducked to avoid the blow, but more magic wrapped around me, holding me in place again.

"They've got Yemeli-lor and Baklinor-ten," one of the powerful dark-elf wizards shouted. "We have to free them!"

Zondia's hand came down on the top of my head, thumb pressed against my temple. Agony lanced into my mind as she once again tried to dig in and read my thoughts. She wished to see the elf who'd given me the charm, to learn everything I knew about her, and she wanted to know if I had truly been duped or if I'd wanted to help that faction of elves all along.

I couldn't stifle a pained gasp as Zondia tore thoughts from my mind.

Sindari had been helping Zav with the dark elves, but he glanced back and saw my conundrum. *Val!*

Growling, Sindari raced across the chamber toward Zondia.

She flung a hand up, and he halted, a wall of magic stopping him as surely as a wall of bricks. *Do not interfere, Zhinevarii, lest you be found guilty of being an accomplice.*

Sindari butted the invisible barrier, then snapped at it with his teeth. *Val? What do you want me to do?*

So much pain bit into my mind at Zondia's rough intrusions that I could barely form words. She'd been reasonable back in my apartment, trying not to hurt me, but now she was furious. After the beating I'd taken, my lungs still struggling to find breathable oxygen in the awful air, I doubted I could have fought her off even if her magic hadn't been pinning me.

Nothing, Sindari. Let her take what she wants.

The sooner she finished the better. A stab of pain accompanied every thought of Lirena that Zondia sucked from my mind, and I was sure I would pass out soon.

A surge of magic emanated from Zav, and the ceiling heaved as ice split. The dark elves trying to get to their allies shouted warnings. Too late. The ceiling collapsed, burying them.

Zav lowered his hands and turned toward Zondia and me. His glowing violet eyes widened with fury.

What are you doing! It came out as an accusation, not a question.

What you are too cowardly to do. Zondia glared back at him, not releasing me.

A battering ram of power struck her in the chest, flinging her away from me. Somehow, that pinpoint power barely stirred a hair on my head. But I couldn't keep from collapsing once her magic released me. I dropped to my hands and knees, nausea and fatigue almost making me puke.

No longer held back, Sindari shambled toward me, blood matting his silver fur, his eyes glazed. I didn't know if the air was affecting him, too, or if it was whatever poison the dark elves had shot him with.

Zav put Fezzik in my holster and picked me up.

Take the scientists and my other prisoners to the Justice Court, he ordered Zondia, who'd recovered from his blow and was glowering at him. *I will take her back to her people.*

She should be taken to the Dragon Justice Court too. Zondia flung a hand toward me. *She worked for one of the rebel elves from the faction that tried to kill you—that did kill our brother.*

Oh, hell. Lirena was one of *those* elves?

She didn't know, Zav replied.

A crack opened up in the ground, the noise as thunderous as a grenade going off.

We will discuss it later, Zav added. *Open a portal, take the dark elves, and get out of here.*

The crack widened, heat and noxious fumes flowing out of it.

Elven Doom

We will *discuss it later*, Zondia said, but she didn't argue further.

She formed a portal, the silver circle filling the shaking chamber with its light. The dark elves that Zav had bound floated through it, and Zondia jumped through after them.

The main exit leading out of the chamber had collapsed. Carrying me, Zav started toward the smaller tunnel that connected with the first chamber, but I wasn't sure we would be able to get out that way either. I'd thrown that grenade to block the tunnel out of that one. Maybe the small one I'd crawled through was still open.

Sindari padded weakly after us.

Go home, my friend, I told him. *I'll call you again after you've rested.*

And after I found out if Zav and I would escape. And if Mount Rainier was doomed to explode. Had we done enough to stop the eruption? I didn't know.

Are you safe alone with him? Sindari asked. *He saw you try to shoot him.*

Zav's face was stony as he strode into the tunnel, still carrying me.

I hope so.

I was sure Zav would forgive me for being manipulated against my wishes. I wasn't sure he would forgive me for welcoming one of the elves who'd worked to kill his brother into my home. What if Lirena had been the very assassin who'd killed him?

I will go, then. I must recover. Silver mist formed, and Sindari faded from our world.

I wanted to throw up. I didn't know if it was from the bad air or just because I was sick that I'd been fooled and could have killed Zav.

When we made it to the other chamber, most of the ceiling had collapsed, and there was no way out. We were trapped.

Chapter 34

"We will have to go another way," Zav said, the steamy gaseous air swirling about us. "The battle weakened the structure of these caves, and your people are even now bombing the main entrance, trying to close them off."

Willard was bombing the caves while I was in here? She must have received orders from a superior officer to do so. With all the rumbling and quaking, there was no way the entire state wasn't aware that Mount Rainier might erupt at any moment.

"What other way is there?" I croaked, my lungs heaving as they failed to filter the toxic air.

Zav focused on an empty point past my shoulder, and shimmering silver light bathed his face, driving back the shadows. He strode toward the portal and sprang through before I could ask where we were going.

My last thought was one of utter fear, as I envisioned landing on the cold marble floor of this Dragon Justice Court and having to explain to his mother and a hundred angry dragons that I'd let myself be a tool for the faction of elves who'd tried to dethrone them all.

A dream-like state washed over me, stars seeming to bend and streak past, like the *Enterprise* zipping along at warp speed, and I had no sense of how much time passed.

My awareness returned as we entered bright daylight, the contrast from the tunnels so brilliant that I had to squint my eyes shut against the intensity. A breeze heavy with the scent of growing things teased my nose, and I gasped in air, *fresh* air. Birdsong came from behind us, and leaves rustled in that breeze.

Zav laid me down, and dry leaves crinkled under me. Unfortunately, the air didn't instantly fix me, and I rolled onto my hands and knees and threw up. At least I hadn't done it while he'd been holding me. Though he was standing close, his silver slippers in danger of being spattered. I tried to shift away from him as my stomach heaved, ridiculously worried about throwing up on his feet.

He knelt beside me, pulled my braid onto my back so I wouldn't hit it, then rested a hand on my shoulder.

"Give me a minute to consider how to heal you," he said. "You were poisoned by the air down there. This is more complicated for me to heal than a wound."

"Thank you." I hoped I could recover, that my naturally robust ability to heal would extend to this, but I would take anything he could do for me. "I'm sorry about… everything."

"I know."

If only his sister did. Right now, she was probably tattling to his mother about how I'd worked with their enemies to try to kill Zav.

"I am annoyed with myself," he said, "for not noticing the trinket before. The compulsion spell was very subtly woven into the existing magic, and I thought little of the presence of a luck charm among the others. You have many charms, and when I look at you, it is not your neck that captures my attention."

Had I been less sick, I might have said I was disappointed by how little sexual allure my neck had, but I couldn't muster the energy.

I pushed leaves over my mess and sat back, hating that Zav was seeing me so weak and hating even more that I'd almost betrayed him, no matter what the reason. He'd just been getting to the point where he'd started trusting me. And now… I didn't know what now. But I feared he would go back to being wary around me. If he wanted to continue working with me at all.

We were on a cliff overlooking a vast forest filled with blue-green foliage that was at once alien and familiar to me, though if Zav had told me the truth about how portals worked, we couldn't be on Earth. The sun setting on the horizon didn't seem much different from my sun, and it painted the sky in richly layered oranges, pinks, and reds. Another time,

I would have appreciated the beauty, but my mind was too busy worrying about what I'd done and what was happening back home.

Zav sat next to me and again rested his hand on my shoulder. This time, magic flowed from his fingers, soothing me deep inside. Soon, my throat felt less raw, and I could finally breathe normally again. My chest ached from the strain of how hard my muscles and lungs had been working. I closed my eyes and slumped against Zav, letting him do whatever he could for me and grateful that he was trying. He'd caught his criminals. He didn't need to be here worrying about me.

I don't know how much time passed, but the sun sank below the horizon, and the birdsong faded. Stars came out, the constellations unfamiliar. As much as I wanted to return to Earth and find out what had happened, my body was too weary to stir. I must have dozed off, for I woke with my mouth dangling open, drool threatening to spill. Zav was sure to be impressed by a mate who puked *and* drooled on him.

"I have done what I can," he said. "Let me return you to your world."

"Thank you."

Though I felt better, I was exhausted, and it was only my pride that kept me from asking for help to my feet. Zav stood nearby, his hands clasped behind his back, waiting until I was ready. The silver of another portal lit up the night. He'd helped me, but he was more distant than he had been before we'd gone into battle, and I couldn't guess at the thoughts in his mind.

That it had been a mistake to kiss me? To sit so close to me in Willard's tent? What if that charm had activated then, and I'd plunged Chopper into his side before I'd had a chance to warn him?

"I must go back to my world to ensure the criminals are properly processed," Zav said. "I'm returning you to a place that will be safe."

"I understand. Thank you."

He inclined his head toward the portal, not making a move to touch me. It felt like a rejection, a silent statement that the relationship I'd only recently figured out I wanted had ended.

Hurt, I took a step toward the portal. But I paused and looked back. I wanted to hug him one more time, even if it was platonic, but I didn't want to see wariness in his eyes. Or for him to step back to avoid it.

Remembering our conversation on high fives, I lifted my palm toward him. Would *he* remember the conversation? Or consider it an acceptable alternative to the too-intimate hug?

It took him a moment to get what I was offering. He hesitated, then pressed a hand to mine. The warm tingle of his power enveloped me, as it always did when we were close. I stepped back before it could tempt me to do something he would reject.

Then I hopped through the portal.

The voyage back was similar, dreams and a fuzzy awareness of stars flitting through my mind, with no ability to control thoughts. Brilliant light once again assaulted my eyes as I came out, sun glinting harshly on ice, and my body winced in confusion. From night to day to night and back to day, all in a couple of hours.

"Thorvald!" Willard stood a few feet away, a radio to her lips.

A helicopter rested on a flat patch of ice behind her. That damn crevasse wasn't far away. The camp had been packed up, but a few soldiers remained, weapons at the ready as they faced the drop-off.

"It hasn't erupted?" I looked warily toward Mount Rainier's summit, the peak still covered in snow and glaciers.

"Not yet. What happened down there?" Her surprise turned to a scowl. "And why did you go down without us? Did they make you? The sister?"

I closed my eyes as temptation sashayed into my thoughts. If I blamed Zondia for my disobedience, Willard might never find out. Zav had been to her office and spoken to her before, but what were the odds that he would go in again and that this topic would come up?

But even if Willard never found out, I would know I'd lied to her, and that would bother me.

"No," I said slowly. "They didn't make me. Zav did point out that you guys might be used against me or him." Which was laughable since *I'd* been the one used against him. Almost used against him. My gunshot hadn't gotten through his defenses. I would feel much worse if I'd succeeded in hurting him, but it bothered me a lot that I'd fired at all. "And you know it's my fear that people I care about will get killed because of me."

"If that had happened, we would have been killed because of the dark elves, not you. We're not invalids. We could have helped."

"By bombing the entrance and helping trap us in there?" I scowled at her, catching surprise on her face again. "Zav told me."

Elven Doom

"I didn't want to. The *president* ordered it." She flung a hand toward the volcano, a few tendrils of smoke wafting up from vents. "This is all over national news now. Were you causing those earthquakes? Were the dark elves?"

A news helicopter flew past in the distance.

"They were, yes." I didn't feel deceitful for putting the blame on them. The dragons throwing magic around might not have helped, but the dark elves were ultimately responsible for all this. "Can we get out of here? I'll debrief you. Their plan was even more chilling than we thought."

I fished in my grimy pockets and pulled out the folded pages I'd taken from their binder.

It only took seconds for grim understanding to blossom on Willard's face. "Yes. We'll leave soon, and you'll give me a thorough oral and written report."

She stalked off, barking orders into the radio. Maybe it was a reflection of my mood and nothing more, but I worried she was someone else who would be more distant with me after this. She'd been in charge of the mission—I'd agreed to that back in her office, even volunteering her to lead—and I'd walked off on my own. That wasn't allowed in the army, and I couldn't pretend I'd thought it would be allowed for a civilian contractor either.

I shivered. The sun had come up and the sky had cleared, but it was colder here than on that nice world where Zav had taken me. As the helicopters circled the summit and Willard's team packed up, I wondered where it had been and if I'd ever get the opportunity to go back there again.

My phone buzzed. Amber.

"Hello?" I answered, hoping the reception held. Maybe thanks to the clear weather, or where I was standing on the mountainside, I had a whopping two bars of reception today.

"Uhm, hi, Val."

She was as awkward talking with me as I was with her. I didn't know whether to be heartened or depressed by our relationship. At least she'd called me. That was something.

"Hey, Amber. Sorry I didn't call back yesterday. I was on a mission out in the wilderness—I still am. My reception is horrible."

"It's fine."

I waited for her to tell me she'd been assailed by Zondia and how horrible it had been, and I groped for what I would say to comfort her. That I'd received the same treatment the night before? My version had been—I dearly hoped—worse. But I doubted that would make her feel better. I worried she resented me for bringing some of my insanity into her life.

"What's up?" I asked after a long silence. "Are you okay? Your dad said someone came by the house and questioned you. It was a dragon, wasn't it?"

Another long silence. I checked to see if the call had dropped. No, she was still there.

"Yeah," she finally said. "The purple one we saw at Schweitzer. I don't like her."

"I don't either." I couldn't remember if Amber knew she was Zav's sister. She'd escaped down the mountain by the time we were doing introductions, and I was surprised she'd seen more than the original three dragons that had kidnapped her. Maybe she'd witnessed some of that battle—and the coming of more dragons—from the trees. Or maybe she'd been able to *sense* some of it.

"She's a total bitch," Amber said.

"I agree." I couldn't bring myself to point out that Zondia was looking out for Zav. That fact wouldn't let me forgive her for bothering Amber.

"Worse than the girlfriend."

"Do you mean Shauna?" I knew she did, unless Thad had picked up a new one in the last few weeks. I doubted it. He wasn't the kind of guy to play the field, and even if he had been, his work wouldn't have given him time for much of that.

"Yeah. She had a fit because Dad wouldn't buy her a BMW. Like, what is she smoking? He wouldn't even buy me the Segway electric skates I asked for, and I'm so much more amazing than she is."

"I agree."

"Really? You think I should get the skates?"

"Uh, that's between you two. I don't think I can afford anything Segway makes."

"I thought assassins made good money."

"It all goes to paying informants and buying new gear. Not to mention replacing thirteen-hundred-dollar rental bicycles that get eaten by dragons."

Amber snorted—it almost sounded like a laugh. "That happened?"

"In Harrison. That's why I was walking on the trail that day."

"Huh. Uhm. There's something I wanted to ask you."

"Yes?"

"Dad said I could have a weapon if you teach me how to use it."

I rocked back. That was the last thing I'd expected her to say. Thad hated weapons and was horrible with them. In the army, he'd qualified for the M-16, since it was a requirement, but only after a bunch of remedial time at the range. He closed his eyes and jerked the rifle when he shot. That was why I'd been alarmed when his buddy had given him a gun when they'd gone searching for Amber.

"Thad said you could have a gun? *Really?*"

"I think he had a sword in mind. A little one."

"Like a fencing foil?" I imagined how underwhelmed Zondia would be if Amber shouted, "*En garde*, dragon!" and sprang at her.

"He didn't say, just that I had to know how to use it well before I could have one." Her tone turned a little sullen. "And that you had to be the one to teach me, because nobody else would know about the magic stuff."

"Ah." I bit my lip, telling myself I shouldn't be pleased that Amber would have to spend time with me, or that Thad was apparently trying to arrange that, not when the reason behind this had to be fear. Her meeting with Zondia must have disturbed her enough that she wanted to be able to defend herself. I hated to tell her that there weren't many swords in the world that would do anything against a dragon.

Still, it would be fantastic if she could defend herself from humans and most other magical creatures that might come after her. If she was now motivated to do so, I would gladly help her learn. And if, at some point during our lessons, she opened up about the events with Zondia, I would be happy to help with that too, even if all I could do was listen and apologize.

"I'll teach you, if you're truly committed to learning." I kept the rest of the thoughts to myself. "It's gotta be like swim team, at least for a while. You have to be dedicated to putting in the time."

I thought of my promise to myself to stay away from my family, lest they be hurt or used against me, but if Amber wanted this, I couldn't say no. Besides, if she learned well and I found a magical weapon for her, she would be able to take care of herself against *most* foes. I could worry less about her instead of more.

"I'm in," she said. "When do we start?"

A lump of emotion filled my throat—I was actually going to get to spend time with my daughter—and it took me a minute before I could answer. "Next weekend."

Assuming the volcano didn't erupt.

"I'll text you a time. And a place," I added, realizing Shauna wouldn't be amused if I hung out in Thad's back yard every weekend, even if I was there for Amber instead of him. Though maybe the BMW request would have Thad contemplating an end to that relationship. I hoped so, for his sake.

"'Kay. Bye, Val."

"Bye," I whispered, feeling a little upbeat for the first time since this mission had started.

Epilogue

"When was the last time someone operated a business out of this establishment?" Nin stood in the doorway, looking around at the broken bookcases and cracked glass display cases left by the previous tenant of Dimitri's new shop in Fremont.

Dust cloaked everything, including my nostrils after I made the mistake of taking three steps in and kicking a drop cloth that had been covering up a bunch of missing floorboards. Rapid-fire sneezes shot from my nostrils, and I imagined how Zav would have reacted if he'd been there, wondering if he needed to apply healing magic to my nasal passages.

But I hadn't seen Zav in almost two weeks, since I'd left him on a ledge in another world and hopped through his portal. How had the turning in of the dark-elf criminals gone? What had Zondia said to his mother about me? And about Lirena? She hadn't contacted me since trying to get me to kill the dragons, and I had no idea if she was still on Earth. Zav had taken that charm, which I hoped had removed her ability to manipulate me from a distance.

"The owner said it had been a couple of years. Something about a mold issue that had to be fixed, and then a previous tenant who didn't pay for months and had to be evicted." Dimitri pushed a bookcase that had fallen over into an upright position. "But she said I can keep all this furniture and use it. It'll be great once I get it fixed up."

"Mold?" My nostrils twitched for more reasons than dust, and a psychosomatic tickle in my lungs made my fingers twitch toward the pocket that held my inhaler.

I had needed it numerous times in the days after the battle, but my lungs had finally settled down and were less reactive. I couldn't imagine how bad it would have been if Zav hadn't done what he could to heal me. Or if Mount Rainier had erupted. There were a few million scientists down there watching it, but the last I'd heard, the quakes had settled down and the threat, at least for now, had dwindled. Nobody had seen any dark elves come out of the collapsed caves, not that they couldn't escape without people noticing. I couldn't help but hope none had made it, though I supposed they could have opened portals and were now licking their wounds on other worlds.

"It was professionally remediated," Dimitri said. "The owner promised."

"That didn't include floor repair?" Nin pointed at the hole I'd uncovered.

"That's not where the mold was. It was in the bathroom." Dimitri waved toward a short corridor in the back. "The bathroom is in great shape."

"That should help you sell yard art and lotions."

"There's a big storage closet and an office back there too. I can do all sorts of things with this space. You two were right to point me toward this location."

Nin and I shared long looks, and I was sure we were both thinking the same thing, that we should have come to see the place in person and not judged it by the listing photos. Photos that must have been taken years earlier, before the dust and upturned furniture had arrived.

I hoped everything worked out with this endeavor. Nin had not only allowed herself to be talked into co-signing on the lease, despite my advice not to, but she had invested in the business in exchange for ten percent equity. Maybe she'd felt better about co-signing, knowing she would have a say in how to make the business successful. She *did* have a good track record with that.

"The foot traffic is amazing," Dimitri continued on, gesticulating animatedly. He was more excited than I'd ever seen him. "We're close to breweries and restaurants, and there's the ice cream shop next door. And it's just a couple of blocks to Gasworks Park."

Elven Doom

Thankfully, kraken-free these days, or so I'd heard. "Don't forget the psychic next door on the other side. I'm sure people come in droves for tarot-card readings."

"It actually might complement my business." Dimitri found shelves that had fallen to the floor and returned them to the bookcase. "People who believe in tarot-card readings should believe in the supernatural and the need to protect their yards from werewolves, vampires, and dragons."

"Dragons?" I asked. "You have devices capable of defending against dragons? And you haven't given me several for my apartment?"

"Well, no," Dimitri said, "but I could put together an alarm system that would let a homeowner know a dragon was on the property."

"It's always nice to have three seconds' warning *before* you're roasted alive," I murmured.

"There are not any coffee shops on this street." Nin picked a route through debris to one side of the room, glancing at the dirty window, the street barely visible through the grime. She spread her arms toward the wall. "If you put in an espresso stand here, you could get more business."

Dimitri's top lip curled. "I wasn't planning to get a food handler's permit."

"It is not difficult. I can show you what is required."

"I don't know how to make fancy coffee."

"You can get a barista. The coffee sales could cover her wages, and in this area, with the right marketing, you could recoup the cost of the espresso equipment within a few months."

"I don't think it's a good idea," Dimitri said.

"One of my assistants is looking to pick up extra hours in the mornings before my food truck opens." Nin ignored his protest as she studied the space along the wall, no doubt envisioning where the orders would be taken, where the coffee would be made, and where the munchies and menu would go. She turned toward Dimitri. "When would your coffee, art, and lotion shop open?"

"It's just an art and lotion shop," he said sturdily, not realizing he'd already lost the argument. "It would be weird to sell coffee with that stuff."

"Not at all," Nin said. "It will make you unique. Also, the locals would come every day to buy coffee. While here, they will be inclined to make impulse purchases such as lotions and dragon alarms."

Dimitri looked at me, a helpless expression on his face. Or maybe that was a please-help-me expression.

"You should sell hard cider too," I told him. "I wouldn't come for coffee, but I'd sit and have a cider."

"I'd need a liquor license to sell alcohol."

"It may be worth considering," Nin said. "Many coffee shops in the area also sell beer. This allows them to attract clientele who do not wish to consume caffeine at night."

Dimitri kept shaking his head, but I was confident this place would have an espresso stand, at the least, the next time I came in.

My phone buzzed. It was Willard, her office number, not her cell.

She hadn't called in over a week. After twiddling my thumbs for three days, I'd taken a freelance gig and hunted down a rabid were-hyena killing livestock—and two farmers—near Centralia. It wasn't as if I couldn't survive without my government jobs, but I'd been wondering if Willard was holding a grudge and might cut me off.

"Hey, Willard." I played it casual.

"This is the secretary of Colonel Willard's office. How may I be of service?"

"Uh." I recognized that voice. "You called *me*, Gondo."

"Yes, but I still like to be of service. Do you need anything built?"

"Maybe. Can you make a shiny new espresso machine from old parts?"

"Val, no!" Dimitri flung up an alarmed hand.

Nin turned toward me, interest in her eyes. "A refurbished unit would lower our startup costs."

"Espresso? I love espresso," Gondo said. "Are you starting a coffee shop?"

"Dimitri might be. I don't think you've met him yet. He's a quarter dwarf and enchants housewares. Do any of your people need housewares?" I nodded to Dimitri, thinking he might thank me for putting the word out about his business.

He slumped against the bookcase, his head clunking a shelf. For some reason, the image of a defeated boxer dangling from the ropes came to mind.

"My people? My people can make their own enchanted housewares. We do, however, require espresso. This is not something that exists on our world, and we do not have expertise in locating your coffee beans and turning them into an acceptable beverage."

"Yeah? Well, tell your friends. When Dimitri's shop opens, it'll be a safe establishment for goblins. Goblins with money who can keep from making off with his tools."

Dimitri closed his eyes. *Maybe I should stop helping him.*

"I will tell them," Gondo said. "Also, let me investigate the possibility of acquiring a broken espresso machine and repairing it. Freysha can help. She is very good at repairing things—for an elf."

"She's still there, huh?" I felt a little guilty that I'd suspected her of plotting against us. But just because Lirena had been the troublemaker on our mission didn't mean Freysha was innocent. It was still possible that someone from Willard's office had warned the dark elves we were coming.

"Yes," Gondo said. "We get along well. She is more goblin than anyone else here."

"Nobody else there is goblin."

"Exactly. Let me give you to the colonel. I believe when she asked me to call you, it was to immediately give her the phone, not to discuss other matters with you. I am getting better at interpreting her scowls."

"Why didn't she call me herself?"

Willard was the one to answer. "My hands were sticky. Someone caused the cake that Sergeant Banderas brought in for Lieutenant Sabo's birthday to explode."

"I did not realize you could not use a blowtorch to cut human desserts," Gondo said in the background. "Goblin pastries are much sturdier."

A door thunked shut, possibly on Gondo.

"How're you doing, Thorvald?" Willard asked. "I heard about the hyena."

"You hear about everything."

"My intelligence network is vast." Her tone turned dry. "Gondo was the one to tell me. He really does know everybody."

"How does he collect so much gossip when he's in your office shredding papers day and night?"

"Only days. He has nights off. He doesn't know if the dragons are gone though. Are they?"

"As far as I know. Zondia took the prisoners away and Zav didn't say if he's coming back any time soon."

"I assume he is since you lip-tangled with him in front of my team. Guys are into that."

"Maybe." I hadn't put everything in my report, like the part about Lirena controlling me through the charm. Or that Zondia had walked in right as I was shooting Zav. "Why? Do you need a dragon?"

"I have a criminal's name on my desk, a kelpie who's been eating fishermen instead of fish. She's also on Zav's list, near the top. He prioritized his criminals for me and color-coded them by levels of dangerousness."

"He's considerate."

"He said I would screw up in assigning you to missions if his directions weren't absolutely clear."

"Maybe I should have said *thorough* instead of considerate."

"I think so. I wondered if you two wanted to work on the mission together?"

"I'm not sure about Zav, but I'll take the gig."

"Also, if you want to arrange a meeting at the coffee roastery, I've been authorized to pay you for your work against the dark elves. Even though you disobeyed orders and made my night hell."

"Thank you. I think."

"I'll send over the details of the new mission. And Val?"

"Yes?"

"Thanks for risking your life down there. I've looked over the papers you gave me, and you're right. Their plans were chilling. I think they were angling to get rid of humanity and take over the whole planet."

"Could that have really happened?"

"We've had worldwide volcanic winters in the past from the eruption of one big volcano, where there was widespread famine because crops couldn't grow that year. If the dark elves had caused a chain of eruptions, yeah, it could have been an extinction-level event. We like to think we've got enough technology to save ourselves from catastrophes, but if you can't grow food for an extended period of time, your civilization is screwed. We could have gone the way of the dinosaurs."

A depressing thought that I didn't want to let linger in my mind. So I opted for levity.

Elven Doom

"That must mean I'm going to get a *big* combat bonus."

Willard snorted. "Don't book your trip to Tahiti yet. I'm going to have to charge you for that carbon monoxide detector you lost."

"That can't be more than a hundred bucks."

"Government equipment comes at a premium."

"Or is it that you're adding a Val-disobeyed-orders fee onto it?"

"I'd never be so vindictive. That comes straight off the bonus."

"Just so you know, if I can't make my rent this month, I'm moving in with you. You've got a guest cot, right?"

"I hope things aren't that dire."

"I'd be okay with the couch."

"I'm not entirely sure you're joking," Willard said.

"Good." I hung up and quirked an eyebrow at Dimitri, who was walking past carrying a broom cloaked in layers of dust. "Do you need another investor?"

"I thought you didn't think this business was a good idea."

"I didn't say that." Not out loud, anyway.

"You got a grim foreboding look when I was showing you the real-estate listings and asking your opinion."

"That's because I sensed Zav was going to show up, and the dinner bill would skyrocket from sixty dollars to three hundred."

"Did it really? Was there wine? Nobody can eat that much."

"I believe he had eight entrees in the end."

"That's amazing. He was in human form, wasn't he? Does his stomach expand more than ours? Like magically?"

"I don't know. He didn't eat any of the vegetables or starches, so there was more room for meat." I tilted my head. "You're not answering my question. I guess that means you don't need more investors."

"Not necessarily, but what made you change your mind?"

Nin came over, took the broom from Dimitri, and gave him a tablet. "I put together a business plan and a conservative five-year projection for you. Please look it over and give me your input."

She went off to sweep.

"That changed." I pointed after her. "You got a better business partner."

"Zoltan is still a partner."

"Will he ever be here?"

"Probably not."

"Then I'm in."

Dimitri raised his eyebrows. "Do you have money?"

"You've seen my change jar."

"That's your savings? I thought that was for tipping delivery drivers."

"I've got real savings and retirement accounts—modest ones—but I wouldn't mind investing in something that's potentially more profitable. How much did Nin put in for her ten percent?"

A familiar aura soared within range of my senses. Zav. I almost melted in relief that it wasn't his sister, but I decided to wait until we talked to feel too much relief. Zondia could be in the area too, or he could be here to inform me that the Dragon Justice Court wanted to interrogate me.

"Five thousand dollars and her expertise," Dimitri said.

"I should have that after Willard pays me." The special government carbon monoxide detectors couldn't be *that* much. "I'll do the same deal. Ten percent and you get *my* expertise."

"Do you know how to be a barista?"

"I know how to shoot anyone who tries to *rob* your barista."

Zav walked into the shop in his human form.

"I also have a dragon ally," I said, hoping that was still true.

He'd held my braid while I puked. If that wasn't an ally, I didn't know what was.

Dimitri stepped back, eyeing Zav warily. "Are you sure? He looks aggro again."

Alarmed, I looked at Zav. I hadn't said anything to him. He couldn't be irritated yet, could he? Unless he'd brought aggravating news…

Zav lifted his chin, his mustache and beard impeccably trimmed, his robe tidy, his slippers immaculate, and the gold chain around his neck polished. He appeared to be his usual pompous and arrogant self, not angry.

"That's his normal expression," I said.

"Are you sure?" Dimitri asked.

"Yeah."

"We will speak in private," Zav told me, ignoring Dimitri.

Normally, I would object to anything phrased as an order, but I wanted to know what he had to say. And I was glad to see him after two weeks without dragons in my life.

"Dimitri, can we use one of the rooms in back?" I asked. "Which one did you say was remodeled and looked nice?"

"Uh, the bathroom."

"Wasn't there an office?"

"Not that was remodeled."

"We'll take our chances."

Zav was gazing around the dust fest, a faint curl to his lip.

"This way, noble dragon mate." I picked a route to the corridor, then poked my head through doors until I found the office. It was only slightly larger than a bathroom.

"You should accept her as a business partner," Nin said from the front room. "Should we ever need her services, she would feel compelled to offer them for free if she is an owner. She is not inexpensive to hire. I know."

"What kind of coffee shop needs an assassin?"

Zav followed me inside and closed the door, so I didn't hear the answer. I did find it amusing that it had only taken Dimitri ten minutes to start referring to his business as a coffee shop.

There wasn't anywhere to sit in the room, shabby built-in bookcases being the only furnishings, so I leaned against the wall and faced Zav.

"Are you okay?" I asked.

The question seemed to catch him off-guard. He paused before saying, "Yes."

He looked me up and down, his gaze lingering on my curvy areas. Or maybe that was my imagination. Then it shifted upward, to my neck—my charms—and I winced as he perused them. Not trusting that I hadn't blindly accepted a new one?

"Have you recovered?" he asked.

"Yeah, I'm good."

"Your volcano has not erupted. I flew over it."

"It hasn't. We're cautiously optimistic that it won't. Did you get your criminals turned in?"

"I did. My mother and sister and two dragons from the Silverclaw Clan were waiting when I arrived."

"Were they pleased?"

"They wished to know what took so long and when the remaining criminals on my list would be brought in." Zav pressed his lips together.

"My brother, who is collecting criminals on another world, has brought in more than I have."

"Distressing."

He lifted his chin again. "I will catch up with and pass him. You will assist me."

"I will. I believe there's a kelpie on your list? Willard wants me to take care of her."

His lifted chin turned into a head tilt. "You do not object to assisting me with my list?"

"Not for now. I owe you a few."

"Owe me?"

"You saved my ass up there."

He glanced at my ass.

"My *life*," I corrected, remembering that dragons apparently had no expressions involving asses and took references to them literally. "I'd be dead if you hadn't charged in to help. Thank you."

His gaze returned to my face. "You are my mate."

"Yeah, but that's a ruse for your dragon buddies. It's not like we're having sex." Memories of our kisses flashed through my mind, but I refused to voice the *unfortunately* that crept to my tongue. "You didn't have to risk yourself to save me is what I mean. I'm guessing your life would be easier if I'd died up there under the ice."

I tried not to think about how close I'd come to that. I'd walked away without any grievous injuries, but when I'd seen my doctor last week and described all the noxious fumes I'd inhaled, he'd said I was lucky to be alive.

"I would not like it if you died," Zav said. "For practical reasons as well as personal ones. You are better at doing research in this forsaken world than I am. You were the one to realize the dark elves were on that mountaintop. It pleases me that you are clever. Usually, a dragon chooses a mate based on physical attributes and her willingness to serve him or her. I chose you because you are a loyal ally in battle, you are good at finding people, and you vex my enemies." Zav looked as pleased with himself as with me, but coming from him, all this was quite the compliment. Especially since we'd started our relationship with him calling me mongrel and vermin.

Touched that he still wanted anything to do with me, I crossed the small office and lifted my arms to offer him a hug.

But he held up a hand. "There is something else we must discuss."

"Lirena?" I lowered my arms.

"*Lirena.*" Zav did more than curl his lip as he said her name. His tone was savage. "Anyasha-sulin is her true name. She is one of the leaders of the faction that attempted to oust dragons from power and started a war with our kind. Many of them were killed when we replaced them with more amenable elven leaders, but some still live, and as you can see, they continue to plot against my kind."

"I see that now, yes."

"I know you did not know who she is." His face was tense, and his jaw barely moved as he spoke the words. "But she is the one who hired the assassin who killed my brother."

I thunked my head back against the wall. I'd been afraid of that. Through sheer stupidity, or naivety at the best, I'd betrayed him, and I'd betrayed him with someone who was a mortal enemy.

"We were the only two born in that clutch," Zav said. "We were close. Closer than I am with my sister and my other brothers—they came from different sires and are younger than I. It is difficult for me to know that this elf was in your home and helped you drive out my sister."

"Hey, I get it. I'm sorry. But it's not like I invited her into my life. I assume she lied to me and isn't my cousin."

He probably wouldn't understand my point of view, but I felt betrayed too. Lirena had pretended to be my relative, to be a member of the family I'd never known, a link to the father I'd wondered about my entire life. She'd even taught me a few things. Yes, she'd been doing it so I would be better armed to attack Zav, but there was a part of me that wished it had been real. I'd never had a sister, and my childhood had often been lonely, with only my mother and my books to keep me company. Maybe that was why I hadn't been wary enough when it came to Lirena.

"I do not believe so. I can research her lineage. Or—" Zav's tone turned to ice, "—I can find her and kill her."

I almost made a joke, asking what had happened to his vaunted punishment and rehabilitation program, but his expression was dark. He wouldn't appreciate any jokes right now. Maybe Dimitri had been right. My dragon was aggro.

"You will tell me if she returns to Earth and contacts you," Zav said.

"I will, but I'd be even more eager to help you if you made that a request and not a command."

He closed his eyes, as if he was struggling to control his temper. If he'd spent the last couple of weeks dealing with his sister and his mother, he was probably in a foul mood. I shouldn't push him, but I also couldn't let him think he could order me around.

Trying to lighten his mood, I added, "If you added the word *please* to your requests, I would be so tickled, I'd take you back to the barbecue place."

He opened his eyes, the anger fading, but it turned into a sad smile. "It is not a good idea for me to let you feed me."

"Because it makes you randy?"

"Essentially. And, even though I am having trouble remembering this, I should not allow that around you. I know you don't have plans to betray me—incidentally, my sister learned that much from her mind-scouring of you—but you are not a dragon. You are susceptible to mind control, and others know of you now and will believe you can get close to me, close enough to kill. We cannot... be that close."

Basically, I was a liability to him. I wished I could argue otherwise, but dragons, dark elves, and elves had all proven themselves strong enough to control me. That made me furious, and I resolved to find more trinkets—or learn how to develop my own powers—so I could stop that from happening in the future.

"So glad I'm exonerated on that front." I glowered down at his slippers. "Zondia ought to know *everything* about me by now."

Zav stepped closer and lifted a hand to my cheek, his fingers warm, a familiar tingle of magic running over my skin. "I am sorry that she hurt you. I would never have allowed that if I'd noticed in time to stop her."

"I know." I didn't think he'd ever apologized to me before. I didn't say it was all right, because it wasn't, but I did say, "I don't blame you."

"No?" There was that sad smile again. "She was only here because I claimed you."

"But you claimed me because you thought you were protecting me. I know that too."

"Yes."

He rested his forehead against mine, and I wanted to cry, because that was his platonic elven-battle-bond gesture. My pompous and arrogant dragon had finally become someone I wanted to date, and he wasn't going to let me buy him ribs again.

Zav leaned back, his knuckles gently grazing my cheek as they dropped. I was certain he would rather be kissing me than doing the forehead thing, and somehow that made it all worse.

I expected him to walk out, but he lingered, gazing at my face instead of my neck this time, his violet eyes contemplative.

"You are not without power, without aptitude," he said. "Perhaps..."

"Perhaps?"

"As I told you, a dragon cannot teach an elf to use magic, but perhaps when there is time, I can take you to your people—your *real* relatives—and they would consider teaching you how to protect yourself from mind manipulation. And to fully learn how to use your powers."

A spark of hope kindled in my heart. "Do you think they would? My father must be... busy."

Or indifferent. He hadn't, after all, sent someone to observe me. Maybe he didn't care about me at all.

"I am certain he is, but there are many elves with the capacity to teach. I will let it be known to them that I will be pleased if one of them trains you. If they are not fools, they know that it is wise to please a dragon." His eyelids drooped, his lashes nearly covering his gaze. "And unwise to *displease* one."

"You're going to threaten my relatives if they don't teach me? That should make me popular at family reunions."

"If you can protect yourself from mind manipulation and I need not worry about getting a dagger in my chest when I am sleeping, *then* you may feed me meat." Zav lifted his hand to the side of my head, his eyes growing bedroom steamy as he developed his new plan. "And *then* we will mate."

I knew I should object to the idea of him bossing around my relatives and forcing them to teach me, but warm magic flowed from his fingers again, making my entire body tingle. I wanted very much to *mate* with Zav. Or, as we said on Earth, drag him into my bedroom for hot, passionate, illegal-in-seventeen-states sex.

As long as I was with him when he was talking to the elves, I could frame things more diplomatically, couldn't I? Of course I could. A porcupine flinging quills couldn't be less diplomatic than a dragon.

"We could look into it," I said casually, refusing to let him know how much I liked this idea and wanted it to come to pass, and not only for reasons related to horniness. He was already full of himself.

"Yes." Zav lowered his hand with noticeable reluctance and stepped back. "I must capture more criminals before taking a break, but once I have turned in more than all of my brothers have, we will take a trip and speak to your people." He glanced toward my shoulder. "You should also see the dwarves and learn about your sword."

A lump threatened to form in my throat. I knew his primary motivation was wanting to have sex, but he could have used his power to stamp his compulsion on top of any that a lesser species might put on me, which would have prevented me from being a danger to him. But he understood that I didn't want that, and he actually cared. He wanted to help me become strong enough to fend off enemies on my own.

I clasped his hands and tamped down my tendencies toward sarcasm to say, "You're an amazing dragon, Zav. I'm glad you're here on Earth with me."

"Good." He nodded firmly. "I will pick you up at your domicile tomorrow, and you will have researched the kelpie and know her location."

"Really?" This return to the practical brought my sarcasm back out. "You're giving me an entire night to find our next nemesis?"

"I am."

"I'm honored to be working with such an understanding and magnanimous partner."

"As you should be. Few lesser species are blessed with a dragon for an ally."

"I'll be ready for you in the morning, but there's something you need to know."

"Yes?"

"My superintendent put up a sign in the apartment building requesting information on whoever keeps destroying the chairs on the rooftop deck. He's talking about installing a camera to catch the culprit on video next time. You may not want to land up there anymore since you can't fit without squishing things."

"If the chairs were placed to the side of the landing pad instead of in the middle, they would not be damaged."

Elven Doom

"It's a deck, not a landing pad."

"A dragon lands where a dragon wishes."

Zav inclined his head, then slipped out, and I had a feeling the next batch of deck chairs would end up as flat as the first two. What would my landlord think when the camera revealed the culprit?

THE END

CONNECT WITH THE AUTHOR

Have a comment? Question? Just want to say hi? Find me online at:
http://www.lindsayburoker.com
http://www.facebook.com/LindsayBuroker
http://twitter.com/GoblinWriter
Thanks for reading!

Printed in Great Britain
by Amazon